ONE LAST MILE

ROGER SALTSMAN

This book is a work of fiction. Any references to historical events, real people, or real places are used factitiously. Other names, characters, places, and events are products of the author's imagination, and any resemblance to actual events or persons, living or dead, is entirely coincidental.

ISBN: 978-1-7372914-0-4 (sc) Amazon
ISBN: 978-1-7372914-1-1 (ebook) Amazon
ISBN: 978-1-7372914-4-2 (ebook) iBooks
ISBN: 978-1-7372914-5-9 (ebook) KoBo
ISBN: 978-1-7372914-9-7 (sc) B & N
ISBN: 978-1-7372914-8-0 (ebook) B & N

Editor: Nomi Isak

Cover Photography: George Mayer

Cover Design: Karrie Ross

Dedication: First, to the Brevard College runners past and present. Second, to all runners, and their favorite trail, road, beach or climb; their own personal Agony Hill. And finally, to the coaches: whose guidance, encouragement, discipline, drive and dedication was not lost on your runners; we remember, and we love you for it; thank you for passing the baton.

In Memory: Jeff Wentworth, Manual Moreno, Gary Young, Tim Brisson, Andrew Keller and Tony Bosclair.

PART ONE

CHAPTER 1

The rutted trail was still damp from the previous week's dusting of snow, with icy white clumps clinging to the shade beneath the rhododendrons. Eric ran ten yards behind his friend Mary as they descended the hill. He kept a close eye on her foot placements, and using that information, he usually followed suit, his feet landing in the same places—most of the time. From experience, he knew that the lead runner had the better view and usually picked the safest spots to run; the trails were fun, but one always had to pay attention. He watched Mary juke side to side, deftly picking her spots, as though she could see with her feet. She was a natural-born mountain goat. Mary could descend the trails faster than anyone, male or female, on the high school's cross-country team.

In alternate bursts, the morning's gusty weather swept over them, the wind scented with the damp-earthly forest and fresh, frigid air from the valley below. When Eric ran the trails of the Appalachian Mountains, the peaty smell of nature's debris connected him to Mother Earth—an experience he missed during his daily training while looping endless miles on the valley's oil-soaked asphalt. He'd prefer to run in the forest year-round—except in late fall when the downed leaves hid roots, rocks and potholes. And then, only after the winter rains had washed away the leaves was it safe to return to the footpaths. Even with those hazards visible, these trails were no family fun hike. The Art Loeb trail, in particular, fell somewhere between a Weekend-Warrior outing and a Pack-the-Ibuprofen run.

The trail bottomed out, and the two dashed along a fifteen-yard swale, using that momentum, like two linked roller coaster cars, to attack the coming ascent. Eric powered his aching legs up the steep 200-yard grinder.

When he crested the next peak, he glanced to his right through a small opening in the trees, taking in the valley below—still beautiful despite its winter-browned landscape. His focus returned to the rocky, rutted path, eyes sweeping side to side, still following Mary's lead. Even on safer, flatter terrain, Eric minimized his sightseeing. He feared turning an ankle on a loose rock or hidden root. A resulting face-plant into the forest floor was a constant fixture in the back of his mind. He knew that any one part of his anatomy could be kissing dirt in a nanosecond if his attention strayed. So far, Eric had escaped serious injury.

Today, the weather's challenging gusts made staying upright trickier than usual. The night before, a late evening cold front had charged into town. This morning its Confederate wind was attacking the ridge, strafing the slopes, and rattling the thin, naked branches of the hardwoods, whistling as it raced through the needles of the pine trees. Eric had expected the forest to shelter him from the biting wind, but there was no protection this day. He had forgotten to wear his knit cap, and his ears were numb despite the shagginess of his hair. More showy than protective, his thin, Adidas-knockoff warmup suit didn't help either. The icy wind bit deep.

Mary, always prepared, wore a green knit cap that brought out the green of her eyes. Her long auburn braid had snuck out from under the cap and swayed between her shoulder blades as she continued setting their pace. She had covered her top layers with a thin nylon rain jacket and wasn't complaining about the day's conditions. They both wore white cotton work gloves on their hands. Before they'd begun their run that morning, he had offered her a bribe of dinner and a movie for her knit cap. She'd gently chastised him, pointing out his lack of preparation.

Eric checked his watch; they'd been running for thirty minutes, which was their agreed-upon turn-around time. They took a short rest, then retraced the same route back toward their starting point—the Davidson River Campground.

The section of the Art Loeb trail they were running was labeled Shut-in Ridge on Geographic relief maps. The mouth of the trail was in the Southwestern section of the Pisgah National Forest, which shared a border with the town of Brevard, North Carolina, where Eric had lived his whole life. He'd been a freshman the first time he'd done this run; now he was eighteen and a high school senior, and he still loved every inch of this trail. Certain sections of this ridgeline path had originally been old roads and herd paths. Starting in Brevard, the trail climbed fourteen miles before it crossed over the Blue Ridge Parkway into the northern part of the forest. From there, it passed by the base of Cold Mountain before winding down and ending near a Boy Scout campground in the county of Haywood, North Carolina. Eric considered it one of the toughest trails on the Brevard side of the Pisgah Forest. For Eric and Mary, it had become their favorite forest trail run.

Nearing the end of their return trip, the two of them descended a set of lazy-sloped switchbacks. They always welcomed the gentler gradient after the beating their legs had endured on the challenging route. When they rounded the last switchback, they shuffled down a steep thirty-yard slope, stopping at a wooden bridge that spanned a small creek.

Mary crossed the footbridge, turned around, and hung her heels off the end to stretch her calves. Eric stayed on the other end. He blew his warm breath into his cupped hands, then covered his ears with them, but found no relief.

He eyed Mary's knit cap. "Sure I can't borrow your cap for this last half mile? My ears are freezing."

She rolled her eyes and shook her head. "I said no before we started. The answer is still the same. You'll just have to suffer."

Amply rebuffed, Eric figured he might as well stretch too, hoisting his leg onto the bridge's railing and then reaching for his toe.

"It's always beautiful out here, isn't it?" Mary said.

Along with Mary's other exceptional qualities, he found her optimism endearing. She would find uplifting things to say in the worst of circumstances. If a wildfire scorched the forest bare, Mary's typical response would be, "Through destruction there is renewal. New pine trees will grow, and the forest will be green again."

After stretching, Eric folded his arms across his chest, trying to keep warm as he watched his vaporized exhales curling into the wind. Winter wasn't his favorite season.

Eric had met Mary four years earlier when she'd first moved to town with her family. When she'd joined the cross-country team, he invited her more than once to run the forest trails with him, but she had declined each time, citing her busy schedule as the excuse.

On a cold, windless New Year's morning, however, Eric received an unexpected visitor. He could remember in vivid detail the frosty morning when she came tapping on his bedroom window. At first he had refused to join her on the spur-of-the-moment adventure because it was the crack of dawn—the Times Square ball having dropped only hours earlier. But in the end he relented. He'd made the original invite; he had to make good on the offer. Besides, Mary's father was sitting in the family Buick waiting to drive them to the forest.

Eric's favorite memory from their first run was a sparkly "Happy New Year" tiara she had worn on top of her knit cap.

Mary called to Eric from the other end of the bridge. "What are you staring at?"

He shook his head. "I was just remembering our first run here."

"Man, that seems so long ago," she said. Then she grinned. "Today is our fourth New Year's run." She bent over to touch her toes. When she straightened, she said, "So how much lead time are you going spot me for our race? You know you're getting a beat-down again, right? Just like last year."

The bet dated back to their founding New Year's Day run.

When they had stopped at this same spot to stretch, Mary had challenged Eric to race the trail's final half mile to the trailhead. Their finish line wasn't the trailhead sign itself, but a wooden and steel-wired suspension bridge. The unique bridge was iconic. Eric's hiking and running friends spoke of it with fond reverence, like Grand Central Station—a demarcation point for the outbound and inbound journeys on the trail.

Before their race had begun that first morning, Mary had agreed to twenty seconds as a head start. Even with that he slowed his pace, so as not embarrass her by beating her by too much. He pulled ahead toward the end to claim his victory. Afterward Mary scolded him for patronizing her. Proud and independent, she wanted no pity, even in fun. When they competed, she wanted him to give 100 percent effort. Eric shared Mary's passion for competition, and the race became their reward after running the unforgiving trail.

Mary and Eric had bet a can of soda that first year as the prize for the winner of the final dash. The second year it had been a milkshake at the Clock diner; the third, it had been a hamburger and fries at the Cardinal drive-in, their favorite hangout. They'd discussed the terms for this year's bet the night before at her family's New Year's Eve party. Since it was their senior year, they'd decided they would celebrate in style, and the loser would buy dinner at a quaint downtown restaurant called Marcel's.

"I don't know, Mary," Eric said, walking up to her. "You beat me last year. I'm sure I gave you too much of a head start."

"No way," she protested, lightly slapping his arm. "I earned that one."

"It was close, wasn't it?"

"You know it was. But hey, Eric, you've gotten stronger this year. I haven't improved much, so you've have to give me extra seconds."

"Maybe so," he said. "How about twenty-eight seconds this year?"

"Make it thirty seconds because of the wind. How about that?"

"Fair enough. Let me stretch some, OK?"

"Aw, you're just stalling," she joked.

He bent over one more time, hanging his heels off the end of the bridge.

This repartee had become part of their game, and he enjoyed it as much as she did. Their tradition was like a rite of passage: They chose the challenging trail to remind them of the hard work it took to be great, and their race at the end was a perfect way to renew their competitive fires for the upcoming track season.

He stepped down off the edge of the bridge. "OK, let's see." He punched his watch to timer mode. "Twenty-five seconds. Right?"

"Noooo!" she said. "No cheating."

Eric cleared his watch, and Mary crouched, toeing an imaginary starting line.

"Runners to your mark—"

"Wait," Mary said, rising out of her crouch. "I can barely hear you, Eric. Say it louder, with feeling, like a starter would. Besides, with these wind gusts it's hard to hear when you speak quiet as a mouse."

"So, you're a movie director now?"

"Shut up and start me," Mary said.

Runners to your mark . . . set—"

Mary sprinted off, anticipating the "GO" command.

"Bang, Bang," Eric shouted, mimicking the two shots of a starter's pistol that signaled the runners to retreat to the starting line. "False start!"

Mary halted twenty yards away, spun around, and threw her hands on her hips, "Roberts, you did that on purpose."

Eric laughed. "You have to wait for the starter's last command."

"Yeah, right," she snipped, tromping toward him. "Come on. You're just trying to mess with my concentration. You have to say GO just after SET. You can't let it hang there like you did."

He waited for Mary to resume her starting position and gave her extra time to settle herself.

"Runners to your mark . . . set . . . go!"

"See you at the finish, loser!" she yelled, sprinting away. Her haughty laugh rang clear despite the turbulent weather.

Eric circled in one spot like an animal in a cage, waiting for the thirty seconds to pass. When he sprinted off, he heard bits of the trail landing behind him—his powerful stride launching chunks of mud and leaves from the waffled tread on his soles.

As Eric blazed the riverside trail, he caught random glimpses of Mary through slits in the dense forest, but he needed to cover more yards before gauging Mary's lead.

The trail's last stretch to the suspension bridge was a comfortable ride. It was sandy where the river had deposited sediment in times of flooding. The welcome softness provided relief for battered feet, without hindering a runner's stride. Eventually the path split through a vast, overgrown patch of briars. When Eric entered the prickly tunnel, the thorns grabbed at his legs. He winced but ignored their assault, blasting right through, not slowing his pace.

Out the other side of the prickly patch, the trail snaked through the trees, hugging the water's edge, the path mined with jutted roots washed bare from the river's overflows. Eric caught glimpses of Mary's knit cap. He had gained on her.

Having trod this last section an infinite number of times he could navigate it blindfolded if necessary. With precise footfalls, like a graceful gazelle, Eric deftly negotiated the downed trees and roots along the river. When he rounded a long open bend in the trail, he spotted her again. He assessed the gap, attempting to calculate his closing pace—but he laughed at himself. Running full tilt already, he knew catching Mary would be tough. She wasn't playing around.

As he closed in on her, his legs aching—Novocain-numb with lactic acid, the universal demon signaling fatigue—he pressed himself for one last burst of speed. He ignored the pain and drove hard to catch her. No matter that it was just a race between two friends, he was just as enamored with winning as she was.

He caught her with fifty yards remaining to their finish line, following behind her for a few moments, sizing her up for a decisive pass around her left side. Savoring his imminent victory, he launched his move. She flicked a sideways glance, found one extra gear in her stride, and kicked hard the last twenty yards. A few seconds later, she thrust a victorious fist in the air as she broke through the imaginary finish line next to the suspension bridge. He crossed a yard behind.

Her face beamed.

He tapped his finger on his watch face. “I should have argued for more time,” he huffed, winking.

“Good race, Eric,” she huffed back. “Happy New Year.”

“Ditto.” He gave her a sweaty hug.

They recovered for a couple of minutes, pacing and breathing, as the wind wicked sweat from their clothing.

Mary patted him on the butt. “Come on, let’s go. I got some parades to watch. And the Rose Bowl later. You’re coming right over after you clean up. Right?”

“Sure. Your boyfriend going to be there?” he said.

“No,” Mary insisted. “Parker’s not coming over until dinnertime at three.”

“Hey,” Eric asked. “Can Pamela come, too?”

“The Freshman?” she said, her voice pitching a bit too high. “You just started dating her two weeks ago.”

“Well, yes, I guess we’re boyfriend and girlfriend now.”

“Already, huh?” Mary chortled, “Yeah, sure, bring her over . . .”

“Great. Thanks.”

Eric started toward the bridge’s steps. Mary dashed ahead of him, giving him a friendly push out of the way. “Whoa, there buddy,” she said, chuckling. “Winners first, losers second.” She sprang onto the bridge, jogged two-thirds across, wheeled around, and waved for him to hurry.

But as he did so, she bounced up and down on the planks, causing the wires and wood to oscillate, making Eric take awkward steps.

“Ha, ha, ha,” she crowed.

“You’re killing me, Mary.” He waited for her to stop.

As soon as she did, he ran toward her. Mary shrieked with delight as he chased her off the bridge at the far end.

They walked parallel to the forested riverbank for the two hundred yards to the tiny parking area. They were quiet until Eric broke the silence. "I'm a little nervous," he said. "I'm not sure I can bring my mile time down to 4:10. And I still haven't gotten any offers from the big colleges."

"Well," she said, "to be honest, lowering your 4:18 mile to under 4:10 might be a stretch for anyone."

Mary's honesty didn't surprise him, but her retort touched a nerve. He didn't want to admit his chosen goal was beyond his reach. Securing a scholarship at one of the country's prestigious track programs had become his ultimate priority. He wanted to run with the best.

"Have you been keeping your weekly mileage up?" she asked.

He stared at the ground.

"You've been slacking, haven't you?"

He nodded sheepishly.

"You know, Eric," she said, less serious, "you're great at making goals, but you have an inherent lazy streak. If you want your goal, you gotta put in the miles."

"Thanks, Mary," Eric said, a smirk on his face. "But be brutally honest."

"Well," Mary said, "between your obsession with beating Trey Allison and applying only to a select group of schools, you're kinda picky, don't ya think? A little too picky, I would say."

"Thanks for the reminder," Eric grumbled. The talented runner from Charlotte, NC—who had never lost to Eric—incensed him only because of Trey Alison's superior attitude, which he threw back into the faces of those he defeated.

"That 4:13 he clocked last year—if I can run as fast as that, as fast as him, I'll definitely have a shot at a good scholarship."

"I'm sure you will," Mary said. She stepped around the gate to the parking lot and turned to face Eric as he followed. "Did you hear?" she said flatly. "Trey signed early with NC State like Jen and me."

"How do you know that?" Eric asked.

"I just heard some people talking."

"You didn't tell me last night?"

"No—Eric." Mary playfully pushed up into his face, then smacked the middle of his chest firmly. "It was New Year's Eve. The last thing I wanted to do was talk about your stupid scholarship."

Eric rubbed the center of his chest. "I guess. But that doesn't change anything for me. I have my own goals. There's nothing wrong with that, is there?" He unlocked the doors of his VW hatchback, then grabbed his dry clothes from the trunk.

"I guess not," Mary said. She came over and placed both hands on his cheeks and squeezed them like a mother talking to her child. "Let's go! You're sucking all the fun out of this day with your scholarship talk." She grabbed her favorite blanket from the passenger seat and wrapped it around her shoulders. Eric called across the roof of the car to her, "What are you smiling at?"

She placed a sparkly tiara on her knit cap, her eyes shining. "Bring back memories?"

Chapter 2

In the weeks following his New Year's Day run with Mary, Eric did not miss a single training day. But, regardless of Eric's renewed motivation from his New Year's run with Mary, he was suffering from a mid-winter malaise due to shortened daylight, sunless skies, and frigid temperatures. Eager to break his funk, Eric had pre-spring adventure on his mind.

One Sunday afternoon in early February, he set out on the roads for an hour and ten minute run. Nearing the end of his route he encountered some college runners who introduced him to a road he never knew about. The two-mile loop had some steep challenging sections which Eric liked. The sparsely populated road was shaded by pine trees and hardwoods, which during the summer heat, would make for a pleasurable run.

Two weeks later, wanting his friends to see what he had discovered, Eric invited Mary, Jen, and Rodney over for an afternoon run. In the winter months, he and his friends preferred running later in the day when the temperatures were warmer. If they could avoid the icy morning temps, the decision was simple.

Rodney was the last to arrive at Eric's house. He met the others at the end of the driveway. Rodney ran cross-country and track but was also a skilled basketball player and starter for the school's team. During basketball season, he would go for short runs with Eric if it didn't interfere with his training or games. "So, Eric, what's this run you been talking about? It's not going be another 'apple orchard' deal, is it?"

"Aw, heck no," Eric said. "This run is harmless. It's *not* going to be an apple orchard deal."

"Well, that run was pretty harmless, too," Jen said, "until Eric decided he wanted to get some apples."

Mary moved in closer to Jen. "I wasn't there. Tell me again what happened?"

"With glee," Jen chirped. She reached out both arms placing her hands on Rodney and Mary's shoulders guiding them closer to Eric like Jen was going to tell everyone a secret. "Well, Mary, as the story goes, and Rodney can attest to it, Mr. Wonderful here—"

"Ahem." Eric interrupted.

"Anyway," Jen said, "we reached the orchard which was our turnaround point, and Eric here gets the brilliant idea to go pick *someone else's* apples."

"But there were tons of apples," Eric said. "They weren't going to miss a few."

Jen ignored his comment and continued her story, saying Rodney hadn't agreed to the apple-picking idea at first, but was OK with it if they made it real quick. Jen herself had thought it was a stupid idea, but she wasn't about to stand out on the road alone in the middle of nowhere, waiting for the boys, so she'd also ducked into the orchard, just a row from the road. She was the first to hear a car pull up. She scurried further into the orchard, toward the boys, to alert them. The three ran to the creek that bordered the orchard and jumped into a patch of briars. They waited for a while before Eric called *coast clear.* But before they managed to untangle their clothes from the prickly branches, they heard foot falls coming from a nearby row of apple trees. They froze and held their breath, peering out at the legs, and guns, of two men who walked just a few feet from their hiding place. By the time it was safe to emerge, the three were covered head to toe with scratches.

Laughing, Mary said, "Oh, Man. Now I remember you telling me that story. I had forgotten about that one."

"But that's not the end of it," Jen said. "After all that, we get a couple hundred yards down the road and Mr. Wonderful says he doesn't want to leave without some apples. Since the guys had to drop them when we ran. So, he tells us to wait. Fortunately, we were out of view of the farmer's house, so me and Rodney wouldn't be seen just standing on the roadside waiting for Mr. Wonderful. Anyhow, he runs back to the orchard, and returns with three apples."

"I know," Rodney said. "I'm not sure whether to call that last move bravado or stupidity."

Mary, standing next to Eric, put and arm around Eric's shoulder and drew him closer, batting her eyelashes at him. "So, Mr. Wonderful," Mary said, mimicking Marilyn Monroe's seductive, breathless way of speaking, "this loop, you say, is no apple orchard run. But where is it?"

Eric went along with Mary's playacting. He pursed his lips and leaned to kiss her. She pulled away giggling. Her question disguised in comedy was underlined with the pall of doubt. After the Apple Orchard run a couple years ago, they always questioned his for details before agreeing to a running adventure. "Come on, guys," Eric said. He spread his arms in front of him, palms up, like a minister inviting the flock to join him on a journey with the Lord. "Aren't you tired of our usual loops? This one is short and fun—two miles at most. The road climbs for a while, circles down, and ties back into itself. A few nondescript homes are up there, but other than that there's not much around."

What road's it on?" Mary asked.

"Foxboro road. You guys know where I'm talking about?"

Rodney said, "I know the road, but I've never been down it."

"OK, people," Jen clamored. "Are we going start this run, or do I need to call Triple-AAA for a map and itinerary? I'm cold."

As they jogged to the starting point of their run, Eric nonchalantly told his friends they should be prepared to breathe a little. Fifteen minutes later, he halted the group in front of the entrance to the property. A metal gate was all that blocked their way, save for the black letters NO TRESPASSING painted on the top crossbar of the galvanized tubing. Eric ducked through a large opening in the gate's steel framing, turned, and motioned for them to follow.

He saw them staring wide-eyed at the black letters. Eric had seen that same look on their faces on previous running adventures he'd taken them on. Jen walked to the fence and said, "They couldn't afford a real 'No Trespassing' sign?" She slipped through the framing and turned back to the other two: "Come on, guys. Let's go."

Rodney let out a sigh, "You never told us we were running on private property. You know I have to be careful where I go. If you know what I mean?"

Eric stepped close to the gate and placed both hands on the top bar. "You'll be OK; you're with us. Anyway, the college runners do this loop, and they've got a black distance guy on their team too. If they run it, there's no reason we can't."

Rodney took a deep breath, "OK."

Mary, standing with feet close together, arms folded across her chest, said, "How many times have you been here, Eric?"

Eric raised his eyebrows and gave her a purposeful smirk. "A few times . . . Come on, Mary. It's harmless."

"That's the second time you've said harmless today," she said.

Jen jumped in: "Come on, guys. It won't take long. Besides, what would anybody do to us? We can tell them we were trying to find a friend's house."

"See?" Eric's voice peaked. "Jen has the right attitude. Besides, the longer we stand around, the more likely somebody will see us."

Rodney and Mary ducked through the gate.

Eric led the group up the road's dramatic incline. Their conversations soon dissipated into rapid huffs. No air left over for words. When they reached the road's apex, each huffing white-vapored breaths like steam engines ready to explode, they stopped and paced a few minutes to let their bodies recover. "Man," Mary said, "That was harder than those hill repeats Coach Miles made us do up Willow road last track season."

"I know," Rodney bellowed. "My calves were sore for two days after."

"I told you guys it was steep," Eric said.

"Thanks, Captain Obvious," Jen said. She walked over to the edge of the road. "Hey, Eric, you know where that trail goes? Ever been on it?"

"No. I haven't," Eric said. He stepped off the road and walked a few yards into the woods to check if it was navigable. He came back out. "It looks OK. What do you think? Want to go explore some more?"

Mary chirped, "I thought we were doing the rest of this loop?"

"The rest is the same but downhill," Eric said. "The trail would be more fun."

"I'm game," Jen said.

Rodney joined Jen and Eric at the edge of the road and peered down the trail. "Man," Rodney said, "you don't have a clue where that path goes. We could get lost."

"We won't get lost," Eric promised. "Besides, I know these trails better than anybody. I think this trail will probably follow the ridgeline that this road crosses and eventually link to a trail back into town. You know how these woods are, there's always a connection to town somewhere. Remember the route we took to John Rock last year?"

"I remember," Rodney said. "We took that trail from the back side of the Willow Creek subdivision. That trail was long and tough. All of us were so tired on Monday's practice. Coach Miles was livid. We couldn't complete his workout."

"Tell you what, guys," Jen said. "If anybody gets nervous, we all have to run back the way we came in. Is that cool with everyone?"

Eric stepped between his friends and stuck out his fist with his pinky finger extended. "Pinky shake, guys. OK?"

Mary's and Rodney's frowns disappeared. They agreed and linked pinky fingers in official agreement.

The trail followed the ridgeline as Eric had hoped, then it descended thirty yards running parallel to its original path. Five minutes later, they halted single file on the narrow path at a fork in the route. Contemplating their next decision, Eric turned and said, "'A road diverged. And I took the road less traveled' . . . is that how it goes?"

"Oh, wonderful," Mary said half-joking. "We're out in

God-knows-where, and you're quoting Robert Frost . . . and, it's 'two roads diverged in a wood, and I—I took the road less traveled by, and that has made all the difference.'"

"Wow Mary, that's impressive," Rodney said.

"Thanks. My ninth grade English teacher, Mr. Gideon, made us memorize that poem."

"So, Eric," Jen said. "Which way leads back to town?"

Eric looked at both sections of the fork, then upward, searching for the sun to find his direction, but he had forgotten that a gray blanket of winter clouds had occluded the sun. "I think we should take the right fork."

"You sure?" Mary said.

Rodney walked past Mary and Jen and examined both trails. "I say we take the right fork. It looks 'less traveled,'" he said.

"You, too, Brutus?" Jen joked.

"All right, enough of the English class, guys?" Rodney said flatly. "But no, I agree with Eric."

"OK, professor," Mary said, nudging Rodney into Eric, "move this school bus along. You guys lead the way."

A few minutes later, when the group reached the peak of a short rise, Eric threw his hand out, motioning for the gang to stop. He turned, put a finger to his mouth, and shushed them before pointing down into a shallow ravine. They piled close to Eric.

Mary whispered, "Eric, what is it?"

Eric pointed again. This time everyone saw it. Below them three whitetail deer, a larger, mature buck and two younger males, were foraging for food among a clump of rhododendrons. Having not heard or seen the runners approach, they continued foraging while their distracted ears flitted back and forth, listening and surveying their surroundings for danger. Eric counted the points on the mature buck's rack and figured it was close to twelve.

"Oh, man," Rodney whispered, "I've hunted many times with my step-dad, but we've never seen a buck with a rack that big."

"Aw, it's like the movie Bambi—but, without the girl deer," she said.

"It's so cool," Mary said. "I've never seen any deer when I've run the trails."

Eric moved aside to give his friends a better view, inadvertently stepping on a brittle pile of twigs, and the debris emitted a sharp ripple of snaps. The large buck's head jerked upward. In that instant, the runners heard a distant rifle crack, followed by a bullet's leaden slug thudding into a decaying tree right about where the buck's head had been, exploding the log skyward. Shards of bark showered the deer as a cloud of lighter particles lingered. The frightened whitetails jolted backward before bolting up the far slope and sprinting over the ridge.

"Hey," Rodney cried, "it's past hunting season. Someone's hunting illegally."

"That's right," Eric said. "Deer season ended last December."

"Can't we tell a ranger or something?" Jen said.

"No, Jen. There's nobody out here," Rodney said.

"We're here. Mary said, gesturing to the group. There are four of us. Doesn't that count for something?"

"Well," Rodney said, "unless a Park Ranger caught a hunter in the act, or with a deer, then no law has been broken. At most, the officer would issue a warning for taking target practice on public lands. But I don't know all the rules."

"Hey, let's discuss this later," Eric said. He motioned for them to follow.

"Wait!" Rodney grabbed Eric's arm. "What if the hunters are up the trail? Think they'd give us trouble?"

Eric scanned his friends' concerned faces. He threw on a smile. "It's OK, guys. I've never had any problems with hunters. They usually give me grief about runners not wearing bright colors during hunting season so they can see us. It'll be OK."

Mary jumped in. "Can't we just go back the same way? Like we said?"

"Guys, we only have a short way to go. There's a turn just up—" Eric caught himself.

"You lied to us?" Jen said. "You've run this trail before!"

His three friends glared, their faces red-cheeked from the cold.

"Look, guys," Eric pleaded. "I know I lied, but you know I'd never drag you guys this far out in the forest and not know where I was going. Besides, we're really close, and I'm sure the hunters will be cool."

Eric saw anger simmering beneath their cold stares, like angry employees learning that their deceitful CEO had lost their pension funds in a fraudulent stock scheme. The four close friends had always kept each other honest, speaking truthful even when those words sounded hurtful; it was tough love. This time, their faces said everything, Eric's adventure was wearing on them.

Then Mary spoke. "I'm getting tired." She slid her sleeve back to check her watch. "We've got an hour until dark. I don't want to go back the long way this late."

"She's right," Jen said. "Let's get going. Eric, lead the way."

For about a hundred yards Eric didn't see any hunters. Maybe they had already moved on and headed down another fork in the trail. As the runners jogged, the path dipped down about six feet and bordered a swale before pitching into a twenty-yard climb. At the crest Eric stopped in his tracks, his friends bumping into him like stacked-up freight cars. Two hunters were walking in their direction, twenty yards distant. Eric, keeping his eyes on the hunters, whispered out of the side of his mouth, "Let me do the talking." The hunters stopped six feet away. Both men were tight-lipped and flushed. They wore camouflage and trapper hats with earflaps. One was a head taller than his partner with a barrel-sized waist and had a trim brown beard. The other was shorter than Eric, and slender too, his full-faced beard dangling down to the middle of his chest. Recognizing these two men outside their hunting apparel would be impossible.

"Hey guys," Eric said, friendly. Ordinarily, if Eric were running by himself and had encountered these two hunters, he'd give them a neighborly wave and keep on running down the trail. Yet, Eric sensed something wasn't right about these two hunters, especially the smaller one, whose beady-eyed look told Eric that he and his buddy knew that Eric and his posse had scared the deer. Eric was the captain of this running adventure, and it was his responsibility to get his friend's back safe. He had to put on a brave face and try not to aggravate these hunters, hoping he and his friends could quickly leave these men to their business.

The smaller man had fixed a cold gaze on Eric the moment he'd approached. The man's gray-specked beard was unkempt and ragged like an overgrown lawn, hiding his mouth entirely. When he spoke the movement of his lips barely made a ruffle in the thick hair. It was like talking to the back of someone's head.

Not returning a greeting, the thin man stepped close to Eric. His blue eyes shone brightly, a stark contrast to his shabby grooming. His eyes—like a cold blue flame—penetrated right through Eric.

"Why'd you scare my deer?" the long-bearded man said in a slow, high-pitched squeal. It wasn't the words the man drawled that unnerved Eric. It was the meanness he exuded. His actions were slow and deliberate, like a man with something to prove.

Eric spoke kindly, flatly, not wanting to alarm these guys any further. He had thought to tell a lie and say they didn't scare the deer, but he decided that plan would aggravate the men more. "Hey, mister, we're sorry if we scared your deer."

"Yeah, that was our deer," the large man blurted in an unconvincing snarl. "We know ya'll scared em'."

The smaller man turned and backhanded the other man's chest. "Shut up, Del—" He caught himself before he gave away his partner's entire name.

Now was a good moment to cut and run and leave these guys to their business. The large man wasn't a threat. Eric sensed he wouldn't hurt a bunny, and besides, he held his gun with the barrel pointing down, no finger on the trigger, unlike his partner. Finger at the ready, the smaller man was too quiet. He fixated on Eric like he was ready to snap, looking for any excuse to do something. Unhinged was the word that came to Eric's mind.

Eric clenched his teeth, trying to quell a trembling spreading down to his legs. Hoping the man didn't notice, Eric faked a tight but cheerful smile and—as politely as possible—said, "Excuse me," then slid a step to his right. He positioned himself between the two men and the outside edge of the trail. He held his gaze on the smaller man and motioned his left arm behind his back for his friends to run around him. "We'll just be on our way, gentlemen."

The gang needed no prodding, sweeping behind Eric before he could gather his next thought. He turned to leave, but the little man grabbed his shirtsleeve and pulled himself close to Eric's face. The man's breath hit Eric's nostrils, and Eric felt his throat tighten. He turned his face away and tried not to breathe the putrid mix of oral neglect and hair cream.

The man maneuvered back into Eric's eyesight. So much for a three-foot personal boundary. A wave of uncertainty crawled up his spine. His first instinct was to shove this guy off the side of the hill and make a mad dash the hell out of here, but what if the other guy retaliated and shot him or his friends? He took a stuttered breath and stared blankly into the flame-blue eyes.

"Well there, mister," the small man said in a low, measured tone, leaning even closer to Eric's face, "seems you're the leader of this gang. Well . . . I got somthin' to say to you." The man took a step back, heaved his rifle to level, his right hand gripping the stock firmly, finger still on the trigger, before settling the rifle's black steel barrel in the middle of Eric's chest. Eric's lungs pulled in a quick breath. This was for real. The man's eyes gleamed, recognizing Eric's fear, his tight-lipped grin cocking to one side. He gave the gun a forward push, knocking Eric back a bit. The scraggy guy then took his free hand and jabbed a bony finger in the direction where the gang had run. Eric turned and saw that Rodney had stopped and was shooing his hand at the girls to move farther down the trail. "You better tell your 'boy' there," the man bellyached, "we don't like his kind in these woods. You understand?"

As Eric held the small hunter's gaze, he saw out of the corner of his eye the bigger hunter taking a step forward. Eric flicked his eyes right, noticing the man's face had turned soft and compassionate.

The tall hunter came closer. "Let the kids go. They ain't done nothin'."

The little hunter spun half toward his buddy, keeping the rifle pointed at Eric. "Shut up," he snapped. "They scared our deer. They gotta pay up."

"Your friend's right," Eric said, looking at the big hunter, searching his face for signs of help.

The small hunter swiveled back to Eric. "What did you say?"

"N-nothing," Eric said.

The small man raised the gun to his shoulder, leveling the barrel squarely between Eric's eyes, his finger tapping the trigger nervously.

This is it. He's going to do it.

The next thing happened so quickly, it took Eric a moment to understand. A shot rang out, and his eyes landed on a large meaty hand wrapped around the barrel of the rifle, which was now pointing skyward. Shock waves of the rifle's report crashed through Eric's body, knocking him back a step. Eric felt his chest to reassure himself that he didn't have a gaping hole in his chest. The gun was no longer pointed at him.

The larger hunter wrestled his friend's rifle away, then plastered the heel of his left hand into the small man's sternum, knocking him to the ground. He turned toward Eric, "You better get going, OK?" Then he flashed a small smile.

Eric dashed after Rodney, thirty yards ahead, who was heading down the trail at a hundred-yard-dash pace. Eric stumbled at first, his legs wobbly from fear. After a few steps, he got his stride under control, though he could barely feel his legs. He couldn't help but glance back repeatedly just in case the little guy had somehow gotten his gun back and was pointing it in his direction.

The girls had waited far enough away from the hunters, out of view, at a bend in the trail. After everyone regrouped, Eric took his lead spot in the front and started to lead his friends out of the forest. But a few minutes later they stopped him and peppered him with questions. He appreciated their concern but insisted they all get out of the woods fast. Though his body craved rest, he knew he wasn't going to settle down until his feet hit pavement; he resumed his lead spot, setting the group back to a brisk pace.

The trail eventually intersected a gravel road. Eric steered the group downhill, back toward town. They passed by a few trailers, one with broken windows, then a bit later, a log cabin with a long low porch across its front. On the porch, bundled in a red blanket, an older man rocked back and forth in his chair, his gaze following them as they passed. Jen gave a little wave, but he didn't return her salutation.

When they came upon a road sign they recognized, Eric and his friends breathed a collective sigh of relief. After their fight-or-flight adrenaline had worn off, they jogged more slowly than usual, lethargic, as if recovering from a hard race. Jen commented that it was nice to have pavement under their feet again. She brought up the subject of what the man had said. One more time, Eric postponed his friends' petitions, telling them to wait until they returned to the house. He noticed his friends' liberated expressions and thought if he explained what happened, he'd rile them up again. They were decompressing, and so was he. Mary started to speak but caught herself and said, "Never mind."

The gang turned onto a road that led to Eric's house, jogging slowly in silence. Eric took a moment to apologize to Rodney and the girls. Then he decided to reveal what the hunter had said, but Rodney didn't react with anger or rage as Eric might have expected. Rodney later stopped the group on a quiet two-lane road after Mary had asked him if what the hunter had said bothered him. He told them, "It's no problem. I'm used to it" He clarified further. "That doesn't mean that I'm not bothered by it. It just means, that I have to take it for what it was. That little guy was mean and he's probably mean to everyone; the racism just added to his anger. Besides, not all people are bad. That big guy saved you, Eric—us for that matter."

On the rest of the way to Eric's house the gang didn't speak. It seemed everyone was processing the previous events in their own minds. For Eric, it was the first time that he experienced racism up close. And while he could never trade places with Rodney to truly understand discrimination, the visceral fear that shuddered through his body when the hunter had the gun aimed at Eric's chest, was as close as he could fathom. Eric remembered back to the news casts of the late 60's and early 70's showing the violent clashes, inhumane treatment and death.

After the girls left, Rodney was about to leave when he said to Eric, "I do appreciate your apology. Remember, I didn't have to go off into the woods with you guys. I could have turned back. And to put it in perspective, your Apple Orchard deal, back a few years ago, Eric, was stealing, and we really shouldn't have done that. But this time we were running in a public forest and we just happened to find the one and only lunatic hunter in the woods."

Watching Rodney drive away, Eric vowed to never press Rodney to do anything he didn't want to, and most of all, never put Rodney in that position in the first place.

Chapter 3

"Winning is not our goal for this season's first meet."

This was what the head track coach of Brevard High School had told his runners on the Thursday before the meet. It was early March, and there was plenty of season left for peak performances. For this initial contest, he wanted his athletes to compete without the pressure of his expectations.

The dual meet was scheduled for Friday afternoon, but rainy weather delayed the start time by an hour. The sun finally broke through and helped dry out the fields, but the long jump pit needed a little extra work to drain the standing water.

Early spring track meets in the Western Carolina Mountains were always cold. A sparse but brave contingent of parents, students, and athletes huddled close, sharing blankets in the trackside bleachers.

In the mile race—five events previous—T C Roberson's top sophomore runner, Randy Wardlaw finished six seconds behind Eric, never challenging him during the closing quarter mile. Eric's winning time was a shade under 4:20, falling short of his junior year's personal best of 4:18. Having beaten Roberson's top miler easily, Eric approached his coming two-mile run, as an uncontested eight-lap time trial.

By the time the two-mile was announced, the sun had long dissolved beyond the horizon, and the glaring stadium lights were no substitute for warmth. An icy tingle still lingered in Eric's nose, and the tips of his fingers were numb despite his twenty-minute warm-up. He sat in the infield, stretching, jealously eyeing his friends, warm under their blankets. His mother was there, too, sitting in the closest bleacher across from the line that would serve as both the start and finish to his race. She was wrapped in a red wool blanket with a hot cup of coffee cradled in her gloved hands. His younger brother, Mark, didn't appear to be in the stands, but Eric envied him at this moment. Mark had finished his pole vault event and was done for the day. Eric wanted this race over soon. He loved his sport, but he couldn't wait for the warmer, body-friendly months.

The last call for the two-mile reverberated from the stadium speakers. Eric jumped up, slipped off his sweats, and tossed them to the infield. He jogged over to the race clerk standing at the far end of the straightaway, where the 100-yard dash runners typically started their races. He checked in. Once the final heat of the 220-yard dash was completed and recorded, the clerk would escort the two-mile runners 50-yards midway up the straightaway for their start.

The starting line crew had assigned the boys the first three lanes and the girls the outer three. Because of the lateness of the meet and the dropping temperatures, the coaches had combined the boys' and girls' two-mile races, for a total of fifteen runners. Holding their races together would shorten the meet and help send the kids home earlier.

The race officials escorted the athletes to their assigned starting lanes. From lane two, Eric looked over at Mary in lane four. To keep warm, she wore a long-sleeve T-shirt under her nylon singlet. Eric and most of the other runners, except for a hardy few, had done the same. Mary sported her customary grim, determined game face. She stared down the straightaway as she paced in one spot in her lane.

"What are you staring at?" Eric called over.

She turned her head, shot him a blank stare, then resumed her focus up the track.

"So how long do you think it'll take before I lap you?" he said with a mischievous chuckle, leaning around the adjacent third lane runner, trying to catch her eyes.

Mary's forward gaze held fast. "I don't care. Shut up, Eric!"

Eric frowned. He blew his warm breath into his cupped hands, rubbed them vigorously, but the cold tingle's pricking his fingers had not gone away. The starter then just crossed the track in front of him with his pistol in hand. "Good," Eric thought. The race would start soon. From his previous cold weather experience, he figured about three minutes into the race his extremities should start feeling warmer. He then sprinted up the track to keep his legs loose. When he returned, Mary said, "Do you take anything seriously anymore?"

"Sure I do."

"Could have fooled me!"

"Aw, Mary. I'm only messing with you. Just having some fun."

"Well, now isn't the time, Eric."

"OK, OK," Eric said. "You know I like to put a smile on your face." He stepped behind the scowling third lane runner and thrust his hand up for a high-five, and Mary batted his hand down.

"Your timing is impeccable," Mary said, but her voice had softened a little.

"That's sarcasm. Right?"

She huffed. "Eric, go back to your lane, OK?"

He stepped back into his assigned lane, then shifted his attention to Randy Wardlaw in lane one. Wardlaw had a three-inch height advantage over Eric and cut an imposing figure on the track, towering over the other runners. Wardlaw's blue and gold racing singlet fit snug around his chest. He had broad shoulders for a tall, skinny kid.

When the race began, Eric and the other runners dashed around the long curve. Halfway down the first-lap's backstretch Eric and Wardlaw were already fifteen yards clear of their trailing teammates.

At the end of the first lap, Eric shifted over to the third lane, slowed his pace, drifting backward. "You all right, Eric?" the other boys asked as they passed him. He didn't answer.

Eric glanced back and spotted Mary tailing a group of four boys. She was thirty yards ahead of the girl's nearest runner, Jen. Roberson had no equal for Brevard's female duo. When she pulled beside him, he eased over to lane two and matched her speed.

"What're you doing!?"

"Thought I'd—run with you—a bit."

"You can't—"

"Yes, I can." He raised his eyebrows when she met his look.

Nearing the end of the second lap, Eric caught the angry stare of his head coach, Rowland Baker standing on the infield near the finish line. Baker's booming voice hammered Eric's ears as he ran past. The coach was barking at decibels Eric had only heard from a Hi-Fi stereo. "Roberts, get back to your race, or I'll yank you off this track."

As Eric passed Baker, he raised his arms in submission.

"Looks like I gotta go," he told Mary.

"Jerk," she growled, before thrusting a fist into Eric's left shoulder, knocking him over into lane three.

Well, so much for fun, he thought. Up the track he spotted Wardlaw rounding the top of the far turn, about a hundred yards away. The gap was farther than Eric had anticipated, but it was nothing he couldn't make back quickly. He accelerated to reel in his opponent.

As Eric chased, he paid little attention to the timers calling the lap splits. To catch and beat Wardlaw mattered most. Each time he passed the finish line, he endured relentless catcalls from Wardlaw's teammates and a few Roberson parents. Turning a deaf ear, he put his head down and zeroed in on the back of Wardlaw's jersey.

After two laps of marking Wardlaw's blue and gold singlet, it became evident to Eric that his competitor's stride was more fluid and efficient than the previous fall, his footfalls rolling effortlessly underneath him. Every inch of his lanky frame devoured the track.

In the next two laps, Eric cut half the distance to Wardlaw, but he began feeling his legs dulling sooner than usual for a two-mile race. The mammoth effort of chasing his opponent was taking a toll. With only a half mile remaining to the finish, and forty yards still between himself and Wardlaw, Eric felt desperation rising in his chest. He tried to focus, to relax—to shut out the nagging self-criticism in his own mind: *How in the world did you dream up the boneheaded idea of giving Wardlaw such a huge lead?*

Despite Eric's deadening legs, he mustered reserves and whittled down Wardlaw's lead to twenty-five yards. Six hundred yards remained.

When Eric turned onto the home stretch, five hundred yards to go, his tall foe was now only five yards ahead. Eric's confidence surged. *Ok, zero-out that gap, Eric. Then you can blow by him for an easy victory.*

He finally pulled alongside Wardlaw's right shoulder.

Clang, clang, clang, the final lap bell clamored.

Eric flicked his eyes left, scanning his competitor's form for signs of fatigue. Wardlaw's eyes held stolid, his pace matching his resolution, steady and locked in, but there were no signs of him starting a kick. Halfway into the next curve, Eric was ready to make a decisive move; it was time to leave this guy in the dust.

But before Eric could turn on the gas, Wardlaw surged. He'd beaten Eric to the punch and now busted open a five-yard lead.

He's got a kick!

Wardlaw wasn't the same runner Eric had handily beat the previous cross-country season. Eric hadn't anticipated this advancement in the sophomore's distance prowess. Eric continued to claw the track, desperate to close the gap.

For the first seven laps, Eric had believed Wardlaw to be a lesser runner, someone he could beat with ease. Now he saw this guy was for real. Eric's seesawing confidence waned again, but he dug deep. Forty torturous yards later, he zeroed the gap and settled in directly behind his opponent. Right now his foe had the driver's wheel. Eric, not wanting to reveal his fatigue, held his position, hoping to play a little hide-and-seek, forcing Wardlaw to lead. Drafting behind his sizable foe would give Eric a chance to recover. Wardlaw towed Eric out of the second turn to start the hundred-yard-long backstretch.

At the beginning of the backstretch, Eric heard Rodney screaming encouragement. Eric gave a quick glance and saw him standing near the end of the long jump pit, close to the track. Eric returned his eyes to his race where he found himself running inches behind Wardlaw. To keep from colliding, Eric buttressed his hands against Wardlaw's shoulder blades and quick-stepped to the right, one lane over, to avoid clipping Wardlaw's feet. From this new angle, Eric drew a clearer picture of Wardlaw's condition: his stride had turned choppy, head tilted back, and his upper body cardboard stiff. Wardlaw's surge must have taken its toll. Eric strained to lift his legs also, to hold himself erect, not lean back, to surrender to the fatigue.

Still confident that he had the better foot speed, Eric steeled himself for a go at Wardlaw, coaching himself for the imminent jump: *Break him now. Stick your move.*

Eric found his reserve strength and accelerated, but Wardlaw countered, matching him stride for stride. Fifty yards later Eric jumped again. Same result. *I can't crack this guy.* Despite Eric's frustrations, he noticed that Wardlaw had matched his previous two surges but wasn't making any counter attacks. That light-bulb moment gave Eric a glimmer of hope even as his legs swung heavier with each step.

A hundred yards later, the two deadlocked runners lumbered out of the final bend—fifty yards remaining to the finish line. Eric was ready to launch one final counterstrike to end this battle. He made his jump, arms churning, legs driving, and edged around a now wheezing Wardlaw. He flicked a backward glance, gauged the gap, then shifted to lane one. A two yard lead would have to do. *Keep your head up. Focus on the line. The victory is yours.*

But Wardlaw wasn't done yet. With a growling grunt, the indefatigable foe surged, sweeping around Eric's right shoulder. Eric shifted right to block the pass, but Wardlaw retaliated, dipping his left shoulder, and throwing a forearm into Eric's side. Eric stiffened to absorb the hit, but he still lurched leftward, his inside foot clipping the track's curb. He stumbled but quick-stepped to keep upright. Wardlaw was coming again and not playing nice. But that suited Eric. He liked a good fight; that was racing. They were like two stock cars—engines whining, bodies scraping, sweeping out of the last turn for a pedal-to-the-metal finish.

Shoulder to shoulder at the finish, inches apart, they hurled themselves toward the line. With their arms laid back like Alpine ski jumpers, they crashed through the finish line, stumbling, arms flailing. Each gripped the other out of reflex, trying to maintain their balance. They eventually halted fifteen yards past the line, both immediately doubling over in chest-heaving exhaustion.

"Tie," A timer called out.

What? Eric thought. He wanted to scream, "Are you crazy?" and run over to challenge the call, but he couldn't right himself.

When he regained some composure, he looked over and saw the timers huddled together, arguing.

Eric headed toward them.

"Get back up the track," an official barked and shooed him away.

"Don't push me," Eric moaned.

The other boys were completing their races, and in a few minutes the girl runners would be coming through the finish to begin their last laps. Race officials scrambled among the stacked-up athletes, attempting to clear the lanes of exhausted runners. Eric retrieved his warm-ups from the infield. He returned to the track's sideline and paced in one spot, waiting for the decision.

Minutes later the head official called out, "Wardlaw First place; Roberts second."

"No way!" Eric shouted. He spun and kicked the dirt. *I don't believe it. I won. I don't care how close it was. I won.*

Someone tapped his shoulder. "Hey, great race," Wardlaw's voice said behind him.

Eric ignored him and kept walking.

"You know," Wardlaw yelled after him, "Roberts, you're a real jerk!"

Not looking back, Eric waved him off. The scorers recorded his name. He snatched his red second-place ribbon and rushed to the outer fence, his stomach churning. He slumped over it, hacking to clear his throat before spitting a thick lugee onto the sidewalk.

Someone patted Eric on the back. "Gweat wace, Ewic."

Eric knew the voice. He craned his neck toward his handicapped classmate. Buzzy Connor stood in front of him wearing a giant smile on his face.

"Not now, Buzzy. Please go away." As far as Eric was concerned, it was never a good time to have Buzzy around. Ever since they were kids, most everywhere Eric went, Buzzy was always tagging along. Eric lowered his head, his stomach roiling again. Buzzy said nothing and walked away.

"Are you all right?" said a man's voice in an accent Eric didn't recognize.

Eric didn't look up. He just continued to hack and cough. "I'm OK, buddy," he managed. *Why does everybody want to talk to me when I feel like crap?*

"Do you always race that way?" the voice asked.

"What kind of question is that?" Eric spat a few more times on the pavement, wiped his mouth with the back of his hand, and righted himself to look at the stranger. The tall, frail man towered over Eric, his white hair poking out from under a baseball cap, its bill shading his gaunt face from the stadium lights. His voice was raspy, like Eric's grandfather had been.

"Oh, I don't know, I was curious."

Eric flailed his red ribbon in front of the inquisitive man. "No. I don't always race that way. I got second place. Does that answer your question?"

"Second place isn't so bad. Sometimes it's the effort that counts."

Eric huffed. "Well, if you like second so much, you can have this." He grabbed the man's thin hand and shoved the ribbon into it, turned, and stalked away.

Chapter 4

Eric woke early the next morning and dressed for running, being careful not to wake his brother, who was still asleep in the room they shared. He grabbed a twenty-dollar bill off the dresser, folded it in quarters, and stuffed it underneath the laces of one shoe and knotted both with double knots.

Before leaving the house, Eric stopped by his mother's room to tell her he was stepping out for a run. He reached to knock on her door but hesitated. Their previous night's confrontation flashed through his mind. After his catastrophe of a race, his mom had confronted him at the track's perimeter fence, demanding he get home at once. "I'll ground you for eternity if you don't get there in under than fifteen minutes," she'd warned. At home she sat him down at the kitchen table and began a verbal assault greater than he had ever experienced—even worse than the time he'd come home two hours after his curfew. During their intense discussion, mostly one-sided on his mother's part, she expressed her embarrassment at his reckless, egomaniacal display at the meet, saying that he didn't seem to think about anyone but himself. She punctuated her diatribe by pronouncing him "a selfish, arrogant teenager."

Eric apologized, but denied all her allegations, which further exasperated her. She stood up, tears spilling down her cheeks, jabbed a finger at him, and screamed, "You'd never act like this if there were a man in this house."

Floored that she'd throw out such a thinly veiled reference to his deceased alcoholic father, Eric stormed off to his room and slammed his door.

Now, as dawn's emerging sunbeams were penetrating the house, Eric took a deep breath before he knocked gently on his mother's door. "Mom, you up?"

"Yes," she said. "Come in."

Eric cracked the door open and peered around the edge. "Hey, Mom. I'm going for a run."

"I kind of figured that. I heard you rummaging around in there."

"I tried to be quiet and not wake Mark up."

"Well, your brother's a heavy sleeper and he's probably used to it, but you being quiet in the morning isn't one of your strong suits," she said with a long eyebrow raise.

Eric grinned. "Sorry."

"Why are you up so early? You usually wake up late on Saturdays, especially after a Friday track meet.

Eric stepped into the room. "I couldn't sleep, so I decided to get my running done early today.

"How long will you be gone?"

"An hour. Maybe two."

"Oh!" she said, startling Eric. Her eyes were flickering with delight. "You're going over to Mary's to apologize, aren't you?" She shifted her pillow so she could sit up.

"Yeah, but I don't think she'll listen."

"Come here, Honey," she said, patting the bed beside her.

He shuffled over and sat down.

"You two have been friends for how long?"

"Almost four years."

"Right. Now, don't you think Mary values your friendship?"

"I guess . . ."

"OK. So, you made a mistake last night. If you apologize honestly, she'll see you mean it."

"You're probably right. But I made her super mad this time."

Mrs. Roberts guffawed. "I doubt it'll be the last time either."

Eric's eyes widened. "Man, Mom, you and Mary should've been twins. You two don't hold back."

His mother cleared her throat. "Well, I can't speak for Mary, but that's my job as a parent—to be honest with you. But listen. Mary's your good friend. She's a smart girl. If you say what you think she wants to hear, she'll read right through your words. Speak to her from your heart. I'm sure she'll forgive you—for the millionth time."

Eric laughed. "I guess you're right." He leaned over and kissed her on the cheek. "Thanks, Mom."

She touched his arm as he started to stand. "Hey, I know I gave you a month-long grounding and more chores to do, but if you're a good boy, I'll reduce your sentence for *good time* accrued."

Eric nodded. "OK, Mom. That's up to you. But you know I'll serve my full sentence."

"All right," she said. "Get going. Have a good run." But before Eric left the room, she added, "You know, you'd have better chances by letting her sleep in. You should do it later."

He gave her a salute, "I'll take that under advisement, Captain."

In the kitchen, Eric toasted a piece of wheat bread and slathered it with strawberry preserves. The meager amount of bread and sugar would be enough to give him a little energy but not upset his stomach while he ran.

His brother Mark appeared, rubbing his eyes.

"I thought you were asleep?" Eric said.

Eric's brother, a sophomore, was now an inch taller than Eric's six feet and still growing. Mark was thin and wiry like their father and looked to be well on his way to reaching their father's height of six feet two inches. They both had brown hair like their parents, but Mark had inherited their mother's blue eyes.

Eric licked jam from his fingers. "You pole-vaulters are lucky," he told his brother. "You don't have to run every day like us distance runners."

"Au contraire mon ami," Mark said, laughing. He had been taking French since freshman year and was always trying to sound sophisticated. "We train as much as you guys do. Not as many miles as you lunatic distance runners, but we lift weights and run sprints too."

Eric set his little dish in the sink. "Well," he said, "let's see how those weight-lifting muscles can power you through fixing the shed with me."

"It's too bad Dad's not here," Mark said. "He could do it."

Eric looked at his brother but said nothing, then walked to the kitchen door, where the family dog, Molly, had been whimpering to go out. "I'll see you later, Mark." He reached down and grabbed Molly's collar and escorted her outside. Eric clipped a chain to the collar of his Golden Labrador. She bolted off the porch to chase the same squirrel for the hundredth time, her chain snapping horizontal at the last second. The annoying, tree-climbing rodent scolded her from the high-rise safety of the pine branches.

"Aw, girl, you never learn, do you?" He sighed. He missed running with her. She had once been his trail running partner, but her arthritic hips kept her in the yard now. Eric called her back to the porch. He rubbed her graying muzzle and said, "Hey Molly darlin'. We'll go for a long walk when I get back, OK?"

After a few stretches, Eric slipped off the porch and strode away from his house, which sat towards the back of its lot surrounded by Maples and pines his father had planted. He turned right on Probart street, uphill, to take the longer route to Mary's house. She lived only a mile and a half from him, but he wanted more time to loosen his tired legs and rid the morning chill from his extremities. Molly's plaintive barks echoed in his ears until he crossed over the next rise.

Eric groaned, feeling the lactic acid nagging his depleted muscles. His shoes scraped the pavement, his legs dead weight. The day after a meet, he knew his legs would give bitter complaint. Like any athlete, he understood it was the price you had to pay to excel.

As he ran, doing his best to ignore the ache, he busied his mind by conjuring an elaborate excuse for his apology to Mary. The only excuse that made sense was that he had wanted to test his fitness by seeing how far he could let Wardlaw slip away before reeling him in. That explanation seemed the most logical. If he were about to use it on another person, someone who didn't intimately know him, he might get away with it . . . but it would never fly with Mary. He reminded himself of his mother's advice. *Just tell her you're sorry.*

After slogging through the first mile, Eric's stride became a bit more fluid, if just a bit. He took the next left, deciding to shorten the loop. The route he chose cut through an quaint older neighborhood leading back to Main Street. He passed the city's maintenance shed, and at the next intersection, he stopped to stretch. As he alternated toe-touches to stretch is leg's aching hamstrings, he gazed across the street at an old dilapidated white house. It appeared, as always, to be uninhabited.

The architecture was generic and unimpressive, but he liked it anyway. The generic, front-gable, two-story house occupied an elevated corner lot situated on a big curve and bordered one other home. From the street, he noticed a forest of overgrown shrubbery surrounding the structure. Through the tangled foliage he thought he saw a sign on one of the front windows. But the only letters he could make out were, "-DEMN-". The letters swirled in his head for a moment then it came to him: It was a CONDEMNED sign. In the past, whenever he had passed the house, a For Rent sign was habitually staked in the front yard.

He took one last look before moving along. But as he took his first steps, a screen door slammed at a house next door, and a gray-haired black man emerged. The man shuffled to the end of his pea-graveled walkway. The older gentleman paused and bent over, one hand wobbling on a cane, his free hand straining for his newspaper. Eric jogged over to the man, who had finally grabbed the newspaper, his other hand quivering on his cane as he righted himself. "Hey, sir," Eric said.

The man's feet scuffed a small step backwards, sending pea-gravel skittering. His aged body unfolded with remarkable swiftness. The tall man settled into a hunched-shoulder lean. His eyes were widened and wild "Geez, you scared the hell out of me. What do you want?"

"Sorry to bother you about that," Eric said. "But, I wonder, do you know anything about that two-story house next door?"

The man peered into Eric's face. His eyes flashed, and a grin spread across his broad face. "Hey, I know you. You're Eric Roberts.

I saw you run last night." He stuck out his hand. "I'm Andrew Butterfields' grandfather."

Eric shook the man's hand. "Oh, yeah Andrew, I know him. He's a freshman. A good sprinter, and quarter-miler, too."

The man leaned closer like he had something to say. "I'm sorry about your race last night," he said, chuckling.

"Thanks," Eric said. "You're not the only one. Everyone in town will know what happened when they read the paper this morning." The man only nodded his assent. "Hey, I don't mean to be rude," Eric started, still eager for and answer to his previous question, "but do you know why that house next door is empty?"

"No," the man said, grimacing. "Sorry, I don't." He stabbed his cane in the gravel repeatedly, steadying himself as he turned around. He shuffled back up his driveway.

Eric watched the man surmount an eight-inch high, rectangular, cement-slab-of-a-front-porch, plop down on a wooden chair and start to unfold his newspaper. Eric, feeling like a pesky reporter wanting to know more, was tempted to press the man for an answer to his question. But he thought better of it and said, "Thanks anyway. Again, sorry to bother you." He turned and jogged off.

"Hey," the man called. Eric, stopped and looked back. The man was waving the newspaper at Eric, pointing at a picture. "You made the front page of the sports section. Big photo and everything."

Eric blinked his eyes hard. The stunt he'd pulled the night before was bound to make headlines in a small town. "Wow," Eric said to himself, "when you go down in flames, Eric, you torch the whole town."

As he continued his run, however, his thoughts were not on the article or having his photo in the paper. The abandoned house had taken up residence in his mind and pushed all other thoughts out. Why had the old man been evasive when asked about the house?

When Eric arrived at Mary's house, he walked the gravel driveway that led to the back of the house. He picked up a few pea-sized chunks of stone on the way. He knew of only one way to wake her without disturbing her family.

With care, he tossed a pebble at her upstairs window. He expected it to glance off the glass, but instead it made a loud thunk. Man, I don't need to break her window, he thought. She's already mad enough at me. He waited a few seconds for her to appear. Nothing.

He poked a finger around in the pile of pebbles in his palm till he found one suitable. He launched a smaller stone at the window, but still, Mary didn't show. He tossed another.

The window sash whipped open and crashed to the top of its frame. Mary stuck her head out, her lips tight, eyes narrowed. "What the hell are you doing here so early?" she said in a whisper.

"Uh, well, I was coming to apologize . . . and I was hoping we could maybe go for a run."

Their fellow teammate, Jen, crammed her head out the window. "Why don't you go home, Eric? She doesn't want to talk to you."

"But—"

"It's OK, Jen," Mary said. "Let's hear him out."

Mary's face had softened, but Jen was still scowling.

An idea popped into his head that might sway Jen's attitude. Jen's boyfriend, Jonathan, was a shot and discus thrower on the track team. He lived six houses away.

"Hey, Jen, how 'bout I go up the street and wake up your lazy discus-throwing boyfriend and see if he'll run with us over at Straus Park? I know Coach Baker gave the throwers and sprinters some distance running this weekend. If he meets us there, he could drive us back. Which means we could all go stuff our faces at the Clock Diner after we finish our run. Sound reasonable?"

Jen's eyes brightened. She dragged Mary back inside. Eric stepped closer to the house to hear their conversation but had no luck.

Jen reappeared. "Ugh. OK. We'll run with you only if you can get Jonathan to come."

"OK, you got a deal. I'll be back soon." Eric sprinted off. As he rounded the corner of the house, he peeked back at the window and made eye contact with Mary. She turned away, embarrassed, but he saw she had a cute little grin on her face. Good sign, Eric thought.

Fifteen minutes later, Eric returned and found Mary and Jen stretching on the front lawn.

"What did he say?" Jen said.

"I can't repeat the exact words, but uh—he wasn't too happy when I pounded on his window. He said he'd meet us over at Straus by the docks on the lake."

Eric noticed Mary and Jen giggling, giving each other furtive glances.

"Hey, what's with you guys?" Eric asked.

Mary looked at Jen. Her teammate pulled her arm from behind her and opened her hand. A red ribbon unfurled. She held it out to Eric.

"What's that?

"You should know. It's your ribbon. I asked the old man for it last night. He didn't want it, but I figured you would. I was going give it to you at school on Monday, but since you're here . . ." Jen tossed it at Eric's feet. "Here you go number two." Mary and Jen snickered.

Eric snatched up the ribbon as though he could make the whole fiasco disappear by hiding the ribbon from sight.

Chapter 5

The Clock Diner's menu wasn't much to boast about, but the place had the best breakfast around—and real ice cream milkshakes too.

Eric and his friends settled into a booth on the sunny side of the tiny restaurant. A waitress took their order, and while they waited for their food to arrive, Eric half-listened while folding his paper napkin a dozen different Origami-like ways, while his friends launched into a debate about the ridiculous Biorhythms theory. Earlier, while they'd waited for a table, Jen had plunked a quarter into a wood-paneled Biorhythm machine that stood enticingly close to the front door of the restaurant. She'd entered Mary's birthdate into the predictive contraption, and an info card, replete with mathematical graphs, instantly jutted out its answer slot.

"Eric," Mary said, "aren't you joining in? You never miss chiming in on a debate, especially on a subject as ludicrous as a Biorhythm Machine."

Eric smoothed out his napkin and looked up at Mary. "No, you guys got it covered." The table quieted.

"What's that mean?" she said.

Now Eric was nervous. Their eyes were on him. He wanted to apologize for his actions the day before, but he wasn't sure he knew the right words. *Remember what your mom said, speak from your heart.*

Eric exhaled. "I can't exactly explain what happened yesterday. But I do know one thing; I embarrassed my team, my school, my coach, and most of all, my mother. And well, my little brother, too. But mostly, he laughs at me." He paused, noticing his friends' faces had softened. "I hope you guys can forgive me."

"Awww," Mary said. She reached across the table, touching Eric's hand.

"I think I'm going to cry," Jonathan said, mock sniffling and rubbing a finger at fake tears in his eyes.

Eric threw his folded napkin at him.

The waitress returned, her arms loaded with plates, perfectly timed to rescue Eric from any more embarrassment. She deftly unloaded their epicurean reward, crowding the tiny tabletop, barely a speck of its white linoleum visible. "You going to eat all that?" she said.

The gang just looked at her and smiled.

"OK," she said, "I'll check on you guys in a bit."

In a flurry of cheap cutlery, they devoured the bountiful feast, not a crumb remaining. During the meal, Eric remembered his mother's advice. His apology was heartfelt. However, his upcoming punishment of pushups and sit-ups the track coach had issued him was minor compared to the protracted suffering he would endure from his friends and teammates. Their lighthearted verbal abuse would continue for a couple more weeks, at least.

When the waitress checked on them, Jen said to her, "I don't think the dishwasher will need to clean these dishes."

Clearing the spotless plates, the cheerful waitress winked and said, "I suppose not."

Relieved that his friends had accepted his apology, Eric took a deep breath and let out a long sigh. His friends' rejection would be more than he could endure. With Eric's mind now more at ease, he found his thoughts returning to the abandoned house on the corner, and the way the old man had reacted to his questions. Earlier, during their group run at Straus, he had described for them his encounter with the man. They reminded him there was probably nothing to what the man said. He was just mad that Eric had scared him and didn't want to talk anymore.

"Hey, you know that house on Oaklawn," Eric said now. "I was thinking—"

"Really, Eric," Mary interrupted. "You and that house again. You've been blabbering about it the whole morning. That's about enough for one day, don't you think?"

"But—"

"Why are you so interested, anyway?" Jonathan asked. "So it looks condemned. Who cares?"

"I mean, really," Jen, piled on, "that house is ordinary. There are nicer houses to fawn over."

"I don't know," Eric said, defeated. "I hoped we could go see what's inside or something. Wouldn't that be fun?" He searched his friends' faces for signs of interest, but their smirking and rolling eyes told him this conversation had hit a dead end.

Eric slid out of the booth. "OK, let's go. I promised my mom I'd fix the backyard shed today. He walked toward the cash register, and without looking back, said, "Don't think I don't hear you all laughing at me."

The snickering ceased.

When Eric walked through the kitchen door, he saw his mother standing on a wooden three-step ladder, swiping a rag back and forth across the large living room window. Rags, and plastic bottles filled with cleaning solution littered the kitchen table. His mother was full out into spring cleaning mode.

"It's 11:30. Where've you been?" Mrs. Roberts said.

He walked into the living room. "I was hanging out with Mary, Jen, and Jonathan at the Clock for a while."

His mother stopped wiping and turned. "You should've been home a few hours ago. I was worried. And—you were supposed to be working on the shed today." She sprayed more window cleaner on the large pane and wiped furiously at one spot.

"Sorry, Mom," Eric said.

She huffed in exasperation. "*Sorry* won't get it, Eric. You've been promising for weeks now to fix that shed. You need to do it today! The rainwater is getting inside and ruining everything."

"Yes, ma'am," he said obediently.

"Oh, and your brother is supposed to help too. Mark's nearly worthless at cleaning the house. He's taken an hour to clean four windows. I think he has Jenna Basset on his mind. Been talking about her all week. You boys only have one thing on your minds at this age," she said.

Mark yelled from another room. "I can hear you, Mom."

"I'll get Mark to help," Eric moaned.

His mother stepped off the ladder. She brushed a few strands of her long brown hair from her face, her blue eyes glaring. She shook her rag at him. "Look, I'm the only parent here. I got to do this all by myself. All I'm asking for is a little help, OK? Can you do that for me?"

"Yes," Eric said.

MR. JENKINS, THE PROPRIETOR of Harrison Hardware, helped Eric load his hatchback at the store's rear loading area. The wooden siding and two-by-four lumber for the shed repairs extended out the car's back end. The store owner helped hold the hatch down as Eric secured it with twine.

Jenkins turned to Eric. "Hey. Would you be interested in working for me again after you graduate in June?"

Eric appreciated the gesture from his old boss. He was a fair and even-tempered guy. All he expected was that you show up on time and not goof off. The money Eric had earned working at the hardware store the last two summers had enabled him to save enough to buy his VW hatchback. "Thanks," Eric said. "I haven't decided on summer work yet."

"OK. Well, I better get back inside."

"Uh, Mr. Jenkins?" Eric said, before he could turn away.

"Yes, son?"

"Do you know the anything about that old abandoned house

over on Oaklawn?" Eric threw a thumb over his shoulder in the general direction.

Jenkins, not answering, turned his attention to the twine that Eric had used to secure the hatch. He tugged at the string. Still not looking at Eric, he said, "Good and tight. You shouldn't have any problems on your way home."

Eric placed a light hand on Jenkins forearm, getting his attention. "I apologize for asking again. But, do you?"

Jenkins's gentle eyes tightened. "You don't need to know nothing about that house, OK, son?" He threw on a quick smile and said, "It's good to see you, Eric. But I need to get back to my business. Let me know if you still want to work this summer, OK?" He turned and went inside.

Eric stared at the back door of the hardware store. Strange, Eric thought. Why was everyone so reluctant to talk about that house?

When Eric pulled away, he headed in the opposite direction from where he lived.

Moments later, Eric stood in the driveway facing the run-down structure. The yard's grass had grown so thick that even a powerful lawn mower would stall out trying to cut it. And the majority of the adjacent hedges had scaled the second story windows. The narrow building still had a cement porch on its left side, but the roof that had covered it was long gone. Only the outline of nails peppering the siding hinted at its former existence. A No Trespassing sign had been duct-taped over the front door's tiny square window.

Eric stepped onto the front porch, then tried to peer into its three windows, but he found no gaps in their curtains. The front door had a hasty patch job of plywood with drywall screws near the handle. Someone must have tried to pry into it. He reached to test the door handle but hesitated. There's nothing to be nervous about, Eric. He jiggled the knob. It was loose but still locked.

Ignoring the shiver in his chest, triggered by his overactive imagination, he decided, Eric set out to investigate the backside of the house. The remaining windows on the left side of the structure had curtains, except one that was nailed over with plywood. When Eric walked toward the back, he noticed that the architecture changed; the rear section seemed to be an addition.

Before rounding the corner to investigate further, he stopped. He spun around to check the surrounding neighborhood. Was anyone watching him? He needed to make this quick.

At the back, he found one window that was open a crack, and the curtain was slid off to one side. He slid the lower sash upward until it stopped. He reached for the window sill to crawl in, but he jerked his hand back. I can't do this, he told himself. It's trespassing. He compromised and peered in the window, but in the darkened interior, he only recognized a toaster on the counter still plugged into a wall socket.

Resisting the urge to explore further, Eric headed back to his car.

An orange sunset fringed the mountain peaks, and the late afternoon air was cooling. Eric and Mark were nailing the last piece of siding to the backyard shed. It had been a harder job than Eric had expected. Once he'd torn out the moisture-rotted section, he'd discovered that the shed's framing needed further reworking. He'd had to return to the hardware store for more supplies.

Now the boys leveled the final plank and hammered the nails flush. Eric eyed the fading skyline, then pointed at the two caulking guns he'd laid out, "We should have enough time to finish this."

Fifteen minutes later, Mark applied the last inches of caulk to the shed. "Hey, Eric, do you miss dad?" he said.

Eric was collecting the tools. He paused and looked at Mark, "I've told you before. You don't understand," he said flatly. He gathered the rest of the tools and stepped into the shed to put them away.

Mark followed him into the shed and laid the caulking guns on a shelf. "Well, I miss him, even if he was a mean drunk." Mark turned and left the shed, leaving Eric alone in the dim light.

"Hey," Eric called after his brother. "I'm sorry. I didn't mean to be short with you."

Mark peeked his head back in.

"I guess we look at dad differently."

Mark came in and leaned a hand on their father's old workbench sitting adjacent the newly repaired wall. "I guess we do." He swiped some sawdust off the table's dusty surface. "Come on, let's get the rest of these tools put away."

After Mark had gone back into the house, Eric flipped on the bare-bulb light that dangled overhead from twisted AC wires. The workbench, was an old discarded rectangular kitchen table his dad had brought home one afternoon. Eric's eyes caught the glint of metal shavings buried in a sawdust pile around the vise clamped to the table. The silver shards sparkled under the glaring light. He pinched a clump of the congealed wood and metal and drew it to his nose, taking in the bitter metal tang and the warm oaken wood mixed with oil. It was like walking into Harrison Hardware, the peculiar mix of home restoration materials all smacking you in the face the moment you enter, or like the antiseptic tinge of a doctor's office. They were places of renewal; all things could be made better there—maybe a can of paint, maybe a prescription, or maybe just a good case of sound advice from a friendly storeowner.

Eric exhaled, smiled softly, brushed his fingers off, then picked up his father's wooden hammer and hung it back on its pegboard hooks, safely inside the black-markered outline drawn by his father when Eric was five years old. Eric traced his finger along the faded ink line, then drew his hand down the length of the tool's cherry-stained handle, before leaving the shed.

Chapter 6

The next day, Sunday afternoon, Eric went to the library to study. After he had finished his Calculus homework, he leaned back in his chair, mulling over the house. Eric knew little of its history, but who would know more? He had thought about searching the microfiche newspaper archives. Sorting through small boxes of film, loading them into the machine and manually scrolling the newspaper's photographs would take hours just to find the information he wanted. He didn't have time for that.

The head librarian, Mrs. Carlson, was shelving returned books two bookcases away. As far back as Eric could remember, she had been a fixture at the library. If anyone knew about this town and its inhabitants, she did.

He walked over, picked up a book from her cart, and when her attention turned to him, he handed it to her. "Hello, Mrs. Carlson."

"Oh, hi Eric, may I help you?" she said quietly, politely accepting Eric's offering.

"Well . . ." Eric paused, not sure exactly how or if he should ask his question but plowed ahead anyway. It was worth a shot. "Do you know the history of the abandoned house over on Oaklawn? You know, the one on the big curve?"

Mrs. Carlson said nothing. She checked the Dewey Decimal number on the book's binding, scanned a row of books, found the correct spot, and shelved it. "I know the one. Why do you want to know?"

Embarrassed, Eric didn't want to admit he had a strange fascination with the structure, so he tried to sound nonchalant. "I was curious, that's all."

"Oh, I see," she said, a treble of doubt in her voice. After a moment of sorting through the remaining books on her cart, she said, "I live on that side of town. When I drive to work, I go through that neighborhood. Why are you interested, if I may ask? It's been empty for a while."

Eric had lucked out. At least she knew of the property. But did she know more?

"Well, I asked an old man, a next-door neighbor about it, and I got the gist that I should just forget it.

She laughed aloud, then covered her mouth to muffle the sound, her eyes flicking left, then right. Having broken her own code of quiet, her cheeks flushed rosy. "Oh, Eric," she whispered, "Well, I'm not surprised. If he's lived next door for a long time, he probably knows more than he cares to tell."

"Really. How come?" he said.

She motioned him to follow her. She steered her cart to another shelf and slid a book into its correct location. "No one wants to rent the house because of the so-called 'ghosts.'" She made quote motions with her hands. "If I remember clearly, a woman was murdered in the house back in '57."

"A murder? Do you know the story?"

Well, . . . its been a while, but I do know the incident took place on the Fourth of July. Her name was Adele Harrison. She and her husband owned the hardware store for which it remains named. Her husband had passed away five years earlier, but she continued to run the business afterward."

Now I understand. That's why his old boss refused to talk about the place just like the old next-door neighbor did. Eric had remembered Jenkins telling him he had worked for the Harrison's before they sold the store to him.

The Librarian had finished shelving her last book. "Eric, I have to get back to the front desk," she said, pushing her cart past him, a distressed look on her face.

Eric caught her with three quick steps. He tugged her shoulder for her to stop and moved in front of her. "Mrs. Carlson, are you OK?"

She strained a smile then patted Eric gently on his shoulder, "I'm fine, Eric. I just have a lot of work to do. Listen, if you want to find out more about the house and all, we have Microfiche archives that will help you out." She turned and steered the cart back to the main desk without looking back.

"Ughh . . . Microfiche," Eric thought.

After Eric had gathered his things he stopped by the front desk to thank the librarian for the talk—even if it only revealed a few small details. She wasn't there. He spotted her in a back office filing some papers. She looked up. Eric waved. She forced a smile, gave a feeble wave, and went back to her filing.

There's got to be more, Eric thought, pushing through the building's front glass doors.

Chapter 7

The Asheville High Invitational, Eric's favorite, was scheduled for the first week in April, six days away. It was Monday, the last day of March, and Eric was eager to relegate his season's first track meet fiasco to the trash-bin of his mind; if there was such a thing. It had been fourteen days of hell since his two-mile embarrassment, but his life was finally beginning to return to normal.

Eric's two-mile race against Randy Wardlaw had kicked off his 1979 track season with a bang—or with a thud, as his brother joked. In the aftermath of his maniacal and ill-conceived folly, he suffered through the ensuing two weeks of push-ups and sit-ups from his head track coach, a grounding from his mother, and a constant barrage of jokes from his teammates. As a bonus, the school's principal had requested that Eric submit written apologies to Randy Wardlaw and T.C. Roberson's track team.

One way to put his past mistakes further behind him was to concentrate on his training, beginning with Monday's fartlek session his assistant track coach Harry Miles had scheduled for practice. The coach had chosen the team's favorite practice venue, which would be held on what was technically a private green space, Straus Park. The local cellophane plant owned the tract, but nobody cared if a few runners were tromping around the grounds every so often. The property had been a summer camp since the 1920s until

Harry Straus, the local mill owner, had purchased the site in 1945 and converted it for his employees to enjoy.

The front border of Straus Park stretched for a half mile along the four-lane highway that led to downtown Brevard. Part of this green space seemed to have been a small golf course in the past, though Eric wasn't certain if the course was a part of the camp back then. Circular outlines of greens and rectangular tee boxes dotted the landscape, their once raised surfaces eroded by time, like sandcastles on a beach barely visible after a retreating wave. The rest of the land was heavily wooded. Two roads, spaced about a quarter-mile apart, led onto the grounds. One of the roads passed close to the boathouse and docks and then led to one end of the lake's eastern dam; the other road ended at a gravel parking area at the other end of the dam.

The boys and girls teams had jogged the three miles from school out to Straus to meet their coach at the car park. Harry Miles's dark green AMC Gremlin rolled into the parking area only minutes after the kids had arrived. He quickly set the ground rules for the team's workout. "You will run for a total time of forty-five minutes. Each runner gets a turn. You can make up whatever type of interval you want but limited to three minutes in time. Of course, your teammates have to try to keep up with you. You can have a *rest* turn if you wish, but only for one minute, then your turn ends and passes to the next runner. The goal is to have fun and be creative. For the three new kids we have here today, this is called fartlek-style training. The Swedish word *fartlek* roughly translates to 'speed play,' which basically means varying the pace to minimize boredom. Hope that's clear enough," he ended with a chuckle. "All right, I'm starting my watch. Have a great workout." The boys headed toward the lower green space near the front of the property, while the girls team set off around the lake.

Coach Miles was middle-aged with an older-man sized waist, evidenced by his belt being down to two remaining notches. He had admitted he was too cheap to buy a new belt, citing his modest teacher's salary. He'd accepted the coaching position for the cross-country team seven years before, when no other teachers wanted the job. Having known nothing about distance running, he'd learned what he could by scouring books on running at the local library and bookstore. He'd also enlisted advice from his fellow coaches and developed a close friendship with an experienced peer—a track and field coach for over thirty years—over at T.C. Roberson High School near Asheville.

Before Eric, Mary, Jen, and Rodney had shown up at cross-country practice their freshman year, in the Fall of 1975, Brevard High School's cross-country teams had no victories and lacked at least five runners to field a full team. After victories mounted, kids came out of the woodwork to be a part of the success. Coach Miles was a humble man and had confessed to Eric that the talent Eric and his fourteen-year-old classmates had brought to the team had enabled his success. He also lamented that he would not likely see that much talent ever again. He said it was fate. Eric and his teammates loved their coach, despite his modest coaching knowledge. Miles was kind and honest, and the kids knew he had their interests at heart, loving them as a father might. Winning wasn't super critical, but he wanted them to have a great time competing.

Miles was a considerate man, but no pushover. He kept track of them on their runs to make sure nobody slacked off. Although he had originally stayed in his car during Straus Park workouts, he eventually decided to walk around the lake to get his own exercise. That led to a discovery of some freshman boys hiding in the woods near the boat docks in order to ditch their workout. After that, Coach Miles purchased a ten-speed bike and began following his runners on the local roads, though, at Straus, his road-bike's skinny tires weren't suited to the gravel road's of the park, so he still had to walk the grounds.

Twenty minutes into the training session, Eric was about to start his third turn in the rotation. He was leading his team counter-clockwise around the lake's circular gravel road. When the boys reached the lake's dam, they turned left to cross over the hundred yard berm. Seventy-five yards across the dam, the girls' team were approaching, jogging slowly; likely one teammate was taking a one minute *rest* turn. As they came closer, Rodney yelled, "You girls run the Hill yet?"

Mary, the girls' team captain, shot back, "Two times already."

The two teams halted a few yards apart.

Rodney, Eric's co-captain, said, "If you gals ran it twice, you don't look tired."

Jen, the girl's second in command, pushed to the front of the girls' group, placed a thoughtful finger on her cheek, smiled, and said, "Don't you guys know anything? Girls don't sweat. We glisten." The other girls giggled.

"Well," Eric said, "if you princesses want to glisten, how about another go up the hill?" He knew Mary was fibbing. They might have run the hill once, but not enough time had passed for two ascents. Mary's boasting was for the entertainment of her team.

Insults erupted from both teams, along with finger-pointing.

Mary raised her arms. "Hold on," she said. "Coach wanted us taking shorter turns, not longer ones like Agony Hill, that would be well over three minutes."

Eric gave Mary a cheesy grin. "If we take three consecutive turns, then it's still the same, right?"

Mary shook her head. "You always have an answer for everything, don't you?"

He grabbed Mary's hand, pulling her to him, his grin still plastered on his face, then threw his left arm around her shoulder, turning her so that both teams were in their view. Eric extended an arm. "Coach said to be creative. Right?" He gestured left to right from the girls to the boys.

Mary squirmed away and stepped back to her team, eyeing him suspiciously. Then she turned to Jen, who nodded agreement. "All right, losers," she said, turning to the boys, "you're on."

Euphoric battle cries flared from both teams.

Meanwhile, Eric had wheeled around looking for coach Miles. "Hey, I don't see coach, but we better move out. He'll go nuts if he catches us together." Eric glanced toward a forested hill thirty yards past the softball field on the front side of the property. "You remember the last time he caught us together? He made us sprint up Golf Course Hill ten times after practice."

"Good point," Mary said. "You guys go counterclockwise around the lake, and we'll go the opposite, and meet you there."

A few minutes later, the two teams met at the entrance to the climb. Like archers in battle, the teams launched condescending verbal first strikes, loosing slanderous arrows at each other, each team attempting to gain a competitive mental advantage over the other. But mostly it was just fun to throw out a few digs before the suffering began.

Knowing their coach might be walking around the bend any minute, they hastily arbitrated a staggered start for the race. The slower teammates would go first, followed by the faster kids to keep everything as even as possible. There were twenty-two runners total—twelve girls and ten boys. Jen and Rodney combined both groups into sets of four. Mary and Eric would wait and go last, after the four groups, their one-on-one race requested by Eric, who had a score to settle for his loss to her back in January at the Art Loeb trail bridge. Jen and Rodney then set off early to be cheerleaders at the top and call out the times for the kids without watches. Many of his teammates liked to hear their time to see if they could beat their personal best for the climb. Eric knew his fastest time for the hill but he rarely ever timed himself. This hill was special; just to experience the climb and not let his competitive urges get in the way, was satisfying enough.

Separated by one-minute intervals, the first group of runners sprinted away. While waiting for his turn, Eric watched his teammates joking with each other, as they kept an eager eye on their watches for their start times. Eric found his gaze drifting to Mary, who was stretching five yards away from him. Touching her toes, her red braid was flipped over. Eric knew he was staring. He always loved her gorgeous athletic legs.

"You're still in love with her," a female voice said from behind him. His ex-girlfriend, Jessica Holman, stepped dangerously close to him, Eric feeling her body heat from the seductive entreaty. Her adoring green eyes peered up at him, her face framed in the trendy pixie-style haircut. She patted his butt and then using her fingertips, traced line up the middle of Eric's back tingling his spine.

"I am not," he said, his voice cracking. Tapping his watch face, he said, "Don't you have to start your turn?" Jessica gave him a playful smile and dreamy eyes before she jogged over to take her turn with the next group of runners.

Eric looked back at Mary, who was hopelessly shaking her head. She turned away to clap and cheer on more teammates. After the last group disappeared in the distance, he and Mary remained. She kept checking her wristwatch, not looking at him.

When it was close to Mary's start time, she walked over to Eric and stopped inches from his right shoulder. She wore a wicked smile, her eyes gleaming flirtatiously. She reached her left hand down, patted Eric's butt, and said lasciviously, "You should've stayed with Jessica, there, Romeo . . . Oh, by the way, you got sixty seconds, dude." She turned and bolted off.

Eric stood Jell-O legged, mouth agape. *Wow. Did I just have two ex-girlfriends flirt with me?*

Jessica, yes, he could understand, but Mary no. Jessica had always wanted him back and didn't shy away from showing it. But Mary was the kind of girl who gave you only one shot. If you cheated or crossed her, that was it; there were no redemptions. For Eric, kissing another girl while he was dating Mary didn't seem like cheating, but Mary hadn't seen it that way. She had given him the cold shoulder for a while, but eventually she'd reopened the friendship door to him. Eric remained friends with many other girls, but he was closest with Mary.

Eric was struggling to regain his calm, still flummoxed by Mary's flirtations. Then it hit him: she was paying him back for messing with her during their previous two mile race on the track. Yes, that was it. *She was trying to mess with my head, tense me up so I can't focus on the race.*

Eric checked his watch. His starting time had passed. He groaned and charged away, gravel spewing out from under his shoes.

The first half mile of the climb was tame. The grade wasn't much worse than a gently sloping driveway. But the second half, replete with switchbacks and a dramatic incline, was what truly defined Agony Hill. Typically, when first-time Agony Hill runners reached the top, whether running or walking, they reacted like children at the end of their first rollercoaster ride; they always wanted to do it again.

Agony Hill's mile-long climb fueled the competition between teammates, each runner knowing their suffering would be over quickly. They loved keeping tabs on each other on their way up, more so on the switchbacks because they could see each other on a switchback above or below them. Once at the top, many took the pleasure of claiming bragging rights, while the others vowed revenge, all in good fun.

Eric's focus had returned. At least he thought so. It was hard to tell when running full tilt. But his mind had cleared, and Mary's distraction was an afterthought.

By the time Eric reached the switchbacks a half mile later, he had caught up to a few of his teammates. Through heavy breaths, he said, "Keep it up," patting them on the back as he passed. Soon he spied Mary, up one level on the next switchback. She glanced down at him, her pained hill-climbing face revealing nothing. Eric knew any runner would have little energy to muster smiles from this point to the top; it was always head down and digging.

At the summit above him, Eric heard the growing cacophony of his finished teammates' supportive camaraderie.

When a hundred yards remained, Mary was ten yards in front of Eric but kept throwing back glances. As Eric closed on her, he was met with a barrage of cheering. His teammates' inspiring calls helped him ground out the last painful yards. Mary checked behind one more time. She surged, and Eric matched her effort. He finally caught her, but in a repeat of her suspension bridge victory in January, she shifted her kick one more gear and pulled away. She crested the hilltop, a yard ahead of Eric, then thrust a victorious fist upward.

Shortly afterward, the last remaining runners crested the hill, their cohorts still wildly cheering. Once everyone caught their breath, they exchanged copious hugs and high-fives. The previous combative repartee had given way to admiration and compassion. They had conquered the climb again.

Eric walked over to Mary. After she finished hugging one of her teammates, feigned a pat on her butt but respectfully held back. He said, "I started too late, or I would've had you."

"Aw, Eric," she said, mocking him, "you're still a loser. Always with the excuses. Not my fault you couldn't compose yourself in time to check your watch."

"Hey," Eric said. "How would you know that?"

Mary chuckled. "Ha, you already know the answer, stud."

"Fine—fine," Eric said, in high-spirited exasperation. "We'll see next time."

Chapter 8

Held on the first Saturday of April, the Asheville High School Invitational was Eric's favorite meet of the season. Since its inception twenty years before, the meet had garnered prestige from the quality and depth of competition. Over twenty schools attended the invite each spring, coming from as far away as Tennessee, Georgia, and South Carolina. If Eric had a choice of venue to set a personal record, it was the Asheville Invitational.

Because of the meet's popularity and the ever-increasing number of schools and athletes attending, the director had to split up events like the mile and two-mile into heats. In Eric's freshman year, his mile personal best seeded him in the slower, second heat. Eric won his heat, and when the two results were combined, he placed sixth overall. He always qualified for the first heat after that. In his junior year, Eric had won the race, defeating a talented runner from Georgia. The two battled out the final lap, Eric edging out the Georgian in a wind-hampered 4:23. This year, he wanted to claim the blue ribbon again. That accomplishment, along with state championship titles in the mile and two-mile, would top off his highlight list for his senior season.

The Friday before the meet, the track team assembled in the bleachers of the Brevard football stadium for their head coach's premeet speech. Rodney, the team's half and quarter-mile star, plopped down next to Eric. "Hey dude, I think it's cool that coach is going to have you run the lead-off leg for the mile-relay team tomorrow."

"Huh?" Eric mumbled.

Rodney playfully slapped Eric on the back of his head. "Wake up, man. The mile relay. You know—track, sprinting, baton exchanges?"

"Hey, I heard you," Eric said. "Sorry, I was mentally running over my races tomorrow—and yes, I'm ready for the relay."

"You know," Rodney said. "We ain't been on a relay team yet this year. Coach has been keeping you in the distance races. Man, you know when we team up, the other team better look out."

"Absolutely," Eric said. He changed the subject. "Hey, remember our Little League baseball team?"

"Wow, where'd that come from? Of course I do. Our team wasn't worth a nickel, but with you batting the 3-hole and me cleanup, we were the best batter combination in the league."

"I miss playing team sports sometimes. It's nice we run track as individuals and still be a team, but it's different when you have to depend on the other guy."

"Sounds kinda the same to me—like our relay team depending on your sorry butt to run a good first leg and keep us close to the lead?"

"Don't you worry, big boy. I'll hold my own. You just make sure you close the deal."

"Aw man, obviously you forget who you're talking to. I'm the Muhammad Ali of the last lap, the closer of all closers, the anchorman of the century—"

"Yeah, right," Eric said, trying to cover Rodney's mouth with his hand.

"Anyway," Rodney said, pushing Eric's hand away. His tone grew more serious. "Do you think you can handle Trey Allison in the mile tomorrow?

"I'll be ready."

"Cool, that's what I like to hear." Rodney high-fived, Eric.

The team's chatter faded, as Coach Baker launched into his premeet speech, his voice chipper, more animated than at his usual no-nonsense, military-style practices—well-organized and always on time. This past week he had been joking with the athletes and other coaches before practice. It was the first time this season that his face had a smile instead of a permanent scowl. It must be the Asheville meet; he knew Baker looked forward to this meet as much as he did, and his excitement showed.

Baker concluded his speech and dismissed the athletes to their respective assistant coaches for their afternoon workout instructions. Harry Miles was the head cross-country coach but acted as an assistant coach during track season, training the distance runners. He assembled his group for a quick chat before he sent them off on their premeet easy run.

"Is everyone feeling good?" Miles shouted.

Eric and his teammates hooted and hollered.

Miles wiped his brow and flipped his sweaty ball cap onto his bald head. He read over a page on his clipboard, then scanned their faces: "Good, everyone is here. Well, let's see . . . we finally have some warmer weather."

"Too hot for you. Huh, Coach?" Devon Daniels yelled from the back.

Miles chuckled and continued.

"Tomorrow is the biggest meet you will attend this season. As you know, I reduced your distance volume this week so you'll be fresh and ready for a good effort. Since everything has gone well with your training, this should be a nice reward for your hard work. I hope you're ready."

"You know it, Coach," Devon chimed in again. Everyone chuckled.

"Also, I'm not putting any constraints on where you run or who with for practice today, so enjoy it. I would like you to run for thirty minutes and finish with ten 100-yard striders on the football field when you come back. Oh, and make sure you stop and stretch about a mile into your run."

It's the beginning of April, and I know we still have a ways to go, but I want to say that I'm proud of the hard work you have put in. And for you new kids—don't let the size of Saturday's meet intimidate you. Remember, the other kids at this meet put their shorts on one leg at a time, just like you."

Murmurs and some eye rolls spread among the new kids.

"All right—tomorrow morning we meet in front of the school at 8:30. Don't forget, the bus leaves at 9:00 sharp. And, if any of you decide to push it, we will leave you behind. And if you miss the bus, that's it—your parents can't drive you over to Asheville. If you don't come on the bus, you don't run, no exceptions. So be on time."

Eric nudged Rodney. "Hey, man, you want to run with the girls today?"

Rodney snickered. "Sure—Maybe Jen will have another present for you."

Eric didn't rebuke this comment. He simply said, "Great." Jen had been pranking him with the whole number-two thing ever since she'd tried to give him back his second place ribbon.

Rodney laughed. "My favorite was last week at lunch." Jen had stood on the table in the cafeteria and bestowed her second-place dance trophy to Eric because he "*so* gracefully came in second." Rodney clapped Eric hard on his back. "That one was good."

"I'll get her back someday," Eric said.

Rodney composed himself. "Aw, forget it, man. You got no comeback."

"OK, OK, let's go," Eric said. "I see Mary and Jen are down on the track already."

Moments later, the four were running down Broad Street and were approaching a gentle incline. The road would peak at the city's central crossroads downtown. Mary and Jen, wanting to talk girl stuff, were tagging thirty yards behind the boys. Meanwhile, Rodney was offering Mile Relay strategy to Eric for the next day's race, and speculating about where their team might place overall.

As they approached the beginning of the grade, Eric saw a black-and-white patrol car pulled up close to the building of a tiny gas station. When he and Rodney neared, Eric saw two police officers interrogating a man sitting on the ground, his back against the wall of the gas station's front office. In one hand the man had a firm grasp on a brown, long-neck bottle. He was looking up at the two officers, gesturing with his arms like he was pleading his case. As Eric watched, not once did the man let the bottle tip over and spill its contents. The unconvinced officers roughly jerked the man to his feet, cuffed him, and escorted him into the back of the squad car.

"That's sad," Eric said to Rodney. "They should treat that guy better."

"You got that right," Rodney said.

Eric and Rodney had been friends ever since Little League baseball, and if anyone understood Eric, it was Rodney. He related to Eric's father issues, Rodney's father having abandoned him and his mother when he was five.

Eric had been ten years old when the police had found his estranged father lying face down in the narrow hallway of his rented trailer, dead from alcohol poisoning. A neighbor had not seen his father for several days and had called the authorities. His parents had separated six months earlier, and he'd only seen his father four times during those months.

As the years passed, Eric tried to come to grips with his father's alcoholism; why his dad couldn't quit; why some people turn mean when they drink. Those questions remained unanswered because he wasn't John Roberts. All Eric could do was move on, one day at a time, or so he thought. But seeing the cops with that drunk guy had opened the tap, and more memories began flooding in.

A couple of months before his father's death, Eric had begun pitching for his baseball team. It was the second of his four years of Little League. While his team's win—loss record tilted toward the loss column, there were moments when the team would eke out a brilliant victory. One night, Eric's team was having one of those star-aligning games, where everything was falling into place. His team occupied the home dugout that night and would have the last at bat.

At the top of the sixth and final inning, Eric's team was up by a score of 2 to 1. He was pitching and on the verge of completing his first full game—all six innings. Eric had collected two outs against the other team's first two batters, but he had just given up two consecutive singles. The opposing team now occupied first and second. His coach called time and came out to the mound. In a show of support, Rodney and the other infielders gathered around the pitcher's mound. His coach wanted to sub him for another, fresher pitcher, but Eric insisted he'd get the last out.

The moment Eric toed the rubber to throw his next pitch, a familiar voice jerked his attention toward the right side of the backstop. His father was hooting and hollering about his awesome son, with one hand's fingers wrapped into the chain-link fencing, his other hand clutching a beer bottle. He incessantly jangled the metal and wood structure as he continued his inebriated over-the-top rooting for his son.

The home-plate umpire halted the game and warned Eric's father to stay back. But his dad ignored the order. Some fathers in the crowd stalked up to the elder Roberts to pull him off the fence, but Eric's father looped slow, awkward swipes at them. The men eventually subdued him before calling the police. After the officers hauled him off, the game resumed.

Eric composed himself as best he could. Determined to finish the sixth inning, he flung his next pitch. After the batter crushed the ball into the darkness over the center field light towers, the coach pulled Eric from the game. Later, when his team came up for their last at bat, the other side struck out the next three batters, ending the game—another loss.

It was two months later that Eric's father passed away.

Rodney nudged Eric's shoulder. "Hey, let's stop at Main Street and wait for the girls."

"Sure," Eric said, relieved that Rodney had jarred him from his thoughts.

When the girls arrived, Rodney said, "What have you two been talking about?"

Jen giggled. "Boys, silly. What else?"

Rodney pressed. "Which boys?"

"Wouldn't you like to know?" Jen hid behind Mary and snickered in her ear. Then she broke away from Mary to flirt with Rodney, poking at his defined, six-pack abdomen.

At that moment, Eric caught Mary's eyes. Her face wore a Mona Lisa smile, not exactly returning Eric's friendly grin. Her eyes refocused over Eric's shoulder, pretending not to notice his gaze.

"Hey, the light changed," Jen said, bringing Eric back to reality. "Hurry up, guys."

From the city's center, Broad Street descended gently for a hundred and fifty yards before flattening out. When the road leveled, they passed a fast-food restaurant, and on the next corner, the sidewalk continued and paralleled an old stone wall, still intact from the local college's original founding. They turned into the school's main entrance, and eventually they stopped at a patch of soft green grass on the shore of a creek that split the campus between the women's dormitory and the gym. A modest cement footbridge spanned the gentle waters and led to the phys ed building.

The gang settled on the soft grass, enjoying the sun's warming rays.

"Oh, man, this feels so good," Mary said.

"No doubt," Rodney said. "I've been counting the days this winter. Summer can't come soon enough."

Rodney was right. The winter seemed to have edged into spring, with March mostly cold and rainy. But the weather was finally cooperating, and with the warming came expectations. Eric now had the post–high school bug. He still had track goals to accomplish, but he knew schools were awaiting his decision concerning a running scholarship. One coach Eric had spoken to stressed that college track programs had most of their scholarships signed by the end of April. This March, calls from Coaches recruiting Eric had increased, all echoing the same message: Sign soon or lose the offer.

Music blared out a window from the women's dorm behind them. It was Friday, classes were over for the day, and the students were already letting off steam.

"Hear that?" Jen said.

"The music?" Mary said.

"Sort of," Jen said. "I mean . . . that's what college is all about. It will be so cool to be on our own. We can play music whenever we want. No parents telling us what to do. No schedule to follow every day. Well, classes and practice, obviously, but you know what I mean."

Rodney, lying next to Eric, said, "Well, it looks like all of us are signed up for college except one."

Eric, eyes still closed, was enjoying the warming rays. "It will happen. It will happen."

"I hope so, dude," Rodney said. "I hope so." He called to Jen on the other side of Mary, "Jen, you want to go to the gym and get a drink at the water fountain? I'm a little dehydrated."

"Sure." Jen sprang to her feet. "All right, guys, we'll be back in a few minutes." She and Rodney jogged across the tiny cement bridge.

Eric tried to relax and clear his mind, but his childhood memories still lingered. Mixed into that were a barrage of thoughts about the following day's showdown against Trey Allison. Images of him and Trey battling it out on the track kept wheeling through his mind.

It was normal for him to use mental imagery to prepare himself for his races, by visualizing different scenarios and picturing himself winning. He had done the same thing as a twelve-year-old in his last year of Little League baseball. The coach had told him this was a good thing to do, that it might help him improve the command of his fastball. Sometimes he would lie awake at night, eyes shut, mentally throwing the ball to various spots around the plate. Today he wanted to relax, but his anxiety kept nagging him.

Alison was the top high school miler in the state of North Carolina, a rank he'd held since his sophomore year. Eric had first met him in a few Junior AAU track meets back when Eric was in seventh grade, noticing then that Trey was heads and tails faster than anyone else. The reason? One was talent, the other was that his father had had him on a regular training schedule since sixth grade. One factor that Eric could control relative to Allison was his own training, but he couldn't control another runner's gift, his pure talent. Trey had plenty, and that worried Eric; would he ever be able to beat him?

"Hey, Eric?" Mary said.

"Yeah?"

She rolled over to her side. "Do you think I can beat that girl from Tennessee tomorrow?"

He shielded his eyes from the sun to see her better, "Sure. You're both equally fast."

"You're being too nice, Eric." She laid on her stomach, closer to him, resting her chin on her folded hands. "Tell me, honestly?"

"You always want the truth, don't you?"

"Come on. You know the way I am. Give it to me."

Eric rolled over, one hand still shielding his eyes. "Well, Mary, she's pretty fast. But I do think you can handle her."

Her face brightened, and she appeared satisfied with his answer. "It's peaceful here, isn't it?" she said. "I could take a long nap right now."

"I know," Eric said. "It's the first day we've had this spring where we can relax. No intervals to do, no tests, and finally a Friday that we don't have a meet to go to."

Mary softly brushed Eric's cheek. "You're a good friend. You know that?"

Chapter 9

The evening before the Asheville meet, Eric's mother made him a nice pasta meal—manicotti and a fresh salad. Later he hung out at the Cardinal for an hour before returning home to relax. Around eight o'clock, Mary called. She asked him to come to the Clock Diner as soon as he could. Eric heard automobile traffic in the background; it sounded like she was calling from a pay phone. Her urgency puzzled him.

The moment Eric pushed through the diner's aluminum doors, he spotted Mary in the sparsely populated restaurant. She was in the last booth at the back of the tiny dining room, wearing a beige long-sleeve corduroy dress and calf-length boots. A blue Peacoat was lying in a heap next to her on the booth's vinyl seat. She must have been on a formal dinner date.

Mary looked up and caught his eye, but when he gave her a friendly wave, she mustered only a weak smile. Her hands were clenched around wads of tissues, and her eyes were red and puffy. Her long red hair draped loosely around her face and shoulders. Eric preferred her hair like this, but he rarely saw it set free from its customary braid.

On the table opposite her a half-consumed chocolate milkshake sat in a puddle of condensation.

He slipped into the other side of the booth, sliding the paper cup to one side. "You all right?"

At first her green eyes brightened, her lips forming a tight smile; then her face fell. “Parker broke up with me,” she said, sniffling. She patted her eyes as more tears spilled, soaking her tissues. She searched in her tiny purse for more.

To see Mary like this was surprising. He always knew her to be so strong. In the past, when someone had broken up with her, she blew it off, each time saying the guy was the one who was losing out.

“I’m sorry, Mary. When did this happen?”

“Tonight. We went to dinner at that new place on Main Street, Marcel’s. The jerk knew the whole time he wanted to break up with me.” She dragged out more dry tissues from her purse, then snapped the delicate case shut.

“Well, at least you got a free meal out of it,” Eric said, hoping the levity might raise her spirits.

Mary’s eyes narrowed.

“OK, OK. Maybe not a good thing to say right now.”

It stunned Eric that Parker would be that callous and he hated that the guy had hurt his friend. Eric wanted to think that he himself had never been so cold-hearted, but he knew better. He’d hurt plenty of girls’ feelings. Even Mary’s. He and Mary had dated early in their junior year, but he had gone out once with Jessica Holman, and Mary found out. She broke things off in a huff, saying that she shouldn’t have gone out with a guy on the team in the first place, let alone one that already had a reputation. “This was a mistake,” she had said. “We never should have dated. It’s my fault, not yours.” Her words had hurt him, but deep inside, he had known that she was trying to play down the pain he had caused her. She and Parker began dating shortly after their split.

“Did he make you pay?” Eric asked, trying one more time for a smile.

Mary snatched a dinner knife from the table and shook it at him.

“OK, not funny,” he said. He put on a cheery face and reached out to comfort Mary’s hands, but she drew them toward her.

“Why do you guys have to be like a bunch of bees, going from flower to flower?” she asked.

Eric had to work hard to hold back a smile. "Like bees, Mary?"

"Yes," Mary blurted. "It's a cliched analogy, *Eric.* But you know I'm right."

"Touché," he said. "All I can say is maybe we're wired that way. Like it's a survival thing. If we don't try to procreate, the species will die, right?"

She grabbed her melted chocolate shake, stirring it aggressively. "Nice try there, Sherlock."

"I don't know. Maybe we all want to be James Bond." Eric attempted a Bond accent: "A cavalier stud who gets any woman he wants and moves on."

Again, she laughed. Eric always managed to make her smile.

Mary swished her liquefied shake in its sweaty container. She frowned, then plunked the cup on the tabletop, "So who does that make me?" She affected an accent as well. "Miss Moneypenny? The secretary that pines away for the guy while he's off on a mission, surrounded by beautiful women?"

Mary's British pronunciation was even worse than Eric's. In many ways, he thought Mary was like Moneypenny: quick-witted, unshakable (except for tonight), a beautiful girl who deserved a good guy.

"So, what did Parker say?" Eric asked.

"Honestly, he didn't say much. We finished eating dinner. Then suddenly he spits it out, saying he'd just started dating Missy Patterson. You know—our pretty head cheerleader. Can you believe that?"

Eric knew her question was rhetorical, but he searched for something positive to say. "Well, it's been said that it's best to go straight to the point."

Mary's eyes narrowed again, and her lips tightened to a tiny frown.

Eric quickly back-pedaled with: "But I think he should have been more apologetic." He sighed; he was back to square one—his comments see-sawing Mary's mood. He continued, hoping some honesty would break her gloom. "Mary, I'm obviously not the best person to say this—I've had my share of callousness before—"

Mary huffed. She flopped back into the booth and jabbed a finger at Eric. "It's always the same. All you guys want are the cheerleaders or majorettes or the girls that dance on the sidelines, you know . . . the Devilgirls."

"The Devilettes?"

"You know what I meant," she said. "I mean . . . Look at me, Eric. I barely wear any makeup, don't style my hair, never paint my nails like all the other girls. Is that what you guys want? A painted princess?" Her wounded face suddenly softened, her eyes holding his, imploring Eric to tell her she's wrong. Mary was sinking, her angry words a signal flare for help. He needed to say something. But finding those special words always eluded him in these situations.

She then looked down at the table, defeated. "Guys don't want someone like me—the studious athlete . . . a plain Jane."

He and Mary had touched on this subject before. He realized in this moment that the past rejections had cut more deeply than he had known at the time. This was just the final straw. He reached over and clasped his hands around hers. "You're perfect, Mary." He wanted to add, "and any guy should be lucky to have you," but it was cliché. Simple was better.

Eric was relieved to see the waitress approach the table. He needed to catch his breath in a conversation where he seemed to keep stepping on the foul lines.

"I don't mean to be nosy," the waitress said, "but I happened to hear you're having a little boy trouble."

"Um," was all Mary managed to say. She shot a glance at Eric.

"Well, what about this boy right here?" the waitress asked, hand extended in Eric's direction. "He seems like a good listener. And it's hard to find a man that'll listen to a woman. Ain't that right?"

Mary nodded almost imperceptibly.

"I think this one's a keeper," the waitress said.

Mary and Eric exchanged wide-eyed embarrassment, his face warming, probably as red as Marys' cheeks.

"Anyhoo, do you two want something to eat?"

"Two more milkshakes," Mary blurted out.

"And some cheese fries," Eric said, happy to give the waitress a task that would take her away from the table.

The cheese fries were as good as ever and helped calm Eric's embarrassment. He was surprised to see Mary suddenly hungry too. When the two had finished off the fries and both milkshakes, Mary said, "I want to thank you, Eric." She tucked her hair behind her ear and dropped her eyes slightly. "If you hadn't been here tonight, I would have been a wreck; my race tomorrow against that girl from Tennessee has me stressed enough."

"Of course I came," Eric said. "You'll be great tomorrow. I know it."

Chapter 10

Eric's car tires squealed, protesting his little hatchback's Grand Prix–inspired turn into the school's parking lot. A few parking rows across the lot, Eric saw the bus doors closing. He whipped the car into a sliver of a parking space between a van and a large station wagon. He jumped out and bolted toward the bus, clutching his track bag against his upper body. Before he reached the bus, Eric's right toe caught the parking curb between the rows of cars. He lurched forward, freefalling. Only through sheer luck did he avoid direct impact with the asphalt, his track bag cushioning the fall.

"Smooth, Eric. Real smooth," he grumbled to himself.

Bus windows slammed to the bottoms of their frames, followed by a cacophony of hoots, hollers, and vibrating metal. Eric didn't have to look up to know that his teammates were hanging precariously out the windows, their hands slapping the sides of the bus. Red-faced, he sprang up, and zigzagged his way through the lot in the direction of the school's yellow transport.

With an ingratiating clawing of gears, the driver finally got the stick shift into first and started the bus forward. Eric jumped up and sprinted hard, catching up to the bus as it motored slowly toward the lot's exit. As he ran alongside, he looked up and saw Coach Baker sitting in the seat closest to the front doors, his eyes glaring out the window, shaking his head, a tight-lipped scowl under his thick mustache.

Eric pounded on the doors as he ran alongside, holding one handle of his track bag in his other hand, which banged against his thigh, like an anchor. The bus continued picking up speed. After all his training leading up to his favorite meet, was he going to miss the stupid bus? Baker really wasn't going to stop for him. Eric should have taken him at his word: If you're late, no luck. But hell if Eric wasn't going to try to make a run for it anyway.

Halfway out the exit, the bus's brakes squealed as the bus lurched to a stop. The doors flapped open. Eric tromped onto the first step, panting as if he had just run his race. The entire vehicle rocked with laughter.

Baker met Eric at the top step. "Boy," he barked, "I'm going to be happy when you graduate. And, for making me stop this bus, starting next Monday, you've just earned two weeks of push-ups and sit-ups before practice. You got it?"

"Yes, sir," he quietly replied.

"I didn't hear you, son."

"Yes, sir," Eric said, louder this time.

"Good. Now sit your butt down here in front so I can keep an eye on you."

"Yes, Coach." Eric slid into the seat opposite his coach's.

"OK, Jones, "Baker said to the assistant coach driving the bus, "let's get this bus moving again." The assistant thrust the stick shift forward and let out the clutch.

Baker, one of the first Black men to graduate from the Air Force Academy in the sixties, had also been a sprinter on their track team, and had served multiple tours in Vietnam, piloting the F-4C Phantom II. He was a disciplined man, had a short fuse, and never used the word "son" unless an athlete angered him. When he said "son" or "ma'am," in his sentence, you knew you were in big trouble. Eric respected the discipline his coach enforced, but once you landed on his wrong side, it took heaps of effort to earn his good graces. Eric now had a few weeks of *boot camp,* so to speak, before that could happen.

Coach Baker looked over at him now, and Eric wished he could just disappear until this ride was over.

"Will I have to hold your hand at the meet, too?" Baker asked. "Make sure you get to your races on time?" He didn't wait for an answer before growling, "Oh, I forgot—you're always on time to your races, just not your practices."

Muffled laughter came from the back of the bus.

Suddenly Jen's voice cackled in Eric's right ear: "You big loser," she whispered. Unable to resist, Eric cracked a small smile. Jen and Mary had called Eric 'loser' so many times, that it now felt like a term of endearment.

Coach Baker turned to Eric. "Son, wipe that smirk off your face. You think this is funny? You want extra punishment on Monday?"

"No, sir."

Baker spun around, "If the rest of you find this hilarious, you can join Mr. Roberts for push-ups and sit-ups, too."

The bus silenced.

By the time the bus picked up cruising speed on the interstate, Eric's stomach was rumbling. He reached into his bag and pulled out one of his mom's homemade biscuits. She had stuffed them with her homemade strawberry preserves, Eric's favorite. One biscuit had survived his track bag crushing, and a second one was flatter but otherwise still intact.

Eric put on his headphones and settled back to listen to his portable radio. Seconds later, someone tapped his shoulder. Mary had slipped into the seat behind him, next to Jen.

"Hey Eric," she said, "I wanted to ask—have you found any more info on the house?"

"No," he said, turning around, pulling off his headphones. "I told everyone what the librarian had said a few weeks ago. I haven't brought it up anymore because you all think I'm crazy."

She propped her elbows on the back of the seat. "No, I don't think you're crazy. A little weird, surely—but not crazy."

Eric was grateful for this softer version of ribbing after having had the whole bus laugh hysterically at his misfortune.

"Listen, I know I didn't sound that interested the other day, but that house has me curious too."

"You?" Eric said.

"Well . . . A little. It's an interesting story. Other than that, though, I don't think looking around inside is a good idea—"

Jen leaned forward. "Hey, I have some information on that house." She huddled closer and hushed her voice. "I went by the Brevard library after practice yesterday and looked for articles about the murders."

"I thought you didn't give a rip about that place, Jen," Eric said, confused.

"I didn't," Jen said. "But all your house babbling made me curious."

"And you didn't tell me?" Mary said.

"Well, you don't tell me everything you do," Jen said.

"Girls," Eric said, impatient.

"Anyway," Jen said. "So, I searched for articles written a few weeks after the murder, and I found one on Mr. Jenkins. Another I found was on the Harrisons—who Jenkins bought the hardware store from. The Harrison article had said that their only son was away at college at the time of his mother's murder. The article also mentioned that the son wanted to sell the store to Mr. Jenkins but keep the family house and rent it. That must be why the he holds on to it. His mom died there. He can't bear to even think about it."

"Wow. So, *that's* why the son kept it all this time," Eric mused. "But do you think there's any other furniture besides a toaster?"

"A toaster? Mary looked at Jen and back at Eric. "You went over there?"

"I did. I kept it from you guys because I knew you would give me crap over it. But yes, the Sunday after we had breakfast, I looked around the property, but I didn't go inside. A rear window was open, so I pulled the curtain over and looked in, but I couldn't make out much."

Jen grabbed Eric's hand and gave it a few quick shakes. "Congratulations. You solved the toaster mystery."

Eric pushed her hand back. "Funny, Jen. But I'd still like

to see what it looks like inside. Maybe the murdered mother is a ghost in there."

"Hold on, Eric," Mary said. "That's not a good idea. It's an old building. It could be dangerous. And besides, it's trespassing."

"I know, but—"

"She's right, Eric," Jen cut him off.

"Well . . . maybe you're right," he said. He was still unconvinced, but he knew there was no point in arguing. He turned around and put his headphones back on, trying to focus on his upcoming races.

Chapter 11

After the bus pulled to a stop in the Asheville High parking lot, Coach Baker stood to address the team.

"I'm always excited when we come to this invitational. I hope you are, too. The coaches and I have tried to peak your performance for this meet, and after that, we'll start a new cycle focusing on the championships. So have fun today. The competition level here is impressive. I hope many of you have personal bests this afternoon.

"OK, I'll go check us in and look over the heat sheets. Also, sprinters, jumpers, and throwers, Coach Jones will have your event schedule. All right—let's have a good meet!"

As everyone rose to gather their things, Baker placed a hand on Eric's shoulder and quietly said, "I don't need to tie a string on your finger today, do I?"

"No, sir," Eric said.

"Good," Baker said with a broad smile. "Thanks for helping us today in the mile relay. I hope you and the other boys will break the school record. Oh, and good luck against Allison. He's a good runner, but I know you'll give him a good fight."

"No problem, Coach," Eric said, relieved to hear those encouraging words. Earlier, on the bus ride to Asheville, Eric reflected about his many screwups these past few weeks, and he was growing tired of them as much as his friends and family were. He had to do better. A competitive race against Allison would be a good start. He wanted to make Baker proud.

Of the two scheduled mile heats, Eric's heat included the fastest distance runners at the meet. The event starter strutted back and forth in front of the lined-up runners like a military officer inspecting his troops. The small, heavy set man, had a pair of ear-muffs draped around his neck which he would later pull over his ears before he shot the pistol to begin the race. Eric stood in lane five. His impending duel with Trey Allison amplified his pre-race anxiety, which now approached nausea. He expected stomach qualms before his races, but to have them with such intensity worried him. To win today Eric had to bring his A game, and he wasn't sure his body would calm down when the race started. There was no way for him to know the answer until he threw his body into the fight. "Come on," Eric muttered, his hand on his belly, "settle down. We need a good mile today."

Standing three lanes to Eric's left was Trey Allison. He stood six feet, just like Eric, but was leaner, probably around one hundred forty-five pounds. Trey's running style was like the Finnish Olympic champion Lasse Virén; the Finn's effortless long-legged stride consumed the track with the speed of a Cheetah. And while Trey's form was nearly flawless, Eric had detected one anomaly, a side-to-side head bob that became more pronounced as he tired.

Eric weighed about ten pounds more than Trey. His muscle bellies were thick, but they tapered off quickly, which gave him a lighter weight-to-musculature proportion, and he had a slight bounce in his stride.

The starter told the runners they could sprint a few times down the track to stay loose, and when they returned, he would start the race. Eric sprinted out fifty yards, his spikes clicking the track's surface. He liked the sound of the metal scratching the asphalt. While wearing spikes on such a hard surface wasn't the optimal choice for his mile race, he preferred their lightness. He wasn't the only miler who wore spikes for today's mile race; Allison and many others sported them too.

Eric turned and walked back. On his left, he noticed the customary grouping of coaches, resting heavily on the track's three-foot perimeter fence, huddled close to the starting line, each clutching their watches. But one man around his grandfather's age caught Eric's attention. The man's dark aviator sunglasses enveloped his gaunt face, hiding his eyes. He also wore a cowboy hat. But what the man gripped in his fist was what piqued Eric's attention the most. He held a silver, hand-wound stopwatch, its blue lanyard draped around his neck. Who used watches like that anymore? Despite the guy's eyes and head being concealed, the man seemed vaguely familiar. Maybe he was a college coach scouting him. Eric let that thought linger before setting it to the back of his mind. He returned to his position in the fifth lane. Eric looked over and gave Trey a steely glare, which his foe mirrored with equal intensity.

Then a male voice boomed from the trackside stands. It was Trey's father barking endless advice at his son. The elder Allison never missed his son's races going all the way back to when Eric and Trey were junior high school age competing in AAU meets. Eric believed that once the runners were on the line, it should be time to quit the guidance counseling and leave the runners to their business, but Trey's father had always sounded like he had a megaphone strapped to his mouth.

"Come on, Trey," his father bellowed. "Go get 'em. Roberts ain't got nothing for you."

The starter dispensed his instructions to the assembled runners. He walked ten yards up the track and took a spot on the infield next to lane one. Raising his starter's pistol high, he commanded, "Runners to your marks—set," and the gun blasted like a miniature cannon, a plume of white smoke drifting skyward. As the runners streaked down their assigned lanes, Eric stormed clear of the pack. At the break line, a hundred yards later, Eric swept over to the inside lane and settled into his pace. He glanced around for Trey, but he couldn't find him. Fifty yards later, Allison showed up on Eric's right shoulder.

For the next two laps, Eric nailed his splits, setting a steady tempo with mechanical precision, a pace that put him a tad faster than his 4:18 personal best. Dictating the race's first half-mile satisfied Eric, but he expected Trey to quit tailing him, move to the front and assume command of the race. Trey had posted a solo 4:13 the week before, so Eric expected Trey would take over soon.

So far, Eric's progress toward his 4:10 goal had been dismal. The previous weekend he had only bettered his best time by a few tenths of a second. His frustration over his minuscule improvement had boiled over into daily grievances to his friends, but they had put an end to his whining by pointing out how pathetic and unconfident he sounded.

The fast-paced first half mile had separated him and Trey from the majority of the field. It would be a two-man race for the final two laps. But there was a wiry, blond headed sophomore from Greensboro leading the trailing runners twenty yards back. The kid had recently made impressive jumps in his personal bests. His name had climbed the state's weekly track and field rankings on a steady basis. Eric figured him to be a future top-level runner. But today wouldn't be his day, not yet, at least.

Normally Eric preferred to run in the front and take control of a race, direct the tactics, or draw another runner into a pace greater than the competitor could handle. But today he was running against a superior athlete, and his patience was thinning. If Trey wouldn't take the lead, at least he should move up and run next to Eric, make his presence felt, earn some respect, not hover behind Eric's right shoulder. It wasn't like Trey was in a large pack of runners and didn't want to show his hand; it was he and Eric, there would be no surprises, and with Trey, being the faster runner, had no reason to play cat and mouse.

Deep inside, Eric wanted to go for broke, give Trey one hell of a run, show him how good he was, but he had set the pace at his current personal best and had little room for such daring, like making an early surge to see if Allison would go with him. Eric reminded himself to be patient. He knew frivolously wasting energy reserves and not saving some for the last lap kick was suicide against an equal or greater foe.

As they entered the third lap, Eric could hear Trey's father yelling: "Go now, go now!"

Eric tried to filter out the older Allison's ranting by focusing on his upcoming lap split.

When the two entered the backstretch of lap three, Eric eased his pace, hoping the shadow on his right shoulder would take the lead. Trey had been drafting behind him for almost two and a half laps now, and Eric wanted some help, wanted Allison to man up and fight him stride for stride. But Eric knew he couldn't make a competitor do anything he didn't want to do.

He's not budging, Eric thought. *Maybe on lap four he'll change his mind. Sit tight . . . If he takes off at the bell, I could draft behind him, he'd pull me along for a fast time.*

The starter's pistol cracked, signaling the start of the fourth and final circuit. Still Trey didn't budge. Eric's shoulders crept upward. *Relax, Eric. Relax. The three-lap split was good. I'll have to start things.* Eric leaned a touch forward, forcing himself to move his legs faster. His pace would be a tad slower than his maxed-out kicking stride, but building to it. He always loved the last lap. The promise of a blistering final circuit excited him. A new personal best might be in the making.

Still leading the race with two hundred yards of blacktop to cover, Eric shot a glance backward. He and his reluctant companion still owned the race. Allison's stride continued matching Eric's intensive final lap push, but Trey still hadn't made a move.

Come on. Go around! Show me your kick!

Still nothing. Eric had to decide. Sprint two hundred yards out with Trey on his shoulder? *No. Wait longer.*

Again, nothing. A hundred yards of asphalt left.

Eric had played the game long enough. This slow dance of a race had come down to a pure hundred-yard dash, and he intended on giving Trey hell every yard. He grunted and blasted hard, his legs wheeling furiously.

Trey matched Eric, edging even with him, but made no further accelerations. *You're in this*, Eric told himself. *Get to that line first.*

In his best sprinter's form, learned from Coach Baker, he pumped his arms down and back. For ten yards, Eric held his own. A surge of adrenaline pumped through his solar plexus as he realized he was hanging in with Trey Allison's speed. Maybe, just maybe, this was his chance to beat him. Then Trey finally delivered what he apparently had been holding back all this time. He simply jaunted away, just like that. More like flying than running, he effortlessly ate up the final seventy-five yard straightaway before Eric's eyes.

Eric eyed the infield race clock as he approached the finish. He leaned forward and dove through the line. The clock read 4:15.

Despite another loss to Trey, his new, more respectable personal best pleased him. *Maybe 4:10 will be doable,* he told himself. And yet, Trey's easy-as-pie victory gnawed at him. Suppressing his disappointment, he tried to be the better man and congratulate his competitor. It was the least he could do. Eric located Trey by the track's perimeter fence, speaking with his father. The elder Allison's face was red, with an angry scowl. Eric couldn't make out the whole conversation. They were alternating between yelling and civil discussion. But he figured this wasn't the right time, so he headed for an exit gate.

As Eric lifted the gate's lever, the crowd behind him quieted, and Trey's words to his father rose above all other sound: "That hillbilly was easy pickings."

Eric spun and glared, but Trey was otherwise engaged. His father had a tight grip on Trey's arm and was jerking him back each time Trey looked away.

At first, Eric wasn't sure if he wanted to go over and deck Trey for the comment, or his father for grabbing Trey's arm. Yet, he did feel a little sorry for Trey, his father treating him like that. Either way, instigating a fistfight at a track meet was something he didn't need right now. He'd be kissing any scholarship chances goodbye.

Eric snapped the latch down on the gate behind him. He headed to where his teammates were sitting. It was time to relax and rest up for the mile relay race, the last event of the meet. Mary was standing by the gate waiting for him, her eyes concerned, expectant, unconsciously fidgeting with her braid. She had stood near the gate while watching his race. Eric had heard her cheering for him each time he passed the finish line.

"Did you see my time?" he said to Mary. "Not too shabby, huh?"

"You ran a good race, Eric. Sorry you lost."

"Thanks.

As they walked to the stands, Mary tapped him on the shoulder. "I heard that 'Hillbilly' comment Trey made at the fence—"

Eric cut her off. "It's nothing, Mary." He put a friendly arm around her shoulder. "I'm not going to worry about it."

When they met up with their teammates in the stands, the congratulations began, and his previous rage melted away. He had executed his race well despite the outcome. He'd bettered his personal best by a decent margin and that was something he could hold his head high about.

On the bus ride back to Brevard, Eric reran the race in his mind. Why hadn't Trey pushed off the front and gone for the victory sooner? Eric understood there were occasions to go for a good time and others to go for the win. But Trey's race wasn't just about winning. What on earth was in the guy's head today? Was he afraid of Eric? Did Trey push only as hard as necessary, to show him he could beat him without even trying, or at any time he saw fit? Eric had never seen a runner effortlessly pull away like it was no big deal. Trey had put three seconds on him in the last seventy-five yards.

It had been a strange race for Eric, but he had to respect the guy's talent. Trey had a new personal record. While he'd clocked an impressive 4:12, Eric thought Trey had a higher ceiling for today's mile race; a 4:10 in Eric's estimation.

Eric stretched out on the bus seat, laid his head on his track bag, closed his eyes, and tried to imagine running faster.

Chapter 12

Eric's teammates, along with the usual Saturday night crowd, had surrounded the Cardinal drive-in restaurant, their vehicles inundating the two-acre property. The resulting overflow spilled into adjacent parking lots, making the modest red-bricked establishment appear to float in an ocean of cars. His classmates had primped, preened, and polished their rides to perfection for the weekly cruise down the city's main boulevard.

Eric's teammate Jonathan steered his blue Firebird into the parking area with Jennifer waving from the passenger seat. The car's ominous rumblings parted the throng of students as he cruised it through the lot, temporarily halting the crowd's chatter. He slotted it into an open space next to Eric's car. Earlier, in saving the spot for Jonathan, Eric had nearly come to blows with another teammate. He talked him down by promising to hold a place for the guy the next time they were celebrating at the drive-in.

Eric ducked into his driver's side window and cranked up the volume on the car stereo. Rodney sat on the hood, chatting with another classmate. Jessica Holman, one of Eric's ex-girlfriends, bounded up to him, wrapping her arms around his waist, pulling him close. "Hey there, Eric."

Her long brown hair draped gracefully over her bare shoulders as her intoxicating perfume infused the cooling air.

Eric reciprocated the hug. "Aren't you cold in that tube top?"

"No. That's why I have my arms around you, silly."

"You've been drinking, haven't you?" Eric said.

"Only a smidgen," she giggled.

"So!" Mary said, standing at the rear of his car. "You cheated on me with Jessica last year when we were dating, and now you're fooling around with her while your *freshman* girlfriend is out of town? I don't think she'd like what you're doing right now."

Eric moved Jessica to one side. "We're only friends. Right, Jessica?"

Jessica grunted. "Thanks for spoiling my fun," she complained as she brushed past Mary.

"You're welcome," Mary said smugly.

In one quick motion, Eric zipped his jacket to his neck. He thrust his hands into the pockets. "Aw, Mary, we were just keeping warm. Why'd you have to make such a big deal about it?"

Eric's car stereo volume shot higher. Startled, Eric bent to see the culprit. Buzzy Connor was dangling in through the passenger-side window and messing with the radio controls. "Hi Ewic," Buzzy yelled.

"Buzzy, leave my car alone. Can't you go talk to your other friends right now?" Eric said.

"I hate you, Ewic," Buzzy screamed, jerking his hand off Eric's stereo and slinking off into the crowd of kids. Mary rushed after him.

"Man, Eric," Rodney said, "why'd you have to be like that to him?"

"C'mon, man," Eric, pleaded. "He bugs the crap outta me, always following me around at school and track meets, always trying to be my friend—I hate it."

Rodney slid off the hood. "So? He wants to be your friend. The rest of us are nice to him, but not you. Well, not counting some of your other buddies at school who play tricks on him all the time. But that's another matter." Rodney's eyes drifted to something over Eric's right shoulder before a hard thump between Eric's shoulder blades knocked him a step forward. Eric spun to find Mary inches from his face.

"You apologize to Buzzy," she spat. Buzzy cowered behind her.

"Can we talk?" Eric said. He grabbed Mary's arm, steering her toward the front of the car.

"What *is* your problem?" Mary snapped.

Eric leaned in. "Keep your voice down. Do you want Buzzy to hear?"

She folded her arms. "Fine."

"Listen," Eric said, throwing a glance at Buzzy. "I've got nothing against him personally. I've told you before. He's just been bugging me ever since we were kids."

"He just wants to be your friend."

"I know, I know. But it's—"

Mary jammed her index finger into his chest. "It's the same old thing with you. If someone isn't 'normal' enough, you can't deal with it—look at the person inside. Like when I first met you, you didn't see who I was—all you saw was a girl beating you at basketball, and you freaked out. Buzzy bothers the hell out of you, but to be honest, you don't have a good reason, and you can't handle that he's a little different."

"Aw hell, Mary, he—"

"Eric," Mary growled.

Eric winced. He could continue the denial, but Mary's truth turned his selfish heart.

Kids in town called Buddy Connor by his family nickname, Buzzy, and not because he couldn't pronounce his birth name as one would think. It was because as a child he would make a buzzing sound when he was trying to read a book or solve a simple puzzle—like he was using the sound to help him focus; his mother called him Buzzy one day when he was very little and it made him laugh; he liked the name and the nickname stuck. Buzzy's struggle to articulate the letter 'R' resulted from an infantile infection. Some of his bipedal motor skills were also impaired. Other children didn't understand his situation and teased him for his odd imperfections. Buzzy also had trouble making friends. Some kids called him a freak or a retard.

Back in Mary's freshman year, she had befriended Buzzy. She noticed that during lunch hour, Buzzy mostly ate alone.

Mary invited Buzzy to eat with her and her friends. Her kind act encouraged other students to accept him. But because Buzzy had to go to "special" classes, some kids still saw him as an outsider, and continued to reject him. Some were downright mean, and others thought it was fun to tease the "retard." Eric was one of them, but for some reason, Buzzy liked Eric despite the way he teased him. Mary had once told Eric that Buzzy could see the goodness inside people. When Buzzy befriended someone, it was because he trusted that person. Half-jokingly she had added that for the life of her she didn't know why Buzzy had chosen *him*.

Eric huffed for a minute but finally surrendered and put on his most charming face. He walked over to Buzzy, next to the car door and said, "I'm sorry, Buzzy. I didn't mean it."

Before Eric had finished the sentence, Buzzy had wrapped his arms around him in an affectionate bear hug.

"Come on," Eric said, wrenching himself away from Buzzy's reconciling embrace. "Let's go. *Invasion of the Zombies* starts in twenty minutes, and I want to play some pinball before."

Mary called to Buzzy, "Hey, champ, why don't you go with Jonathan, and Jen and I will go with Rodney and Eric. Is that cool with you?"

"Yeah, awesome!" Buzzy said. He had wanted a ride in Jonathan's car from the first day Jonathan had brought it to school the previous fall.

Jonathan jingled his keys. "Come on, Buzzy, let's go."

"We'll follow you," Mary suggested.

Jonathan's blue Pontiac Firebird was a Smokey-and-the-Bandit, Highway State Trooper-beating hunk of machinery with a golden Firebird logo on the hood. And it was fast. Eric followed the beautiful car, chuckling at Buzzy hanging out the passenger window screaming at the top of his lungs, "Faw out, faw out, fastew, fastew!" Suddenly, the car fish-tailed, rocking sideways, its spinning rear tires billowing white plumes. Jonathan burned the tires a few more seconds before easing the throttle to settle the Firebird down, cruising at a sensible speed the rest of the way to the theater. As the Firebird's speakers blasted out a southern rock song on Jonathan's 8-track stereo, Buzzy belted out his best rendition of the ballad, while still hanging precariously out his window, waving to anyone who noticed.

They found parking spots on the same side of the street as the movie house. Buzzy jumped out of Jonathan's car and thanked him for the ride. He bobbled over to Mary as fast as his uncoordinated legs could carry him.

"Did you see, Mawy? Did you see how fast we went?"

"That was cool, huh, Buzzy?"

"Yeah, weal cool."

While the gang waited for the theater to empty from the previous showing, they bought their refreshments and headed over to the pinball games. Buzzy had wanted the largest popcorn container, but Mary had orders from his mother, and she persuaded him to buy a smaller one. Jonathan, Eric, and Rodney hovered over a pinball machine next to a side wall, as Jennifer and Mary chitchatted. Buzzy watched the game while earnestly fidgeting with a small gold charm on the necklace he was wearing.

"Hey," Buzzy interrupted, "I've got a spowts question. And—and anyone who can ansew it, I'll buy them some candy."

"Go ahead," Rodney said.

Jonathan flapped the machine's paddles back and forth, launching the silver ball through the top-level gate, accelerating the game's chimes and chirps.

Eric's guilty conscience was still needling him, so he decided he would make a goodwill offer. "Tell you what, Buzzy, if we can't answer it, I'll buy you *your* favorite candy. How's that?"

"OK. Who whew the only U.S. twack athletes to win the gold medal in the 5,000 and 10,000 metew distance waces?"

They gave each other collective glances and shrugged.

Buzzy giggled with happiness, and Jonathan and Rodney couldn't help but laugh along.

"It was Bob Schul in the 5,000 and Billy Mills in the 10,000," Buzzy shouted with delight. "All in the same Olympics!" He slapped the glass of the pinball machine like he was laying down a dangerous bet.

"Buzzy, move your hand, I can't see!" Jonathan said.

"Was that the '64 Olympics?" Rodney asked.

"Yes," Buzzy said.

"Hey," Eric interjected. "Give Buzzy a turn, Jonathan. I'll give you a quarter."

"That's OK," Jonathan said, his eyes still glued to the tabletop. "Buzzy, slide in here before the ball drains." He released one flipper while flipping the other one to keep the silver orb alive.

"Cool, thanks," Buzzy said.

Within minutes Buzzy had posted a huge score and racked two free balls. Buzzy's expert pinball skills impressed Eric. As he watched Buzzy rock back and forth with the ball's momentum, Eric noticed that the charm on his gold necklace had a unique shape.

"Buzzy, what's on your necklace?" Eric asked, curious.

"It's a . . . it's a . . ." Buzzy stuttered, ". . . It's a winged foot," he finally said.

"Really? That's cool," Eric said.

"Real cool," Jonathan said. "It looks like Mercury's winged foot, like the kind we have on our varsity track letters. Who made it?"

"My, mom said a jew . . . jew . . ." Buzzy stumbled again.

"A jeweler?" Jonathan said.

"Yeah."

"Pretty cool, Buzzy. Your mom has good taste. When did she give it to you?"

"For my biwfday, yestewday."

"Very nice," Rodney said, patting Buzzy's back.

"Thanks," Buzzy said, beaming. Distracted by the attention, his last ball drained into the center hole below the paddles.

"Sorry about your ball, Buzzy," Eric, said, putting a friendly arm around him, steering him toward the theater door. "Come on, Mr. Pinball Wizard. The movie's about to start."

After the movie let out, the group huddled next to their cars and chatted before heading home. Rodney and Mary, who had left their vehicles in the parking lot at the Cardinal, would ride back with Eric and Buzzy. Jonathan was taking Jen home. After they said their goodbyes, Jonathan spun his tires one more time as he peeled out of his parking space, his friends cheering as the Firebird roared away. Eric pulled out onto the road shortly afterward. When he reached the next street, Eric made a quick right turn instead of continuing straight and turn at the downtown crossroads.

"Dude, why'd you take a right?" Rodney asked.

"You're not taking us by that house, are you?" Mary asked, clearly knowing where the road led.

"What house, what house?" Buzzy asked.

"Man, Eric, we don't need to go look at no haunted house," Rodney said.

"Haunted house? I want to see it." Buzzy said.

"C'mon, guys," Eric, whined, "I only want to look at it for a second. There may be nothing to the rumors, but aren't you curious to see if any ghosts are in there?" He peered into the rearview mirror at Buzzy and Rodney and then looked over at Mary. None of his passengers spoke. Buzzy's face reflected a confused enthusiasm, but Mary and Rodney's frowns expressed volumes.

"Come on, guys," Eric pleaded.

"Eric, this isn't like some treasure hunt," Mary said. "That house has been abandoned for ages. It could be dangerous."

The minute Mary finished speaking, the dubious, specter-riddled home came into view. Eric whipped the hatchback into the driveway, skidding to a stop a few yards from the cement porch. He grabbed a flashlight he had stashed under his seat. "I'll only be a few minutes. If you all don't want to come, that's fine." He climbed out, shut the door, and leaned back in the window. "I thought you guys would be interested, but I guess not." The moment he turned to walk away, Buzzy lifted the driver's seat release and threw the backseat forward. Eric reached in the window and pushed the seat back into place. "Stay in the car, Buzzy."

Eric hustled up the driveway and jumped onto the old cement

porch, skipping its three steps. He switched on his flashlight and pointed the round beam at the structure. A corner streetlight blinked erratically, but a bright, full moon helped illuminate the house's yellowing white paint.

"Come on, Eric, we all have eleven o'clock curfews," Mary yelled, leaning out the passenger side window. "It's twenty-five till. We don't have time for this."

Eric raised a finger and gestured one minute.

Through the dim light, Eric could just make out Mary's righteous indignation; he knew that face well. She groaned and slipped back into the car. He pointed the flashlight beam on his wristwatch. She was right. Their curfew clock was ticking. He looked in his car's direction. Mary was turned in her seat, toward the boys in the back.

"OK, one quick look," Eric said to himself. He jumped off the front porch and sprinted to the back of the house. The same kitchen window he had opened on his prior visit was now closed. Had someone shut it since his last investigation? He eyed the window sash and saw that the latch was unlocked. With both hands he pressed his fingers into the upper corners and gave an upward thrust, the frame moving an inch or so. He then reached down and slid it upward till it stopped.

Before Eric climbed in, he checked to his left and right before scuttling up into the opening. Eric grabbed the window's threshold with both hands, leveraged his forearms against the sill, then pulled himself through the opening before rolling onto the floor, his flashlight knocking from his hand. He snatched the flashlight before it rolled too far away and waved its beam corner to corner.

No specters, but the toaster he'd seen on his prior visit was still sitting abandoned on the linoleum counter, its chrome gleaming despite its coating of dust. The toaster and a white refrigerator, minus its doors, were the only appliances in the room. The kitchen was no more remarkable than the house's exterior. The gray painted metal cabinets were flaking off paint chips exposing layered years of color choices. The black-colored countertop complimented the black-and-white checkered flooring. Eric slowly opened several upper cabinet doors, his mind filled with horror movie visions of a mouse or rat jumping out onto him, but he found only crinkled, desiccated shelf-lining paper.

The kitchen had two doorways, one directly across the room from the window and the other to his left.

A chill crawled Eric's spine the moment he stepped through the left doorway. Once in the room, his tension eased when he saw the ordinary décor. A gold-chrome chandelier hung from the ceiling, and a deep-red oriental-themed wallpaper decorated the walls of what looked like a small dining room. He padded across the room to another doorway. Eric stepped cautiously through the opening, his flashlight beam leading the way, light beginning to fill the next room. Eric jerked back, his chest sucking in with a sudden halt. From the corner of his eye, he saw a lone figure lying on the floor next to the fireplace. Once his flashlight illuminated the supposed figure, Eric exhaled. *It's only a sleeping bag,* he assured himself, relieved. In the hearth was the ashen remainder of a wood fire. Two cheap-grade wine bottles sat empty at the side of the mantle.

Eric thought of the drunken man at the gas station. Was this where that guy lived? *OK, Eric, keep it moving,* he told himself, thinking of his friends waiting in the car. He would just check out the upstairs real quick before heading home.

He discovered a set of stairs not far from the front door. As he approached the staircase, the odor of rotten wood tinged his nostrils. On his way up, about five steps below the second floor, he noticed a hairy patch of pale-green mold growing on a couple of stairs. He shined his light toward the ceiling and saw a basketball-sized hole where a water leak had penetrated the plaster. He leaped over the rotted steps to one step above the patch and slowly padded up to the upper floor. He glanced into two empty bedrooms, then headed to a room adjacent to the staircase. The room was large and had its own attached bathroom and a modest walk-in closet. *The master bedroom,* he thought. After completing his disappointing ghost-less adventure, he decided it was time to hustle back to his friends. But first he would look out the room's front window to check on Mary and the boys. He tugged the curtain aside and noticed Mary standing on the porch, close to the front door. Then Rodney climbed the three steps up onto the porch. Buzzy must still be in the car.

Eric had an idea. He turned off his flashlight and set it on the floor. He then released the latch of the lower window sash and, with both hands, he slung the window upward until it dead-ended with a loud thud.

He ducked through the opening, holding onto the frame's side-moldings, leaning out as far as he could. "Muahahaha," he bellowed.

Mary shrieked. She spun toward Eric, clutching her chest.

"Man, that was so great," Eric yelled down. "You should see the look on your face."

"You're an ass," Mary screamed at him.

"I was only trying to be funny."

"It was horrible, Eric."

"I'm sorry," he said.

"Is Buzzy with you?" she said.

"With me? I thought he was with you. Isn't he in the car?"

"No—he's not. That's why I'm asking *you*, Eric," Mary said, exasperated. "Did he follow you into the house?"

"I'm sure he didn't . . ." Eric trailed off. "Wait, I hear something. Hold on . . ."

Eric grabbed his flashlight, flicked it on, and shone the beam through the bedroom doorway. "You there, Buzzy?" he called out.

"Ewic, Ewic, y—you up thewe?" Buzzy's voice drifted up from the lower floor.

"Yeah, but—"

"I'm coming up!" Buzzy shouted.

Eric heard the dilapidated steps groaning and creaking as Buzzy started tromping his way up the staircase. Eric's mind raced. Stairs were difficult for Buzzy with his awkward gait. And it was dark too. He wouldn't see the two rotted steps.

"Almost thewe, Ewic!"

"Buzzy watch the stair . . ." Eric rounded the doorway and directed his flashlight's beam downward just in time to see Buzzy's foot sink into the rotted patch. Buzzy lurched sideways into the railing, the creaking wood bowing, but holding. Then the decrepit banister issued a series of cracks and pops, beginning to buckle under Buzzy's weight.

"Help me, Ewic!"

Eric dropped his flashlight to grab the doorframe with his left hand. His fingers strained to grip the molding as he extended his right arm. Possibly blinded by the flashlight's beam, Buzzy's arm wavered, searching for Eric's hand. After repeated swipes, Eric's hand grazed Buzzy's wrist, but he could not clasp it, his fingertips only skimming across Buzzy's shirtsleeve. Then a sound like a fastball smashing through an oak bat rang out as the banister shattered. "Ewic," Buzzy shrieked, as he spilled over the edge.

Buzzy's howling voice seemed to yank Eric from the door jamb. He lurched forward, planting a foot right in the spot where Buzzy had been. As Eric fell, the glint of the hallway's brass chandelier caught his eye. In a flash of pure reflex, he swiped at the chain suspending the decorative ceiling light, but the thin metal loops were no match for his weight. The links snapped. And like a marionette cut from its strings, unable to check his free fall, Eric crashed down onto a long, narrow table in the hall. His right leg hit first and bent under him like that of a jumping hurdler, his foot pried back, tendons ripping in his knee. His left leg hit second, ankle rolling over, bolts of pain rocketing up his spine.

He wailed as he collapsed to the floor, thrashing for a few seconds before curling into a ball, groping simultaneously for his ruptured ankle and torn knee.

The flashlight had followed Eric's trajectory, having rolled off the stairway and ricocheted off the table and wall before tumbling to the floor. It rolled to a stop near Eric's head, the flashlight's beam illuminating a lifeless body. Buzzy lay contorted on his back, one arm pinned under him, eyes open, his mouth agape. A pool of blood was creeping out from under his skull. His charm, the winged foot, gleamed in the light's faint glow.

Chapter 13

A short line of green caps and gowns, the remainder of Eric's classmates, waited for the principal to call them forward to receive their hard-earned diplomas. They shuffled along one side of the gym toward the stage, Eric hobbling with them on his aluminum crutches.

The outdated building, packed with parents, teachers, and students, had no air conditioning. Instead, fans were staged at various locations around the gym, but they provided little relief from the unrelenting heat. The audience was aflutter with folded bulletins as people fanned their faces.

Eric's proud mother waved to him from the center of the crowd. He returned an unenthusiastic wave. His brother hooted and hollered his name, along with the dozens of other parents and relatives screaming their own children's names.

The principal, Mrs. Eckerd, looked uneasy despite her best attempts to present a happy face to the graduates. As the ceremony progressed, her time announcing the graduates sped up. Meanwhile, she continued to pat her handkerchief at the beads of sweat collecting on her forehead.

Eric tugged at his collar to loosen his tie. He had gained weight after his accident. Unable to engage in any aerobic sports, he had taken to lifting weights to give him something to do and to relieve his stress. It became Eric's way to cope. He worked out in the school's weight room in the afternoons when the track athletes were at practice. He could do the bench press, lift dumbbells, or other upper body exercises while sitting down at the universal machines, avoiding involvement of his broken left ankle or tendon-torn right knee.

His friends Mary, Rodney, and Jonathan had now received their diplomas. Jen, standing in front of him, was bubbly and squirming with excitement. She turned around. "I'm so excited. Aren't you?" She wheeled back around to face the stage.

"Yes," he said, mocking her tone, "*so* excited." He had no desire to hide his disgust.

She spun, eyes flashing. "Eric Roberts, what's gotten into you? You've become the biggest bore since your accident. Frankly, I'm tired of it." She glared at him until principal Eckerd called her name, at which she spun around and pranced the three steps up to the stage and accepted her diploma. She gave the administrator an over-the-top hug and curtseyed to the crowd, leaving people in giggles.

"Eric Roberts," the principal announced.

Bracing himself heavily on his ungainly metal appendages, Eric eyed the stairs, hunched his shoulders, and lifted the crutches onto the first step. He hated using these things.

Eric's right knee had healed. He used his right leg to steady himself on the stairs before hefting his left leg. His doctor had just cut off the cast a few days prior, but he still had to wear a boot for one more week before he could lose the crutches. The audience hushed as he surmounted the stage. Under the weight of his effort, one of his crutches squeaked against the backdrop of quiet, as Eric suffocated in his misery. The audience's silent pity magnified the tension, making the room feel hotter and smaller.

He could feel their eyes boring into him. He could only imagine what they were thinking. *Poor old Eric. It's such a sad thing that his busted ankle, but he really should be in jail for killing Buzzy. Pathetic gimp, serves him right.*

Unable to bear their pitying eyes, Eric zeroed in on Principal Eckerd. He hobbled across the stage, unceremoniously shook her hand, grabbed his diploma, then rushed to the platform's steps. The audience murmured.

Eric stopped at the top of the stage's three steps before carefully negotiating them. As he worked down, one step at a time, to the third and final tread, a man's voice rang out from the back of the gym—"Killer!" Eric looked up as everyone's eyes darted toward the shout, but he couldn't identify who had cast the insult. Boos and hisses radiated from the audience, and the man fell quiet. Distracted, Eric misjudged the distance down to the floor, his right crutch grazing the edge of the last step. When the crutch's rubber end hit the floor, he bobbled and spun halfway around before falling backward, landing on his shoulder blades, his crutches flying in opposite directions. One caromed into some parents' feet in the first row, and the other clamored across the floor in front of the stage before banging to a stop against a far wall. The crowd gasped, and the room hushed.

"We know you didn't do it, Eric," a voice in the distance called. "Don't listen to him." Someone returned a vulgar rebuke, then insults accelerated as the audience became unglued.

Eric lay frozen on the gym's glossy hardwood as though he'd traveled back in time: spread-eagle on his back on the dreary, grayed-out oak floor of the dilapidated house, Buzzy's lifeless, contorted body lying next to him. Instantly his chest tightened as if an Anaconda was squeezing it, and phantom pains started throbbing in his healed ankle and left knee, the faux pulses riding up his spine. *"Please someone. Please, get me up," Eric forced out.*

Principal Eckerd hollered in vain into the podium mike, attempting to quell a crowd that was hurling jeers and epithets through the room. Eric snapped back into the present and twisted over to right himself. Still, before he could, Mr. Anderson, the head football coach—a towering guy who could likely bench four hundred pounds—swiftly grabbed Eric under his armpits and hefted him to his feet.

Fortunately, Eric's fall had caused him no physical damage. He had landed on his shoulder and upper back, his impact no worse than a hard tackle in a football game with his friends.

"You all right, Eric?" the coach asked, helping him gather his crutches, diploma, and brushing off his dusty jacket.

"I'm fine, Mr. Anderson. Thanks for the assist."

Once the coach had determined Eric had no critical injuries, he set out to aid the school's now-desperate principal. "Attention, everyone," his voice boomed as he walked to the front of the stage. The crowd quieted some. "Attention!" he yelled again, louder this time, and the murmurs ceased entirely.

"Thank you. Now let's restart this graduation. Remember, we're here for the kids. If you have something to say, write a letter to the newspaper. If you have a problem with that, you'll have to take it up with me." He turned back to the stage. "It's all yours, Principal Eckerd."

"Thank you," she said, dabbing at her drenched forehead. Her voice a bit wobbly, she spoke the next name on the roll into the mic.

As the principal called the final students forward, Eric hobbled his way to the outer lobby, where the graduates were to assemble for a class picture before a final procession back onto the stage. The photo would hang in the principal's office for a year before moving to the cafeteria, where trophies and class pictures were kept for the students to view.

As soon as he entered the lobby, Eric's classmates crowded him, peppering him with questions about his fall and the man who had verbally accosted him. To escape the attention, he excused himself to the bathroom, but he ended up feeling embarrassed for hiding out in there.

When he emerged from the bathroom, he crossed the hallway to the water fountain. He rested his crutches against the side of the fountain and bent over to take a sip.

"You killed my nephew," a voice boomed down the hallway—eerily familiar.

Eric looked left toward the shout and saw a gray-suited man

stalking toward him, his hard-soled shoes clapping heavy, growing louder every step. The guy was small, with a whiney voice. *Buzzy's Uncle?* Eric had never seen the brother of Buzzy's mom, but he did know he lived about ten miles away, halfway between Brevard and Hendersonville. That's who had shouted at him during the ceremony? The interloper clomped to a halt, standing inches from the water fountain, his mouth tight-lipped, snorting like an angry bull. Eric straightened and searched the man's cold, reddened eyes.

"Why'd you kill my nephew?" the uncle said, grisly and glaring, maniacal even.

A sweet stench hit Eric's nostrils, and the hairs rose on his neck. It was the smell of hair cream. The man's face was pasty white below the cheekbones, with a distinct tan line, like he'd just shaved his beard. The guy was small enough for Eric to whip him in a fight, but his mind went to his broken ankle and newly healed knee, and he was flooded with a feeling of vulnerability—just like he had felt as a child when his towering father became angry. Fighting this lunatic would be crazy right now. He needed to flee, and fast. As Eric turned for his crutches, the man clapped a hard flat hand on Eric's chest, stinging his skin like a paddle hit.

"Hey, what's your problem," Eric said.

The guy grabbed Eric's lapel, and another smell mixed in with the hair cream. Foul breath. Eric peered into the man's blue eyes, and it hit him. This was that scrawny hunter from the forest trail. The sting of that incident multiplied Eric's anger, and he tipped past the point of caring. On the forest trail there had been guns, and his friends to protect, but not now. Now he felt he had nothing to lose—ankle be damned.

"Let go of him," Rodney yelled, racing up as Eric was about to drop his crutches and defend himself, but the man maintained his grip on Eric's lapel. Rodney grabbed the uncle's narrow wrist, latching tight. Rodney's eyes were burning fierce with anger, the likes of which Eric had never witnessed from his gentle friend. Rodney thrust the base of his other palm into the center of the man's chest, slamming the aggressor into the cinder block wall and pinning him there. Both of Rodney's hands were now on the uncle, and he added to the squeeze on the guy's wrist until the assailant's mouth gaped to cry out, but the uncle's quivering lips could only manage a faint whimper. Finally Eric's lapel slipped from the man's grasp, and the uncle crumpled to the floor.

Eric mounted his crutches and charged toward the lobby, the sturdy but delicate construction of the crutches creaking and popping under the strain. Then he plowed his way through the outside doors. As he neared a row of cars, Rodney swept around and stopped him.

"Hey. What happened back there?"

Eric, not making eye contact, adjusted himself on his crutches. "Nothing. Look, I need get out of here. Tell everyone I'm sorry for not staying for the class picture."

Rodney grabbed Eric's shoulders. "Where are you going?"

Eric took a long stare across the parking lot, turned back to his friend, "Nowhere. I'll catch you later. OK?"

"Yeah. Sure, man," Rodney said. But as Eric turned, Rodney stopped him. "You ain't going to do nothing stupid, are you?"

"Don't worry," Eric said. "I'm all right. Really." He started to turn away but stopped. Eric let out a long breath, momentarily closing his eyes trying to collect himself. "Rodney," he started, his voice calmer but still pitchy from his sky high adrenaline. "I'm sorry I rushed out. I've somewhere to go right now—OK? And, thanks for your help back there."

Rodney didn't say anything at first. He had those distraught eyes when a person feels powerless to help. "Sure, man. Do what you have to do."

The flatness and frustration in his friend's words squeezed Eric's heart. He started to speak but caught himself. There was nothing more to say that would make this less hurtful for Rodney. Eric turned and headed to his car.

Eric opened his car door and chucked his crutches over to the passenger side, causing them to ricochet off the window and dashboard. He ripped the Velcro straps off his boot and tossed that in, too. Eric sped out of the parking lot, the car tilting hard left on the turn, tires squealing.

He obeyed the speed limit at first, but as one red light blurred into another, rage built inside him. He was trapped in this town like a proverbial mouse in a maze. Everywhere he turned was an emotional dead end. Over the past few months, he had come to dread speaking to anyone, fearing the constant *Buzzy death* questions and allegations. That old house was his curse.

Two deaths had occurred in that immodest structure: Buzzy and Eric's life as he knew it. Eric's only motive that night was his curiosity about ghosts. But why didn't I wait to go to the house alone? Why didn't I just drop the whole thing? It was such a stupid obsession that came at too dear a price. Man, I just want to go back in time and start all over again.

The moment Eric's car zoomed through the next red light, a sudden constriction gripped his chest, like the anaconda was squeezing again. At each exhale, his chest tightened further. Through watering eyes, he vaguely realized the next signal was red. Eric jammed the brakes, nosediving his compact to a stop. Once the car ceased rocking back and forth, Eric closed his eyes trying to relax. *Breath, Eric. Breath.*

By the time the light turned green his breaths were slightly slower and deeper; the snake had uncoiled some but hadn't slid away yet. He drove slowly to the next signal and turned left passing through the two pillars marking the entrance to the Pisgah forest. He wanted to be alone for a while and he knew just the spot.

Once his car entered the forest, dappled spots of sunlight dotted the road. A patchwork of bright flashes illuminated the car's interior as the compact plunged through the late afternoon spectacle. His breaths smoothed and became deeper. After reaching the Art Loeb trail head parking lot, Eric strapped his boot's Velcro straps tight around his ankle. Leaving his crutches in the car and loped slowly along the Davidson River to the bridge where he and Mary had their New Year's Day race. Eric went out to the middle of the wire-suspended crosswalk, sat down and splayed his legs over the edge of the wooden planks, still holding onto the thick wires in front of him. The air was warm and the cooling of the evening was still a few hours away for this time of year.

It was quiet. The summer fishing crowds wouldn't arrive all together for a couple more weeks. His jacked up heart rate was still thumping in his neck, but holding to a little under a hundred beats a minute, he guesstimated. He gripped the bridge's wires and leaned his chest forward against them. He looked down at the gurgling river trying to lose himself in the glassy water. The river's ceaseless motion seemed to draw his anger out of him. What had just happened to him? This was supposed to be his graduation day not Eric's mental apocalypse.

He closed his eyes and listened to the river and nature; birds flittering in the bushes nearby, the wisp of the breeze rustling the hardwood's spring leaves.

Still unable to completely pry his mind from his current situation, he reflected on these last few months. He felt like the third act of a his play had just ended. It was one thing for him to incur a scholarship-losing injury and witness the accidental death of a classmate, but to have Buzzy's Uncle assault him twice, vaulted his story to the 'Thriller Movie' level. Not an accolade Eric wished for on any level. All that was left was for an intrusive *narrator* to give a moral summation of the protagonist's actions. The narrator in this case would be Eric's doctor, and he would also repeat the words he told Eric the morning after his accident: "There's a high probability that you may never be able to run seriously again. If your ankle heals properly, you should be able to have a normal life. But you will need to be careful. If you fracture it again, the harm could be irreparable. You might even have to use a cane for the rest of your life."

Sadly, Eric's three-act tragedy wasn't derived from an overactive imagination. He had a new reality: his life would never be the same. But what was he going to do? Get a job? Go to college? Unfortunately, none of those choices included running.

And running was all that mattered—and he would never do that again.

Chapter 14

The next morning, Eric's car idled quietly at the Main Street intersection. Through a thin, wispy fog, he stared at the traffic light dangling motionless from its cross wire, the top light beaming crimson. Eric was eager for green. It meant forward and freedom. A few more lights and it was nonstop interstate to his Uncle Joe's house in Mount Pleasant, South Carolina, a tiny hamlet on the northern shore of Charleston harbor.

Eric revved his car's gas pedal. The meek exhaust note reverberated from the minuscule muffler, echoing off the storefronts, briefly interrupting downtown's Sunday morning tranquility. Eric squirmed in his seat, fidgeting with his steering wheel, anticipating his impending freedom. Still, reflecting on what he was leaving, and how he was doing it, nagged at him, making it hard to enjoy the moment.

After the graduation incident, and Eric's flight to the Art Loeb suspension bridge, he had only been there for an hour before Rodney had found him. Rodney had organized a search party of sorts. Apparently Eric's friends had been worried that he'd done something rash.

Back home, the instant he stepped through the kitchen door his mother confronted him and, without warning, slapped him in the face. But after tempers calmed, he apologized and promised never to disappear like that again. She forgave him reluctantly but listened to his newly hatched plan. His uncle had offered Eric a summer vacation down at his place after graduation, but no date had been set. His mother wanted him to stick around for a while, but Eric's new plan was to leave the next morning.

"So soon," she said. Then she sighed and sat back in her chair. She gave a small nod. "Maybe this is what you need." Perhaps some time spent with her brother would be the perfect thing to snap Eric out of his funk.

Eric rubbed the welt on his cheek. "You really smacked me, Mom."

"The strength of love," she said. "You had me worried out of my mind."

While it comforted him to stay with family in Mount Pleasant, he couldn't suppress his nervousness at striking out on his own. He had never traveled alone on a long car trip before. Still, he smiled. The excitement about his impending freedom was overriding his misgivings. He looked across the intersection toward Mary's house. *Maybe I should go over there and say goodbye in person,* he thought. *Maybe throw a few pebbles at her window for old times' sake?* The light blinked green, but his foot still pressed the brake. He stared down the long, empty street. He shifted his foot to the gas pedal, but the street light flashed to red again. He cursed out loud, annoyed with how rapidly the light had changed. Was he having second thoughts?

While he groused about the slow-changing signal, a green car appeared out of the fog and approached the intersection before pulling to a stop on the opposite side. It was Mary!

He gave a hopeful glance at the signal, but the crimson beacon held steady. He pounded his steering wheel. "Come on. Come on, light. Turn!"

"To heck with this," he said, first looking right then left before flooring the accelerator pedal. The little compact car roared across the intersection and pulled to a stop parallel to her driver's window.

Their windows rolled down together. Mary spoke first. "I want to talk to you—"

Eric pointed down the street. "Turn your car around and park by the sidewalk near the gas station."

At the next driveway, he swerved the hatchback to a screeching halt in the station's entrance. He threw the car into park and pulled the parking brake. He strapped his walking boot onto his left ankle. Leaving his crutches in the car, he waited on the sidewalk next to a public bench.

Mary approached but kept her distance, stopping at the other end of the bench. She was clutching a tissue in her hand, and her eyes looked red and puffy. Her reticence to come closer and engage Eric puzzled him. Her in-your-face style of confrontation was uncharacteristically absent. "Are you OK?" Eric said.

"No, I'm not OK," Mary said. "I'm upset."

"At what?"

"Quit playing dumb, Eric."

"You're upset with me . . . that I'm leaving."

Mary's face softened, "Don't go, Eric," she pleaded. "Stay here a little longer. You can go to your uncle's later in the summer."

He edged closer. "I need to get out of here, Mary." He reached for her arm, but she spun away and sat down on the bench with her back to him. Without looking, she said, "What, Eric? What are you so afraid of?"

He circled around in front of her. Mary looked up, her eyes begging. This time she spoke more softly: "Don't you want to spend time with me before I go off to college?"

"Yes. I do, Mary . . ." Eric's voice trailed off, words failing him. Mary's doleful entreaty had sapped his endless excuses.

She stood up. "Doesn't seem like it," she snipped.

"I told you last night—"

"You didn't say jack last night," she said. "All you said was you were leaving to spend the summer with your uncle down in South Carolina, and when I asked why you changed the subject."

"I don't know . . . I had packing to do last night. That's why I cut our talk short . . . Look, I'll be back soon. You'll see . . ."

"I *thought* we were friends," Mary said.

"We *are* friends."

"If we're friends, then why are you leaving so soon. Why the rush?"

"I'm not in a rush," he said, exasperation seeping into his voice.

"No? I think calling your uncle yesterday and leaving the next morning kind of counts as a *rush,* Eric."

Tell her the truth, he thought. He lowered his voice. "I need a break from this miserable town. I can't take all the stares and whispers anymore."

"Is that what these last three months have been? About you feeling like everyone is against you? Buzzy's death, is that it? You think you're the only one who feels guilty? What about Rodney and me? Don't your 'miserable' friends have any say in the matter? Or are you the only one?"

Her barrage of words had caught him by surprise. Eric wanted to respond, to tell some lie, something that wouldn't hurt Mary's feelings. Her desire for answers was the precise reason for him to leave quickly. No explanations. No hassle. No lies. It was painless that way.

She eyed him hard. "Is that the way you feel about me? I'm one of your 'miserable' friends?"

The word sounded so harsh coming from her, and he felt himself becoming flustered. "No, that's not what I meant . . . Aw, never mind." He threw his hands up at her and tromped over to his car and got in. He circled his car around the gas station's lot and pulled his driver's side close to the sidewalk near Mary. Leaning out the window, he said, "Please understand, Mary, I have to get away for a while."

She stepped close to his door, putting her hand on his arm. "When are you coming back? You *are* coming back before I leave for school—right?"

"Of course. I'll be back in time." He slipped his hand into hers. "I'll give you a call, OK?"

Her eyes said she didn't believe him.

"I better go. My uncle is waiting for me." He pulled away, waving goodbye out the window.

Eric pulled to a stop in the right-turn lane. Before he made the turn, he leaned out his window and took one more look at Mary, who had sat back down on the bench. She jumped up when she saw him look her way. She took two hopeful steps toward him, but he drew his head back into the car and stared at the annoying blinker light ticking on and off. He slapped it down and reached up to angle his rear-view mirror so he could see Mary. She had collapsed back onto the bench, her knees pulled to her chest, one hand brushing tears from her cheeks.

Lord, why is this so hard? Eric scrunched his eyes and threw his head back against the headrest. He flipped his blinker back on, blinked back the tears, and pulled away.

PART TWO

CHAPTER 15

Eric's summer vacation with his uncle had gone past Labor Day—long past. Twenty-three months after Eric's hasty hometown departure, the rock band Led Zeppelin had broken up, Mount St. Helens volcano blew off its north face, and President Jimmy Carter had forced the US Olympic team to boycott the 1980 summer games in Moscow, Russia.

Near the end of Eric's first summer away, had asked his uncle Joe if he could stay longer and Joe had graciously accepted. That August, he had ditched any thoughts of a college education. He assured his uncle that he would look for employment or maybe enter a technical school once Dr. Doughton cleared his ankle. Living in a new city seemed like a good way to put his past behind him. Nobody recognized him here, and nobody asked him probing questions about Buzzy. Most people he'd met only wanted to know where he was from or which of the state's college sports teams he supported, and that suited Eric just fine. With his decision finalized, he settled in, content to put off a return to Brevard. The only complication brought by his decision was the fallout from people he'd left behind. Infuriated, his mother didn't speak to him for a month.

For the seven months following the removal of his cast, Eric had obeyed his doctor's orders and hadn't run a step. On his Christmas visit back to Brevard, during the winter of 1979, Eric had his final appointment with Dr. Doughton. He had waited nervously as the doctor examined his X-rays. Then Dr. Doughton had palpated Eric's ankle and flexed it gently this way and that. "Any pain?"

"No."

The doctor looked up. "It's healed well enough, Eric."

It took the full length of the office visit for Dr. Doughton to clarify what "well enough" meant. He said Eric had healed better than he'd expected and told him he could now resume normal activities, but that he needed to ease into everything very slowly. As far as running went, if Eric decided to pursue that again, he was to start gently and only on level surfaces. Throw in a day off every four days for the first four weeks. And he cautioned Eric to keep his distance to a minimum for a while.

"So, do you still think competition is out?"

"Only time will tell. That's a ways off. Don't rush it." Then he warned Eric that there was always a possibility that the ankle could break again. Those words sent a chill up Eric's spine.

Then the doctor offered him an unexpected bit of hope. He said he'd seen a patient with a similar fracture who had returned to competition without recurring ankle pain. Eric grabbed onto that handful of optimism and kept it close.

Dr. Doughton gave Eric his home phone number and told him to call if he had any ankle pain at all. Before Eric left the office, the doctor said he was proud of him for having followed his rehab instructions. Then he had a nurse teach Eric the proper way to wrap his ankle with athletic tape for support.

On the evening after Eric's December appointment, he met Rodney, Jonathan, and Jen at Donnelly's pub. Mary was absent because she was spending Christmas at her Grandparents' house in Apex, North Carolina, a small town outside of Raleigh. Jen had also let slip that Mary was still mad at Eric and would likely not attend, anyway.

At first Eric was excited to hear about his friends' college adventures. But when it came time for Eric to elaborate on his new life, there wasn't much to say other than he was working and his ankle had healed. His life was boring compared to theirs. They did encourage him to come back to Brevard and go to school at the local junior college, and maybe run again, but he clarified his situation, reiterating that he wanted to work for his uncle's home remodeling business and that a higher education wasn't a priority anymore. His friends good-naturedly pushed him to rethink his plans, but when Eric gruffly defended his decisions, they backed off.

Eric didn't stay in town long, leaving for South Carolina the day after Christmas. It was a long, lonely drive.

Shortly after the world had pinned their 1981 calendars to the wall, eighteen months since Eric left Brevard, a pink envelope from Mary arrived in the mail. Inside it was a letter that made him reconsider his decision to stay in Charleston.

It was May now, an early Friday morning. Eric had prepared to travel back to Brevard well before noon. He wanted to get his apartment hunting started early. The previous Monday, he had received an envelope from his mother stuffed with newspaper clippings of *For Rent* ads she had cut out of Brevard's local newspaper. She'd circled listings she thought might fit Eric's budget.

In truth she wanted Eric to come back home to live with her and Mark. And she said so again in a heartfelt, handwritten letter she'd included with the clippings. But he had made his decision to live on his own and planned to stick with it. On their last phone conversation he had made his decision clear to her but promised to visit her often.

Eric unpinned the last poster from the wall of his room in his uncle's house. The early morning light refracting through the open blinds lit up the wall. In his mind's eye, like a ghost from Eric's past, a rectangular silhouette—a visual apparition—seemed to remain on the white-painted sheetrock. The poster was a photograph of his running hero Steve Oberlin, the current American record holder in the mile at 3:49. He carefully rolled up the poster and slid it into a cardboard tube where he'd already stored the posters of Jim Ryun and Steve Prefontaine. These superstar runners had been like sentinels over Eric's life as he had softened from his former athletic fitness. Like the slow crisping and curling of his poster's desiccated edges, he had aged some too. He could never go back to who he was, but he could change, and he knew that time had come. It was time to go home to Brevard.

He set the tube down on the naked mattress and checked himself in the full-length mirror hung on the back of the door. Stroking his full mustache, he smiled, then pressed a hand against the bulge in his T-shirt as he contracted his abdominal muscles. This didn't entirely omit the bulge. Eric frowned—only twenty and already a paunch. He smoothed his hair back, checking that his pony tail was securely tucked into its rubber band. Satisfied, he grabbed his keys from the top of his dresser, along with a towel, and headed out to his car.

Eric drove east toward the ocean. He was heading for a tiny barrier island beach community called Daniel Island located a mile and a half across the tidal flats from the mainland town of Mount Pleasant, where he'd been living with his uncle for nearly two years. His little car buzzed down the city's central boulevard as a light southwestern breeze brushed the fronds of the nearby Sabal palmettos.

Eric was going to miss this place. The area's history, the sultry summers, the salty ocean air, and his ex-girlfriend, Melissa. He pictured her sitting in the passenger seat, the car's windows open, the humid air sweeping her long reddish-blond hair back, a few unbound strands draping delicately across her face. He had dated her for a year and a half, an all-time record for Eric when it came to relationships. Her favorite place was the beach. When the weather was warm enough, she and Eric spent most of their time at the shore. She loved to eat at Poe's, a little restaurant wedged in among the cluster of bars and shops—a hundred-yard strip that was the extent of Daniel Island's downtown. Melissa, now a senior at the College of Charleston, was graduating in a few weeks, before heading back to her home state of Massachusetts. That was that; neither of them wanted to be bound by a long-distance relationship.

He crossed over the swing-bridge onto Daniel Island. Once he had slipped through the one-gas-station downtown, he took a left and kept an eye out for the town's only water tower. The tower marked the general location of his favorite beach access point. He pulled his car off the road at Station 22.

Eric got out, propped his left foot on the door sill and unlaced his shoe. He took it off, then grabbed a roll of athletic tape he had stashed in the door's side pocket and promptly taped his ankle. He pressed the taping all around to make sure the seams were sealed and his taping wasn't too tight, cutting off his foot's circulation. Eric crammed his doctored ankle into his left shoe. He locked his car door, then bent over and looped his car key into the laces of his right running shoe. He cinched his old training shoes with a double knot before stepping off the road onto a sandy path. He walked through a tunnel of wind-scarred scrub oaks that had become familiar to him as the forest trails back home. When he cleared the foliage he stood squinting at the brilliant sun of a clear blue sky. The path connected to a boardwalk that led to a dune covered with sea oats. At the end of the wooden walkway, he stepped off and stood next to a vertical four-by-four post sunk into the sand. Toward the top of the post was the carved number twenty-two.

As Eric walked to the water's edge, he passed two teenage girls sunning themselves on large beach towels covered with yellow daises. He turned right and walked the grey, hard-packed sand south toward Charleston harbor. The tide was low and slack. There was virtually no incline to the beaches on Daniel Island, so a rising tide was quick to reclaim the beach. When hanging out at this beach, Eric always had to be careful how close he placed his gear to the water. If he wandered too long, he might return to a soaked towel.

Eric liked surfing this beach, and he also enjoyed walking the strand when he needed time to think. Back in Brevard, a vigorous run up Agony Hill had always been an excellent venue for sorting out his problems. But this picturesque barrier island would more than do in Agony Hill's stead.

The ocean breeze was warm and slightly humid. Eric was wearing a pair of green nylon running shorts and a large, surf-shop T-shirt. This morning he had dug out his old pair of running shoes from the bottom of a cardboard box. They'd been crushed flat from the weight of his old sporting gear, and the shoes' nylon uppers were brittle. He'd flexed their foam soles, examining the extent of abuse incurred. The rubber waffle soles had hairline cracks, but the foam was still intact.

As Eric walked, his feet flopped hard with each footfall as if wearing a new pair of leather dress shoes. The nylon crackled with every stride. His training shoes had seen better days, but these were the only pair he had.

Ever since the accident, Eric hadn't been able to bring himself to purchase a new pair of running shoes, only to be used for walking. Once the doctor had given him the all-clear, he'd still waited until now before considering his first attempt at a distance run, taking the extra time to make sure his ankle was at its full strength. After he had started working for his uncle's remodeling company, the extended time on his feet lifting and moving construction materials daily helped strengthen his body, especially his legs and ankles. Yet, he still balked at buying a new pair of training shoes. He just couldn't get past the feeling that he didn't deserve them. Buzzy was dead, and Eric had only suffered a fracture. When he even pondered the idea of running again, that was the thought that surfaced: *Buzzy is dead.* Running and Buzzy's demise seemed inextricably linked.

After a half mile of walking down the beach, his shoes' foam midsoles softened, and the insoles reformed to the contours of Eric's feet. A chill tingled his skin. He wanted to bolt into a full run. But he stuffed that feeling. He reminded himself to be careful. If he plunged too hard and deep back into his old training habits, he might reinjure himself. He knew his penchant for wanting things yesterday. He always found it difficult to resist those impractical urges.

Eric was now passing a national landmark, Fort Moultrie—a series of seacoast fortifications put to use from 1770 to 1947. Exploring the Charleston area was like stepping through the pages of a history book. He couldn't go a quarter mile in any direction without bumping into something historical. He had visited many national park sites, along with taking in a requisite number of walking and carriage tours in downtown Charleston. He had fallen in love with the city and its saga. At first, those intriguing charms were enough to keep Eric in South Carolina. He thought Charleston and its surrounding towns were a great place to start over, build a new life, but now his heart's desires burned anew.

His first order of business, once he returned home to Brevard, would be to make amends to his friends and family. Second, if he began running again, Brevard was the proper place to do it. Before his accident, when he still fantasized about becoming an Olympic runner, he imagined using Brevard as his home training grounds. With flat valley roads for fast runs and mountain trails for strength and endurance—each only a short jog away—an athlete would have the tools to become the best they could be. Plus, the area was beautiful. Eric may have been a little partial to his hometown, but he could imagine no better place.

The shoreline curved right, the long bend forming the north end of Charleston's harbor mouth. On his left he could now see Fort Sumter, Charleston's old iconic bulwark, sitting lonely on its tiny harbor island, still symbolically guarding the city against naval invasions.

Eric walked until the beach narrowed to the width of a single traffic lane. He stopped and looked across the harbor one last time at the Charleston's church-spired skyline, then turned around and eyed the curved shoreline. He pictured himself standing on the starting line of a track about to start his race. He had visualized this starting-line moment often in a recurring dream, usually on a familiar track he had raced on in high school. But in every dream sequence, the moment the starter's gun fired, he startled awake, soaked in sweat, pulse throbbing in his temples. He never took the first step.

Eric took a deep breath and leaned forward, falling into his first running step, but he drew up and stopped.

"Come on, Eric. You can do this. What are you afraid of?"

He eyed the shoreline again.

In his mind, he knew the answer to his own question. He feared the truth. If he reinjured his ankle, his future as a serious distance runner would be an afterthought. That thought paralyzed him more than any prerace jitters he'd ever had. His stomach turned, and a nervous tension stiffened his limbs.

But he knew only one way to ease his nerves. It was to start.

Searching for the motivation to plunge himself into a bone-chilling pool of uncertainty, he rocked back and forth in one spot. At last he blew out a breath and confronted his doubts and fears. Finally he was off and running.

He held his pace to a touch faster than walking. He kept his footfalls flat, barely bending his ankles. A half mile later, his calves were tight, and his lower front quadriceps, just above the knee, had a creeping soreness. A throbbing pain also daggered the center of his chest, a sure sign that his circulatory system couldn't even keep up with Eric's plodding.

Keep it slow, Eric. His mind was picturing speed—his legs rapidly circling underneath him, his pony tail flying behind him. But his body was voting for the couch and a good movie. Five minutes later he reached the north end of Fort Moultrie. He stopped to rest and check his ankle. He pressed his fingers hard against the joint connections, probing the ligaments. Relieved that his ankle was holding up, no pain, Eric resumed his run.

The refrigerated container ship's bow now pointed toward the harbor and would soon meet the tugboats. As Eric lumbered along, he had noticed that the rapidly subsuming tide had erased his previous footprints. In the distance, the island's water tower had grown taller. Figuring he had a mile to go, he continued trudging.

Eric had said good-bye to his uncle that morning before Uncle Joe had gone off to work at his construction company. Joe had been gracious in taking Eric under his wing. After Doughton had given Eric the go-ahead to resume normal activities, his uncle had taught Eric the construction trade. Eric knew that having that work experience might come in handy if he ever needed a job.

In the distance, approximately a football field away, Eric could see the two girls with the colorful daisy towels still sunning themselves in the same spot. He stopped and pressed his fingers around his ankle—still no pain.

Eric did a quick self-assessment: His shoes were cracked and brick hard, his running shorts were skintight, and he wore a large T-shirt in an effort to hide his twenty-five extra pounds. He was in a sorry state.

He thoughtfully rubbed his mustache. Sorry state or not, he decided for one more test of his ankle. He would sprint a hundred yards, about even with where the girls were. *OK, it's now or never, Eric.*

He launched himself forward, but instead of blasting away from his imaginary starting line like a svelte, nimble sprinter, he found his body's additional pounds held him down like one of those lead jackets that dentists make you wear when taking X-rays. The container ship now entering the harbor was probably moving faster than he was at this moment. Like the ship, Eric wished he had a whole fleet of tugboats to assist him.

After overcoming his weight-handicapped inertia, his legs moved a little faster underneath him. When he reached half the distance to the girls, unable to bear the pain in his calves and remain on the balls of his feet, his brick-hard shoes clapped on the hard-packed sand. Five or six strides later, he abruptly halted, his youthful but neglected body crying in pain. He bent over and threw his hands on his knees. Several moments later he righted himself, but he continued to wheeze like a three-pack-a-day smoker.

Twenty yards up the beach, a well-tanned man, wearing only a pair of running shorts and shoes strode in Eric's direction. The lithe runner, maybe a few years older than Eric, gave a polite nod as he glided past. The runner had well-defined six-pack abs, and his quadriceps muscle striations shimmered under his Coppertone skin. Eric barely heard the scratch of the man's footfalls on the hard-packed sand—his stride efficient, body erect, posture perfect—a seamless symphony of movement. Eric groaned and wondered if he could ever look, or run, like that again.

As Eric shuffled past the two girls, he saw them giving each other furtive glances, their hands covering their mouths, whispering and giggling. The two reminded him of Mary and Jen after Jen had given him his second place ribbon. Were they talking about him? He didn't dare look them in the eye. But surely the girls had witnessed his pathetic sprint down the beach. Dejected—metaphorically beaten down and worn out like his shoes—he thought: *Eric, it's going to be a longer road than you think.*

Eric scanned the dunes for his beach entry point. The waist-high station markers, when viewed from the shoreline, looked the size of a kid's plastic Wiffle ball bat and were always hard to spot. Sometimes trying to remember where, precisely, he had entered the beach proved challenging.

When Eric reached the marker, he stopped, turned, and faced the ocean. He made a mental picture of the shoreline. "Beautiful," Eric whispered. He would miss this beach.

BEFORE HE PUT THE city limits behind him, he wanted to pay his respects to the owner of the Run and Race shoe store first.

The proprictor, Irv Batten, was an icon in the Mount Pleasant running community. He had founded the Mount Pleasant Running Club. By the time Eric had arrived in the summer of '79, the club was three hundred members strong. The club also held Tuesday night interval-training sessions on an asphalt track in old downtown Mount Pleasant.

After Eric had wandered into Run and Race a few times to thoughtfully examine the wall of running shoes—yet leave each time without buying a pair—Batten finally approached him as Eric inspected a racing flat. Eric's hand was jammed inside the shoe, his other hand flexing the forefoot. "If you're going to fondle my shoes," Batten said, "I expect a dinner offer, at least." Eric laughed, his face flushing. Drawn in by the owner's easygoing nature, Eric stayed on for a conversation with Batten and ended up confessing the full story of his accident. Batten understood Eric's plight but encouraged him not to turn away from the sport he loved, even if he couldn't run himself. Batten also asked Eric to come out and help time the runners at the Tuesday night track workouts. Eric took him up on the request and had shown up almost every week since.

Today when Eric arrived at the store, one lone clerk was in the front of the store taking foot measurements from the one and only customer. Eric walked to the store's back office.

Batten stopped writing entries in his ledger and looked up in surprise. "Eric, aren't you supposed to be working?" Standing to greet

Eric, "Ohhh I almost forgot, you're heading home. I'm sorry. I've been so busy lately. It completely slipped my mind."

Eric shook his hand. "That's OK. I'm sure you always forget your best customers."

Batten smiled broadly and rolled his eyes. "I would if that said customer had ever bought a pair of shoes from me." Both of them chuckled.

"Seriously, Irv," Eric said, "I've come to say goodbye, but also to buy a pair of shoes."

Batten's voice raised a few merry octaves, "Oh, anything for my best customer. Come this way." Batten turned Eric and steered him to the wall of shoes.

Eric settled on a new pair of shoes, burgundy red, each shoe emblazoned with the silver colored, S-shaped logos. At the counter, he opened his wallet to pay cash. Batten threw up his hands. "Your money is no good here."

Shocked, Eric implored, "Irv, come on, I gotta pay, please."

"No," Batten insisted, shoving the shoes across the counter, "you're my friend. It's my gift to you. It's my way of saying good luck."

Eric's throat knotted. "If my ankle holds up, Irv, I'll make you proud. I promise."

"I know you will," Batten said. "OK, now promise me you'll come back and visit, all right?"

"I will."

Batten came around the counter and walked Eric to the front door. The two shook hands. Batten leaned a bit closer and looked Eric in the eye, "Be careful, OK?"

Chapter 16

His favorite spot in Straus park had always been the northern shore of a little man-made lake. The slopes of the Pisgah Forest buttressed the lake's edge, which surrounded the park like two warm hands, the old pines and hardwoods sheltering Brevard's little treasure. He stood there now, watching dragonfly's flitting in and out the lake's brushy edges as Water Skaters glided across the smooth surface. Beneath his feet, Allison Creek, the lake's spring fed water source, continued its journey through a clay pipe under the gravel roadway as it fulfilled its round-the-clock job of filling the tiny reservoir.

On the circular path that bordered the lake, Eric spotted a dark-haired man jogging with an unusual gait. Dark sweat patches under the runner's arms had nearly merged in the middle of his chest.

The man came to a stop in front of Eric with a goofy but cheerful grin on his face.

"Do you know where Agony Hill is?" the man asked. "This is my first time in this park. I moved to town a few weeks ago."

"Hey, is your leg all right?" Eric asked.

"Oh, that," he said, glancing down at his foot. He pulled the knee of the leg in question to his chest, as if trying to show Eric his flexibility and fitness. "I'm fine. I've had this problem since I was a kid, but it doesn't bother me much. Thanks for asking." His eyes then narrowed and his buoyant grin fell. "Hey," he said in a secretive voice, "is Agony Hill as hard as people say?"

The man was like a little boy, Eric thought. Like a kid asking an adult a question but not wanting to hear the answer. What the man wanted to be told was that Agony Hill was creampuff run and that all the tough talk was just overblown hype.

Eric chuckled. "Well," he said. "I don't know who you've been talking to. It's tough, no doubt, but it's short, roughly a mile long, so it won't be too bad."

"Yes, I've heard similar," the man said. But I needed a second opinion. I haven't been running much lately."

Eric purposely coughed into his fist, and said jokingly, "Yeah, me too." Realizing he hadn't answered the man's first question, he said, "Oh, I forgot to tell you. Agony Hill is down that path around the lake. Take a right and the next left. When you see two small metal posts with a wire between them at the start of a gravel trail, you have the right one."

"Got, it. Thanks. I appreciate the directions . . . Oh, by the way, my name is Bill Kest. It's nice to meet you . . ."

"Eric. My name is Eric Roberts. Pleasure to meet you too. Goodluck."

Bill gave a friendly wave and jogged off.

Eric watched the runner shuffle around the bend. He looked down at his tight T-shirt and placed a hand on his belly. *The guy's in better shape than I am, Eric thought. At least he's running. That's more than I can say. One half-assed beach run won't cut it.* He bent over to touch his toes. Still a little sore from the previous day's run, the effort made him grunt in pain. *Man, I got a long way to go.*

Eric walked in the same direction the man had gone. Minutes later he stood at the foot of the graveled trail. Eric hopped over the low hung wire between the two poles and began hiking the trail.

Images of kids racing the hill flew into his mind—he and his running brethren hoofing it up the one-mile path. At the top their bodies would be screaming for oxygen. But, once they recovered, their prior torment was always worth the climb.

Within moments his brow broke out in sweat, and he was only walking. He hiked about a quarter mile, then stopped, bent toward his toes again, and this time, his muscles had warmed, allowing him to stretch far enough to grab his toes.

He imagined running up the mile-long climb, driving his body to the limit, and a shiver of excitement coursed through his limbs. He knew it wouldn't be wise to attempt that, not today, but he hadn't lost his love for his sport. He released and audible sigh and retraced his path back to his car.

"OK, IT SOUNDS LIKE a great place," Eric said. "I look forward to seeing it. I'll see you at two." Eric hung up the receiver at a gas station phone booth across the highway from Straus Park. The man had told Eric the apartment for rent was a renovated barn loft, and the location was at a children's summer camp, a quarter mile off Highway 64. It was affordable, and Eric would be moments away from the trails of the Pisgah Forest. He was thrilled by the idea of having his own apartment—his first time living on his own.

He had some time to kill, so he decided he'd go downtown to grab a bite to eat at Donnelley's Pub. While Eric was keen on getting back in Mary's good graces, he needed more time to consider what he would say to her. A late lunch at Donnelley's would also give him the chance to catch up with his old soccer coach, who owned the pub. Eric had played on the bar's soccer team for a couple years when he'd been a little kid. He'd never taken to the game, but he later got to know John Donnelley better. On November 12th, the fall of his senior year of high school, Eric had turned the legal drinking age for North Carolina. He'd spent many a Saturday night in the bar with two other eighteen-year-old high school friends.

He opened the VW's hatch and adjusted his surfboard so it would stop banging the back glass while he drove. He'd considered selling the board or leaving it with his uncle down in Mount Pleasant, but he liked having it with him. It would make a nice decoration to hang on the wall or from the ceiling in his first apartment. He threw an old blanket over the board to help shield the waxed surface from the sun and drew down the hatch, but he stopped when he noticed that a packet of photos had spilled out of one of his boxes. He scooped them up to file them back into their envelope, but he couldn't help flipping through them first. The picture at the bottom of the pile was of him and his ex-girlfriend, Melissa, at one of her college parties, celebrating a friend's birthday.

On a warm September evening, that first fall in Charleston, Eric had met Melissa at a trendy college bar on East Bay Street in downtown Charleston. Melissa was a college Junior two years older than Eric. Later in their relationship, she had confessed that she didn't usually date guys younger than her, but she said Eric was different. While she couldn't exactly put her feelings into words, Eric guessed it was because he was not part of her college crowd, and that made Eric exciting to her—sort of like purposely dating a boy her parents wouldn't approve of. He loved his time with her, but because he wasn't college student, he had always felt like an outlier, no matter how often he tried to convince himself otherwise.

She and her college friends were having fun and moving along with their educations—as were his friends—yet Eric had chosen the working man route. There was nothing wrong with that, he knew, but soon he concluded that he had to decide: go back to school or make a serious commitment to working long-term for his uncle's renovation business.

For nearly two years, coming back to Brevard had been far from Eric's mind. When speaking to his friends on long-distance phone calls, he'd grown tired of having to repeatedly tell them how his ankle was doing and whether he was running again. A few had been willing to spend the nickel to call him at first, but everyday conversations with Eric were brief. He didn't want to discuss the past, and he had little to say about the present unless it related to sports or a favorite TV show. As the days passed by, Eric's promises to write or call his friends eventually slipped by the wayside. In the last year, he had not spoken or written to any of his friends from Brevard. He always found a convenient excuse—that he didn't have time to sit down and write a letter or that long-distance phone calls were too expensive.

Melissa had told him he was pigheaded for not dealing with his past. Back in February when the two had been drinking at a little pub down on Daniel Island, Eric had confided to Melissa that he was having nightmares about Buzzy and the house. Until then, he had kept his issues to himself, thinking he could just get through it. Besides, during his day-to-day activities, his life seemed normal enough. Lately, though, the nightmares had increased. One day, while helping his uncle rebuild a staircase in a stately antebellum mansion down along the Battery section of downtown Charleston, Eric had been the cause of a close call. Working near the top of the staircase, he'd laid down a skilsaw too close to the outside edge of the stairs. His foot bumped it, and the tool tumbled off the edge. Eric reached for the cord as it spooled after the saw, but by the time Eric clamped a grip on the wire, the saw had already clipped the shoulder of another worker. Fortunately, the guy only needed a few stitches and was left with a large bruise for a few weeks. The accident shook Eric, and his uncle let him go home early that day. That night, once his anguished mind settled down enough to let Eric finally sleep, he had one of his worst nightmares. The scene was the same as always, Buzzy falling from the stairs, but this time Buzzy was holding onto the cord and Eric couldn't grab it. It felt so real that it took Eric a long moment after waking up to convince himself it had only been a dream.

The frequency of Eric's nightmares increased, with insignificant things triggering them, like the certain sound of cracking wood or the sight of a dilapidated old house. At first Eric thought his subconscious was overreacting, and assumed these episodes would go away. *You're not crazy,* he had told himself. Eric decided he would continue to take the athletic approach to his troubles. He would put his head down, keep swinging at the plate, so to speak, and eventually he would break out of his slump; everything would work itself out. Eric had determined to put his past behind him *his* way.

Eric slid the set of pictures back into their envelope and placed them into their box. But before he closed the hatch, he reached into the same box and pulled out a pink envelope. After he settled into the driver's seat, he opened and reread Mary's letter she had sent last January.

Dear Eric,

How are you? I'm good.

I hope you are doing well down in Charleston.

I thought about you today. It's New Year's Day, and I ran the Art Loeb Trail. The weather was a little crappy. It was like our senior year, but not too bad. Last year the weather was perfect, sunny, no wind, and I wanted to run it, but I just couldn't do it without you there. Not that you could have run it, I know, but it would have been nice to have you there hiking nearby or something.

I'm sorry you won't talk anymore. I thought we were friends. I still don't understand why you left. I guess it's like you said, sometimes we need to get away for a while.

It seems like you don't want to continue our friendship. I feel like you've moved on already. And, well, I guess it's time for me to move on, too.

I didn't write this letter to bash you. I only wanted to tell you this is the last time I will write. If I don't hear from you after this, I will assume you don't want to be friends anymore.

Sincerely,
Mary

Eric thought back five months previous when he first read Mary's letter. He stared through his windshield, running her words over in his mind. Would she take him back, be a friend again after the way he'd acted? Why should she? He hadn't spoken to her in close to two years now, even though she'd written him half a dozen times. He had written back, but only once. It was at the end of his first summer down south. He wrote that August, telling her he was staying longer at his uncle's place, and he wouldn't be coming home before she set off for college.

Remembering their heated confrontation the last time he'd

seen Mary at Brevard's downtown crossroads on that June morning after graduation, he swallowed hard. After the way he'd left Mary sitting on that sidewalk bench, he could have at least called her the following August to tell her he wasn't coming back yet. It would have been the more personal thing to do, and would've meant more to her than some one-page letter that had taken him five minutes to scribble down. He hadn't even included a plausible excuse for not coming to see her. While the letter had done its job—provided the minimal communication necessary, avoiding another potential argument with her over the phone—he surely had hurt her feelings all over again. His stomach tightened, a queasy wave welling upward to his throat. He swallowed back the bile. He felt worse now than he had when seeing Mary in his rearview mirror, sitting all tucked into herself on the bench.

Eric knew his actions had pushed him far down on her friends list, if not off, but he had to have hope. She had extended an olive branch with her letter, and that was more than he could say for himself. *Why didn't you write her back last January?* he thought. There was only one way to find out if she would ever talk to him again. Mary's final exams would be over by now, and she'd be back home from North Carolina State for the summer. He changed his mind and decided to stop at her house before heading to Donnelley's.

The closer he drove to Mary's house, the more his trembling increased. Once there, he sat in Mary's driveway for a few moments trying to gather himself. There were no other family cars visible. He found his courage and walked to her porch and mounted the steps. He stood at the edge of the porch and stared at the doorknob. "It's only Mary," he muttered to himself. She won't be that mad. Will she? She'll understand. *Get a grip, Eric.*

He stepped to the door.

As he reached for the doorbell, the trembling returned. He finally pressed the button and heard the bell ring.

Only silence, no footsteps on the wooden floors, only the faint sound of the family's tabby cat, Nickel, meowing on an adjacent window ledge. When no one answered, his trembling ceased. Why was it so hard to apologize to someone? Off the hook, for the moment. He backed his car out of the driveway and headed for the pub.

As Eric's car approached the pub's parking lot, he passed by the rusty metal and wood bench on the sidewalk where he and Mary had said their last goodbye. He grimaced. It was one more reminder of the past. Everywhere he had driven today he'd recalled specific things he and Mary had done or experienced together. Like the time he had taken her to the downtown sporting goods store to show her what kind of clothes she should wear for winter running. She had been so cute and naïve.

He went into the pub and ordered his lunch. As he ate, he tried to picture what Mary might look like now. People change; he had. Maybe she wore her hair shorter now or liked different clothes. Would they have anything to talk about?

Chapter 17

The man Eric had spoken with about the apartment had told him to look for a large wooden sign with red letters reading CAMP RIVERLAND. He said to take a right and at the end of that road he would find a large farmhouse, and a barn with an apartment on top.

Having grown up in Brevard, Eric knew the approximate whereabouts of the camp, but he'd never traveled down the road that led there. This was surprising because he had crisscrossed most every patch of asphalt in Brevard, but not this one. He was excited to see this hidden corner of his home turf, almost like going on a treasure hunt in his own backyard.

Eric steered his car onto the property, crossing over an old, no-longer-needed cattle grate which sent a rattling shudder so violent through his vehicle, that half the loose change jangling in his center console's unused ashtray, vibrated out onto the floorboards. As he drove in the direction of the farmhouse, he saw a small lake off to his left with a few cabins nestled near the far shore. The camp looked to be larger than he'd anticipated, and he wondered if it extended to the foothills of the Pisgah Forest. How had he and his friends never discovered this property on their adventure runs in high school?

When Eric pulled up to the beige two-story farmhouse, he noticed a light-blue Dodge Polara with a white vinyl roof parked next to the back porch. The early '70s model was the size of a tank.

He looked in the driver's window to examine the car's interior. *Wow, a classic,* he thought—no dents or rust spots.

The old farmhouse steps creaked as he made his way onto the back porch. A large window filled the backdoor's top half. A warped, wood-framed screen door sat ajar. Eric pulled open the screen door and knocked. No answer. He tried again. Seconds ticked by, and still, no one answered. The window on the door was partway open. He peered into the window and shouted, "Hey, anyone home?" Again, nothing. "Man," Eric said, slapping his hand on the porch post. "I come all this way, and he's not here."

He walked the house's perimeter, but he found no sign of anyone. He checked his watch to make sure he wasn't too early. Nope, right on time. Maybe the guy had gone out to run an errand and had lost track of time.

Eric looked across the yard at a two-story barn sitting forty yards away. It had two large black doors that faced the house. Left of the doors was a wood staircase that scaled the outside wall to the apartment. That was it, the place that was for rent. He walked over to see if he could peer into the apartment windows.

From the top of the stairs, Eric saw that the windows were curtained. No way to see inside. He twisted the door handle, and the latch clicked open. "Aha!" He glanced around and then stepped inside to have a quick look. The apartment was spartan, just as the man had described it. The rafters and wall studs were exposed, unfinished—definitely built cheap for the summer camp season, not for cold winters. But if the price was right, Eric could make do. A set of upper and lower cabinets sat adjacent to the door, the lower with a sink and a faucet. A small single-door fridge was wedged between the cabinets and the adjoining corner. There was a full-sized bed, already made with an Army-green wool blanket on top, a nightstand, and a plush chair in one corner. He liked the compact but cozy space. He walked over to check out the bathroom.

"Are you Eric?" a voice called from behind him.

Eric jumped and spun around to see a tall silhouetted figure in the doorway.

"Sorry. I didn't mean to sneak up on you," the elderly man said, stepping into the room.

"No one answered the door at the house, so I decided to have a look around. I found the apartment open."

"That's OK. I was over at the cabins tending to some woodwork. I lost track of time. Sorry I kept you waiting."

"I'm Eric Roberts," Eric said, walking over to the man.

The man was over six feet, Eric guessed, and slim by the way the man's shirt and trousers draped loosely, tied narrowly with a thin brown belt. The man had a full head of white hair except for a little thinning on the top. Eric shook the man's thin bony hand, and the old guy returned a firm, confident grip.

"Oh, forgive me. I'm Miklos Ionnos."

"Miklos what?"

"Ionnos. It's Hungarian. I've been in this country for a long time, but my accent still gets a little thick at times. Let me know if you have trouble understanding me."

"Your accent actually sounds familiar to me. Have we met before?"

"Oh, well, I don't think so. There are many Hungarians here in the US. Maybe you heard it on TV or something . . . no, I don't think we've met before."

"Could be. Anyway, I like the apartment. You said the rent would be lower in exchange for some work you needed. Can you tell me more?"

"Come downstairs. We'll talk," Mr. Ionnos said and headed back down the stairs.

Eric followed close behind.

When Mr. Ionnos neared the bottom of the stairs, he stumbled and pitched forward. Eric grabbed the railing and with his free arm reached for the back of the man's shirt. His fingers snatched at the loose shirt finding purchase. He closed his fist and held firm as the man's freefall snapped the clothing taught, fabric ripping as Eric pulled him back.

Once the man was upright Eric held him around his chest until he was steady on his feet. The man's panicked heart pounded under the palm of Eric's hand.

The landlord turned. His eyes wide with fear. "Thank you, Eric. I don't know what would have happened if you weren't here."

"You're welcome. Now let's get off these stairs."

When they both had descended, the man turned and pointed to the loose board.

"You see? I need help around here," the older man said. "I've meant to fix that step. I didn't think it was that bad yet."

Eric bent over and investigated the plank. "Yes, loose nails on one side. That's easy to fix. You should replace the board. It looks a little rotted."

"I think you're right," Ionnos said. He gestured toward the open barn doors.

Eric followed him inside to where an old green tractor sat.

"Have you ever worked on engines?"

"Some minor things like changing a radiator or A/C compressor," Eric said, "but not any engine rebuilds or stuff like that. What's the problem?"

"It won't start."

"Is it getting spark?"

"I think so, but I'm not sure. Can you look at it?"

Eric examined the tractor while Mr. Ionnos stood close by, watching intently. Eric knew from experience with his well-weathered car to start by checking the typical high-wear items. He ran his hand along the tractor's wires and connections. When Eric checked the distributor, the wire's sheathing appeared cracked and brittle. He located the center wire from the coil and tugged gently. It broke loose with a puff of dust.

"There's your problem," Eric said, pointing to the top of the distributor cap and the broken wire. "The wires are old; they just need to be replaced."

"Well, now, I feel a little stupid," said Mr. Ionnos. "I've never been good at figuring out mechanical or electrical problems, though. I appreciate the help. I can swing a hammer, but anything with a motor, I have problems." He patted Eric on the back. "Come, come," he urged, beginning to guide Eric toward the house. "We must sit on the porch. Have some sweet tea. Then we will talk."

When they stepped onto the porch, Mr. Ionnos said, "Please, please, sit down," gesturing toward a set of old rocking chairs. "I'll be back in a minute." He disappeared into the house.

When Eric lowered himself into one of the old rockers, it wrapped around him like a comfy blanket. The chairs were handcrafted of thin branches and leather, and to Eric's surprise there was no creaking or cracking as he gently rocked to and fro.

Mr. Ionnos returned and handed Eric a large glass of iced tea before settling into the other chair. A circular table matching the chairs' construction sat between them. Eric poked at the animal skin top, still taut despite its apparent age. "Your furniture is cool. How old is it?"

"Close to a hundred years, I've been told. The previous camp owner said the farmers left all the furniture with the property. So, most everything here is original and handmade. There's a four-post bed upstairs that is a work of art."

"Wait a minute," he said, getting up. "I forgot something" When he returned from inside the house he handed Eric a folded pamphlet then sat back down.

He pointed to a camp promotional document Eric had unfolded, "I run this boys camp. I purchased the property back in 1975 with a minority partner; he's a professor at the local college. But now that I'm a little older, I need help taking care of the property. I had a regular man helping with the maintenance and other odds and ends, but he moved away recently. So, I decided I would try to find someone with good carpentry and mechanical skills who would do the work in exchange for a cheap place to stay. You have a good comprehension of motors; how is your knowledge of carpentry?"

"It's great. My uncle Joe—that's who I worked for down in Charleston—taught me a lot. He has a construction firm that does home renovations. So, there isn't much I can't do. He got me a job with a construction company over in Hendersonville now that I'm moving back here—he knows the owner."

"So, you'll be working full-time?"

"I will," Eric said. "How many hours a week does it take to maintain the camp?"

"It can be busy during the summer when the campers arrive. Something always breaks. But after that it should calm down, there's usually only routine maintenance to take care of during the winter. And if all goes well, next year it won't take much to ready the camp for the coming season.

"So, on the phone, you mentioned a one-year lease?"

"Yes, a year's lease. Is a hundred and fifty a month OK?"

"Sure, that's reasonable," Eric said. But he was uneasy about not having a concrete answer as to how many hours or work would be required. "Excuse me, Mr. Ionnos, I don't mean to be rude, but you never answered my question about the hours needed for the job."

"Oh, that," the old man said. "Well, it varies—it can be anywhere from ten to twenty hours a week. And you can call me Miklos. 'Mr. Ionnos' is too formal."

"Sounds good to me," Eric said. "So, Miklos, first and last month's rent?"

"Yes," his new landlord said.

Eric pulled a wad of hundred-dollar bills from his pocket, counted out the money, and handed it over.

Miklos took the money and stuffed it into his pocket without bothering to count it. "When would you like to move in?"

"Can I move in today?" Eric asked. "All my stuff is in my car."

"Sure. I can help if you like."

"Suit yourself. I don't have much." Eric walked over to the back of his car and lifted the hatch and carefully drew his surfboard out.

"You should have left your surfboard in Charleston," Miklos said. "You won't get much use out of it here."

"Don't remind me." He set the swallow tailed, twin-fin down

on the grass. "My uncle wanted me to sell it to him; he loves this board. But I couldn't convince myself to leave it behind."

"When I lived in California," Miklos said, "I tried surfing a couple of times, but the water was too cold for me."

"You surfed? Really?" Eric said, a hint of skepticism in his voice.

Miklos raised his eyebrows and smiled. "I wasn't always the old man you see before you."

Eric laughed. "Sorry, I didn't mean anything. I hear the waves in California are awesome. Here on the east coast, it's flat most of the time."

His new landlord grabbed the board. "I hear surfers on the east coast have to wait for hurricane season for good waves, no?" Miklos said. "Come on, let's find a good place to hang this in the apartment. You don't want to ding it."

Once Eric unloaded everything into his new apartment, he decided a small reward was necessary. He chose to go by the Cardinal and grab a treat before driving to his mother's house. He pulled into the Cardinal's parking lot and squeezed his car between two jacked-up four-wheel pickup trucks. A note taped to the menu board stated that the intercom system was out of order. A carhop skated by, and when she had finished with another customer, Eric flagged her down. After the young girl took his order, she gracefully glided back to the order window to relay the message. When she returned with his apple turnover, he tipped her and slid down in his seat to enjoy his treat.

The front door to the restaurant opened, and a group of five girls came out and made their way along the cement walkway that separated the restaurant's two rows of parking spots. The gang was boisterous. Eric instantly recognized their faces from high school. One still had her back turned, but it didn't matter—he knew who it was. Her once long red hair was now shoulder length, and she wore it in the currently popular shredded-out punk style. *So much for the old Mary,* he thought. The girls stopped in front of their cars and exchanged goodbye hugs. The group separated with four of them making their way to one car, while Mary walked in the opposite direction—toward Eric.

Eric gripped the steering wheel, twisting it back and forth as she walked in his direction.

When Mary was directly in front of his car, she gave a cursory glance his way and continued walking.

Doesn't she recognize me? Eric thought. *My car has to be a dead giveaway.*

She stopped in front of a blue compact car and waved to her friends as they rolled out of the parking lot. She slid her key into the drivers-side door and looked his way again. He detected a small smile on her face.

He leaned out his window. "Hey, Mary!"

Her smile dissolved. She quickly turned away, rushed into her car, and cranked the motor. She started backing out, but then stopped, put the car in drive, and brought it back to the curb. She rolled her window down and stared at Eric. Still, she said nothing.

How weird, Eric thought. *Two old friends, and we can't even leave our cars to talk to each other.* Stiffening his courage, he jumped out of his vehicle and strode over to her.

"Hey there," she said robotically, her vacant eyes assessing him from head to toe.

"I'm back."

"I can see that," she said flatly.

He looked around the parking lot, searching for some words of inspiration, but nothing came out. It was like the first time he had tried to ask a girl, out in sixth grade. He had frozen, suddenly losing access to language. The girl and her friends had giggled and walked away.

Mary threw her car into reverse but still held her foot on the brake. "Look—if 'I'm back' is all you can spit out, then I gotta go." She raised her foot off the pedal, and the car began to roll back. Eric walked with the car, placing a hand on the top of her doorsill. "Please, Mary. Please."

She slammed the brakes. The car halted, rocking back and forth on its springs. "Please, what?" She snipped. Her eyes flicked down to his hand still on the doorsill.

He jerked his hand back like it had been burned. "Agony Hill."

"Huh? Agony Hill? What are you talking about?"

"No . . . I mean . . . Don't go."

"Look, Eric. I don't have time for this."

"I'm running again. Meet me at Agony Hill. We'll run it like old times."

She blinked her eyes a few times then bellowed, "Is that all you can say to me after a year and a half? No phone calls, no returned letters—and all you blurt out is 'Agony Hill?' Are you serious?"

"Wait. Even better," Eric said. "Race me up Agony Hill. Please. It'd be more fun."

"*You*—want to race me up Agony Hill? Look at you," she said, an edge in her voice. "You're a mess, with your long hair and fat face." She leaned out her door, "How many pounds have you gained, anyway? You don't look in shape at all—when's the last time you ran? And what about your stupid ankle? Didn't the doctor say you shouldn't run again?"

Eric grunted at each of her blows, but he kept silent until she finished her barrage of insults. He puffed out his chest and looked her square in the eye and halfway lied. "I can run on it," he said. "The doctor cleared me. I tried it out a few weeks ago."

"Is that so? How many times have you run since?"

"Well . . . a couple times."

"A couple of runs, and you think you can race me up Agony Hill?"

"Yes," Eric said reluctantly.

"OK, mister. What day and time?" she said. There was that edge again in her voice, but this time her eyes were softer, looking off into the distance, her head gently nodding agreement with herself, her mind's eye already deriving satisfaction from Eric's future suffering.

Eric hadn't pictured their first conversation happening this way.

He had dug his own grave, though, and Mary's caustic remarks didn't make an easy reconciliation possible.

"How 'bout eight tomorrow morning?" he managed.

She jabbed a finger at him. "Fine, tomorrow then. Better be ready. And don't be late, either." As her car backed out of the parking space, she leaned out the window and chirped, "I see Charleston has done a lot for your conversation skills."

Her tires squealed as her car banked hard out the IN DRIVEWAY.

Chapter 18

The home Eric had grown up in was a rectangular ranch-style with two bedrooms and two baths. As he drove up to his old house, he noticed that the avocado green exterior appeared dingier than the previous time had been home, over a year before. The 950 square feet was a big reason for not wanting to move back in. He didn't want to share the same tiny room with his brother again; he liked being on his own and enjoyed having his own space. But, to spare his mother's feelings, he never told her it had anything to do with their home being so small.

Eric pulled his car into the driveway and shoved the gear shift into park, then eyed himself in the rearview mirror. "Some day you had, Eric," he said. He didn't even know how to feel about the day's events, but he didn't have time to sort out his feelings, because the kitchen door burst open, and his dog and his mother rushed out, mobbing him the moment he stepped from his car. Molly launched her front paws onto his chest, knocking him back a step.

"Aww . . . you missed me, didn't you, Molly?"

His mother squeezed him tight. "Eric. You're home."

"Love you, Mom," he whispered down to her ear.

"Have you gotten taller," she asked, standing on her tip toes, reaching to the top of his head.

"Still the same, mom."

"Hey, your car's empty. Where are your things? Did you find a place already?"

"I did. It was the first one I checked out today. It's perfect, so I gave the guy the money and moved in."

"Where is it?" She asked.

"It's off 64, down at the Riverland Summer Camp."

"Is it nice?" she asked. "Will it be warm in the winter?"

Eric steered his mom toward the house. "OK, OK, mom. Enough questions for now. I'll tell you more over dinner." As they stepped inside, Eric asked if Mark was around.

"No, your brother's over at a friend's house right now. But he can't wait to see you. He should be home any minute," she said.

"Man, Mark's a senior now. He must be insufferable, huh?"

She rolled her eyes. "I seem to remember another insufferable senior who used to live here."

"Touché, mom."

Mark arrived on time for dinner, armed with a million questions for his older brother, which Eric patiently answered. After dessert, Mark asked Eric if he'd like to play video games with him on his new game console. Eric said he would, but said to give him a few minutes.

As Mrs. Robert's was clearing the table, Eric said, "Mom, can we talk?"

She unloaded the dishes into the kitchen sink then returned to the table, her face wearing a suspicious frown. "Since when have you been the talkative type?"

"Come on, mom. Please?"

She set another dish in the kitchen sink and sat down near Eric.

On Eric's drive back to Brevard, he had had plenty of time to think. Two years earlier, his mother had been rightfully furious with him for not returning home and continuing his college plans, even minus a running scholarship. He had apologized, and she had accepted it, but deep down, he knew he hadn't meant it, telling her only what she wanted to hear. This time, though, it was different. She deserved an honest, heartfelt apology.

Eric reached over and cupped her hand. "Mom, I'm sorry for being a real butthead these last two years."

"What are you apologizing for?" she asked, a confusion on her face.

"I did some thinking on the way back home. I want to start clean. Sometimes I think that I only told you what you wanted to hear back then. And . . . I've felt guilty."

"Look, son." She clasped her tiny hand over his. "Everyone has little hills to climb as they go through life. Yours was bigger than most, but you made it. Now, if you want to apologize I accept. But there's no need. It's all a part of a parent's job. You have to be there for your kids—and you have to let them go when that's what they need. That's why I didn't fight you when you wanted to go down to your Uncle Joe's. I knew it'd be good for you and him to spend time together, and for you to have a little space from this town. Lord knows I didn't think you'd stay for two years, though. I was pretty miffed about that."

Eric laughed. "I know. You wouldn't talk to me for a month."

"That's right. But those were the choices you made back then. You came through it, and I'm very proud of you. You're all grown up now. And that's all I've ever wanted—for my boys to be strong, respectful young men." His mom patted his hand and turned in her chair to stand.

"Mom," he said, grabbing her arm gently. "Can I ask you something?"

"Lord, child, what is it?" she said with a cheerful expression. "You're awful chatty tonight."

"Mom . . . did you love Dad?"

"Wow, that's a question out of the blue. Why are you asking that?"

"I just wanted to know, that's all."

"Of course, yes. I loved your father."

"How can you say that after everything he did?"

"Listen, your dad was a good man. He did the best he could. He just couldn't break his alcohol addiction."

"I don't understand, Mom. How can you love a man that neglects his wife and . . . you know, is not great with his kids?" Eric's mind flitted across his childhood, threatening to land on a particular incident, then another. He pulled his focus back from the dicey stuff, things that would upset his mom, and settled on something relatively safe. "I mean, the guy passed out more than once in the driveway with the car door open."

"Eric," she started, reaching across the table to get his attention, her motherly eyes peering into his. "When you get into a marriage, or even in a serious relationship, no one ever knows how it's going to turn out. Everything starts out rosy, but like with your father, it can suddenly go off track in a hurry. Later, when he admitted he had a drinking problem, he attended AA meetings for a while, but one day your father quit, saying he didn't need their help anymore. I was disappointed, but I was glad he had at least tried. Some people won't even do that much. But yes, I still love him. And I hope you'll find it in your heart to love him, too." She paused for a moment. "I'm sorry I didn't talk to you or your brother more about all that . . . I guess I was trying to protect you two."

She turned her attention toward the living room, holding her gaze on the wall of plaques, ribbons, and photos of Eric and Mark's athletic prowess. Looking back at Eric, she said, "You know, your dad would be very proud of you. He always said you were a fast-little thing. It was always hard to catch when you were a young boy."

Eric hadn't thought about his father in a while. He appreciated his mother for finding the bright side to their bitter memories. He forced a smile, "Thanks, Mom."

Eric helped finish clearing the table. "Mom, can I help you with the dishes?" he asked.

"Oh, no, honey. That's OK. Go and play video games with your brother. He's missed you—Hey," she said , her tone changing—infused with excitement. "Have you seen Mary yet?"

"I can't say I actually *saw* her in the normal sense of the word."

She nudged his elbow. "What's that mean? Come on. I need details."

"It didn't go well."

"And?"

"I blurted out some stupid things, and now I'm racing her up Agony Hill tomorrow morning."

"Oh . . . Well . . . It's never easy with you, is it?" his mother said, laughing. "Does this mean you've been running?"

"I did, once. My ankle feels great, though."

"I know the doctor said you could run a little bit, but don't you think it's still too soon?"

"I think I've waited long enough, Mom," Eric said. "My ankle's fine."

"OK," she said, turning back to the sink. "It's your life."

"Come here, Mom," he said, reaching for her hand. "I know you mean well, but I'm an adult now. I can make my own decisions. I'll live with the consequences."

She turned back to him. "I know, son, but I can't help it. I worry about you."

"I wouldn't have it any other way," he said, wrapping his arms around her. "OK . . . I'm going to go hang out with Mark."

"Have fun," his mom said. "Oh, and I can't wait to hear how the race comes out. Who should I bet on?"

Eric didn't answer, but he grinned and waved his mom off and headed for his brother's room.

His mother called after him. "Mary's going to whip your butt, you know that?"

"We'll see mom, we'll see," he said, as he headed down the hallway.

Chapter 19

When Eric arrived at the Strauss parking area, he saw Mary standing beside her car's passenger-side door, glowering. She eyed her wristwatch, and grimaced, leering at Eric, arms clenched across her chest.

Eric opened his door. "What?" he chirped. "I'm only a little late."

She flashed a wan smile. "Still the same ole Eric."

Eric grunted then reached back to his rear seat to retrieve a shoebox and a pair of socks. He stepped barefoot onto the parking lot, tossing the shoebox onto his driver's seat.

This morning's starting on a cheery note, Eric thought as he put on his shoes. Once he had snugged down their laces, he probed his ankle's tape job to make sure it wasn't too tight; no numbness. He then chucked the shoe box over to the passenger seat and closed the car door, then turned to Mary.

"You ready?"

Eric folded his arms, mimicking her. "Do I look ready?"

She stepped closer, eyeing him up and down, and said, "I'm always ready." She continued to one-side the conversation as she walked around to the back of Eric's car. "When you put your *new* shoes and socks on, let's run a couple of laps around the lake to warm up before we hit the hill, all right?" Eric didn't appreciate her condescending lilt.

She stopped at his passenger window, leaned down, checking out the inside. "Fast food breakfast this morning?"

He glanced at the breakfast wrappers still littering the passenger seat. "About an hour ago. I should be OK. I didn't eat much."

"Well . . . at least you won't be hungry."

Eric snapped the double knot tight on his shoe, slammed his door, and shot Mary a dirty look across the car's roof. "Hey, why are you so sore at me? I'm trying to be friends again."

"By racing me up Agony Hill? Seriously?"

"Fine then. Let's get this over with. I know you hate my guts right now. Not that I blame you." Eric took off before Mary could respond.

A hundred yards into the run, Eric glanced back to see if Mary was coming. She was sprinting to catch him, her face still wearing a permanent scowl. Once Mary drew close, she didn't run beside him, settling for a spot just behind his right shoulder, outside his peripheral vision.

Halfway around the lake, she started running beside him. Her face was stiff, eyes stoic. *Strange,* he thought. *Maybe she really does hate me.* She hadn't responded at all to his last comment. The clawing of fingernails on a chalkboard would sound better than this brutal silence. Fortunately, there was a spot of good news: halfway around the second lake loop, his legs—still sore from his beach run—were loosening up.

To conserve his energy for the hill, Eric purposefully turtled his pace, a shade above walking speed. His pedestrian pace had Mary champing at the bit. Mary, finding it difficult to slow her natural tempo, kept surging in front of him. Finally having had enough of Eric's tortoise shuffle, she strode off, saying she would meet him at the foot of the hill.

As Mary's graceful form disappeared around the next turn, his mind started grappling with the dreaded affair he had created. Eric's heart was throbbing hard, and a pain knifed through his chest. But he was running on level ground. The worst was yet to come.

As he approached Agony Hill's entrance, he saw Mary leaning against a nearby tree, stretching her calves. He smiled inside, remembering their senior year team practice and the race up Agony Hill that day. Eric loved this course, and he knew she did too. But her angry words were eclipsing his memories of this revered climb. Even more intrusive was one insistent thought: Mary was about to hand him his sorry, out-of-shape, ass. He wanted to ignore that ultimate reality, but he had made his deal with her.

He stopped at the entrance to the climb: the two wire-connected metal posts. He bent forward at the waist to touch his toes, painfully stretching his rear hamstrings, stifling his groans, so as not to seem more pathetic to Mary than he already was.

Mary looked down at Eric's feet and smirked, "Can you turn the lights off on your new shoes?" She shaded her eyes, as though blinded by the newness of his training flats.

Well, at least she's talking, he thought. "Hilarious," he said, but in truth he was grateful for the return of Mary's signature humor. "You better wear your sunglasses 'cause you'll see nothing but the back of my heels on the way up," he said, unable to blunt the clichéd words spilling from of his mouth, which rang false in his ears. Even a child could see through his machismo.

An alarming gurgle announced itself in Eric's stomach. He covered his mouth to stifle the sour belch.

"*Nice*, champ," Mary chirped. "You getting sick? Sure you want to do this?"

"I'll be . . . fine," Eric burped out, immediately trying to swallow back the acidic bile burning in his throat.

"Fine, it's your funeral—you ready to go?" Mary checked her watch for the third time since Eric had arrived.

Again Eric's stomach rumbled a vehement regret at his breakfast choice. He knew better, and it wasn't like him to eat so much before a run. But for some reason he had convinced himself that a two-pancake-and-sausage breakfast wouldn't hurt.

Eric gestured toward the low-strung wire between the metal poles that gated the gravel path. "OK, let's start this thing."

Eric jumped the wire first and shouted, "Go!" before Mary had even touched down. He sprinted full out, hoping to create a decent gap in the first few hundred yards. He knew she would eventually close in on him, but he had nothing to lose.

A quarter mile later, he listened for Mary's footsteps. Nothing. He glanced back, but couldn't find her. Where was she? *She's suckering me,* he thought. *She'll make me run all the way to the top, thinking I have her beat, and meanwhile, she'll be cruising back home in her car.* But no, he knew Mary. She wouldn't be that cruel . . . would she?

The sound of crunching gravel behind him interrupted his rhetorical missives. Mary chided him as she blazed past. "I really like your pretty new shoes. See you at the top—*if* you make it."

Man, she's deriving way too much fun at my expense, he thought.

A few agonizing minutes later, Eric reached the half-mile point, lungs heaving, chest aching as he continued to slog up the path. Why had he ever said the words *Agony Hill?* His partying and bar-food diet the last two years hadn't helped matters any. His weight gain hung like a jello weight belt strapped around his waist. Every direction his body moved, it slid the other way. Elementary physics: opposite equal reaction.

Eric knew the first half of Agony Hill was modest and forgiving. But the steeper second half loomed. Having memorized the remaining switchbacks in high school, he had to keep his mind on the current turn, focusing on the here and now to take his mind off the pain.

Mary's shrill voice called down to him from a switchback above him. "See you later, loser. I'll be waiting at the top!"

Eric wanted to cave, turn around, concede defeat, but he couldn't let her be right. With some pride remaining, he fought to continue, but his body had other ideas. *Maybe this one time*, his body pleaded, *it's OK for me to give up,* he conceded. *It's not worth killing yourself over.*

After one more switchback, Eric gasped out, "I'm done. You win," His lungs were desperately rounding up every available oxygen molecule.

Mary, thirty yards ahead, stopped, spun around. "Are you kidding me, Mister 'I want to race you up Agony Hill'?" she yelled. "That's all you got? No way. I didn't leave a warm bed on a Saturday morning to race your sorry butt up this hill for you to quit on me halfway. I don't care if you crawl, you better hump your Fat Albert butt all the way to the top, or I'll kick it all the way back down."

The moment Mary's tirade ended, Eric clutched his roiling stomach, lurched forward, and spewed his breakfast onto the trail.

"Oh! That's pretty. Good. Get it out. Are those pancakes? Don't forget, there's another quarter-mile to go dude."

Eric loathed her right now.

After the violent spasms ended, he heard her chanting, "I'm going to beat you. I'm going to beat you." He would love to prove her wrong, to show her his fitness, but evidently that wasn't happening. Even though he had already conceded defeat—that admission being embarrassment enough—he just had to win back a modicum of respect. He had to make it to the top.

Before he resumed, he checked his ankle. He rubbed vigorously, pressing hard against the fibula. There was no pain. Relieved, he resumed his plodding pace up the hill. He noticed that his unplanned stop had helped more than expected. His leg muscles had recovered a bit, his feet a touch lighter as he hefted one foot, then the other. But it wasn't long before he was struggling for breath again. As though it were yesterday, images of past hill ventures flitted through his mind—Eric and his friends practically flying up the hill—but today his ordeal was dragging on like a plot-less movie. He didn't remember the hill ever having been this hard. He yearned for his old physique. Only two years had passed, and he had devolved into a fitness nightmare. His false bravado in front of Mary had displayed his insecurities about his future as a runner. He had a long road ahead to become a great runner again—assuming his ankle would hold together long enough to get him there.

When he finally rounded Agony Hill's last turn, he found Mary sitting on a cement bench, her elbow propped on her knee, chin in her hand, a satisfied expression on her face.

Exhausted, he bent over with hands on his knees. When he finally could look up at her, he panted out. "You . . . don't . . . have to be . . . so gleeful about it."

Her face hardened. "You got what you deserved."

Eric groaned and rose slowly, his heart still thumping. He donned his best James Bond accent. "It's lovely to see you again, Miss Moneypenny," he said, coughing. "I want to thank you for the delightful thrashing you gave me this morning."

Mary jumped up, fists lightly clenched, her chest bowed out in defiance. "Don't think for one minute being funny gets you off the hook," she said, unconvincing, her tone hinting at humor.

Eric imagined that she wanted to make up as much as he did right now, but she had a lot to say. He knew he had to stand there and silently take it. If there was one thing he'd learned from his ex-girlfriend Melissa, it was to shut up sometimes and try to listen.

"What was this all about, anyway?" she demanded, her voice hard again.

There was a long pause. Eric lowered his eyes, trying to call on the courage to tell her what was in his heart. He glanced up at her. "I missed you," he said, and then dropped his eyes again, uneasy with revealing his feelings.

"Aw, that's rich. I bet you tell all your floozies that when you want to make up." She looked away into the woods for a moment then turned back to him, "You didn't miss me," she hissed. "You have to have a friendship to miss somebody. You slunk outta here like a scared dog with your tail between your legs. You dumped everybody including me—oh, and one more thing, your long hair and mustache look went out ten years ago.

Mary was resilient in matters of the heart, but she would hit back hard, defend herself when necessary. He had been in verbal tiffs with her in the past, but never on the receiving end of a sledgehammer blow like this. It tortured his heart far more than running up this hill had. But he had to take it if he wanted to make amends.

Mary spoke again, her voice a bit softer now. "And then you stopped talking," she said. She looked away, and her voice broke as the next words fell from her mouth. "And . . . that really hurt . . ." Her voice trailed off.

"Mary," Eric said, taking a small step toward her, "the real reason I asked you to race me up our here wasn't—well, there wasn't any thought at all, but I'm sure you already know that—the idea just blurted out of me."

Mary was sniffling, her eyes welling. He took another step forward, edging carefully closer, wanting to comfort her but uncertain if she would accept comfort—or anything else—from him.

"When I saw you at the Cardinal, I panicked," he said. "I knew you were mad at me, and I didn't know what to say to make you forgive me. Challenging you to race Agony Hill was all that came to mind. Pretty stupid, huh?"

"Yeah . . . pretty stupid, you jerk." Mary wiped at a tear. "I'm glad you did it, though. I'm sorry I was so hard on you."

"You aren't that sorry, are you?" Eric said.

"Well, half-sorry—you did deserve your punishment."

"Yes, I'll give you that."

He wanted to hug her right now, but he held back. He had to be sure she would accept his touch. He couldn't take the rejection if she refused his hug. He moved another step toward her until he was standing two feet away.

She turned her gaze downward, looking at her feet, or maybe just avoiding his eyes.

"Mary," he said softly.

She lifted her head, her eyes softer, blinking back the wetness.

His own eyes stinging with tears, Eric fumbled out the words, "I'm really sorry, Mary . . . and I know I don't deserve your friendship . . . but I hope you'll reconsider—"

She wrapped her arms around his waist and began sobbing into his chest.

He held her for a long time. The warmth of her embrace melted away his apprehension. He had realized during his lonely years in Charleston, that having Mary's forgiveness would be a crucial first step to deliver himself from his demons. He needed her in his life.

"I missed my friend," he said into her hair.

"Me, too," she said.

Chapter 20

The upper half of Agony Hill's grade wasn't so steep as it was continuous; there were no level spots for a runner's respite. On the way up and down, a runner had to keep an eye on the un-maintained gravel road, gutted in spots, by past rivers of rainfall.

As Eric and Mary jogged tentatively down the hill, he kept an eye out for the road's dangerous gullies waiting to turn his healed ankle. He realized that even with his ankle taped, he had taken a big chance today; he wasn't running on a safe, even surface. A fresh injury would surely crush his newfound running ambitions. So far, his old fracture was holding up; no pain on the downhill impacts.

When they reached about midway, Eric suggested they walk the remaining distance. Mary agreed.

"So, what brought you home?" Mary said.

"Well, a redheaded friend sent me a letter and gave me an ultimatum."

"And you listened to her?" she said half sarcastically.

"Not entirely. It had been on my mind for a while. I had to decide what I wanted to do with my life. And I'd overstayed my welcome with my Uncle, too. The hardest part was splitting up with my girlfriend. Though she wasn't that upset. She was a senior in college, and we both knew we would have to go our separate ways, anyway. But your note didn't hurt any."

"That's sweet," she said. She paused, and her voice became solemn. "Do you ever think about Buzzy?"

"Yes. All the time." A small rutted section appeared on the road. Eric slowed his walk to let Mary get around it. "When I left Brevard, I was in a panic. I felt I killed Buzzy."

"It was an accident," Mary said.

"But he was the Connors' only child, and I was the one who took Buzzy from them."

"That's not true."

"Maybe, but I should have been watching out for Buzzy."

"It's as much my fault," Mary said. "Mrs. Connor entrusted me with Buzzy. I know he was a grown kid and everything, but, still, his thinking was more like a child. If I were a better friend, I wouldn't have lost track of him. I would have gone into the house immediately and searched for Buzzy. The Connors relied on me to look out for him, and I let them down."

Her admission made Eric feel doubly worse. He remembered their downtown confrontation where she called him out for being selfish, thinking he was the only one responsible or affected by that night. He didn't want to hear it back then, but she was right, and his not calling or talking to her afterward had hurt her more than anything he had suffered.

"Like you said, I kind of *dumped* everybody, including Rodney" Eric said. "Do you know how he feels about Buzzy?"

"Rodney seems pragmatic. He understood there were lots of things that could've gone differently, but he doesn't seem to dwell on it. Though, when we talk about Buzzy, I think it still haunts him a bit."

"You know," Eric said. "It's strange. The couple times I spoke to Rodney on the phone that first summer, we didn't talk about Buzzy. I think both of us were avoiding the subject."

The two walked in silence for a while.

"It'll never leave us, will it, Mary?"

She looked at him. "No . . . I don't think so."

BACK AT THE PARKING LOT, while Mary was gulping down a sports drink, Eric stole behind her and gently took her free hand.

"Mary," he said, "would you like to go to a movie with me?"

She pulled her hand away. "Maybe another day."

"How come?"

"Nothing," she said, avoiding his gaze. She slipped into the driver's seat of her car. "I just don't have the time," she said and closed her door.

"I see. Next time, I guess." He turned and walked away. But before he got to his car, he charged back to her door and rapped on the glass. "C'mon Mary," he begged. "It's me, Eric!"

Mary rolled down her window halfway. "I'm not sure," she said, her eyes pleading with him to understand.

"What, you dating someone or something?"

"No," she intoned, but her eyes flitted back and forth.

"How about a run tomorrow?" he said. "My new boss told me about this cool place that has a waterfall—he says it's beautiful."

She smiled, but the pleasure didn't make it to her eyes. Eric sensed dishonesty in her blank stare, though he couldn't decipher what it was.

"OK," Mary said. "What time?"

"How 'bout nine? That way you'll have enough time to make it to church at eleven."

Mary grinned weakly. "Sure, nine is good. Look, I better go. Looking forward to tomorrow, though."

"Cool. I'll call you and give you directions tonight."

She waved and pulled away.

Her sudden detachment puzzled him. Had she not forgiven him? Didn't their hug mean they were good now? Eric opened the hatch of his car, grabbed his water bottle, then shut the hatch again. As he drank, he realized how impatient he was being. He'd been gone for two years and now he'd shown up out of the blue. Should he expect her to turn cartwheels because good old Eric was back?

He sat on the hood of his car and rolled his left foot in a circle, mentally checking his ankle, then circled it in the other direction. No pain. He closed his eyes, feeling the sun on his face. He had made minor progress with Mary today, but it had taken two days of hell to achieve it. Even when angered, her piercing yet truthful words sounded like music to him. He had forgotten how she laughed at his stupid jokes, and how powerful and decisive her tone could be when she felt challenged. He was relieved they were talking again.

Chapter 21

Eric was sitting on Miklos's back porch sipping the last of his hot tea when Mary's car pulled up to the house. He rose, opened the house door, and handed the empty cup to his landlord, who a moment before had been peering out the door's window. "Miklos, we won't be too long."

Eric rushed off the porch and met Mary at the front of her car. "I'm glad you made it," he said happily.

"Well, you seem chipper," Mary said. "Too much caffeine this morning?"

"No, just excited that you're here. Hey, we better start; I don't want you to miss the eleven o'clock service."

Mary turned her attention to where Miklos was standing in the open doorway. She waved at him. "I'm Mary."

"Nice to meet you, Mary," Eric's landlord said, waiving back. "Don't let me hold you two up. Go have a good run. Eric will bring you around for dinner sometime, no?"

"Yes—I hope so!" she responded cheerfully.

Mary and Eric jogged the two hundred yards from the farmhouse to the property's entrance. They turned right on the gravel road and headed toward the forest. A tiny creek paralleled the road. Orange tiger lilies, halfway open to the morning sun, were a beautiful contrast to the thorny green thickets along the water's edge.

They heard bugs buzzing and birds flitting around in the dense brush. The two jogged lazily, in no hurry.

A mile from the camp, the tree-lined road climbed the length of a football field before leveling out to a dead end. Two houses to the left shared a gravel driveway. Dogs barked ferociously from inside one house.

Miklos had described to Eric what the entrance to the property would look like: leading onto the property was a desiccated asphalt road which was straddled by two large wooden gates, with iron hinges, mounted on granite pillars. Eric recognized them as soon as they came into view.

"There's the entrance," he said, pointing to the gates.

Nailed to the top cross bar of the left gate was an ominous NO TRESPASSING sign, which Miklos also mentioned was nothing to worry about. Next to the left gate was a obscure green metal sign that was peeling paint in strips, and any lettering once there had either faded or dropped to the ground. The driveway's once oil-black surface was bleached white from the sun and cracked like a shattered windshield. Weeds and scrubby bushes were making slow progress along the cracks.

"How long has this place been here?" Mary asked.

"Don't know exactly," Eric said. "It's not part of the camp, so Miklos isn't sure either, but he said he figures it's thirty or forty years. He found it during a hike when he first moved here."

Looking past the gates Eric saw that the ramshackle driveway sloped upward and followed the contours of the terrain before it disappeared into a thick tunnel of rhododendrons and pine trees that shrouded the road. On the right, the embankment sloped down dramatically. Eric could hear water rushing below.

"What is this place?" Mary asked, looking around.

"Miklos thinks it was a retreat sometime in the past."

"You know, I'm a little nervous about that no trespassing sign."

"We'll be fine. If anyone asks, we can say we got lost in the forest, and this is where we came out."

Mary gave Eric a tight-lipped snicker. "Man Eric, you and no trespassing signs. It's like a welcome mat to you."

Eric chuckled and said, "Come on. Let's go."

They walked around one side of the gates—their road-wide span only for keeping autos off the property—and started jogging the hill. Their feet shifted on the asphalt's segmented pieces, sliding on the original crushed-rock base underneath. Eric focused on the sound of the rushing water on his right. Every few feet, he caught glimpses through the gaps in the rhododendrons of an empty lake some sixty to seventy feet below them. He also saw a creek, noting that the lake's once captive water source, was now left to find its natural course along the silted lake bed, snaking through sprouting trees and bushes. Eric tried to picture the forested depression when it had been full of water.

When they crested the incline, they found remnants of parking spaces off to the side of the road and crumbling brick foundations of the buildings that had once been there. A wall of granite stones lined the perimeter of an outcropping. "Man, it looks like a tornado came through here and wiped everything away," Eric said.

As the two continued their jog, they noticed a steep set of granite stairs leading down to the empty lake. The paused to investigate and maybe take them down to the bottom (a playful mud fight crossed Eric's mind), but when noticing that sections of the rough-cut stone were missing and looked dangerous, they reconsidered. After that the roadbed they were running on curved right, crossing over the lake's former spillway. From there, the road rose steeply into the forest.

They paused next to the dry spillway and surveyed the area. Eric eager to see the falls Miklos had described, became impatient and grabbed Mary's hand and led her toward a trail a few feet away.

"Miklos told me the falls would parallel the creek and should be a quarter-mile down this path."

They bounded off the paved drive and down a wooden set of moss-covered stairs to the path below. They navigated their way along the overgrown trail as it paralleled the creek. The deeper they progressed into the ravine, the higher the walls loomed—forty or fifty feet on either side. Soon they saw only the morning sun's fractured beams struggling to illuminate the forest floor.

The growth along the creek was thick, and Eric slowed down to hiking pace to part the lush, overgrown branches, holding them so they would not spring back and smack Mary in the face.

He pushed his way through a last thicket of rhododendrons and turned to make sure Mary made it through. Nearby, water from atop a rocky outcropping cascaded gently down a stair-stepped set of strata.

The waterfall spilled into a small pool before overtaking a battery of rocks and slipping toward the empty lake.

"Wow, Eric, this is beautiful," Mary said. She leaned close and clutched his arm. "I'm so glad you showed me this place." She looked around. "Hey, look, there's a bench. Think it'll hold us? It looks a little rotted, but otherwise strong enough."

"Let's give it a try," Eric said.

They walked over and gingerly tested their weight on the bench before settling down. The sound of the water flowing over the rocks was relaxing, and for the first time since Eric had returned home, the tension between Mary and him was back to zero. That was the magic of the forest. The farther he ran into it, the farther he could leave his worries behind. It calmed him to be here with Mary, away from the world.

Eric sat silent, listening to the birds calling. Mary was quiet, too, taking it all in. He caught her glance a few times, but each time he turned away.

Mary broke the silence. "I wish I could have talked to you when I got hurt last cross-country season." She did not look at him when she spoke.

"I remember that. You wrote me a letter about it last fall."

"I had a rough time. I'd never been injured before. I felt indestructible."

"You're OK now, though, right?"

"Yeah. It wasn't too bad. It was a small tear in my Achilles tendon. It healed fast, but it crushed me when it happened. I know it's not the same as what happened to you, but I think I appreciate what you went through."

"I guess it's not so different," he said quietly.

"Listen, Eric," she said, turning to him. "I'm sorry I was so hard on you yesterday. Your not being there these last few years hurt. I needed to talk to you, hear your voice—and you wouldn't even return my calls."

"I know," Eric said. "I regret that. I was selfish and pigheaded. I was running from everything.

"Are you still running?"

"No, at least I don't think so. I'm trying. But I do know you being here helps. I missed talking to you too, and I'm sorry I wasn't there for you."

"I appreciate that, Eric. It's nice to hear."

They fell into silence for a while. Eric decided to change the subject.

"Hey, guess who I ran into last night at the grocery store?" he said "Our old teammate Jessica Holman."

"Jessica? I haven't seen her in a while. What's she up to?" Mary asked halfheartedly.

"Oh, she told me she has a job south of here, over at the DuPont x-ray film plant. She said it's a bit of a drive, but the pay is good. And she also said she's renting an apartment over by where Jen lives."

"That's nice," Mary said.

"Are you OK?" Eric asked.

"I'm fine. I just remembered I need to get back. I'll be late for church."

Eric eyed his watch. "You have plenty of time."

"I know, but I volunteered to help out with the flower arrangements before the service, so I need to be there early . . . I should go." She stood. "Thanks for bringing me out here. It's a cool place." She turned and started back along the trail.

Eric thought she might stop and turn and wait for him. But she didn't. He sat on the bench a moment and watched her disappear into the rhododendrons. These last two days had been an emotional and physical roller coaster. The moment he thought he was earning Mary's good graces, she was pulling away. Had he said something wrong?

When driving home two days before, Eric had envisioned his and Mary's make-up scene. They would hash things out. There would be some yelling and fighting, but afterward that would be it. They'd be good. He sighed, then sprang up and dashed through the bushes to catch up with her.

Chapter 22

Two weeks later, Rodney finally arrived home from college after competing in the NCAA Regional Track championships. Eric called him, and the two agreed to meet Saturday afternoon at Donnelley's for a one o'clock lunch.

On Eric's drive over to meet Rodney, the glaring *E* on his gas gauge demanded his attention. He drove into the nearest gas station and pulled up to the pump. Parked on the other side of the pump-island was a faded blue, late-model Ford 500. Gaping softball-sized rust holes dominated the car's rocker panels. Eric hopped out and peeked into the car. The steering wheel was large; that meant this car had no power steering. A bare-bones model.

He stepped into the station's tiny store and handed a ten-spot to the woman at the front counter. He turned to walk out but he stopped dead cold at the sound of a little boy's voice: "I want a Nuttew Buttew baw, please, Mom." The way the boy spoke sliced right through him, striking an eerie resonance inside him, like a tuning fork hitting the wrong note.

"Darlin'," the young mother said, with a heavy Southern drawl, "I don't have the money for a Nutter Butter Bar." The child stiffened, his lower lip quivering, eyes welling.

Eric's breath was caught in his throat, his eyes welling too. He reached for the counter to steady himself.

The woman behind the register scrunched her face. "Hey, you all right there?"

It took Eric a moment to answer. "I'm fine," he lied. "I have blood sugar problems. I'll be OK." He couldn't let on that a little boy's plea for candy had nearly buckled his legs. Eric rushed over to a nearby cooler, slid open the top door, and dug out a bottle of coke. He took it to the counter. "I think I need a little sugar pick-me-up."

Eric paid for the coke, but before he left, he turned to the little boy's mother. The boy now stood half behind her, his arms wrapped around her leg.

Eric, always respectful and polite, especially to a mother who looked high school age, said. "Excuse me, ma'am. I couldn't help but overhear your boy wanting some candy."

She reached down to her son, pulling him closer. "Yes," she said tentatively.

"I'm sorry. Please don't be afraid. I only wanted to help. I wondered if I could buy him the candy bar he wanted." Eric looked at the woman behind the counter as if she could vouch for his character. She gave a reassuring smile and nodded to the mother.

The mother looked down, tousled her son's, hair and said, "That's a real nice offer, but me and my boy ain't no charity case if that's what you're saying."

"Oh, no," Eric said. "That's not it at all. I can explain. I wanted to do something nice for him. You know, a kind act."

The mother brushed her disheveled blond hair out of her eyes, looked down at the boy again, "You still want that candy bar, son?"

The boy's eyes flew open, and he nodded hard.

"OK, go grab the one you want."

The boy was sprinting down the candy aisle before his mom had finished her sentence. Eric watched him straight-arrow to the specific candy. The boy could have found it blindfolded if he had to.

The mother looked back at Eric with mournful eyes. "You don't know how much this means to him . . . We've been on hard times lately. My husband hurt his back and couldn't work, so we've had to do without. It's hardest on my boy, though. He doesn't understand."

"I'm sure everything will work out," Eric said.

Eric paid for the candy, and the three walked outside. While Eric pumped his gas, the little boy stared at him out the open window of his mother's Ford, a chocolate-painted grin on his face. When the mother drove off, the boy waved—his smile and gaze steady.

When Eric walked into Donnelley's, he looked up at the clock behind the bar: 1:03. He scanned the place for Rodney. But where was Rodney?? He was never late.

Eric ordered a beer from the bartender.

"You OK?" she asked.

Was his disappointment that obvious? Eric threw on a half-smile, and gave her a couple quick, *You got me nods,* and said, "I'm fine." He pointed toward the far back of the bar. "I'll take a booth back there."

"Sure thing, hun."

Eric slid into the plush vinyl booth and sat facing the door. The place was busy, and he noticed that the owner, Mr. Donnelley, had installed an additional TV on the wall behind the bar since his last visit in December, a year and a half back. The Atlanta Braves were on one set and the other was a soccer match.

The day before, when Eric had spoken to Rodney, his friend caught him up briefly on his track season. Rodney had said he'd raced well at the Regionals, but he hadn't reached the qualifying standard for the 800-meter run and wasn't able to advance to the Division One Championships in Eugene, Oregon, two weeks after.

The abbreviated backstory of Rodney's track season had excited Eric. He had missed talking track with his friend. Besides Rodney's first love of basketball, track came a close second.

However, Rodney's muted tone of voice during their conversation, made Eric feel that he wasn't enthused to hear from him. Had Eric taken their friendship for granted? He had expected fire and fury from Mary, but he figured Rodney would understand; they had been friends since childhood. A friend could forgive another, right?

Eric checked the wall clock again:1:10. The paper coaster under his beer glass was swelled with water. Eric downed the last half-glass of beer and flagged the waitress for another beer. Eric picked up a diet-sugar packet, but having read its ingredient list five times already, he threw it back into its tiny bin. Eric saw Donnelley wave to a customer coming through the front door. No Rodney.

The waitress appeared minutes later. Her pen hovered over her order pad, "You ready for some food?"

"I'm OK for now."

"OK," she said. "I'll check on you in a bit."

The front door closed with a heavy whump. Rodney entered, wearing a white T-shirt with large orange letters on the front that read UNIVERSITY OF TENNESSEE.

It was twenty minutes after the hour. "Finally," Eric whispered, relief washing through him. His friend hadn't bailed on him. Eric slid out of the booth, stood up, and waved to grab his attention.

As Rodney approached, Eric saw a shorter Afro and broader shoulders. He'd surely been working out. He even looked taller.

Anticipating a man-hug from his old friend, Eric put out his arms to accept a reconciling embrace. Rodney quickly slid into his side of the booth. "Hello Eric." Rodney said, formal and distant.

Eric's stomach dropped; this might be harder than his and Mary's first encounter at the Cardinal. "Hey, Rodney, how's it going," Eric said, trying for cheerful, hoping Rodney would return the same.

Rodney leaned back into the booth's vinyl cushions, raised his eyebrows, and chortled. "Man, you look like crap. Long hair, mustache, and a fat—"

"Don't say it," Eric said. "I know what I look like. Anyway—did you come here to give me crap or what?"

Rodney laughed. "Mary told me you were a mess, but now that I'm here, I would call it a disaster."

Eric's blood was boiling. "Man, I don't have to sit here and take that. I was trying to be friends again." Eric edged out of the booth.

Rodney reached across the table and grabbed Eric's arm. He burst out laughing. "Dude—dude, come on. I'm only messing with you. Relax."

Eric sat back down. "So, you were just giving me crap."

Rodney rolled his eyes. "Eric, don't be so insecure. What did you expect? Me welcome you back without any grief? Ain't happening, brother."

"I guess," Eric said.

"Anyway," Rodney started, "Mary told me you two had a run-in at the Cardinal. I cracked up when she got to the racing Agony Hill part. You know, I really like Mary, always have. She don't take crap off nobody."

"That's for sure," Eric said. "Did she put you up to this?"

"Yeah, the whole thing," Rodney said.

"Seriously? Eric blurted.

"Jeez, Eric, you're too easy," Rodney guffawed. "No, Mary had nothing to do with it. Though, when I tell Mary this, she'll wish she'd been here to see your rosy red face."

Eric didn't need to touch his warming face to know it had turned three shades redder. In a half hour span, Eric had gone from grief to anger to embarrassment. It was like he had sprinted the last hundred yards of an emotional mile race, his heart rate pegging at two-hundred beats a minute. He slumped back into his seat.

"I'm sure she would," Eric said.

"Hey, what's wrong?" Rodney said. "I was only teasing."

"I know, I know," Eric said. "But . . . something happened on my way over here. It hit me again but in a different way."

"What happened?" Rodney said. "Did you crash your car or something?"

"No, nothing like that. Then Eric told him the story of the little boy at the gas station. "You know, he talked just like Buzzy. And it really threw me." Eric said he was happy to buy the candy for the kid. But now, he wondered if he was just trying to make himself happy. The candy gift was his small way of trying to make up for the past.

"You know," Rodney said. "It didn't hurt to perform a kind act even if it was a little selfish on your part. But the fact that you did it is a good thing. Maybe you can start putting that whole night behind you."

"I hope so," Eric said, buoyed by his friend's words. If anyone might understand Eric, it was Rodney. When Rodney was five years old, his father had abandoned him and his mother. Rodney had told Eric he could vividly recount that day—his father telling little Rodney he'd be back in a few minutes before driving off, never to return. To Rodney's benefit, his mother had remarried, finding a kind, respectful man. Rodney always said that his stepdad was a truer father to him. But Rodney had remained suspicious of people who made promises. He had to know you well before he'd let you emotionally close to him. Eric was one of the few friends Rodney trusted.

That memory hit Eric hard. He had blown off his friends for such selfish reasons, and Rodney, if anybody, deserved better from him.

"Hey, Rodney," Eric said, "I'm sorry I didn't keep in touch. It won't happen again."

"That's cool, bro," Rodney said, smiling. "We'll always be friends. I knew you were going through some things but didn't think it would take this long."

"So, can we put this all behind us," Eric said.

"I guess. Sure. I'm still going to give you crap for a while, though."

"And how long will that be?"

"I'll let you know."

Chapter 23

The day after meeting with Rodney, a Sunday, Eric got in a five-mile run, then spent the better part of the afternoon mowing the camp's athletic fields and common areas. Miklos wanted them in pristine shape for the next week's campers. Once the tractor-mower was parked in the barn, Eric took a quick shower and hurried over to his mother's house. Mrs. Roberts was making the boys dinner. Afterward, he and his brother were planning to have a boys' night at the house. A movie Eric had seen during his senior year in high school was scheduled to show again on TV that night. He was fired up to watch it again; the *Jericho Mile* was all about running.

In a few weeks, Mark, now a high school senior, would be crossing the stage to accept his diploma. In the time Eric had been away, Mark had developed into a stellar pole vaulter. This year his brother had missed winning a state title by an inch—literally.

Per the boys' request, their mother had made them their favorite dinner—navy beans and ham—and on the side, a square of sweet cornbread drizzled with hot syrup. Eric welcomed the home-cooked meal. With most of his meals consisting of cold sandwiches or spaghetti, the change in his daily fare was like dining out in a fancy restaurant; *Madame Roberts's Café* had the best food on the planet. Once the boys had devoured their second and third helpings, their mother headed off to her bedroom to read.

After dinner, Eric and Mark staked out their respective ends of the family couch. With the tractor-mower's dull vibrations still echoing in Eric's bones, his body melted into the cushions, which satisfied a deep yearning for horizontal respite after working a long weekend of work at the camp. He'd spent the previous day repairing broken bunks in two of the kids' cabins. Miklos had told Eric he'd stay busy this summer with repairs on beds, door handles, porch railings, and anything else young boys could climb or hang onto.

The family dog, a Golden Labrador named Molly, her muzzle gray, nosed at the boys on the couch, her thick tail wagging happily, and as always nearly knocking the boys' drink glasses off the coffee table. With the boys' help she worked her way onto the sofa. She nuzzled between them, laying her head in Eric's lap.

"She missed you," Mark said.

Waiting out a set of car and detergent commercials before the movie began, Eric took in the old living room. The greenish wood paneling his father had installed years back now seemed garish, dated. The old stereo console was also antiquated, but it still had a purpose. The left side opened for playing records, and the right side served as a stand for their color TV. The screen was fifteen inches diagonally, small compared to the current nineteen-inch sets being sold in the stores, yet tonight the picture size didn't matter. Eric would watch the *Jericho Mile* on a six-inch portable if he had to.

The movie's plot centered around the character Larry Murphy, who was doing time for murdering his father, and he dealt with his incarceration by running circles around the prison yard every chance he got. The guy could run fast, but no one knew how fast until someone took a stopwatch and clocked him racing around the "track"—fourteen times around the garbage cans, a prison-yard mile. Turned out he was not far off from a four-minute mile. "Lickety-Split" the inmates called him.

"Hey, Eric," Mark said, chuckling. "He looks just like you . . . has raggedy-ass hair. . . except he's—"

"Not fat," Eric said, holding a grim face for a few seconds cracking a smile.

Later in the film, the prison inmates help build him a real track—a wide, leveled-out clay surface and no more garbage cans—so he can try to qualify for the Olympic trials, which he eventually does. However, the US track authorities have no plan to let him attend, which leads to a tense scene where the head US Track authority confronts Murphy about his past. The man goads Larry until he gets the answer he wants. *Yes,* Larry says, exploding, *if the conditions were the same, he'd kill his father again if it meant his stepsister could be free from a monster like that.*

When the scene faded to black on the TV screen, Eric sat frozen, practically holding his breath. He could feel his pulse rising, with tension mounting in his chest. Larry's defiance at the crucial moment moved Eric, making him feel the anger Larry felt, an anger Eric had been carrying for a long time. Both he and Larry had been robbed of their dream but in entirely different ways.

The movie cut to a commercial. Eric sniffed back the welling emotion, then rubbed his eyes as though some dust had gotten in them. He got up, telling Mark he had to go to the kitchen to splash some water on his eyes to get the dirt out.

In the culminating scene of the movie, Larry runs a sub-four mile in the prison yard, beating the time of the number-one miler in the country. When Larry sees his results on the stopwatch he's been clutching during the run, he hurls the time piece at the far wall, where it explodes, slow motion, into dozens of shiny pieces. Watching this, Eric could feel every ounce of the protagonist's rage. But underneath the anger, there was also pity, regret, and fear. Perhaps he, like Larry, would never make his dream happen. Perhaps some force that held authority over him would block his rise to the heights he'd always dreamed of. Maybe he was destined to pay for his past actions, with his yearned-for goal as collateral.

The movie affected Eric differently this time because he'd watched it through a different lens. Two years before, he'd seen it simply as a terrific running movie; he hadn't noticed the subtle themes. This time, he understood it was about more than running; it took a look below the surface of a man's life, shedding light on his mistakes, his frustrations, his hopes and dreams; but Larry never got a second chance.

Would Eric get that second chance? From where he sat, his aspirations felt as distant as the end of a life sentence. The sensation of zooming around the track at wondrous speeds felt out of reach. Eric was taking baby steps, but his future as a distance runner was uncertain at best.

"Man, that was great," Eric said, standing up. "Hey, can you walk me out?"

Mark scrunched his face, "Since when are you so formal? *Can you walk me out?"* he repeated.

Eric gave his brother's shoulder a playful shove. "I'll tell mom goodbye and then meet you outside."

When Eric stepped off the back porch, Mark was standing behind Eric's hatchback, keeping an eye on Molly as she sniffed around the yard. When Mark saw Eric, he said, "What's with the hang-dog face."

Eric gave him a weak smile. He then stood on his tiptoes to look his brother in the eye, who was now a full two inches taller than Eric's six feet.

"Quit stalling, Eric, and yes, I'm still taller than you." Mark pushed down on Eric's shoulders, taking back his two-inch advantage. "So what's so important?"

Eric didn't answer immediately. Should he tell Mark what was on his mind? Was it that important, or should he just let it go? No, he thought, if he was going to put his past behind him, he had to get this off his chest.

"Listen, Mark," Eric started. "I need to tell you something about dad." He leaned back against the hatch of his car. Mark whistled for Molly to get back in the yard.

"About dad?" Mark said. "Since when do you care about dad?"

"I don't," Eric said quickly. "It's not what you think."

"Then what?" Mark said.

"OK, OK, it's about what happened to me when I was eight."

Mark didn't speak. He nodded for Eric to go on.

"I'm not sure why I need to tell you this, but when I saw that scene in the movie where Larry was explaining his father's murder to the counselor, it really got to me. And later, where he said he loved his father, and talked about sitting on his dad's shoulders when he was little, I suddenly felt this feeling my gut. I nearly lost it."

"I noticed," Mark said softly.

Eric felt his cheeks flush. He pushed himself off the car and paced one tight circle, breathing deeply to collect himself. Finally he told his brother his story.

Mark had gone to sleep. Eric was still up. His father had finally come home, having stopped off at the bar after work. Reeking of alcohol, his father sat at the kitchen table, across from where Eric was coloring in a coloring book. His father was already angry, himself grumbling on about how his supervisor was a jerk. Eric had seen his father drunk before, but didn't really understand why he was always angry when he drank, sometimes yelling at the TV set or at his mother for some little thing she hadn't performed to his expectation. Today Eric's mother had missed work to stay home and take care of Mark, who had a bad case of the flu. She hadn't gotten around to cleaning the house, which irked Mr. Roberts. Then he exploded because the food on his plate wasn't hot enough.

Eric's mother snapped. "Well, if you'd been here for dinner," she said, "you'd have a hot plate of food." She reached to pick up the plate, and Mr. Roberts grabbed her wrist. He squeezed hard. "Stop it, John," She whimpered.

Eric had never seen his father hurt his mother. Anger yes, but he'd never seen him raise a hand to her. "Leave mom alone," Eric blurted out.

Mr. Roberts turned to his young son, his eyes flashing. "Did you just sass me, boy?"

"I didn't—"

John Roberts stood, his chair toppling over behind him. "Wait, here," he grumbled, stalking toward the hallway.

Fear crawled up Eric's spine, the hairs of his neck bristling. He knew where his father was going—the hall closet.

Eric looked up at his mother. She was clutching a kitchen towel in her two hands, under her chin like she was praying with Rosary beads. He could see the fear in her eyes.

The pall of his father's heavy steps closed in behind Eric. And then his dad grabbed his arm, jerking him out of his seat like a rag doll, Eric's chair splaying onto the floor. Eric grasped at the air, his coloring book swept off the table.

At first Eric wrestled to get away, but he stopped when he saw the paddle his father had dug out of the hall closet. He was spinning it in his hand, randomly stopping its rotation. The wooden paddle was flat and round, with a narrow handle.

Mr. Roberts wrenched Eric upward, pulling him off his feet.

"Dad," Eric pleaded, his tiptoes barely scraping the linoleum. "It hurts—"

"How many?" his father growled, his narrowed gaze so hot it felt like it was burning Eric's face.

Eric tried to look at his mother.

"*Please*, John. Don't," Mrs. Roberts pleaded.

Mr. Roberts leaned closer, his rage flashing from his bloodshot eyes. "Don't look at her—answer me." His torrid breath slurred spittle, stinging Eric's face like hot needles. Mr. Roberts spun Eric farther around so he couldn't see his mom. Eric wanted to be a superhero right now, to grow suddenly taller and stronger than his father, to have the power to make things right. That paddle was like a super villain; if you couldn't avoid it, you were going to suffer a whole lot of pain.

"I—I don't know," Eric mumbled.

"Wrong answer." Mr. Roberts whipped Eric around, then threw him at the kitchen tabletop, bending him over at the waist, pinning him down, chest first, his powerful hand pressing hard in the middle of his back.

Afterward, Eric couldn't remember how many paddles he'd taken. He had blacked out. Though he did remember his mother rubbing his bottom with some kind of cream to ease the pain. Luckily, his little brother had never seen what had happened, still fast asleep after their mom had given him some medicine.

That night was the beginning of the end for his parents' relationship. His mother could take whatever verbal or physical abuse Mr. Roberts dished out in her direction. But abuse directed at the kids was off the table; the man had crossed the line. Mr. Roberts hadn't just spanked Eric; he had meant to hurt him.

After that, his parents' arguments became more frequent. And soon the paddle that hung in the hallway closet went missing. Eric suspected his mother, but he was hesitant to ask, not wanting to remind her of that ugly night. Although Mr. Roberts never paddled the kids again, his drunken rages persisted, their mother taking the brunt of it.

"So, Mark," Eric said. "That's what I wanted to tell you."

Mark didn't speak at first, his eyes looking away, as though scanning for something inside his own mind. He looked back at Eric. "I sort of remember it."

"You do? But you were asleep."

"Not totally," Mark said, "I was sort of half-awake, I think, because I remember you screaming and crying. And dad yelling too. I just never knew what happened."

"How come you didn't say anything later?"

"There wasn't any reason to, Eric. I didn't remember that much, and it really didn't stick in my mind. And . . . I could say the same thing to you."

"Yeah, I guess you're right."

"But I'm glad you told me. I can see why mom never talked about those awful memories. She was trying to protect us."

Eric bent over and pet Molly, who had been sitting close to the boys' feet. "I better get going," he said. He gave Mark a hug. Both boys held on longer than the customary quick man-hug. It was as though a wedge had been pulled out from between them. A wedge Eric hadn't known was there.

Chapter 24

Athletically, Eric was at zero again. His mortal, beer-drinking, soft-couch-and-a-good-movie body had long forgotten the exhilarating sensation of hurtling itself around a 440-yard oval approaching speeds of fifteen miles per hour.

Five weeks earlier, Eric had raced Mary up Agony Hill. On the way back down he had become conscious that he was risking injury to his ankle on the uneven terrain. Yet, the following day, he did the same thing when he ran the creek-side trail to the falls with Mary. In a sobering moment, he had acknowledged that he was putting his personal life ahead of his running future; he wasn't thinking things through. Thankfully, Eric had been blessed with a sturdy musculature and rarely twisted his ankle on forest runs. Back in high school he had teammates who avoided the forest almost entirely. They couldn't run the trails without turning an ankle.

Going forward Eric made a decision. He would confine his running to the track—with its smooth, predictable surface; that way he could ease his ankle into the rigors of distance running while reducing his fear of reinjuring his ankle. And so, for thirty-two afternoons Eric circled the same white-lined blacktop and came out of it with a newfound appreciation for swimmers. He'd always wondered how they could endure daily training, lap after lap, with the same monotonous view of the bottom of the pool. He would never again say swimmers had it easy. Having built his distance mileage up to thirty-five miles a week, Eric was ready to venture out onto the roads.

On a Friday of his fifth week home, heavy rain canceled his construction work. While today was an unfortunate monetary loss, Eric welcomed the respite from his daily toil, taking advantage of his free time to get in a distance run, but first he went straight back to bed for some extra sleep. His eyelids grew heavy, and he drifted off while another deluge of rain snare-drummed the apartment's thin metal roof, sheets of water cascading off its gutterless edges. At nine o'clock, he awoke, padded to his front door, and pulled it open. Fifty yards across the property, Eric saw the camp's lake, its surface glassy, mirroring the surrounding landscape—an image vivid as those of the California high Sierra mountain lakes he'd seen in the pages of National Geographic magazines. A light blue sky peeked through a blanket of gray clouds, hovering just above the treetops, a streak of sun breaking through, casting a double rainbow, one end fading into the picture-perfect lake.

A half hour later, Eric emerged from his apartment wearing a T-shirt, running shorts, and training flats, his left ankle taped lightly like Dr. Doughton's nurse had shown him. Cool, humid air surrounded him, infusing his skin, a tingle charging through his muscles. From the top of his stairway landing, Eric saw lines of kids filing out of their cabins and carefully walking down the soggy hill, dressed in rain coats, a few carrying umbrellas, on their way to their First Period activities. The camp was now in its second week and in full swing, and would remain a bustling beehive of campers until the second week of August.

Eric performed some cursory leg and calf stretches before jaunting down the wooden treads, launching off the second to last step into a brisk run, determined to get his miles in before more rain returned.

Because Brevard lay in a small valley, with a population of a little over 5,000, Eric had few training routes available to him on the local roads. His favorite routes looped around the valley floor. Back in high school he had memorized every mile marker on all those routes, backward and forward. Even after being away for two years, he hadn't forgotten them. Most of his loops used the main highway, Route 64, which led into Brevard from the west. From the camp he'd connect to his favorite seven-mile loop; Eric had re-clocked the loop in his car, accounting for his new starting point, not from the home where he had grown up.

A couple minutes later, Eric reached the divided four-lane highway, paused at the edge of the pavement as a semitruck whooshed by, whipping Eric's long hair horizontal. He looked to his left and right, punched the timer button on his watch, then dashed across the busy thoroughfare, dodging in front of a car by a decent margin. Still, the motorist laid long and hard on the horn.

Eric strode off, cruising comfortably in the highway's emergency lane. In spots, where the gullies, overflowed, water sheeted gently across the slanted roadbed, reflecting a silver sky. Eric's shoes splashed through the wafer-thin streams as his legs circled swiftly, in a perpetual rhythm, the cold water flicking up from his heels, soaking his back. A half mile later, he took a sharp right-hand turn, angling back toward the quieter, less-traveled valley roads. The two-lane blacktop, which paralleled the chemical plant that Mary's father managed, was dead flat like a drag strip.

Eric was having trouble slowing down. He knew a fast run might be at hand. This *feeling* wasn't new, but it might as well be. It was as foreign as it was familiar, like reuniting with a long-lost friend. He hadn't felt it in so long. He'd been trapped inside a body that felt heavy with constraint. But the feeling was coming on now, and it was *freedom*! That's what it was. Pure freedom, to put one leg in front of the other, effortlessly, smoothly, painless—his shoes lightly touching the pavement, then flicking off quickly, and back around again. If Eric would let himself go emotionally, he would be choking up right now, just as he had watching the *Jericho Mile* again. It was one thing to run laps around a quarter-mile track like a goldfish in a bowl, with no escape. Running the open roads was like a salt-water-aquarium fish being thrown back into the ocean.

Relief from captivity to swim unencumbered, no more barriers, a new start at life.

His first mile marker came into view—a parking lot entrance sign directly opposite the chemical plant. Glancing at his watch, a giddy excitement jolted through his body—a 5:55 first mile. He was moving faster than he'd thought.

At this point, a decision had to be made. Did he hold his pace, keep the pedal down and push the tempo as long as he could? Or back off, slow down, ignore this incredible feeling? He needed no deliberation. The simple answer was: Go for it!

Being this fresh and rested on a training run had rarely happened for Eric back in high school. Most of the time, he was weary from the accumulated daily fatigue his body incurred. But every so often—if his body was willing and weather conditions were right (low wind and cool temperatures), he'd push the pace, see if he could beat his fastest time for whatever loop he was running at that moment.

When Eric had days like this in the past, he always felt like he was riding a rocket ship to the moon—free sailing, no atmospheric molecules colliding against the hull to slow you down—you just had to set yourself in motion. After his legs had developed a consistent rhythm on the drag-strip-like road in front of the chemical plant, he felt locked in, relaxed, he was running on autopilot. Next, the road teed into a jagged intersection, and Eric juked right, then left through the quiet interchange. A hundred yards further he crossed a small metal bridge, beginning his favorite two mile-stretch of this seven-mile loop.

The river Eric had crossed over at the steel bridge was named the French Broad. Two hundred yards later he saw the watercourse return from its jigsaw meandering, paralleling the blacktop for a while before veering off, continuing its daily sojourn among the fertile puzzle-pieced farmlands the river's sediment overflows had created.

The road soon came to a long, shallow S-turn—a kiddie-rollercoaster rise and fall of the terrain. With the power and speed of a Ferrari, Eric strode into the rise, barely needing to touch the gas pedal, his pace never impaired from the modest inclines. Among the remaining series of turns, he hugged the outer lane line to avoid unwary drivers on the blind corners.

With the curves behind him, Eric relaxed and enjoyed the straight open road, occasionally glancing to his right, taking in the verdant blanket of crops now thigh high in the fields. Before he knew it, his favorite section was over.

He turned right to start a 200-yard stretch before he'd leave the valley bottom. Moments later, he crossed a cement bridge back over the river, the bridge's far end denoting his three-mile mark—nailing the last mile at a 6:05 clocking. Eric's confidence swelled, satisfied to be holding a six-minute-mile pace. To clock approximately eighteen minutes for the first three miles of his favorite seven miler wasn't bad for one month of distance training. But could he hold the pace? And for how long?

He would find out soon; his final test was just starting, the road beginning its mild upward tilt for a lengthy half-mile ascent toward the city's center. Barely a minute into the climb, Eric's body complained about its added weight and two years of neglect. . . of course, he'd been training the last few weeks on flat ground. This was his first test of running a hill, and it was not going well from the start. Like all good athletes, he focused on what he could do and not what he couldn't. Doing his best to block out his suffering mentally, he focused on the white lane line at the edge of the road, not looking up and see how far he had to climb. Ever since his misguided forays up Agony Hill and into the forest with Mary—which his ankle had luckily survived—he'd been running on the level surface of a track. As he chugged along it became clear to him: he would always have to be careful about his ankle. Even now at a prime athletic age of twenty-one, his youthfulness couldn't be taken for granted anymore.

The hill crested at a three-road-intersection, the level surface allowing his body to recover. His pace picked up, his heavy breathing abating, and he settled into flatland tempo again. He raced through downtown, dodging passing shoppers on the sidewalk. Now and again, he glanced at the storefront windows and checked his running posture as he dashed by. Before he made a final right turn at the downtown crossroads, he assessed his pace at the next mile mark in front of Donnelley's Pub, logging a fourth mile split of 6:25. Thinking back to high school, on this same hill, Eric never dropped over five seconds to his pace. Considering his low fitness level, relative to his past, the twenty-second time drop wasn't all that bad.

His personal best time for this seven-mile route was close to a five-minute-mile pace—in November of his Senior year in high school, right after his cross-country season had ended. He wished he always felt that spry in races. One rare moment that always stood out in Eric's mind was at a dual meet his junior year in high school. The school's track, where the meet had been held, had a smaller 330-yard track because they didn't have enough land to install a proper 440-yard oval. Being 110 yards shorter didn't pose any difficulties when keeping track of runners' races. The track was marked to the adjusted difference—five and one-third laps to the mile.

Eric had felt great that day and easily led the race. When he finished, he had a new mile PR by one full second. But moments afterward, he was informed that the finish line was in the wrong spot. Annoyed at first, he dismissed the supposed error, logging that race as an unofficial record, correct distance or not. Afterward, he expected that feeling to reoccur in a future race, but it never did. He had many great races in the remainder of his high school career, his legs feeling fresh and powerful, but never like that day on the 330-yard track.

Halfway into the fifth mile, fatigue besieged his legs, his body's aching mortality dragging Eric back to the present. The *feeling* was gone now. The slowing always came fast once the leg muscles had their fill of lactic acid. He reached the fifth mile mark thirty seconds slower than the fourth. Unable to sustain his previous six-minute pace, he throttled himself back to a 7:30 mile tempo and cruised home.

As Eric ran the remaining miles back to the camp, he put this morning's run into perspective. For his body to fully adapt to high-level anaerobic racing or training, he would likely need at least three to six months of quality training under his belt. When his pace had fallen off around the fifth mile mark, the slowdown hadn't been a surprise. But he was glad he hadn't ignored his body's spryness, even knowing he had a slim chance of sustaining that pace for a full seven miles. Sometimes you have to let the dogs run, he thought. While he had seen some fitness progress, he knew there were a crap load of miles to tread, and pounds to lose, before he could reach for greatness again.

When Eric returned to his barn-loft apartment, the warming sun was drying out the landscape, the humidity thickening the air. He dragged a kitchen chair outside to the building's tiny staircase landing, sat down, propped his feet on the railing, and downed a sports drink. The old Eric was still in there. He only had to keep training and see if he could summon a bit of magic to resurrect his high school self. Only faster.

While Eric's modest seven-mile effort motivated him, he could not translate his enthusiasm into more miles per week. Although his goal was to work up to at least seventy miles a week—his weekly distance in high school—he had to do so slowly careful not to spike his mileage totals and risk injury. Raising his mileage at all, however, was turning out to be a challenge. His two jobs kept cutting into his training time. Daily he came home from his construction job physically depleted. Some days he returned home unmotivated to do anything constructive; he'd collapse onto his bed and watch TV for the rest of the evening. He couldn't coax himself to set foot out the door. If he missed training during the week, he tried to run a few extra miles on the weekends. Once he had made a dent in the camp's repair list and the campers had gone for the summer, he would recover the lost mileage.

Eric still aspired to find a college that would offer a fully paid scholarship for a top caliber runner to complement their team. He had been that kind of runner back in high school, and in time he could be again. He knew it was pure fantasy to try and secure a school by the coming fall; he would need a minimum of six months to log the hundreds of miles required to develop a monster-sized lung capacity required for racing; the following spring was a more realistic expectation. In high school, he had been selective with college choices. This time he was open to any option; from Junior College all the way up to NCAA Division I.

When Eric began to search for prospective colleges, he was honest with the coaches about his injury. Many coaches in the surrounding states were familiar with his plight; the loss of his scholarship prospects after the accident had made the news in the southeastern running circles. For those who didn't know, Eric gave full details, but stressed his excellent recovery to soften their doubts. But he knew at the outset that the medical history he was now laden with would present obstacles in the running world.

One coach he spoke with described him with brutal honesty, lacking any hint of irony, as "damaged goods."

"Granting a partial or full scholarship would be difficult at best," the coach had said.

Undaunted, Eric pressed on, presuming there had to be a coach out there who would comprehend his circumstances and make him a reasonable offer. After umpteen calls and letters, most coaches iterated the same response: "We can give you a little money, but you'll have to prove yourself before I can make a solid commitment." Many coaches remembered him from high school, but his past success meant little to them. Without the pedigree of verifiable road race times, Eric had nothing to put on the table that would earn him a full scholarship.

Eric expected he could be in good shape by spring at least, and for that matter, in spite of his current state of fitness, he knew he had the underlying talent to help those schools he had contacted, but his opinion didn't matter. The coaches didn't want to risk thousands of dollars on a *broken athlete* with an untested ankle.

After ending another frustrating conversation with yet another coach who told him his previous injury was a liability, Eric grabbed his receiver and bashed it against the phone base, cracking the plastic case. He chucked the receiver toward the end of his bed, but the curled line yo-yoed it back, grazing Eric's face as he ducked out of the way. He flopped onto the bed, pushed his face into his pillow, and screamed.

After he had lain there for a few minutes, staring at the rafters of his tiny apartment, he rolled over searching for another object to inflict his frustrations on. He spied Mary's pink envelope on his nightstand. He snatched it up and flung it across the room like a Frisbee, where it careened off the far wall and landed in the sink full of dirty dishes. Horrified the instant he had done it, Eric jumped off the bed and yanked the letter out of the water. He sighed with relief: only a single corner had gotten soaked. While he blotted the envelope with a towel, an idea sprang into his head.

Chapter 25

An hour later, Eric was standing on Mary's porch. They had spoken only twice after their run to the falls. On his first call, they had made idle chit-chat, and the tension in Mary's voice had relaxed, but the second time he had called their conversation was icy, and her voice distant. He had asked her out to dinner, but she turned him down. "We're still friends, but I think it's best if we don't see each other for a while," she had said, with no further explanation. Her words stung him. He had thought they were making progress, but now she was acting weird, and he didn't even know what he had done. He was determined to make it right, whatever it was.

Mary's mother answered the door. They chatted, Eric sharing brief details of his past two years. She said it was all right to go upstairs to find Mary. At her door he raised his hand to knock but paused when he heard her voice. She was talking to someone on the phone: "I miss you. I wish I could see you. No, you say it first . . . Love you, too. Bye." *Is she dating someone?* He immediately scolded himself for eavesdropping, even if it was unintentional.

He knocked.

"Come in."

He opened the door.

Mary was reclined against her bed's headboard, legs stretched out with cotton balls stuffed between her toes, letting her pink nail polish dry. She wore a blue and white striped pair of nylon running shorts and a pink cotton tank top.

Mary snapped a scrapbook closed. "Eric! What are you doing up here?"

"I'm sorry, your mother said it was OK to come up."

"Augh," she huffed. Without making eye contact, Mary rose, brushed back her wild, shoulder-length, rock band-inspired hairdo, and smoothed her tank top in the dresser mirror. "I've told her a hundred times not to do that. What if I were naked or something?"

"Look, I'll go," he said, pulling the door closed. "I can see it's a bad time. I only came by to say I'm sorry."

"Wait."

He pushed the door back open.

"Come in, come in," she said hurriedly, cheerfully.

She patted the foot of the bed, and he sat down slowly.

"I'm glad you came," she posted herself against the headboard again, one knee pulled close as she removed the cotton balls from between her toes. When she was done, she tossed the cotton balls into a waste can, then sat cross-legged facing Eric. After an awkward moment of silence, Mary said, "Hey. I'm sorry about our phone call a few weeks back."

"It's fine," he said.

"We haven't gotten off to a good start, have we?" Mary said.

"No, I guess not," he said, grabbing one of her knick-knacks off her dresser and fiddling with it. "It seems every time I've tried to talk to you, I've screwed it up."

"But—"

"Let me finish," he interrupted her. "It's . . . That, over the last two years, I've been running from my troubles. And now that I've come home, I don't want to do that anymore, but we can't seem to communicate. There's so much to say, and I want to spill it out all at once. But now I recognize that I shouldn't be thinking of myself—I should let you say what you want to say. I want to make amends." He paused, and looked her in the eyes. "I want to ask for my friend back . . . for the third time."

"I think you have."

"Well, in that case, since you're not primed to kill me anymore, how about you accept my dinner offer?"

"Yeah, sure, I'll ask my mom. We don't have any specific dinner plans tonight, so I think she'll be fine with that."

Eric and Mary chose Marcel's on Main Street for dinner. The maître d' seated them at a table on the porch. Twilight's shadows lengthened as the sun dipped behind the mountains, but the air was warm and pleasant.

"You know, it's nice to eat here again," Mary said. "We haven't been here since after the New Year's bet our senior year."

"I never could beat you, could I?" Eric said.

Mary smirked then hid her face behind her open menu.

"I remember I had the risotto," she said. "It was so delicious."

In high school, not counting Marcel's, he and Mary had formally dined twice—once with a group of friends and the other a double date. But this wasn't high school anymore. Mary was different now. Her hair and clothes had changed, and she was wearing makeup and nail polish on her fingers and toes. Eric hadn't been there to witness her transformation. To be the friend he should have been.

"When did you start cultivating the punk look?" he said. "I liked the old Mary."

"Well, I'm not that girl you knew in high school anymore. I wanted to change my look." She flipped her hair back. "You know . . . be a little prettier than the old plain Jane I used to be."

"I mean, I do like it," Eric said. "You seem more grown up. Sophisticated, in a punk kind of way."

Mary laughed. "Nice save, Eric. Just so you know, you're the only one I'd let get away with a comment like that."

Mary's honesty was the thing he had missed the most. His girlfriend in Charleston had a bubbly personality and was fun to be around, but she wouldn't tell you straight out when you were acting like a jerk like Mary would. She'd hold on to her thoughts for a while before she'd open up. When she did, she always gave you the truth and Eric did appreciated that.

"You look pretty tonight." His voice cracked.

Mary blushed, turned her head, and brushed her hair behind one ear. As she did so, the top of her blouse opened a little further, revealing a gold winged-foot charm dangling from her necklace.

"Is that Buzzy's necklace?" Eric asked.

"Oh, I meant to tell you," she said, now fiddling with it. "Mrs. Connor gave it to me last summer. She wanted me to have it since I was Buzzy's best friend."

"Mrs. Connor was right. Buzzy liked everyone, but you were his favorite."

"You don't mind, do you?" Mary said. "I mean . . . Wearing the charm in front of you."

"It's fine, Mary." And he meant it. "I'm glad you have it. It's appropriate."

She leaned back in her chair. "Whew, I'm so glad. To me, it symbolizes what we've gone through, and our friendship too. I wear it all the time. Even when I'm running. I wanted you to know that I had it. But I was afraid I might be taking a risk by wearing it tonight."

"It's fitting, Mary," Eric said, smiling, then he cleared his throat, and rearranged his flatware next to his dish, trying to get the courage up to ask. "So . . . who were you talking to on the phone?"

"You were eavesdropping?"

"No! Yes. Sorry. I couldn't help it."

"Well, Mr. Nosybody, if you must know, it was my boyfriend."

"Oh . . . that's cool," Eric said, trying not to sound too interested. "Have you dated many guys at college?"

"A couple," she said unsentimentally. "You said *you* had a girlfriend?"

"Yes, but like I told you, we went our separate ways before I left. We couldn't keep up a long-distance relationship with me living here."

"Did you love her?"

"I think so . . . I'm not sure. Melissa was really nice, and we had a lot of fun. She always said I was more fun than the boys at her college. I think she felt that way because I wasn't in college and was outside her circle of friends. Not sure if I'd call it a 'bad boy,' attraction but something along those lines."

Mary smirked and rolled her eyes. "Well . . . I don't know if I'd go that far. But you do have a mystical long-haired hippie thing going for you, and a mustache, too. You look mature. Girls can't resist that."

Eric's face warmed. "I guess I've cultivated a different look since high school, too."

"So . . . what did Melissa look like?"

"Around your height."

"That's it? What color was her hair? Was it long or short?" He stirred his risotto. "Uh . . . it was strawberry blond and long."

"Sounds nice. Did she play sports?"

"You're going to pry this out of me whether I like it or not, aren't you?" Eric asked.

"I'm trying."

"You know the desserts here look really—"

"Quit stalling," she said.

"She was a runner."

"A runner, huh?" Mary said, raising her eyebrows, voice rising with intrigue. "Did she want to run with you?"

"Yes. But I did tell her about Buzzy and everything that happened back in high school. She begged me to start running again, but I still didn't feel confident about my ankle, even with Dr. Doughton's all clear."

Eric hadn't minded the personal life questions, but now he felt a little awkward. Mary wanted details, and he wasn't prepared to go further down this path. "Hey, can we change the subject? It's only been a while since we broke things off, and I'm feeling a little weird discussing her with you. Is that OK?"

"Sure. What do you want to talk about?"

"Well, I wanted to tell you about the colleges I contacted."

"And?"

"A big zero. The coaches all say the same thing. I'm damaged goods."

"Did they really say that?."

"Not so much. It was easy to read between the lines. I'm trying not to stress over it, but it's been frustrating hearing 'no' repeatedly. I got so mad today that I took it out on my phone. It still works, though, but now it has a giant crack in the case. I can barely dial the thing."

Mary's eyes widened. "You didn't break any other innocent appliances, did you?"

"No, that was it." Eric rolled his eyes. "But I couldn't convince any of the coaches I talked to that my ankle would survive the mileage load required to run competitively again. After I thought about it, I would've said the same thing. Business is business, right?"

"Have you talked to Coach Winters at NC State? I'm sure you've heard he left Brevard College to take the coaching job there, right?

"Yeah. My mom told me he took a new job."

"I'm certain he would give you a shot. I can put in a good word for you."

Eric shifted closer to the edge of his seat. He laughed mischievously. "It's funny you say that. I was hoping we could call Coach Winters together. You know—give me moral support. Do you know his home number?"

"So," Mary said laughing, "I see how you are. You didn't come to my house to apologize after all. You wanted me to pull some strings?"

Eric laughed with her. "Well, half true. I wanted you to be there. You know, in case I try to break anything else."

She smiled. "Sure. Glad to help. I have his phone number at my house. We can call him from there if you want."

"What about the long-distance charges? I can give you the money for it."

"Don't worry. You can make it up to me later. But, you better not break my phone," she said, shaking a friendly fist at him.

From Mary's room, Eric dialed the coach's number and waited for it to connect. The line picked up after a few rings.

"Coach Winters, this is Eric Roberts. I'm sorry to bother you at home. I ran for Brevard High School a couple of years ago?"

"Eric Roberts? Oh, Eric! I remember. What a surprise. How did you get my home number?"

Eric covered the speaking end of the receiver with his hand. He whispered to Mary sitting on the bed next to him, "He wants to know how I got his number?"

"It's OK," Mary whispered back. "Tell him it was me."

"Mary Kline gave it to me."

"Oh, I see. That's fine; So what can I do for you?"

Mary angled herself close to Eric, and he tipped the phone away from his ear so Mary could hear the coach's voice She gave him a thumbs up.

"I hope I'm not disturbing you," Eric said.

"I'm not busy. What's on your mind?"

Eric searched Mary's eyes for courage. "Go on," she mouthed. He took a breath and then came straight out with his request: "Coach, I wanted to ask you for a scholarship." It was a bold move, he knew, but there was no sense wasting coin if there were a slim chance the coach would let him run for the team. Coach Winters hesitated. Eric pulled the phone further from his ear and gave Mary an "it doesn't sound good" look.

Then Coach Winters started asking questions. Everything about Eric's last couple of years; work, mileage, where he was living, if he had any road race times to show during that time—critical data any coach would need to evaluate an athlete. The coach listened as Eric summarized his condition.

"I see," Coach Winters said and then—duplicating the other coaches' responses, he explained that he couldn't give him a scholarship. The news sunk Eric's heart. But the coach proposed an alternative. By the time Eric hung up, he was optimistic.

"What happened? I couldn't hear everything," Mary said.

"He said I have to run a 4:05 mile by the end of May next year before he will consider giving me a scholarship."

"Partial or full scholarship?" Mary asked.

"Full."

"Full! Wow. A 4:05, huh? But hey, you can do it. You're two years older now, and you're stronger. And your ankle seems OK, so far. I'm totally sure you'll make that time."

"Besides the 4:05 mile," Eric said, "he wants me to complete a year of college before he'll consider me, so I'd have to do one year at Brevard before I can transfer to NC State. He also mentioned he could pull some strings with Admissions at Brevard College."

"That's cool. The school wouldn't admit you this late without Winters's help, though it's not like you had bad grades or anything. You had a B+ average when we graduated, didn't you?"

"Yeah. And it'd help that I'd be an off-campus student. They won't have to find me dorm space."

"I'm so excited, Eric. If you go to State, we could hang out like in high school."

"Let's not move ahead of ourselves, Mary. There's still a ton of work to do."

"I'm sure you'll do it," she said.

"Ever the optimist, huh?"

"Always."

PART THREE

Chapter 26

It was early August. Eric had made his final tuition payment to Brevard College. He knew the sizable outlay was an investment in his future, but he felt financially naked. His balance stood at less than half of his preferred thousand-dollar threshold. He would need to be careful with his money, but he was all in now. His fall semester would start in a few weeks.

Over the length of the summer, Eric had limited opportunities to interact with Mary or Rodney. His friends both worked at Christian summer camps; Mary's camp was over near Asheville, and Rodney's was near the town of Cashiers west of Brevard. Eric's two jobs made hanging out with his friends nearly impossible.

At the end of the camp season, Crystal, a former member of the track and cross-country teams, and a close friend of Mary's had invited Eric to an end-of-summer bash at her parent's lake cabin.

The lake cabin resided on a modest hundred-acre lake. The lake was set off deep in the woods, shrouded heavily by pines and hardwoods. About twenty-five homes surrounded the private property. The majority of the cabin owners were from the lower elevations who desired a place in the mountains to cool off during the oppressive Southern summers.

When Eric arrived, several party guests were floating in the lake on humongous truck-tire inner tubes. Enjoying the lake's cool water was the best place to be when the muggy, late-summer doldrums had settled in. Eric dressed for the occasion wearing a new pair of surfer shorts and a tank top he had bought at the mall. To compliment his summer look, he coupled these with a pair of flip-flops and a pair of aviator sunglasses.

The festive event would be a nice break from his hectic summer schedule and take the edge off his worries for an evening. He followed the stone path down toward the dock. Mary scampered up the path. "Eric!" she said and hugged him. "I'm glad you could make it."

Many beers and a few hours later, Eric, along with Rodney and a few other guests, were in the lake bobbing around on inner tubes. Mary and some girls were sunning on the dock. Suddenly an engine's rumble grew louder and silenced, car doors slammed, and two young men made their way down the path toward them.

"Man, Rodney, you know who that is?" Eric said. He handed his beer to Rodney, propped his sunglasses on the top of his head then grabbed the dock's ladder to pull himself closer. He slipped out of his inner tube and climbed up onto the dock. He turned to Rodney, "That's Trey Allison! What's he doing here?"

"Allison?" Rodney said. "I don't know. Doesn't he live in Charlotte?"

Eric looked back up the path and saw Trey give Mary a hug and a kiss.

Eric flashed a weak smile at Rodney's and said, "So *that's* why Mary's been so weird this summer—she's been dating Trey."

"And, so what?" Rodney said.

"You sure Mary didn't tell you? You guys keeping secrets from me?"

Rodney's face scrunched. "C'mon man . . . serious?"

"She can't *seriously* be dating him. *Can she?"*

Rodney shot back, "I think someone's jealous."

"I am not, we're just friends," Eric huffed. He started for the path.

When Mary saw Eric coming up the path, she quickly pulled away from Trey, turning and giving Eric an apprehensive look.

"Well, well, well, look who we have here," Trey said when he recognized Eric.

"What are *you* doing here?" Eric snipped.

Trey put his arm around Mary. "Why do you care?

I came here to see Mary. I wanted to surprise her." Trey quickly kissed her cheek.

"I *don't* care."

"Well," Trey said, gesturing at Eric. "Don't you have some beer drinking to do or something?"

Mary stepped toward Eric and grabbed his upper arm with both hands, trying to pull him away. "Come on, Eric, go back to the dock." Eric shoved her hands down and moved into arm's length of Trey.

"Man, Roberts, I almost didn't recognize you—going for the mountain man thing? Heard you were running." Trey poked at Eric's stomach. "Not at racing weight yet, I see."

Eric slapped Trey's hand away and shifted closer, fists clenched, leaning up into Trey's face, but Rodney grabbed Eric's arms, and Jonathan—who had just stepped out of the cabin—joined in the effort, and the two men dragged Eric back a few feet.

Eric shook off his friends' grip and stalked back over to Trey. "I *should* hit you, if only for what you said at the Asheville track meet."

Party music blaring from the cabin halted with an ingratiating scratch as someone dragged the stereo's needle off the record. Drawn to the commotion, the party guests descended to the path, encircling the two, whispering and muttering.

Trey's friend, intent on protecting him, lunged at Eric, pinning him in a bear hug, arms at his sides. Jonathan and Rodney swept in and wrestled him away.

"Let me go," he screamed, as the two grappled with Trey's broad, muscular defender.

Mary squeezed between Eric and Trey, holding them at arm's length, stiff-arming both their chests.

Trey squinted. "Asheville meet? What remark?"

"You don't remember the Asheville meet our senior year?"

"Hell, no. Are you insane?"

"Remember . . . you were talking to your dad after the mile race," Eric began, determined to make Trey admit the truth so that Eric's anger and actions wouldn't be meaningless. "He mostly screamed at you, but then you called me a hillbilly and said I was easy pickings.'"

Trey's eyes narrowed. "I remember. So what?"

"Eric," Mary said, pushing him back a step, "you need to leave. You're drunk."

"I'm not drunk."

Mary pointed to his car. "Well, I want you to go, anyway."

"Fine," Eric spit out, "if that's the way you feel about it." He turned and retrieved his towel from the dock, then stalked past the partygoers, kicking rocks and everything else in his path. But before passing Mary, Eric paused for one last shot. "He's a jerk, Mary. You knew that. But I guess you're not picky about who you date, are you?"

Mary grunted. She tromped over and poked Eric's chest. "You're one to talk. How many tramps have you dated? That's the pot calling the kettle black."

"Never mind. I'm outta here," Eric said. He spun his car's tires as he peeled away. Behind him a cloud of gravel dust floated into the air, the flecks lingering in the late afternoon sunbeams streaking through the woods.

Chapter 27

Still fuming about his party dismissal and Mary's love interest, Eric wasn't ready to go home yet. He wanted to wind down, but his stomach pangs kept ringing his five o'clock dinner bell, which further irritated him because he had missed the party's hamburger and hot dog grilling. The end-of-summer blowout had been a bust—so he headed for the bar. Eric pressed his weight into the heavy wood door at Donnelley's Pub. Its triangular iron hinges groaned as it swung open.

"Eric!" Mr. Donnelley shouted as the door closed with a thump. The short, plump bartender came to the end of the bar to greet him. "How are you? How's the running?"

"Hi, Mr. Donnelley," Eric said as he settled onto a barstool, his eyes still adjusting to the darkened lighting. "Running? Not bad. I can't seem to stay consistent, though."

"So, you're not running every day?" the bar owner asked, drawing a pint of Eric's favorite beer from one of the nearby taps. He placed it on a coaster in front of him.

"Thanks," Eric said. "Well, yes. The main reason is that I'm exhausted every day. This construction job I have in Hendersonville is wearing me out. And working for the camp owner where I'm staying hasn't helped, either. The camping season is over now, but he still finds things for me to fix."

Donnelley removed a few empty glasses and wiped the counter. "Well, I'm sure you'll work it out. The last time we talked you said you had till next May to get that time you want for the mile, right? I'm sure things will slow down in the winter. You can train hard then. Right?"

Eric took a long draw of his beer and wiped the foam from his lips with the back of his hand, "I sure hope so."

The bartender scanned the room, "Hey, I have some beer kegs I need to move to the coolers before the crowds come. We'll talk later, OK?"

"Sure, no problem."

"Oh, you hungry?" Donnelley said. "You want your usual, Angus Swiss Burger and fries?"

"Yes. I'm starving."

"Great. I'll be back shortly," Donnelley said.

Eric was sitting at the front corner of the bar, facing the wall. He turned on his seat to see who else was there. Only a handful of patrons occupied the place. Two couples were laughing and enjoying themselves in the booths toward the back. A group of four had entered the bar and grabbed a booth along the opposite wall. The room was quiet except for the clinking of quarters the new group was plunking into the jukebox. A dark-haired man wearing jeans, a cotton Madras shirt, and a black baseball cap sat a few stools away, next to the wall.

The dark-haired man picked up his beer and headed toward Eric. Moments earlier, Eric had noticed the guy scribbling in a notepad. Was he another reporter? After word had spread that Eric was back in town, a journalist had tracked him down, trying to weasel a story out of him. He couldn't understand how Buzzy's death still counted as news two years later. He had sent the reporter on his way.

"I'm Bill Kest," said the man. He set his notepad and beer glass on the bar remained standing.

"Oh, hi, I'm Eric. Nice to meet you."

"I remember you," the man said.

"You remember me?"

"I do. I met you at Straus Park back in May."

Eric sighed. He had contemplated the emotional stakes when returning home. There would be questions galore. Repressed memories, some more painful than others, would rise from their graves. Here was yet another person who wanted to dig into the past. To be fair, Kest simply wanted to talk. But Eric wanted to tell this guy he'd had a bad day and wasn't in the mood to talk, but then he reconsidered.

"You remember last May? I know it wasn't that long, but I've been so busy, I'm lucky if I can remember last week," Eric said.

"May I sit down?" Kest asked.

Eric shifted a few inches away from Kest, giving him room to take the stool next to him. "Sure."

Kest eased onto the barstool and ordered another beer. "Well, I'm good at remembering faces. Maybe this will jog your memory: I was the guy with the limp."

"Oh, yeah, now I remember you," Eric said, visualizing the guy with the strange gait who wanted to run Agony Hill. "How did the run go that day?"

"Well, it was tough but fun. It's the perfect length. I've been up Agony Hill couple more times since."

"It is fun, isn't it? But if you like that run, I have a much harder one for you. It's in the forest. It's called the Art Loeb trail."

"I think I've heard of it. "I'll put that one on my to-do list," the man said, laughing.

Discussing running cheered Eric up—along with learning of the man's newfound enthusiasm for Agony Hill. Still, Eric wasn't particularly in the mood to be social at the moment.

Donnelley brought Bill's beer and Eric's dinner over.

As Eric began eating, Bill said, "Pardon me . . . I don't mean to be nosy," he said, "but I couldn't help but overhear your conversation with the bartender . . ."

"And?" Eric said contemptuously, digging into his meal, and not meeting the man's polite entreaty.

Hearing the hostility in Eric's voice, Bill slid his seat a few inches to the side, giving Eric some space. "I'm sorry. I didn't mean to bother you. I've been trying to write this book." He lifted his notepad, displaying it like a lawyer holding up evidence in a courtroom.

"Oh—I'm sorry," Eric said, swallowing a bite of his hamburger. "I've had a crappy day. I apologize. I shouldn't be taking it out on you."

Bill laughed. "No apologies necessary. If you need your space, I'll go back to my seat."

"Stay, stay," Eric said. "What were you saying about your notepad?"

The man smiled and settled back into his seat. "I come here to write. For a different atmosphere, you know?"

"What are you writing about?"

"Well . . . it's about my life, and how I got here today."

"You grew up poor and won the lottery?" Eric joked.

"No," the man chuckled, "Wasn't that exciting. I had a major head injury when I was ten and was in a coma."

Eric stared at him. "Seriously?" he said through a mouthful of fries. He had never met anyone who'd been in a coma before. So many questions sprang to mind.

Encouraged by Eric's interest, Bill told him the whole story. The odds of him recovering had been a thousand to one. His doctors had concluded that the severity of the resulting injury would leave him nothing more than an invalid for the rest of his life. But he recovered, he explained, even excelling at lacrosse in high school. He said he'd received an athletic scholarship from a major university and later earned a master's degree.

After hearing Bill's story, Eric began revealing his own life's trials and tribulations—slowly at first, as he questioned whether he should dump his avalanche of pain and guilt on this unsuspecting stranger. But Eric was lonely, and Bill was a good listener and seemed trustworthy and kind. They spent the next few hours trading histories. Eric related to this guy who had had to climb out of a dark hole after an accident and rebuild his life. And that seemed to make Bill understand him too.

Finally they ran out of things to say, and for a few minutes, they both stared at the TV screen, watching a taped game of Mr.

Donnelley's beloved soccer team. Bill turned to Eric and leaned in with a serious look on his face. "I have a question for you."

"What's that?"

"Are you ready to start your life again?"

"What do you mean?"

"Well, let me explain it this way. To me, it sounds as if you're ready for a change. You told me you missed all your friends and Mary, too, right?"

"Dude, you should be a reporter."

The man laughed, but he kept his gaze focused on Eric. "You want to run again, don't you? You said you'd tested your ankle out and it's strong again. But you mentioned you're not sure if you're willing to make the needed effort—or even the sacrifice it takes to achieve the goal the coach set for you."

"I mean, sure, I've had my doubts lately. My running is going well, but it's still not where I want it to be. Running a 4:05 mile is no Sunday stroll."

"OK, so it's a little hard. What are you waiting for?" Bill leaned back in his seat. "Pardon my honesty, but if my past has taught me anything, it's making no excuses for what has happened in one's life. No one ever knows how things will turn out. If you don't chase your dreams, you'll regret it for the rest of your life."

Eric slumped back. "But I'm not sure—"

"There are no buts, Eric," the older man said, interrupting him. "You either do it or don't." He paused, then spoke more softly. "Eric, you're a smart young man who had dreams once. Dream again. Change your direction."

"Change my direction?" Eric said.

"Bill slid his empty beer glass toward the drink rail next to Eric's two empty glasses. He then turned on his stool so he faced Eric more squarely. "I have an analogy for you. Have you ever read *Moby Dick?* Do you remember the captain of the ship in that book?"

Eric laughed. Finally his high school English class seemed relevant. "I have. It was Captain Ahab of the Pequod. He was obsessed with killing the Great White Whale."

"That's right. I ask because metaphorically you have to be like Captain Ahab . . . well, maybe not that crazy, but equally determined."

Eric smiled at the analogy.

"Eric, only you can achieve your goal, and only you will answer for it if you don't. Perform everything to your utmost ability, and if it doesn't come out as planned, believe me, you won't look back. I wasn't supposed to amount to anything, but I was determined not to let some little limp hold me back. I set my goals, forged ahead, and succeeded. Peculiar as it sounds, it helped that I spent time in a coma; it meant that I had a newfound appreciation of life after I recovered. And maybe that's what it takes. Maybe we need to come to a stage in our life where we are tired of making excuses, and we decide to go after what we want. You already made a change by coming home. Don't give up now."

After a long silence, Eric spoke: "Thanks, Bill, for talking to me today. You're right. I need to make a change."

"I'm glad. And you're welcome," Bill said, waving to Donnelley for his check.

"You know," Eric said, "I felt a little weird at first telling you all this stuff. But it's been cathartic. I should be paying you, like a psychiatrist or something."

"Don't feel like you owe me something." Bill smiled. "After all, I was the one who pried into your life. I thought you hearing my story might help you out.

Bill slid his stool underneath the bar. "Anyway . . . I should go. My wife is probably wondering what's happened to me. I'm surprised she hasn't called the bar yet."

"Take care," Eric said. "And good luck with your book. Maybe I'll see you in a road race someday."

"Probably will . . . See you later, Mr. Donnelley!" Bill called across the bar, waving. He threw some money on the bar, but before he stepped away, he looked at Eric closely. "You 'll be all right getting home?" he nodded to the three empty beer glasses by the drink rail. "With the beer, I mean."

"I'm good."

"OK, be safe," Bill said, heading for the door.

After Bill was gone, Eric shoved his empty pint glass to the edge of the bar and flagged Donnelley for his tab.

Chapter 28

In Eric's half-asleep daze, he believed the clattering door and windows to be his alarm going off. He swiped at the alarm, which he had not even set, knocking an empty beer can off his nightstand. The aluminum container clinked as it rolled toward the far wall.

"Eric!" Miklos yelled, banging on his front door. "Eric, get up!" The apartment's weathered windows rattled in their frames.

"What?" he shouted back.

"I said, get up! We're supposed to finish painting the barn this morning."

"Oh, my head," Eric groaned quietly. "Can't we do it later?" he yelled hoarsely.

"No, we can't do it later. The weather has cleared. It has to be today. You promised."

Eric slowly rolled out of bed onto his hands and knees. He grabbed one of the bed's sturdy bed posts and righted himself. He shuffled to the door, cracked it open, barely sticking his head out. "Give me an hour, OK?"

"You look like—"

Eric raised his hand.

"Drunk last night, no?" Miklos said.

Eric scrunched his eyebrows. "That's a good assessment."

"Don't be a wise-ass."

"Sorry."

"Look, I'll give you half an hour. Take a quick shower, and for God's sake, get some water in you. It's supposed to be in the mid-90's today." Miklos turned and stomped down the staircase. At the bottom, he spun and looked back up at Eric, "Oh, and by the way, you need to move your car."

"Why?"

"Because," he growled, "you parked it inches away from my drivers-side door last night."

Eric rubbed his forehead. "Aw, jeez, I'm sorry Miklos . . . I'll move it as soon as I come down."

Miklos did not acknowledge him.

Grimacing, Eric gently closed the door. He had never seen Miklos angry like this.

Miklos had a type A personality. He always had something planned, whether it was camp related or personal. And he had one big pet peeve: he was a stickler for being on time. So far Eric had pleased Miklos on that account, until today.

Eric liked living with and working for Miklos. He also enjoyed the many conversations they had while working together, tackling the camp's frequent repairs. However, being a moment's notice or a building away from Miklos had its disadvantages. Eric wanted his camp work done with and not be so conveniently accessible.

Half an hour later, Eric emerged from his apartment dressed in cutoff jeans, a T-shirt, and a red bandana wrapped around his head. He grabbed a ladder from the barn and propped it on the opposite end of the barn wall where Miklos had begun painting. He collected a brush and a half-full paint pale that Miklos had set out for him and ascended the ladder.

Miklos laid his brush on the top of his paint can and said, "I'm taking a break." He walked over to a plaid, aluminum folding chair. The chair's delicate aluminum frame and aged nylon straps issued a cacophony of pops and creaks as Miklos settled his weight.

"Man, when are you going to throw out that old chair? You're going to fall through it one day," Eric said.

"I like it. It has charm. And besides, I'm too cheap to buy a new one."

"I could repair it for you. The hardware store has straps and eyelets."

"Thanks, but I'll be fine for now."

"Suit yourself. But don't come to me when you get hurt," Eric said, chuckling.

"Hey," Miklos said, suddenly changing the conversation. "How was the party? Did you see Mary?"

Eric descended the ladder, shifted it over a few feet, and resumed his spot near the top. "I saw her. I almost got into a fight, though."

"Who with?"

"Trey Allison."

"Oh, you've told me about him. He's the runner who always beat you, right? Why was he there; didn't you say he lives in Charlotte?"

Eric was surprised Miklos remembered Eric's casual mentioning of Allison, but his boss had a keen memory. He could recall details of novels both he and Eric had read with incredible depth while Eric had forgotten the book's key moments entirely.

"He does. He came to surprise Mary. She's dating him."

"That why you almost got into a fight?"

"No . . ."

"You sure? Not because they're dating?"

"Mary and I are just friends."

"Sounds like you drank too much and were a little jealous?"

"I only had a few beers . . . Mary kicked me out of the party, so I hung out at the pub for a while before coming home."

"A few?"

"I wasn't that drunk."

"Not how it looks to me." Miklos jabbed his thumb toward their cars. "I bet you couldn't park your car that close to mine being sober."

"OK, so I was a little drunk. But I've been far worse. I'm a little dehydrated, that's all."

Eric dipped his brush deep into his pail and pulled it out. "Hey, Miklos, can you bring me some more paint?"

Miklos grabbed a fresh gallon can and removed the lid. He brought it over to Eric, now standing at the base of the ladder. "Here you go, Lazlo."

"Lazlo?" Eric poured the paint into his pail. "You mean Eric."

Miklos's faced turned red. "Oh, sorry, I meant Eric."

Eric gave the gallon can back to Miklos. "Easy mistake."

Eric wondered if Miklos had had a brain freeze or he if it was senility kicking in. But we all forget things occasionally he reminded himself. Miklos was a quiet, if not shy man. He rarely initiated conversation, but was easy to get to know him once you got him talking. But there was one subject Miklos declined to discuss, his wife and son. They both had passed away within months of each other—his son from a car accident and his wife from cancer. When Eric had pressed him for more details about his past, Miklos politely refused.

Miklos hurried back to his chair, set the can on the ground. "Are you hungry?" he asked.

"Yeah," Eric said.

"I'll make you a turkey and cheese sandwich if you want one," Miklos said.

"Definitely. Thanks."

As Eric continued to make progress on the barn. Miklos brought out the sandwich and another for himself. They practically inhaled their lunches and set right back to work. Miklos had a nice setup for painting: long wooden poles with rollers and tall ladders. It made the chore more manageable. Still, the relentless sun dictated a pedestrian work pace.

By 10:00 a.m., Eric was shirtless, and his sweat had darkened ninety percent of his shorts. All week Eric had endured the torrid heat and humidity at his construction job in Hendersonville and today was a duplicate. He pictured himself floating on an inner tube in the cold waters of a local river, but his refreshing visualizations didn't relieve his current conditions. Eric usually liked helping

Miklos, but today his dehydration, hangover, and toiling in the sun, had sapped the pleasure from this barn beautification project. He had little choice, so he pushed on.

Three hours later, Eric was finishing the last corner near the roof. "Hey, I have a question for you," he said. "I may have asked you this before, but did you ever play sports in Hungary? If so, I can't remember what you said."

"I think I did tell you." Miklos laughed. "I played some football in the schoolyard as a kid. Oops, I mean *soccer*. I mostly read a lot. I was a bookworm, as you Americans say, but that's all. Speaking of sports: how's your running coming?"

"Oh, it's great. Getting in lots of mileage. I hope to run in a few college cross-country meets this fall to gauge my fitness."

"You're still a little heavy, aren't you? You need to lay off the beer and fast food if you're going to lose some weight."

Eric turned and scowled at him. He dipped his brush into his can. "It's coming down . . . Aw crap!" he shouted.

"What's wrong?" Miklos asked, sounding worried.

"Nothing, I need a rag. I spilled paint on myself, and I dropped my rag earlier."

Miklos picked up the rag lying on the ground next to the ladder and handed it to Eric. "So, you're still coaching yourself?"

"I have to. I can't afford to pay for a coach."

"Can your high school coach help?"

"He said he doesn't have the time. He offered to give me a workout plan, but I can do it easier for myself."

"Have you made any plans?"

"Not yet. I'm trying to increase my mileage slowly. I figure I'll start serious training in September. I need to find some running books or something. I'm sure training for college races is different from high school. They race farther than typical high school three-mile distances. They're either five miles or 10,000 meters. That's—"

"6.2 miles. I know," Miklos cut him off.

Eric laughed. "Oh, yeah. Hungary is a metric country," he said, stepping off the last rung of the ladder.

"You know, I'm sure the training won't be that much different," Miklos said. "Isn't running just running? You have to run a little longer for college cross-country, that's all."

Eric lowered himself into an equally dilapidated twin of Miklos's folding chair. "You might be right. You appear to have a pretty good idea of how sports work for a guy that didn't play anything but soccer as a little kid."

"Well, Eric, you get to be my age, you learn a few things," Miklos said. "I taught high school in California, so I saw many of the school's sports teams play. I do like watching sports. Plus, my best friend was a math teacher who coached the track and cross-country teams. He talked track all the time. More than I wanted to know."

"I see," Eric chuckled.

"The barn looks great. It looks like a whole new building. Thanks for the help," Miklos said. "So, how far are you running today?"

"Should be ten miles. This run will give me my best weekly total yet: forty-five miles."

"That should take just over an hour, no?"

"Yeah, that's about right. Hey, you sure you didn't run before?"

Miklos picked a few dirty paint rags off the ground near the barn, continuing to speak. "Like I said before, my friend back in California was a running coach," Miklos tossed the rags into a metal trash container near the open barn door, then turned to Eric. "He always talked about how fast his kids were getting. Afterwhile, I picked up on the mile-pacing—Are you running the roads?"

"I guess that makes sense—No. I'm going to run in the forest to stay out of the sun. Also, my ankle hasn't had any pain and seems back to normal, and now would be a good time to test it on the trails."

"I see. You can go now if you want. I'll clean up—let me know how the run goes."

"Thanks. I will." Eric said and trotted up the stairs to his apartment to change.

DESPITE THE LUSH, TREETOP canopy, specks of sunlight pierced through, dotting the forest floor. The dense tropical weather was like trying to run through a sauna—it was rough. Eric's hangover headache was gone, and he had some food in him. *I'll be all right,* he told himself. *I've had enough water.*

When he had run the trails in high school, Eric had started at points in the forest near the ranger station or the fish hatchery. But to connect to the same trails from where he lived now, he had to use different paths. He examined the relief maps of the area he purchased a few weeks ago and discovered when he had run the Pisgah Forest trails in the past, he had passed close to this camp without knowing.

Today he planned on making it to a shelter located deep in the woods—a small A-frame structure built as a hikers' refuge for foul weather or injury. He figured it was approximately five miles one way. He planned to keep an eye on his watch and limit his time, just in case he'd underestimated the distance.

A short distance into Eric's run, thoughts of his high school races occupied his mind. His favorite had been at the state course at McAlpine Park over in Charlotte. It was flat and fast, except for a steep and nasty little hill smack in the middle of the course. It was an idyllic creek-side setting that transported a runner to a different place. One could quickly forget that outside the park's border a vast city loomed. Eric's mind flitted to the upcoming cross-country season, just weeks away. Despite the sweltering heat, chills still raced through his body in anticipation of his first autumn cross-country race.

Thirty-five minutes after his start, Eric arrived at the shelter. His lips were a little dry, and his mouth parched. A creek was only yards away, but he decided he would pass on the water until he returned to the camp.

On the way back down the trail, Eric noticed that the air

drawing across his tongue felt dryer in spite of the air's highly saturated state. He tried a quick swallow but gulped nothing, barely able to move his tongue that seemed bogged down in pasty saliva. His body was hotter, too. He wondered if the air temperature had increased. He had been mildly dehydrated on long runs before, but his thirst had to be from the August heat. About two miles from home Eric found himself slowing involuntarily, and his head started spinning. He stopped and rested for a minute before moving again. His legs swung slowly like two rusty pendulums. His stomach twisted, torquing hard. He stopped again, and his stomach settled. He checked his pulse and found it higher than average, but he chalked that up to his long work week in the sun. *I just need to take it easy and not push the pace, that's all,* he told himself. He tried to run again, but halted at a pine tree a few yards later, bending over, one arm braced horizontally to hold himself up, his other hand clutching his side.

"I knew I should have gotten some water back near the shelter," he muttered. *Don't panic, Eric,* he told himself. *Come up with a plan. Keep walking, and you'll make it back okay.* But when he rubbed a hand across his dry forehead, the gravity of his predicament gripped him. He knew what heat exhaustion was, having had a mild case of it as a kid when he was marching with his Cub Scout troop in a Fourth of July parade. He was pulled from the group and immediately given water, and he remembered sitting for a long time in a chair, occasionally bending over to try and alleviate the dizziness. But now he was critically dehydrated, maybe approaching heatstroke.

Eric limped another mile before he had to stop again. Waiting for his stomach spasms to subside, he rubbed at the crystallized sweat appearing on his face and torso. The white salt patches felt like fine sand between his fingers. Chronically dizzy now, approaching paranoia. His thoughts raced. *Got to make it home.*

He tried to run but managed barely more than a walking pace. Cotton-mouthed, he wheezed as he plodded along the hilly trail, remembering a book he had read years earlier. The 1800s era story chronicled the plight of a whaling ship's survivors after a sperm whale had attacked and sunk their vessel. The account intricately detailed how thirsty and disheveled they had become after their interminable time at sea without food and water to sustain them. The men so wracked with delirium growled at their rescuers, convinced that they were trying to steal the gnawed bones that littered their boat—their most precious possession by that point. This thought put fear into Eric. His leg turnover increased, but not much. He had lost track of how far he was from home and prayed that he was close.

Then Eric recognized the trailhead at the gravel road, and he was flooded with relief. The sunlight reflecting off the road's light gray macadam hit his eyes as he stepped from the forest canopy. He stopped, shaded his eyes, and waited for them to adjust. He bent over, hands on his knees, groaning and wincing as his stomach twisted again. To quell the pain, he pressed on his belly, but it was no use. Eventually, the pain subsided of its own accord, so Eric resumed his walk to the camp, his pace still a weak shuffle, gravel dust rising behind him. *Just a quarter-mile to go,* he thought.

Eric held both hands on his hips as he walked on the gravel road, trying to steady himself, but his head and body bobbed back and forth like one of those glass-tubed drinking birds they sold at gas stations. When those black top-hatted birds dipped their red-headed beaks down into a glass full of water they always popped back up the next instant, starting the bobbing process again. Unlike the birds, if he fell, he didn't think he could get up again. *Don't fall,* he told himself. *Whatever you do, don't fall.*

THE HUM FROM THE window-mounted air conditioner was a soothing lullaby. Eric rolled onto his back, tugged the blanket close to his chin, and sighed. It must be fall—the first cold snap of the season. He half-opened his eyes and saw Miklos standing over him.

"Oh, hi, Miklos. What are you doing in my room?" Eric muttered.

"You're not in your room," Miklos chuckled. "You're in my room."

Eric's eyes sprang wide. He blinked hard a few times and rubbed the sleep from his eyes.

"You should see the look on your face, Eric. You must have been dreaming." Miklos laughed.

"What am I doing here?" Eric asked, groggily.

"You don't remember?"

Eric thought for a moment. "Oh, the run. I remember you giving me water, and the cold towels but I don't remember much after that."

"Your memory isn't bad considering your condition. But, yes, once you cooled off, you fell asleep. You're feeling better?" Miklos asked.

Eric inched himself backward to rest against the headboard. "I think so, but I still feel like a truck ran over my body. I'm tired like I could go to sleep as long as Rip Van Winkle."

Miklos chuckled before a semi-serious expression came to his face. "It was hot and humid today. You came close to heatstroke, but you'll be fine. No trip to the hospital for you today," Miklos said.

"Man, I've been a little dehydrated on runs before . . . but never that bad," Eric confessed.

"Well, your hangover didn't help, which was your first mistake. And, in the future if you're working outside and have to run, you could plan a route where you can find water," Miklos said.

"You know, I did have a chance for water near the shelter, but I thought I was fine. I won't do that again." Eric picked up a glass of water from the bedside table, held it out like he were making a toast. "I'm drinking water every chance I can." He took a sip of the water. "This dehydration scared the hell out of me."

"I'm sure it did," Miklos said. He came closer to the foot of the bed. "Hey, I do have question?"

"What's that?" Eric said.

Miklos pointed to Eric's feet and said, "How come you didn't tape your left ankle? You should have if you were running the trails."

"I didn't?" *Is my ankle injured again? I don't remember that.* Eric threw his covers aside and pulled his legs out to see.

Miklos reached over, grabbed his left ankle, and probed it for pain. "Does this hurt," he asked, moving his fingers from place to place.

Eric was relieved that nothing hurt. "I can't believe I forgot."

Miklos helped Eric slide his feet back under the sheets and adjusted Eric's covers over him. "I think you answered your ankle strength question, but I'd stay away from the trails for now."

"I will," Eric said, his tension easing.

"You're hungry, no?"

"Yes, I'm starving."

"Good. I have some meatloaf, green beans, and mashed potatoes left over from yesterday. How does that sound?"

"Thanks, that'd be great. Oh, hey. How'd you know what to do? I mean, with my dehydration?"

"You can't be a camp owner and not know these sorts of things," Miklos said. "Kids are always getting a little dehydrated. I learned to prepare. I had one bad case a few years ago, and ever since I've made sure the kids take breaks and drink plenty of fluids." He turned and left.

"Don't forget the ketchup," Eric called after him.

"You American kids and your ketchup," Eric heard him mutter as he walked down the hallway.

Twenty minutes later, Miklos arrived with a serving tray bearing a plate of food and a bottle of ketchup. He stayed in the room while Eric ate until a phone rang in a room across the hallway. Miklos rushed to answer it, leaving the door open a few inches. Eric had never been in that room before because the door was always shut and locked. He didn't think it was a camp office. His boss used a larger room on the other side of the house where he conducted business. Curious, Eric leaned forward a few inches to glimpse into the room, but Miklos was blocking his view.

When Miklos moved away from the door, he pulled a chair out, took his seat, and turned on a desk lamp. Through the sliver of space, he saw gold-and silver-colored objects, but his vision was too restricted to tell what they were. He slid his tray forward and bent over for a better view, but before he could recognize anything, Miklos spotted Eric's curiosity and quickly closed the door.

Moments later, the receiver settled in its cradle. Miklos stepped into the hallway and shut the office door firmly behind him, then locked it before returning to the bedroom. "You can stay here tonight if you like."

"Thanks, I'll take you up on that. I could use a good night's sleep in a cool room."

"Yes, I agree." Miklos pointed toward the hallway. "I will be over there if you need anything." He came over, retrieved the food tray, and turned to walk out of the room.

Eric picked up a picture from the nightstand of what appeared to be a younger Miklos, his wife and a little boy standing in front of a car. "Hey, Miklos. How come you don't talk about your wife and son? Is this them?"

Miklos sighed. "I'll be back in a minute." When he returned, he grabbed a chair from a nearby desk and sat down near the bed. Eric handed the picture to him. Miklos stared at it for a few seconds before saying anything. He rubbed the picture's glass gently with his fingertips as if he could reach back in time. "OK, I will tell you."

"It's hard to speak about it, but will do my best," Miklos said. "My wife was undergoing cancer treatments at the time of our boy's car accident and was in remission. When the news of his death came, she became inconsolable after that. I tried everything. We took a vacation here for a change of scenery from California—"

"And her cancer?"

"She gave up."

"Gave up? What do you mean?"

"A few months after our son died . . . My wife became increasingly apathetic and refused further treatments. She lost the will to fight the cancer after Lazlo's death.

"What was your wife's name?"

"Her name was Priscina." Miklos's eyes were glistening now.

Eric regretted having pushed him to speak about it. "I'm sorry, Miklos. I shouldn't have asked." Eric placed a hand on the old man's arm.

"It's all right. Don't be sorry. There's nothing wrong in asking. It's me. I'm still trying to deal with it. I should speak more about it, not keep it to myself. You're a good kid, a good friend."

Miklos rose. "Well, you get some sleep, Eric. You've had a rough day. But if you're not tired yet, you can watch some TV." He pointed to the small set, sitting on the dresser near the bed. There's not much on right now. The only good things are some sports: boxing and a big track meet over in Oregon." He walked across the hall to his office, unlocked it and closed the door behind him. A moment later, Eric heard the familiar sound of a typewriter. The earlier glimpse of gold and silver objects and the locked door heightened Eric's curiosity. *There must be more to this guy than he lets on,* Eric thought.

Eric turned on the tiny black-and-white TV in the room and watched for a while, but his dinner had made him sleepy. He turned off the set and closed his eyes. *Today was a close call,* he thought, as he faded toward sleep. *I was lucky to have Miklos.*

Chapter 29

A few days later, Eric searched the local library and bookstore for running books that might help him with self-coaching. The few he discovered were more like *jogging* books—useful guides for beginning runners. He did not find an in-depth kind that explained intervals and how to best use them. His old high school cross-country coach had lent him one book from his collection, but it contained information similar to what he found in the library. His coach had explained a few of the theories, which Eric understood, but when it came to applying the science, he wasn't sure where to start. He couldn't decide how to coach himself. His coach had confessed that much of his style had come from trial and error. *Maybe that's what I need,* Eric thought, *to go out there and figure it out on my own.*

One evening Eric enlisted Miklos to time his half-mile repeat workout at Straus Park. But it was a disaster. He ran one repetition too fast, adjusted, and ran the next one slower. He never knew where he stood with the pace. Should he run more of them, but slower? Or do fewer, but faster?

Eric understood the fundamentals of distance running. He needed to build a distance base—long-distance runs to build up aerobic endurance—and add some form of anaerobic work such as intervals and up-tempo runs. However, he had never planned or trained for one event that would take place almost a year later. In high school, track and cross-country were two distinct seasons, and training for them was different. Cross-country season was more toward strength and endurance, and many workouts were performed on the grass at Straus Park. But during Track season the team trained primarily on the school's 440 yard oval, only occasionally going out to Straus. Back then, all of Eric's daily training routines were planned by his coach. Eric found coaching—or, in this case, self-coaching—to be harder than Coach Miles made it look. Eric wasn't sure if he should start track training now or wait till later.

Frustrated by his seesaw interval repetitions, Eric cut his workout short, and he and Miklos walked back to their cars.

"So, what do you think, Miklos?" Eric asked.

"Me? I don't know what you're doing when you do this interval stuff. You only wanted me to call out your interval times."

"I know. Humor me."

"OK. I think you don't know where your starting point is. You were all over the place today with your times."

"That's pretty perceptive. I think you're right. But how do I find out what my starting point is?"

Miklos shrugged. "Maybe we should call my coaching friend in California. He might know."

Again, with the California track coach reference, Eric thought. *He's hiding something.*

When they reached their cars, Miklos slipped into his large Polara and cranked the window down to let the heat out.

Eric grabbed a towel out of his car and wiped himself down and threw on his T-shirt. He walked over to Miklos's car. "Hey, I was wondering what those objects were that I saw in your room across the hallway last night? Weren't they trophies or something?"

Miklos's eyes widened. "Oh, those were pictures, some photos of family and friends." Miklos wasn't making eye contact with Eric.

"Why do you keep it locked all the time?"

"You're getting a little nosy, Eric," Miklos snipped. "It's none of your business."

"Hey," Eric said, pointing to the passenger seat of Miklos's car, "what's that?"

Miklos flicked his eyes right, then back to Eric. "It's my mail." He reached and flipped the bundle over.

Eric flew around to the car's passenger side, opened the door, and grabbed the rubber-banded bundle with an issue of *Track & Field News* folded around the outside. He shook it at Miklos. "Why is *Track & Field News* in your mail?" he asked.

Miklos stepped out of the car and glared at him across the hood. "I like to keep up on sports, what can I say?"

Eric stormed back to Miklos, grabbed one of his hands, and thrust the mail bundle into it. "I don't believe you. Nobody has a copy of *Track and Field News* lying around if they weren't a coach or a runner."

Miklos tossed the mail bundle onto the front seat, shut the door. He then reached into his trousers and pulled out a small pocket knife, opened it to a small blade and started digging at his fingernails. Without looking at Eric he said, "There's more to it than you know."

You're a coach, aren't you? Those are trophies in that room across the hall, right?"

Miklos snapped the knife shut. "Yes, they were. I didn't tell you—"

"You've been lying to me this whole time. Why?"

"I never lied to you."

"But you didn't tell me—"

"I didn't tell you because I knew you'd act this way—that you would bug the crap out of me to coach you. You are my employee and my tenant. I wanted to keep it that way. Besides, many runners have been able to train themselves to greatness without a coach. It takes a special individual, and many have done it."

"So, I'm your employee and tenant. So what? I just wanted some help. That's all." He stormed over to his car and sat on the hood.

"I know Eric, but I'm too old to coach anymore. I don't have the drive like I used to . . . and . . ."

"And what? You knew I needed a coach. You could have helped me out. But you kept it a secret instead—"

"And . . . I don't think you have the dedication."

Eric jumped off the hood and pressed his palms together like he was praying, shaking them at Miklos in supplication. "Yes, I do. Really. I'll run every day. I'll do anything you say. I promise."

"I'm not so sure. I haven't seen much effort over the last two months. You jabber on about how you want to be a great runner, but most times that you go for a run, you come back early. You don't run as far as you set out to. And you skip days, too."

"How do you know that?" Eric said, surprised the old man had noticed.

"I wasn't a coach for over thirty years to not notice these things."

Eric was speechless.

Miklos sighed heavily and folded his arms across his chest. He turned his head and stared off into the distance.

"Come on, Miklos. Help me out."

"I can't," he said, not engaging with Eric.

"Can't, or won't?" Eric demanded.

He turned back to Eric and eyed him grimly, "Both"

Chapter 30

Eric startled awake, Molly's shrill bark ringing in his ears. "Hush, Molly," he groaned as he pulled his pillow over his head. He had forgotten how loud she could bark and the apartment's bare walls did nothing to abate her volume. His family's dog had been visiting, as his mother had wanted Eric to take her for long walks on the campgrounds. Molly was aging and gaining weight.

Molly continued baying at the apartment door.

"Come out," Miklos yelled through the door. "I need to talk to you."

So that's why Molly wasn't listening. "What do you want?" Eric screamed. "I'm tired."

"It's important."

Eric grabbed Molly's collar and whipped the door open. "What? It's early."

"I will coach you."

"Serious?" The anger had slipped from Eric's voice.

"Yes, but on one condition. You have to run a mile in under 4:40."

"Piece of cake. I can run that in my sleep. When?"

"In one hour—meet me at the Brevard track at nine," Miklos said, then turned and hurried down the stairs without looking back.

"Wait! Give me a week—"

Miklos spun. "You want me to coach you?"

"Yes."

"Then be there on time."

As Eric walked the fifty-yards from the gym's parking area, he saw Miklos standing on the track, hands in his pockets, staring downward. Miklos was wearing a cowboy hat and a pair of dark sunglasses. He had never seen Miklos wear that hat before. He usually wore a beat-up John Deere ball cap. Eric paused, then it hit him. The cowboy hat; the track meet at Asheville; the old stopwatch. He was the guy with the old stopwatch.

Eric stepped onto the asphalt track clutching his old track spikes, one in each hand.

"Morning," Eric said.

"It's 9 A. M. Good," Miklos said flatly. "But a dedicated runner would have been here earlier to warm up and be ready to go."

Eric frowned. "I had to drop Molly off at my mom's. I was still on time, and—"

"Put your spikes down and go do three miles to warm up."

"But—"

"You're wasting my time. Now go!" Miklos barked, pointing toward the cornfields not far from the track. "Four laps around the fields should be enough."

"OK," Eric said pathetically, chucking his spikes to the infield. He jogged off, grumbling. The college owned the fields but leased the land out for farming. The path around the fields was wider than a car and had two deep tractor-wide ruts cutting along through its center. The college's track coach used this area as part of its home cross-country course and for longer-distance interval training.

Eric returned after four laps, his T-shirt clinging to his body. He pulled it off, tossed it to the side of the track, and stretched.

Miklos, sitting on a set of wooden bleachers next to the track said, "I want you to do ten easy-paced one-hundred-yard strides on the infield with a hundred-yard jog between each one."

"Man, he's not even my coach yet, and he's already barking orders," Eric muttered to himself.

After Eric did the striders, he returned and collected his track spikes, and sat down on the nearby bleachers to unlace his training shoes.

"You won't need your spikes," Miklos said.

"What? I always race in spikes."

"You can run a mile under four minutes and forty seconds in your training flats," Miklos said dryly.

Eric huffed, stood up and heaved his spikes across the track to the infield for the second time.

Miklos stood up. "Are you ready?" he asked.

"I'm ready," Eric shot back. He walked over to the starting line in the middle straightaway, directly in front of the bleachers. The track setup was old-school. New or converted tracks had the starting line closer to one curve.

Miklos pulled out a silver-colored hand-wound stopwatch from his pants pocket. There it was. That old stopwatch.

Eric crouched into his starting position in lane one.

"Go," Miklos ordered.

A lap later Miklos called out, "Sixty-seven flat."

Eric's muscles were a little sore from the prior day's intervals, but because he hadn't done too many, his legs still had enough reserves for this test.

Seventy-two seconds later, Eric passed the half-mile mark with a total time of 2:19. He had slowed some on the second trip around, but he was still confident. He was one second under a 4:40 pace.

At the end of Eric's third circuit, Miklos shouted, "3:33. You're plus three seconds."

Aughh, that was an ugly lap. Lost too much time, Eric thought. His easy-peasy 4:40 mile was turning out to be harder than he'd thought. His slowing wasn't from tired legs; his poor, underdeveloped anaerobic fitness and lack of interval training was the culprit. His body wasn't handling the heavy circulatory demands his muscles needed. He would have to grit this last lap.

When Eric had 220 yards remaining, Miklos yelled across the infield, "Four minutes eight seconds." Eric needed to run this last half lap in less than 32 seconds to make it under 4:40.

He rose on his toes, leaning forward a little and pumped his arms.

Come on legs, Eric encouraged himself.

Eric lumbered across the finish line, stumbling from exhaustion. "What—was—the—time?" he managed to get out amid his huffing and puffing.

"Four minutes, thirty-nine point six seconds," Miklos said.

"That's—the hardest—thing—I've—ever—done," Eric gasped. He paced around, waiting for his body to recover.

After a minute Miklos motioned for Eric to come closer. When he did Miklos reached up to his neck and pressed his fingers near the carotid artery and started his silver stopwatch. Eric knew he was counting his pulse for six seconds and multiplying it by ten for a rough measure of his heart rate's recovery after a one-minute rest.

"Heart rate still north of 170," he said. "But that's not unexpected. It will improve. I'm sure you know that."

"Right."

Miklos pulled out a mini-notepad, jotted something down, then slipped it back into his pocket. "Your mile race for your scholarship won't seem this hard," Miklos said dryly.

"I hope not!"

"Long time since you ran fast, no?" Miklos's tone friendlier now.

"Too long."

"Your ankle appears to be strong enough, but I will bring you along slowly."

"OK, Coach."

"Go walk one lap around the track to settle yourself then run a mile warm-down," Miklos said. "Meet me at the room you saw the other night, OK?"

"Got it. But I have a question before you leave," Eric said.

"Sure."

"That was you at my track meets wasn't it?"

Miklos nodded. "I thought you would have figured it out earlier. What was the trigger?"

"The cowboy hat."

Chapter 31

Eric stepped into the doorway of Miklos's den and immediately discovered his new coach's treasure trove of history, plus some impressive connections to famous people within the running community.

The crowded little office had a spacious roll top desk that occupied the corner opposite the door. Beside it sat a wood card table and matching chair. The other chairs were vintage, along with most of the furniture in the house. The rolling chair that matched the desk was still in great shape despite its cracked veneer. A large, cushy armchair filled out the other corner.

But it was the walls and shelves that revealed Miklos's history.

"Eric, if you're going to stand there with your mouth open, at least come in," Miklos said, rocking himself back and forth in his chair.

"Unreal," Eric said as he approached one wall of pictures and trophies. "This is the coolest thing ever."

"You're quite the wordsmith."

Eric pointed. "No, I mean, look at this. One, two, three . . .. Eight, you had eight California state champion cross-country teams?"

"Yes."

"Man, that's hard to do in any state."

Miklos rose and crossed the room to where Eric stood. "Those were good times. I had a bunch of good boys over those years."

"When I figured out you were a coach, I didn't know you were *this* good. And wait—is this you and Tim Donaldson?" Eric was examining an autographed picture of the runner in a row above the championship photos. Donaldson was standing next to Miklos in the shot. "That's amazing!"

"Yes. Me and Tim. It was a magical day."

"Wow, he was the second guy to run the mile in under four minutes in high school!"

"You know your running history."

Eric was amazed. How could this guy know so many people? The few faces in the wall of pictures that Eric recognized were Bob Schul, Bill Dellinger—now the head coach at Oregon—and Frank Shorter. But there had to be lots of famous runners on these walls. It was like standing in the running hall of fame. Eric had experienced the same sense of awe as a kid when his parents had taken him to the Football Hall of Fame in Canton, Ohio; he'd tried to read as many plaques as fast as he could before they'd had to leave.

"Why don't you have a seat in the armchair over in the corner," Miklos said.

Eric eased into the comfy seat, splaying one leg over one of the massive arms. "So . . . when do we start?"

"Hold on there a minute. We have things to settle first." Miklos rolled his desk chair across the room closer to Eric. His welcoming smile slipped from his face. "This is not a democracy. It's a dictatorship. What I say goes. If you're late, and you don't have a good excuse, you will do extra work. Understand?"

"Yes."

"And you are to run the workouts exactly as I have written them—no changes unless I change it or we agree on a different way. But I'll have you know," he held Eric's gaze, "there won't be much discussion when it comes to workouts. Is that clear?"

"Yes."

"Good. Now we get to know each other."

"Like an interview?"

"Yes and no. I want to ask you a few questions. First, what is your goal for all of this?"

"To run a mile under 4:05 and get a scholarship."

"OK—a noble quest. Will I be able to help you?"

"I think so."

"Wrong answer. If you don't believe in your coach, you'll never reach your goal. Next question. Do you believe in yourself?"

"Yes."

"Do you believe in me?"

"Yes," Eric said, giggling a little.

"OK, now we understand each other." Miklos rolled his chair back to his desk. "Now, you told me that you had been accepted to Brevard and will start classes soon?"

"Yes, it's all set. I paid my tuition for this semester, and the financial aid office said I'd be eligible for assistance next spring."

"What about work?"

"I need to find another job. I can't go to school, do a construction job part-time, and still try to run. It's too exhausting."

"Have you started looking?" Miklos said.

"Some," Eric said. "But nothing serious yet. I told my plans to my boss, and he said I could work fewer hours if I needed to, but I'd prefer to have a job in Brevard, so I wouldn't have to commute."

"That's nice of him," Miklos said. "I've been mulling over your work arrangement too, and regarding what you just said, I may have a deal for you. I'm willing to lower your rent to make it easier for you to take part-time work. How does that sound?"

"That would help a lot. Do you know anyone here in town that needs a part-timer?

"I do. I have a friend who does cabinet work. He needs help in the afternoons and occasional weekends for installs. I spoke with him this morning, and he said he could use a guy with your skills."

"That's perfect. Thanks. So, wait, you had already decided to coach me before we even went to the track? This little mile test was just to make me sweat?"

"Something like that. I don't like to take on a runner until I've seen him run."

"How'd I do?"

"D for fitness and an A+ for effort, but your attitude needs work."

"I'll get on that, Coach."

"Also, you drink too much beer," Miklos added. "But we'll discuss your diet later." He stopped talking and smiled.

Eric's head spun as he tried to process the new information he had learned over the last two days. He walked across the room, pulled out the wood chair from under the card table, and sat down. "How come you didn't tell me sooner? I understand why you didn't want to talk about your family, but why not the running?"

Miklos's eyes widened at Eric's blunt query, but he nodded consent. "It might be because the running part still ties in with my California life. A poor excuse, no?" Miklos asked.

"Maybe. But I'm sure I'm ahead of you in that department with me running from my problems."

"I like your honesty," Miklos chuckled. "You might be right. I owe you a better explanation than that. Why don't you sit in the chair over in the corner; it's comfortable? My story might take time."

Eric crossed the room and sank back into the cushy chair.

Miklos rolled his chair a few inches closer to Eric, shifted in his seat, tilted back, and folded his hands in his lap. "I think you have to know my story from the beginning—starting with how I came to this country—for you to be able to see it all in perspective."

"It all began at the 1956 Olympics in Melbourne, Australia," Miklos said. "I was the assistant coach for Mihaly Igloi, and the Hungarian track and field team as well. At the time, our country was in the middle of a revolution, and the Soviet Union had entered our country to stop the uprising. Our Olympic team had left for the Games before the Russians arrived. So here we were in Australia with an invasion of our country happening back home."

Miklos then got up and pointed out pictures to Eric of Mihaly and Lazlo Tabori on the wall above his desk. He sat back down and continued to explain that when the Olympics had completed, Mihaly and Lazlo had decided to defect, along with forty-plus Hungarian athletes, many seeking asylum in the United States. Tabori was one of the three famous Hungarian milers, the two others being Sandor Iharos and Istvan Rozsavolgyi, all world record holders at various times.

Before Miklos and the team had left for Melbourne, he had wanted to defect as well. He had not discussed it with anyone at the time, except with his wife, and she agreed that if the opportunity arose, Miklos should go, even if she couldn't be with him. She had been willing to risk personal persecution for what Miklos might do. They had wanted a better life and a chance for freedom, both knowing his defection might be the only way. Miklos had been terrified, but he and his wife knew that staying in Hungary was not an option anymore.

Miklos paused, then turned in his chair to the mahogany-colored bureau, opened the drawer, and pulled out a photo album. He turned back around, then flipped open the album to a specific page, finding it in seconds, as though he had the scrapbook's contents memorized. He handed the open book to Eric, then pointed to a picture. "That was a few years after we defected. We'd settled in Los Angeles." Igloi, Tabori, and a younger Miklos were standing on a track in L.A. before a team workout.

Eric began to flip through the book, but assured Miklos that he was still listening.

Miklos laughed, then continued, saying that athletes would come from all over the U.S. to train with Igloi, and that Jim Beatty and Bob Schul were the most famous proponents of his training.

At the mention of the legendary runner Schul, Eric closed the book and listened more intently.

Miklos said Schul went on to use Igloi's training methods to design his own workouts. Schul coached and trained himself to victory in the Olympic 5,000-meter race at Tokyo. "That shows what kind of man he was," Miklos said, "strong of heart and character."

Miklos stayed with Igloi for a few more months, but because the coaching paid very little, he needed to find extra work. He worked odd jobs, anything he could find. And because companies in the U.S. wouldn't accept his degrees from Hungary, Miklos enrolled in Los Angeles Valley College to earn a teaching degree and improve his English.

His new life in America was going well, but he missed his wife and son terribly and had been working hard to get them out of Hungary. Finally, two years after his defection, he succeeded in getting them to the U.S. When they arrived, he continued coaching with Igloi another year until his teaching credits were completed, then left Igloi to take an assistant cross-country and track coaching position down south at a San Diego high school. Social studies and math were the subjects he taught, also noting that he'd always been good at math.

Eric shifted in his chair, sinking a little deeper, as though he were in a plush movie theater. Miklos's story was fascinating.

The head coach at the high school eventually left, hired away by a local junior college. The high school offered the position to Miklos.

Miklos gestured toward the wall of pictures and, in an uncharacteristic show of pride, said, "I guess you can tell I was successful." Then he winked, and gave the credit for his success away: "I learned much from Igloi, and I also studied other coaches like Woldemar Gerschler, Arthur Lydiard, Percy Cerutty, and Franz Stamphl. Over time, I developed my way."

"What *is* your way?" Eric asked.

"It's a secret," Miklos said, his eyes glowing with pride. "As for that picture of Tim on the wall . . . Yes, I had the fortunate experience of coaching the second high school runner to go under four minutes in the mile. He was a dedicated athlete. That was in 1966. Seven years later, I retired from coaching after my men's team won its eighth state title. In that last year, I only coached cross-country. I left the program in the hands of an excellent assistant coach, John Delaney. He had run here at Brevard College. That's how I came to know about this area."

"So, as I told you the other day, I came here with my wife after my son's accident. We stayed a week and fell in love with the town. We made tentative plans to move here when she recovered. But . . ." His voice trailed off, and he heaved a sigh. Then he picked up the picture of her he kept on his desk. He handed it to Eric. "Here's another photograph of my wife, Priscina."

"That's a nice picture. That's Looking Glass Falls behind her." Eric said.

"Correct." Miklos said.

And this is my son, Lazlo." Miklos handed him another picture off the desk. "We didn't name him after Lazlo Tabori. It was just a pleasant coincidence. Tabori was my favorite of the three Hungarian runners.

"Your son was a good-looking kid. He resembles you."

"That's what my wife always said. I always thought he looked more like her."

Eric handed the pictures back, and Miklos set them neatly in their respective places on the desk. Miklos cleared his throat. "Well, that's it. That's my story. I did skip a few boring details, but I can tell them later if you like."

"Sure. So that's when you bought the camp? And came here?"

"Right. And now I have another mouth to feed."

"Don't worry, I won't let you down," Eric said. He wrangled himself from the chair's deep cushions and got up. "I should go. You're probably tired after all this talking."

"I am a little tired—thanks, Eric. We'll talk more later."

Before he left the room, Eric said, "I've come to understand in the past few weeks that I can't do this by myself. I had some good runs, but I couldn't string together a real training routine. I didn't even know where to begin. I'm grateful that you're willing to help me. I'll do whatever you ask, Coach."

"You just run, Eric. I'll take care of the rest."

Chapter 32

In high school Eric had been a dedicated, persevering runner who never ceded to any athlete he faced. Despite his self-imposed exile, his competitive spirit had never disappeared, continuing to smolder deep inside him. Down in his semitropical paradise, his isolation from his family and friends had reminded him of what he cared about most. They were the missing puzzle pieces of his life's picture. Without the people he cared about—and who cared about him, too—he was incomplete. Running had also been missing from his life. Now it was back; he had been given a second chance. Still, Eric felt alone in his burden. In his high school years, living under his mother's roof, he'd had some financial security. Now he was on his own. His financial and athletic destiny landed squarely on his own shoulders, and if he should fail, there was no backup. Yes, he could move back in with his mother, but he wanted to determine his own destiny. Besides, he knew his mother had enough on her plate taking care of his brother.

He needed that scholarship . . . but he had to succeed to get it. Creeping doubts kept tapping him on the shoulder. Could he summon the same grit and determination he'd had in high school?

For two weeks now, Miklos had scheduled Eric for one long-distance run per day, that's all. While his summer mileage had rarely broken thirty-five miles a week, Eric believed he had enough fitness to start speed work and he felt Miklos was holding him back by scheduling only distance runs for his weekly routine. Eric craved intervals in any form—long, short, on the track or off, but anything fast. He wanted to train fast because the mile was fast—and so was racing it in four minutes and five seconds.

Miklos regimented Eric's training, requiring him to record his weight and his resting pulse rate when he woke in the morning and before he went to sleep at night. Miklos didn't track what Eric ate, but he told him if his weight didn't come down, he would monitor his meals too. And Eric had to be on time for practice, including any of the Saturday morning coaching meetings that Miklos required.

It was early September, and fall classes were in full swing. Eric was adjusting to college-level work, his semester starting with two quizzes the first week. College, he quickly learned, started with a bang, unlike the high school pace where students had more time between assignments and tests. He studied every night and on weekends. There was no time for goofing off. He could already see that college professors didn't coddle unprepared students. Monday through Friday his schedule was full—classes, work, running and study. Also, as part of his coaching agreement with Miklos, the two would sit down once a week and discuss Eric's upcoming workouts. During these meetings, Miklos also talked over Eric's college progress. His coach offered tutoring assistance if needed, reminding Eric that college came first, then running.

The next Saturday, Eric arrived on time for his meeting with Miklos—8:00 am sharp. He stood in the doorway to Miklos's "hall of fame" (though his new coach had frowned when he'd first heard Eric call it that).

Miklos was sitting at his desk with his back to Eric, writing in a notebook with a pencil. Eric rapped on the door frame, announcing his presence.

Miklos spun his chair to face him, still holding the pencil. "Come in, Eric," he said.

Eric stepped in and flung himself sideways into the armchair in the far corner, throwing his legs over one of the chair's arms. This was now his designated position in Miklos's office. "So boss, what's the plan for today?"

Miklos raised his eyebrows.

Eric straightened some in the chair. "Sorry. Morning, Coach."

"Morning to you too, Eric," Miklos said. Moving quickly to the business at hand, he said, "I've considered your idea about the North Carolina State Cross-Country Invitational over in Raleigh. October would be a good month to start racing, see where your fitness stands. I already called the coach. The course sounds flat and fast. The two-hundred-runner field should make it fun."

Eric's attention piqued, he moved to a more normal sitting position in the chair. "That's great, Coach. That will give me a month to prepare for it."

"Yes, we'll continue your weekly distance and threshold runs up to race day," Miklos said. "As I explained at our first practice, I want you to build a consistent practice routine and stay away from any form of intervals right now. I will use this race to gauge the starting point for your next round of training."

"But," Eric said, "can't we train hard for this race, then start over from there. If it's my only race, I want to make a good showing. I don't want to be embarrassed."

"Eric, you're not seeing the larger picture—"

"But Coach, you have this extensive experience—with the amazing Mihaly Igloi. He coached so many world record holders, right? You surely have the knowledge to whip me into shape and get me ready for that race. I want to run fast again. Can't we do it this one time?" Eric searched his mentor's eyes, but they were stolid and fixed. Miklos was tapping the eraser of his pencil into the palm of his hand. Eric had thought his compliments would eek a smile out of Miklos, but nothing.

"Eric, I appreciate your enthusiasm, but you have to let me coach you. Now is not the time for intense interval training for one race."

"Please, Coach," Eric moaned.

"You're awfully impertinent this morning, Eric."

"I'm not being—"

Miklos snapped his pencil down on his desk. He stood, glared at Eric, and said, "Go grab some water, or use the bathroom or whatever you need right now and meet me at my car in ten minutes. We're going to the track." He walked out of the room.

"Yes!" Eric said under his breath, jumping out of his seat. He was starting interval training with a highly successful coach. Eric couldn't wait to see how fast he'd become. But that glare from Miklos concerned him.

Miklos didn't say a word on the car trip over to the track. The silence made Eric feel like he was riding in a funeral hearse. He couldn't help but wonder what Miklos had in store for him. Would he have Eric run 8 X 440 or 4 X 880 or mile repeats? What was his secret strategy? Until now, Miklos had always explained Eric's workouts ahead of time. Miklos was a planner. He ran his camp with clockwork precision. Weekly, he prepared his camp staff for every positive or negative situation during the camping season.

When they arrived at the college parking lot, Miklos draped his stopwatch's blue lanyard around his neck, then adjusted his Aussie style cowboy hat. He grabbed the handle of a gallon thermos jug sitting on the seat next to him, and without a word got out of the car, shut the door firmly, and set off toward the track.

The morning was cool but not cold, and the sun was bright in the sky. The hot summer temperatures had not yet waned to the cooler fall climes. Today's early September high was to be eighty-five degrees.

After walking to the midpoint of the track's straightaway, his coach set the jug down on a small set of wooden bleachers and sat down. Eric stood before him, eager to learn Miklos's workout plan, hoping his new coach's mood was improving.

Miklos stood up. "Come with me," he said, walking across the track. Once they reached the grass at the inside edge of the track, Miklos stopped and faced Eric. "You are ready to start your training, no?"

"I am, Coach," Eric said.

"Ok, first thing. Give me your watch."

"My watch? Why? Can't I time myself?"

Miklos held out his hand. "No questions. Give it to me."

Eric unlatched the watch and handed it to Miklos, who pocketed it in his trousers. Miklos lowered the brim of his hat and exhaled a deep breath. "OK, your warm-up will be twenty minutes of easy running around the infield of the track. After you've done that, stretch for ten minutes. Next, do fifteen one hundred yard striders on the infield. Once you are finished, we will start."

That's not so bad, Eric thought. Not much different from any warm-up he had done in high school. He took off his T-shirt and chucked it to the infield, then turned to Miklos. "Hey, how will I know my twenty minutes is up? I don't have my watch."

Miklos grabbed his stopwatch and turned its face toward Eric. "I'll tell you when."

Eric was a little annoyed at Miklos's tone, but he put on a smile. "Oh, right. I'll see you in twenty." Eric took off to run his warm-up.

When Eric finished his last strider, he returned to Miklos for his instructions.

"OK, Eric," Miklos said, "here is your top-secret Igloi workout. The example I'm giving you is of a typical morning workout Igloi might have had his runners do. And, to keep this in perspective for you, his elite level runners trained twice a day. The afternoon workout was usually two hours long, not including the warm-up."

"Wow. OK," Eric said. "Sounds good. Will we train twice a day soon?"

"Slow down, Eric." Miklos said. "We'll get to that. Let's focus on today." He paused. "Here is what I want you to do. In total, you will run twenty full laps. It will be kind of like a structured fartlek run, where you vary the distances and pace."

"Sounds fun. Like my teammates and I did in high school over at Straus," Eric said.

"Yes, of course. But you won't be taking turns like you did with your teammates."

"I see," Eric said. "So, like a ladder of 440, 880, 1320, and mile and back down. Something like that?"

Miklos pulled out a folded piece of paper from his shirt pocket and handed it to Eric. "Not exactly."

Eric unfolded the paper.

Repetition Group:

4 x 110 yards, medium speed, 50-yard jog
2 x 150 yards, good speed, 100-yard jog
2 x 60 yards, hard speed, 100-yard jog

Jog between sets.

Complete five sets of the repetition group until approximately 20 laps are completed.

15 x 110 yard striders for warm-down.

Eric understood the sets and figured it shouldn't be too complicated, but he didn't grasp why Miklos had set no time goals for him. And what did *medium, good,* or *hard* speed mean? "Coach, aren't you supposed to give me times to run for these distances?" Eric asked. He handed the paper back to Miklos.

"There won't be any timing today," Miklos said. "You can determine your pace. Run whatever your current state of fitness can handle. Run whatever your body feels. And because this is your first time, you can walk between your reps instead of jogging if you wish."

Still a little confused, Eric asked, "If you're not timing me, why do you have your stopwatch?"

"It's for me," Miklos said. "I'll keep an eye on you and let you know if you're running too fast or too slow."

"I see," Eric said. Then rereading the workout sheet, he said, "Hey, Coach, what does, *medium, good,* and *hard* speed mean?"

Without a word, Miklos extended his hand for the workout sheet, and Eric handed it to him. Miklos folded the paper neatly, then stuffed it into his front shirt pocket and took off his dark Ray-Ban-style sunglasses, placing them in the same shirt pocket. And like a professor giving a student a textbook answer to a question that the professor expected the student to know already, he said, "Similar to what I said previously, you decide the pace for those general definitions."

Eric scrunched his face in confusion.

Miklos's face softened and he looked Eric in the eye. His voice softened too, regaining its friendly, *reassuring coach* tone: "Don't worry, Eric." He placed a hand on Eric's shoulder, steering him toward the starting line, "It's not as difficult as you think. You'll be fine."

"If you say so," Eric said, "I'm ready if you are."

"You can start anywhere on the track you want," Miklos said. "I'll put the water jug on the infield next to the first lane. By all means, drink some water if you need it. I may be demanding, but I'm not a sadist."

Eric launched into the set of 110's, cruising through them at a pace slightly faster than he might with some striders for his usual after-workout cooldown. For the next set of 150's he dialed up is pace, and after the second one his lungs were working hard, but he felt he could get through the 60-yarders by walking between sets as Miklos had allowed. The walk between repetitions helped, but it was after the second 60-yarder that both hamstrings of his quadriceps twinged, tightening with soreness. *I'm already in trouble,* he thought. From now on he decided he was not only going to walk between sets; he was going to slow down. He would not get through four more sets if he continued at this rate.

While Eric managed his way through the set, he busied his mind adding up the total distance for each group of repetitions. He came up with approximately 1460 yards, which was 300 yards shy of a mile, give or take a few yards here or there.

As Eric walked the 100-yard recovery before starting the next repetition, he looked over to the bleachers and noticed Miklos sitting there writing in his notepad, the blue lanyard of his stopwatch dangling outside his trouser pocket. Having no time reference was driving Eric crazy. He wasn't sure how fast to run. How fast was *medium* or *hard* or *good* speed? "Based on your current fitness," Miklos had said. But how would he know if someone wasn't timing his repetitions? He wanted a reference, especially after what he'd experienced with those two painful 60-yard bursts.

After a couple more laps around the track, walking past Miklos again, Eric got up some nerve and called out to his new absentee coach, "Miklos, are you going to coach me, or what? Can I get some times here?"

Miklos looked up from his notepad and said from behind his dark sunglasses, "You're doing fine. Keep it up." Miklos pulled his stopwatch out of his pocket and set it on the bleacher seat next to him.

Isn't this guy going to coach me? Man, he just pulled out that stopwatch to placate me. Pretend like he was doing something. Eric grunted as he started into the next set, his anger becoming as painful as his hamstrings. *Crap, I could've come out here and done this myself.*

When he reached ten laps—two-and-a-half miles—his legs were as tight as piano strings. And what made matters even worse was he didn't know how fast he was running. Was he paying the price for running his first set too quickly? His new normal was a pitiful pace barely faster than a brisk walk.

After another set of 60-yarders, Eric could no longer sprint. And the more his legs ached, the angrier he grew at Miklos, who still hadn't said a word, continuing to sit on the bleachers, watching.

The morning sun had risen fast, the heat of its infrared rays bearing down on Eric's shoulders. It couldn't be past ten thirty. But it felt like noon in the desert. Walking his subsequent recovery, Eric scooped up the water jug, unscrewed the top, took a quick swig, then poured half the jug's water over his head, the water sheeting across his skin, cooling him as the hot air barely wicked away excess body heat.

Twelve laps into his workout, Eric's body was officially toast, kaput, blasted. He had nothing left.

When he approached the end of his fourteenth circuit, Miklos walked out onto the track and said, "Time to stop."

Eric waved a hand at Miklos. "No, coach, I can do it . . . a few more laps."

Eric tried to continue, but Miklos grabbed his arm and pulled him over. Eric didn't resist, too exhausted for more of his false bravado.

Miklos handed him the water jug, the cap still off. Eric hefted the jug to his lips and gulped a few quick swigs. Next, he dumped most but not all the container's remaining water over his head. He walked over to the bleachers and sat heavy onto the aluminum seat. He set the jug in his lap, cradled his arms around it and stared catatonically toward the infield.

After a few moments, Miklos came over and sat down next to him. "How are you feeling?"

Eric turned his head slowly. "Coach, I'm totally blown. My legs are so sore."

"Eric," Miklos said, softly, "do you know why I had you do this workout today?"

"I think so," said Eric, now back to staring off into the middle distance.

"And why was that?"

"That I need to be patient and listen to what you tell me to do."

"Yes, that's true." Miklos took the water jug from Eric and handed him his T-shirt, which Eric put on. "I didn't make you do this workout out of spite. You are a talented runner, and when you put your mind to achieving your running goals, nothing else matters or gets in your way."

Eric motioned for the water jug. Miklos handed it to him, and Eric tipped it up and slugged down more water. He set the container back onto the ground next to the bleacher.

Miklos gently nudged Eric's knee for his full attention. "Listen, I have no doubt I can help you win your scholarship, but you have to let me do my job. Let me do the planning and worrying. You enjoy the running. I can teach you a lot, and right now I'm thrilled

I took you on as my new protégé . . .. I haven't been this excited in a long time. I've realized that I missed coaching."

At this moment, Eric understood Miklos's coaching style. He was all business, but he wasn't like one of those coaches who scream or rant to motivate you or shame you because you didn't do the workout as fast as expected. Miklos understood, and he didn't berate an athlete when he was down only to make a point.

"Thanks, Coach, I appreciate it."

"You're welcome," Miklos said. "One more thing. Listen to me carefully when I say this. There is no ultimate workout, and there is no perfect coach. Each athlete and coach must find out what works for them. And a runner doesn't have to do some maniacal 60-quarter workout to total exhaustion to achieve greatness. It makes for great fiction, but people in the real world don't work like that, and neither do I. And, you being exhausted from a workout that your body's not ready for won't make you succeed. It's consistency. And it's my job to keep you healthy. Remember, keep to the basics, never get ahead of yourself.

Eric smiled. "Understood, Coach. You know what—and I'm not being impertinent—but I'm really starving right now. Can we go to the Clock? I'm craving a triple stack of pancakes, sausage, and some eggs too."

Miklos laughed. "That would be a great idea."

Chapter 33

It was October and Eric was ready for his cross-country debut. During the previous two months of training with Miklos, Eric had adhered to his coach's strict running schedule and was consistently running fifty-five miles a week. Miklos continued to build Eric's weekly mileage slowly, but no interval training yet. For a few weeks now Miklos had him running some of his distance runs at a faster pace—*up-tempo*, as it was called in the running community. Miklos explained that he would use Eric's performance in the 10,000 meter cross-country race to determine his aerobic starting point. Eric chose Raleigh to make his debut partly because Trey would be there, but even more important, he wanted to watch Mary's race and afterward try to mend their tenuous relationship.

On Eric's first effort to reestablish communication with Mary, he, in classic *get-out-of-the-doghouse* fashion, had sent her a cheerful bouquet with a card and left several messages with her roommate. She'd finally called him back. With each successive conversation, her cheerfulness had emerged; it seemed the incident at the lake was slipping into the past, where it belonged. Still, he knew better than to resurrect the subject of her dating Trey. It was a sensitive issue between them now, and he wanted to keep her happy. The last time they'd spoken, she'd told him she looked forward to him coming to the meet and watching his race. He was relieved that their friendship seemed to be moving back on track.

Mary's 5K race started at 10:15 a.m., and Eric's 10K race was at 11:00. They had agreed not to meet up before the race to minimize their pre-event distractions. The mid season meet was a pivotal event for Mary's team. NC State was battling for the Women's Atlantic Coast Conference title this year, and beating top-ranked University of North Carolina here would give Mary's team confidence for the conference championships held in early November at Duke.

Eric was restless on the morning of the race and lonely. He searched the competition area for friends or competitors he might remember from high school. He found two familiar Asheville High runners and chatted with them for a while. Incidentally, he also bumped into Randy Wardlaw, who was now a freshman at Wake Forest, majoring in Computer Science. Eric apologized for his behavior after Wardlaw had beaten him in the two-mile race back in Eric's senior year. Wardlaw said he understood and appreciated Eric saying that. He told Eric he was glad to see him running again and wished him good luck. Afterward, Eric set out to find a spot to make camp. He secured a location close to a row of pine trees and spread out a towel in the soft, dry needles that had accumulated around the trunks. The location was strategic: he wanted to see Mary and her team, but stay in the shadows and be far enough away to remain unnoticed.

As Eric watched Mary talking with her coach and teammates, he realized she wouldn't have seen him anyway. She was laser focused on her team and their upcoming race which was thirty minutes away.

Later Eric went for a jog around the course to familiarize himself with the terrain. It was his first time competing on his own. He wished Miklos were here, but his coach had decided not to come. He wanted Eric to test himself alone.

As Eric neared the end of his twenty minute jog, he saw a group of runners in red warm-ups cresting a small hill in front of him. It was Trey Allison and the NC State men's team jogging their warm-up. The sight restoked Eric's competitive flames, blotting out his low spirits.

Eric respected Trey as a runner, but it was how the guy talked to people that bothered him. Trey was smug and cocky, and he wasn't shy about letting people know where they stood with him athletically. He always came across to Eric as a guy with something to prove, and he seemed unable to recognize other runners' talent. As Eric reviewed Trey's character faults in his mind, he landed on a memory of Mary saying similar things about Eric himself. He cringed at the thought that he might be as arrogant as Trey. Maybe Mary's judgments had been hyperbole; she could get that way when she was mad.

He sure hoped he would he be able to fix things with Mary. On the car ride over, he had practiced saying everything he wanted to tell her, but if Trey was around after the races were over, he'd have no alone time with her to be able to say it. As he finished his warm-up, Eric saw Mary and her team set off for the starting line. He followed to watch.

Eric watched the first mile of the women's race before he had to get back to the starting line area to check in for the men's race. Mary and her team were looking good; he saw a handful of red jerseys near the front.

Mary had a spectacular race. She showed off her superb closing speed by sprinting past three girls in the last hundred yards. Eric smiled, knowing he had been on the losing end of her lightning quick leg turnover many a time. He noted that her team's top five runners had finished in the first fifteen places out of the two hundred-plus runners that started. The impressive placings gave them an excellent chance to win the competitive invitational. Her team's accomplishment wired them with excitement. They jumped up and down exchanging generous high fives. Mary had improved since high school—faster and stronger now, a consummate leader for her team. She had, in fact, been elected team captain this year.

With his race only minutes away, Eric's stomach became uneasy. He didn't mind, though. Without those prerace qualms, he might as well knot the laces of his spike's together and heave them up onto a power line to hang for eternity. Losing that apprehensive reminder meant that he lacked the drive and determination to push his body to its limits—the supreme desire to win. He cared how he performed, and without this emotional trepidation, he would merely go through the motions.

The 6.2 mile course he would be running today wasn't challenging. It was flat, and the one part that might present any challenge was a wooded area with a few twists and turns. *This should be a fast one,* he thought.

Miklos had given Eric strict instructions not to push the pace. Because a six-mile race was twice the length of his high school races, Miklos gave him a reasonable per-mile pace to aim for. He said the longer-distance races took patience and an even tempo to succeed.

Eric found the starting line at one end of the school's practice field. He navigated his way through a sea of thinly clad competitors milling around their chalked starting boxes. He found his assigned starting box, the last slot on one end; the rest of the teams were on Eric's right. A man using a bullhorn bellowed the final call for the athletes to assemble at the start line. As the teams lined up in their respective places, runners sprinted out and back from their assigned positions trying to shake out the last of their pre-race nerves. Coaches gave last-minute instructions to their teams before retreating a few yards up the sidelines to wait, their stopwatch buttons poised with anxious fingers. Eric's assigned starting position was for runners not associated with a college team. Three other runners joined him. Two wore generic running clothes and looked to be non-scholarship runners from the college who wanted a chance to run a collegiate race. The third looked like the African runner Eric had seen on the unattached runner list. The Kenyan was slim and wiry and looked like he could run on a feather. Eric felt heavy standing next to him. Through his singlet, Eric pinched a small roll of fat on his abdomen. He had come a long way, but Miklos said he still had seven more pounds to shed.

"So, are you on the Richard Simmons diet?" an accented voice said behind him.

Eric turned and saw the Kenyan smiling good-naturedly. He decided not to take offense. "Oh, my fat. That's a good joke." He smiled back. "My weight is coming down, but I'm not there yet. I only started training a couple of months ago."

"I'm Jonathan Kogo."

"I'm Eric Roberts." They shook hands. "Hey, haven't I seen you in a running magazine. Aren't you a road racer? What are you doing in a cross-country race?" Eric said, half joking. He knew from the score of running magazine articles he had read that many of world's elite runners participated in cross-country races occasionally. Unfortunately, they couldn't make a living running on the softer surface. Road racing was where the money was.

"My coach wanted me off the pavement for a while. A change of pace." he said, "It's part of my coach's long-term plan."

"Well, good luck."

"You too."

Eric resumed his position and eyed the long straightaway. He flicked a sideways glance across the line of runners. They looked just like he felt, agitated with energy and impatience, pacing and shaking tension from their muscles. The runners were crammed together, multiple rows deep, two or three men wide, in their narrow, five-foot starting boxes. Called forward by the starter, the multitude drew toward the chalked line as one shapeless mob. Frozen to stillness by the starter's subtle pause, the swarm of runners was then released by the blast of the gun. Eric lunged forward, trading elbows with his fellow competitors, the front-runners, all grappling to gain the best position before the first turn. The pack rumbled past the spectators like a pack of wild beasts fleeing hunters. The ground's vibrations reverberated through the soles of his spikes.

Eric and the other competitors made a diagonal beeline for an orange cone at the far-right corner of the rectangular practice field a hundred and twenty yards away. The gangly, horde would make one full loop around the perimeter of the field before they would exit through one of the field's chain-link gates. He found himself on the extreme left of the starting field, but he was content with his position. He had avoided the middle crush and would have to deal with only a few people on his right side when they approached the first bend. The fleet-footed racers continued trading elbows. Some runners had to lean into shoulders of other competitors trying to stay upright as the throng slowed for the first ninety-degree turn. Eric and the other competitors crushed tight around the marker but finished the turn unscathed. After completing the field's circuit, they filed out through a small gate.

Having escaped the field without incident, Eric found himself in the front group—a position he always liked—with Kogo cruising next to him. *I'm not supposed to be here,* Eric reminded himself. *I'm supposed to stay back and relax.* But he pushed the thought aside. He had fallen into the typical procedure for a cross-country race—go out fast, secure a good position, and settle into a bearable pace. Challenging the elite front-runners was acceptable for the seasoned, well-trained hierarchy expected to claim one of the top spots, but Eric wasn't one of those runners yet. Miklos wanted him to hang back and run a steady first three miles, and if he had the reserves to do it, ratchet up the pace after the fourth mile.

There was another half mile of open ground before the course took a right turn into some trees. Despite the brisk first-mile tempo, Eric found it difficult to hold back his fluid stride. An intense competitor, he never wanted to be the straggler in the herd. But he reminded himself of his coach's orders and throttled back his pace. He drifted back, letting the faster runners pass.

Suddenly someone jolted his right shoulder, knocking him off his stride. "Roberts . . . Trying to race with the big boys?" someone said in his ear.

It was Trey Allison, along with the rest of the NC State team in tow. Eric restrained himself, saying nothing. Trey let some of his teammates pass while he kept pace with Eric. "Take it easy," Trey said. "Don't want to break that ankle again." He pushed ahead to catch his team. Kogo continued commanding the pack fifteen yards farther ahead.

Another quarter-mile passed as Eric watched the crimson jerseys of the State team diminish in the distance. Like a bull to a red flag, unable to collar his pride and pace himself as his coach had instructed, Eric grunted and sped off after the Matador—Trey Allison.

Kogo set the race tempo by escorting the pack through the first mile. As Eric closed the gap between him and Trey's teammates, he heard the coaches and course timers yell 4:45 as the first group passed them. Eric came through at 5:00.

By the time Eric had caught the tail end of the front pack, the Kenyan had surged off the front. Eric guessed Kogo's time separation from the front pack was ten seconds now. Eric held his spot for another quarter-mile before sprinting to a front position next to Trey.

"Roberts, you again?" Trey needled him.

"Thought you . . . needed . . . the help," Eric managed.

"Better have the legs."

A minute later, Kogo drifted back to the group. Eric was skeptical. Kogo couldn't be tired. He must be surging, testing his fitness and recovery, or trying to soften up his competition. His suspicions proved correct. Shortly after taunting the lead group with his presence, Kogo charged away, putting a good fifteen yards between him and the pack. Trey and Eric looked at each other. Trey nodded in the lead runner's direction. "Go for it." Despite Eric's redlined, anaerobic battle to stay with the lead group—and even though he knew better—he couldn't resist. He burst out to catch the Kenyan.

Kogo's eyes widened when he noticed that Eric had become his new companion. *Well, hell,* Eric thought. *I'm shocked that I'm here, too.* Kogo threw Eric repeated inspections. A quarter mile later, the Kenyan took off again. When Eric responded and caught him, Kogo returned to a reasonable pace. *This isn't so bad,* Eric thought, convinced his fitness was holding, as he ignored the raspy wheeze starting to whistle out of his mouth. Again, Kogo blasted off. Eric matched Kogo's surge and hung on intrepidly for another hundred yards, but the Kenyan's last blast doomed him. By the time the three-mile mark approached, the Kenyan had carved a thirty-yard gap between them. Eric glanced back. The main pack was closing on him. When Kogo crossed the three-mile mark, Eric heard the timer's faint call: 14:30.

Eric came through ten seconds later, and as he did, he took an opportunity to assess the damage he'd done to himself. He wanted to glance back, but the increasing rumbles of footfalls hitting the back of his ears told him that the pack was on his heels.

"Done already?" Trey chirped as he sped past.

Eric's pace faltered, dropping back through the pack like a lead weight falling to the ocean floor. He had run three miles faster than his body could handle, especially at this stage in his training. And now, approaching energy bankruptcy, he still had another three miles to go. It wasn't how he had imagined today's race. Now he would suffer these last three miles like the end of a bad marathon. And Eric had experienced a bad marathon. He had entered one in his junior year, but lacking the full appreciation of the distance and his physical limits, he had gone out too fast, and his body had bonked at mile eighteen. Interminable was the appropriate description for those the last eight miles. *Miklos is going to kill me,* he thought.

Eric had at least one bright spot in this race. Randy Wardlaw had kindly patted Eric on the back as he passed him and said, "Keep it going, Eric." Considering how Eric had treated him two years prior, Randy's kindness helped make his embarrassment tolerable. Well, at least until he faced Miklos's wrath.

And what would Eric say to Miklos? *Sorry Coach, I couldn't help myself. I had to show Trey how fast I was.* Eric had to learn to control himself. If he were to achieve his 4:05 mile goal, he would have to rein in his impatience. Back in high school, he ran in the front of his races, but he was playing with the A-league boys now. College runners at this level had equal or better talent than Eric.

A mile later, Eric realized the way he felt was no blown-up marathon ending. It was more like an exhausted husky in the

Iditarod race, trudging through deep snow with a sled in tow. But even worse than his exhaustion was his emotional embarrassment. He stared straight ahead, not looking spectators in the eye when he passed them.

When he finally crossed the finish, some kind spectators threw him some "Atta boy" and "Good job" comments, but there was no thrill. He missed the intoxication of winning.

He noted his unspectacular time with a frown and headed for the water table.

After his body settled and he had downed some fluids, Eric dashed off to gather his things and set out to find Mary. He checked the area where her team had camped out, but her teammates said she was with her parents. He caught sight of her walking through a back gate onto the practice field with her track bag slung across her shoulder. He raced across the field to catch up with her.

They exchanged nervous greetings. Then, to move the conversation forward, Eric asked how her team had finished.

"We got a two-point victory over North Carolina." But then Mary switched the subject and asked why he had gone out so fast in his race. Eric shrugged, not sure himself, but said that he wasn't looking forward to his next conversation with Miklos.

Mary giggled but assured him he'd figure it out.

They walked together in silence along the fence line of the practice field. He stopped her and turned. "Mary," he began, his stomach knotted like before his races, "I want to tell you something . . ."

"I'm not seeing Trey anymore," she blurted.

The breakup surprised him, and yet he was relieved. Eric had thought Mary and Trey were close. When Eric had spoken with her the last couple of times, Mary had never let on that anything was wrong between her and Trey. "What happened?"

"Come on, let's sit down," Mary said, and she led him to metal bleachers near the fence. "Before I tell you, I want to say something. I know you think Trey's a jerk and everything, but he's a good guy. He has his flaws, sure, but so does everyone."

"I still don't see how you could date a guy like that."

"Eric—you don't understand. You need to step into another person's shoes before you can criticize. He's had a rough life. His mother ran off with another man when Trey was little, so his dad had to raise him on his own."

"I didn't know that," Eric said.

"And," Mary continued, "his dad was a former track star in high school and college. He lives vicariously through Trey and has pushed him into running since he was a kid. Trey has thought of quitting; running isn't fun for him anymore."

"If he's such a good guy, though, how come you're not together?" Eric said.

Mary looked away, tapping her hand nervously against her thigh. "He almost hit me."

"See—"

"No, Eric," she cut him off. "You're judging again."

"OK, OK," Eric said. He stiffened and inched back to give her space.

Her voice calmed. "Trey said he's never hit anybody. His anger seems to revolve around his father. He's revealed a little to me about their relationship, and I won't go into specifics right now, but I can say they don't see eye to eye right now."

"What happened between you two?" Eric said.

"It was on a Friday," Mary said, "at a party at one of the frat houses. He got jealous that I was talking to a guy for a long time. Back in my dorm room, he confronted me. We started yelling at each other, and he raised his hand. The second he did it he jerked it back and apologized. I could tell that he felt horrible, but later, as we talked, I discovered that I didn't love him—and not because he almost hit me. We weren't on the same page. We split up that night."

Eric thought back to the night before the Asheville track meet back when they were in high school and her boyfriend Parker had broken up with her. Here Eric was again talking to her about another breakup. Though, this time she wasn't asking for Eric's comfort or consolation. Was he just another one of her *disappointments* in a long line of failed relationships? "Speaking of lousy guys, Mary, why do you put up with me? I've been a real pain these last few years. How come we're still friends?"

"You know why," she said, clapping a hand on his thigh. She jumped up, grabbed his hands and pulled him up to her. "It's because, Eric, you try hard. When someone finally gets through your hard head," she said, tapping her pointer finger on Eric's forehead, "you try to change. Maybe not as fast as that person would like, but you do. That's a beautiful trait. A lot of people can't or won't do that."

Eric loved how Mary could wrap up a compliment inside of a personal assessment; how could you dispute your faults when the imperfection was what she endeared about you.

"Listen, Mary. I'm sorry about you and Trey. It's not for me to judge. It's like you said, I'm sure he's a good guy underneath."

"Thank you. If you want to know the truth, though, we didn't mesh well anyway. I thought about ending it last summer, but for some reason I stuck around."

"I want to tell you something," Eric started. His mind swirled with everything he had coached himself to say to her. "I had this big speech planned, but now I'm not sure I need to say it."

She leaned in closer, Eric sensing she was already two steps ahead. She had always been like that. Would he ever catch up?

"Tell me," she said softly.

Eric paused, focusing on a runner doing his warm-down run. He returned his gaze to her eyes. "First, I know I apologized to you on the phone when we started talking again, but I want to tell you again, in person." Eric's words were flying out of his mouth like he was rushing to tell a 911 operator that his house was on fire. He held Mary's gaze a moment longer, letting her beautiful green eyes settle him. "I'm sorry about what I said at the party and nearly getting into a fight with Trey. It was rude and reckless. The guy may have said a crappy thing a few years back, but I didn't need to confront him. I should have been the better man; I should have let it go."

Mary waited.

This is so hard, Eric thought. But just like the last three miles, he had to keep going. "Second, I think I've figured everything out. Why you and I have always fought so much . . . It was mostly my fault, though, I'll admit . . . it's that . . ."

Mary's eyes opened wider.

". . . a selfish part of me doesn't want anyone else to be with you. I never understood it until recently. You've always been there through all my idiocy, more than I deserve, I'm sure."

"That's not the most romantic line I've ever heard, but it'll do. I love you too, Eric Roberts," Mary said, reaching her arms around his shoulders and hugging him tight. "You know," she whispered in his ear, "you may not be the smartest guy at times, but you do always manage to come around.

Chapter 34

After Eric had returned home the day after the Raleigh cross-country meet he gave Miklos the news about his race. Eric's first words were, "I went out too fast, and I blew up." Miklos replied, "It seems your running fitness is *still* not the only thing we need to work on." His coach said no more. He pulled out a writing pad and pencil and wrote down any race time-splits Eric could recall. Miklos then sent Eric out for a distance run and told him to come back to his office after he was done. When Eric returned, Miklos handed him a sheet of paper listing his next four weeks of training. He also said that running the forest trails would be off limits. Eric's training would be restricted the road and grass—and some occasional workouts on the track, for now.

From that mid-October until the end of December, his coach had focused on developing Eric's anaerobic threshold level, which included performing intervals of a half mile or longer. His coach timed his splits as he did tempo runs along the valley roads, and long intervals in Straus Park. And for a change of pace, he took Eric over to the college for mile repeats around the cornfields. But Eric's favorite workout was doing half-mile intervals around the scenic lake in the back section of Straus Park.

There also was one other road workout that Eric had found devilishly hard and fun in a masochistic sort way. Miklos would drive out to a certain location a few miles from the camp and Eric would run there to meet him as part of his warm-up. For the workout, Miklos would give Eric the distance for the next interval and at what time. Miklos would drive the interval's length and stop to call out the time when Eric arrived. As the workout progressed, Miklos would vary the distance and time goal of each repetition. This workout was a total length of twelve miles. Eric loved the challenge of trying to meet his coach's expectations.

In a blink the Christmas season had past, Eric and Mary had rung-in 1982 at Donnelley's pub, and Eric's first Indoor track season was a week away. Mary was to drive back to Raleigh from her winter break on Sunday, January third.

On the Saturday before Mary's departure, she and Eric were walking back to Mary's house after a trip to the Cardinal for a soda and chocolate soft-serve cone. The sky was a crisp blue, and the afternoon sun warmed their faces. The two were sharing their treats, Eric holding the soda and Mary the ice cream.

Despite the five hour car-trip between them, Eric and Mary had managed their distant relationship as best they could. Eric wrote letters regularly, and they alternated long-distance phone calls every other week.

"It was nice spending the day with you," Mary said. "And I really liked running with you again. Can you believe it's 1982 already?"

"I know. Where'd the time go?" Eric said.

"The holidays flew by too," she said. "I wish I didn't have to go back to school already."

"We had a good break, didn't we?" Eric said. "I have to go back to school, too—just not as far away as you do. You should transfer."

"Ha, ha. Me repeat my first two years of college just to babysit you? Good luck on that, bud."

Eric suddenly realized how ludicrous his statement had been, even in jest. He wished they weren't so far apart. He wanted to be with her and not five hours away.

She placed the cone near Eric's mouth for a bite. "You know, it's too bad we won't have any indoor meets together."

"That would be cool if we did," Eric said. "Miklos decided to keep the indoor schedule closer to home, partly because we can't afford to travel far. But mainly he wants me to race in smaller venues, so there is less pressure—so I can get my feet wet with racing and winning again. And Miklos also said he wants me to execute different race tactics this indoor season—like running from behind and not always taking the lead, pushing the pace. He keeps telling me I need to learn patience."

"You think?" Mary said. "He's turning out to be a good coach, huh?"

"He has a different approach than I'm familiar with," Eric said, "but it's growing on me."

They turned the corner at Main Street and approached the sidewalk bench where he and Mary's confrontation had taken place two years earlier.

They turned at the same instant and looked at each other. Eric spoke first. "Seeing that bench used to give me chills, but now it reminds me not to run away from my problems."

Her eyes softened into a smile.

Eric pulled her to him with his free arm, "I guess the next time I'll see you is on spring break? Or are you going down to the beach?"

"I'll try to get home for a few days, but I have a meet that week. Can you believe that? There should be a rule—no college sports on spring break."

Eric laughed and held out the soda for her to sip. Eric then asked Mary for a bite of the chocolate soft serve. She put the cone in front of Eric's face. As he leaned forward to bite, she pulled it away but still held it close to his lips. He tried again, but she continued the tease.

"Ah, so you're going to play that game!"

"Teaching you patience."

"That's not patience. That's cruelty." Eric swiped at the cone, but she jerked it away and sprinted down the sidewalk.

"You better eat that cone now, Mary," Eric said playfully, sprinting after her. "'Cause' I'm going to push it in your face!"

She glanced back, and when she saw him gaining on her, she screamed, turned, threw the cone at him, and kept on sprinting.

Chapter 35

During Eric's eight-week indoor track campaign, January through February, Miklos had entered him in four meets, while he spent the other nonracing weeks busting his butt training. After his first indoor race, he had told Miklos his legs had no zip. But it didn't take long for his speed and turnover to come back to him. He won two of his three remaining races. The victories had been a confidence boost. And because he had gone to smaller, less competitive indoor meets, Eric wasn't stressed and could focus on his performance and training.

Eric had enjoyed his first indoor track season. More important, he was thrilled to be "treading the boards" for the first time. He had heard that description used by the sportscasters on televised indoor track meets. Wood was the first surface used for indoor tracks, and the moniker had stuck even after rubberized versions had replaced the timbered constructions.

Eric's first indoor meet was at the University of Tennessee at an ALL-COMER's meet the track program held for smaller colleges. Chills bristled his skin the moment he stepped onto the 176 yard, flat oval. He couldn't wait to lace up his spikes. The 10-laps-to-the-mile track was located inside the college basketball team's Stokely Athletic Center. The track's rubber surface circumscribed the basketball court on the cement floor. The track had no banked curves like the ovals he'd seen on TV, but the style of construction didn't matter; he was racing again.

Rodney, who was attending Tennessee on scholarship, promised to come by and see Eric at the track meet. Unfortunately, Rodney had track practice that day and was unable to catch Eric's race. They pledged to catch up again at Tennessee's home invitational track meet this coming April, which, Miklos had scheduled Eric to attend.

A few weeks later he and Miklos traveled to Virginia Tech. Eric ran on an old wooden track that the school had purchased and reassembled in its Field House. With banked curves and eleven laps to the mile, it also sported a coated rubber surface. The bouncy plywood construction had its quirks, with some sections firmer than others, causing an occasional wobbly leg give-out, jolting a runner's rhythm. Other than that, the old track was a blast to race on.

Eric had known that the indoor season was not the time to peak. He would focus on his outdoor season results. At the end of February, after his fourth indoor race, he had told his coach he was eager to begin to his outdoor crusade. His best indoor mile time took place at his new favorite venue: the bouncy Virginia Tech track. His 4:12 there had been great motivation entering the outdoor season.

By the time Eric's indoor season had ended, he realized he had changed more than he had anticipated. Under Miklos's supervision and profound coaching expertise, he had reaped the benefit of the wisdom that came with his mentor's age and experience. With Miklos's encouragement, Eric was limiting his drinking to special occasions and had begun eating healthier meals that included more fruits and vegetables. He had also followed Miklos's suggestion that he purchase a breakfast and lunch meal plan at the college cafeteria so he wouldn't have to spend time cooking. Eric was beginning to feel like he had a grandfather and father all wrapped into one.

March began Eric's outdoor season, and the weeks flew by as quickly as the indoor season had, with no regard for whether Eric wanted it to or not. In the remaining months until the end of May, Eric tried to make each day count.

During this time, Eric spent more of his daily workouts on the track relative to his previous indoor training regimen, which generally included longer intervals on the roads around town or out at Straus Park. Miklos explained to Eric that his track workout designs combined what he had learned from his mentor Mihaly Igloi including his experience coaching his eight state champion teams in California. Eric slowly had come to accept whatever type of workout Miklos chose to have him perform. It didn't matter; he had to trust his coach. And, so far, Miklos was delivering as promised. Eric's heart-rate recovery was lowering each week. One test Miklos liked to use to test Eric's fitness was a timed 8 X 440-yard workout with only a 50 yard jog between reps. Eric executed the interval session two weeks ago, and his average interval split for each 440 rep had dropped by an average of two seconds. He was making great progress.

By the end of March, Eric had whittled his mile time down to four minutes and ten seconds. Another time drop came shortly after, on the first weekend of April at a large college invitational at the University of Tennessee. He placed sixth in the mile with a time of 4:08. That was only 3 seconds above his target. This performance resonated with Eric for one reason other than the improved time. From the gun, Eric had struggled to handle the race leader's pace. When the pack began the fourth and final lap, Eric was in eleventh place, trailing a group of eight runners. Thirty yards off the front were two dominant sub-four-minute milers assured to win the race. When Eric's pack approached the middle backstretch, the sprinting began, and the group strung out. With 250 yards remaining, Eric still held the eleventh place, still struggling to improve his position. Desperate for motivation, Eric glanced across the infield at Miklos standing by the finish line. He remembered what his coach had preached during their training sessions: *Training the mind is as vital as the body.* Eric eyed the line of runners and set his sights on the last one. He said to himself, *Get one, then the next.* To Eric's surprise, he reeled in five runners within the final half lap. To secure the sixth spot, he inched past one last runner at the finish line. His closing burst in those crucial yards blew his mind. Eric had never dug that deep before. Afterward, he felt he could summon that courage again. *Success begat success,* Eric thought.

The Monday after the Tennessee race Miklos summoned Eric to his office to discuss his future meet schedule. Eric found his coach digging through a morass of papers—what looked to be schedules and notes—on his desk. He sported a heavy tweed sweater and beside him was a half-full cup of tea with a squeezed lemon wedge lying in the saucer.

"Hey Miklos, what's with the heavy sweater?" Eric asked as he approached the desk. "Are you sick?"

Miklos slumped back in his chair and took a sip of his tea. "I'm OK. It's only a little chill. Some hot tea and lemon and a good night's sleep should take care of it."

"OK, if you say so," Eric said reluctantly.

Miklos slid a piece of paper across the desk closer to Eric. "Well, I've checked, and it's as I suspected—we've sort of run out of meets for April. For the time being, at least."

"It's because of the conference meets, isn't it?" Eric asked, pulling out the chair from the card table.

"Yes. The meets are restricted to college athletes only; you cannot run unattached." Miklos tapped at a spot on the piece of paper. "But, here's the *sort of* part. I called around, and there's one meet in Greenville in two weeks that should do the trick. The coach down there is trying to raise money for a new track."

Eric pulled the page closer to read the smaller print. "They've invited a bunch of top-caliber runners, including Steve Oberlin." Both Miklos and Eric were well aware that Oberlin was the national record holder in the mile. "Oh, man, that is so cool. I would love to meet him."

"I feel that's the race where you could make your 4:05," Miklos said, now leaning his elbows on his desk. "I've never been one to over-prognosticate for my runners, but this race should have the right caliber of competition to push you to a higher level. Plus, right now, it's the best I could find."

"That's OK by me," Eric said. "And it's close by, too. We can go down that morning." But the impending finality of his coach's findings made his blood rise. "Coach, what if I don't make the time in Greenville? Are there any meets after that?"

"That's a good question," Miklos said. "After the conference meets, the athletes who qualified for the regional contests go to those. The runners who haven't qualified *can* go to 'last chance' meets."

"Does that mean what I think it means?" Eric asked.

"Let me elaborate. Any runner can go to the regional meet if they can beat the NCAA qualifying time standard. If a runner accomplishes that goal at a sanctioned meet, he can take part in the Regional contest. And of course, the runner must better the mark before the deadline to send in his entry.

For now, there's only enough time after your Greenville meet to fit in another contest before the schools have go to their regionals. And yes, that means you will have only one more shot after Greenville.

Many times in the previous eight months Eric had contemplated the finality of his quest. The day after Coach Winters had set Eric's goal date, Eric ripped out May from his calendar, circled the thirty-first and had pinned it to the wall next to his bed. Now the approaching climax of his nine-month journey sobered him. He couldn't fathom where the time had gone. Only last August Miklos had given him his initial mile test, and now May was around the corner.

Miklos handed him a paper he'd fished out of the pile. Eric scanned the document.

"Raleigh! My last chance race could be in Raleigh? That seems appropriate, I guess. But isn't there anywhere else I could go?"

"There is one at Georgia Tech, the same week, but if you don't make your goal in Greenville, I recommend the Raleigh, NC State meet."

"Why's that?" Eric asked.

"I'll tell you in a minute," Miklos said. He stood and began pacing around the room like a college professor. "As you know, a coach instructs and mentors an athlete through each facet of training: intervals, rest, recovery, and so on. But a coach must also nurture the psychological component of a runner's athletic performances."

"I love it when you start talking like a professor, Miklos. All you need is a podium in front of you."

"Shh, I'm on a roll. Listen to me." He continued his lecture. "Athletes' performances are often driven by the stage setting. Running the mile in Oslo, Norway, for example, is a big deal. Why? Because the runners know the conditions and atmosphere are conducive for a world record attempt. That's why so many athletes set records there."

"I understand. But how does this apply to me?"

"It applies to you, Eric," Miklos said, "because racing at NC State in front of your potential new coach, with everything on the line, could make the two- or three-second difference in your time. I don't think you'll push as hard if you race at Georgia Tech. High stakes are what can truly make a runner's effort great."

"Good point. But I hope it doesn't come down to that."

"Me either. I'm sure the Greenville race will be the one."

Chapter 36

The Monday before the Greenville race, Eric and Miklos had planned to meet at the college track at 4:30 p.m. for an interval workout. The weather was cold, but the morning drizzle had stopped after lunch. Eric called from a pay phone inside the Student Union and reported to Miklos that a few wet spots remained in the first lane, but the standing water should pose no problems. He knew from experience that Brevard's track had one drawback in rainy weather; over the years the asphalt-coated surface had become so hard and smooth, it was slick as ice when wet. But Eric planned on using an old pair of gum-rubber-soled racing shoes he had used in high school. They would help his feet stick to the slippery surface—at least until the rains returned. For now, the track was usable, with only a few puddles to navigate.

As Eric waited for Miklos, he sat on the bleachers next to the track, one leg straightened along the metal bench as he reached for his toe. Then the other leg When he heard the slam of a car door, he eyed his wristwatch; it was 4:40 p.m. In what felt like minutes, Miklos shuffled the fifty yards from the parking lot to the track. He stepped onto the black asphalt clutching an umbrella in one hand and his favorite stopwatch in the other.

"You all right, Coach?" Eric asked. "You look pale." He wanted to tease Miklos about being late, but he sensed this wasn't the time. He knew Miklos had been in and out of bed all week, but his mentor downplayed it, even though Eric had urged him to see a doctor. Miklos had insisted that it was only a cold, nothing to bother about.

"I'm fine, Eric. I'm sorry I'm late—I fell asleep." Then Miklos broke into a coughing fit.

When the coughing settled, Eric said, "We can try another time if you're not up to it." He was concerned now. He'd never seen his coach this sickly before.

It's only a cough," Miklos said in a dry, gravelly voice.

"But I—"

"I'll be *fine*," he said firmly. "Now let's get started." He hacked a few more times, propped his umbrella against one leg, and pulled his jacket tighter around his waist, zipping it to his collar. He lowered the front brim of his Western-style hat before searching his jacket pocket. He pulled out a small sheet of paper and handed it to Eric:

6 x 330 - 3 medium, 3 hard effort, 100 yard jog
4 x 440 - in 62 seconds, 150 yard jog
8 x 220 - 2 easy, 4 medium effort, 2 hard, 100 yard jog
1 x 880 - in 2:04, 440 jog
2 x 440 - under 58 seconds

Eric studied the paper and then handed it back to Miklos. "OK, Coach. I'm ready." The length and times of the workout would be the most challenging interval set he had done since they'd started training together. But Eric trusted Miklos. If he wanted Eric to do this, then he would do his best.

As the workout progressed, Eric experienced normal fatigue and accelerating lactic acid levels in his legs—but it wasn't until after the end of the 880 yard repetition that doubts crept into his mind. Hellish demons of anaerobic-bankruptcy were raging through is body and mind, especially in his beleaguered legs. Eric knew the quarter-mile repeats under fifty-eight seconds would be a challenge. He feared he would let his coach down if he couldn't match his goal times. When he returned after his one-lap recovery jog, he asked Miklos if he could skip the last two. "My legs are toast."

"No, you must finish this!" Miklos erupted. "You have to suffer before you can savor victory." His eyes had reddened, and his face appeared more gaunt than usual. Eric wanted to ask how he was feeling but decided not to agitate him by asking again. Clearly Miklos didn't want to talk about it. This was the most on-edge Eric had ever seen him.

"To the line," Miklos commanded.

Eric stepped forward, placed his left foot near the line. Miklos gave the command, and a touch less than fifty-eight seconds later, Eric crossed the line. The drizzle returned, small puddles appearing on the track's surface. Eric paced until Miklos ordered him to the line for the final circuit.

"Coach, I can't—"

Miklos turned, his red eyes narrowed, "You will," he commanded. "If you want your scholarship, you will do this."

Eric gave Miklos a cold stare, but he walked to the line, crouched into his starting position, teetering some, then steadied himself. *"Focus, Eric, focus,"* he whispered to himself. Dog-tired as he was, this was when he appreciated Miklos; this was what coaches were for—to help you push beyond what you could achieve on your own.

Eric charged down the track for the last grueling interval, concentrating on one hundred yards at a time. To mentally conquer this lap, he pictured himself running the anchor leg of a mile-relay race. Eric visualized a phantom competitor, ten yards ahead, laying down a fiendish pace. He knew that in a relay race some pacing restraint was necessary or you might blow up. Pacing? Who was he kidding? There wasn't time for sensibility. Numbing lactic acid had invaded every cell of his body, and he was on the verge of mental and physical bankruptcy. He drove into the last half circuit hell-bent on vanquishing the demons raging inside him. They smelled blood and were dancing around Eric as he lay prostrate on the sacrificial alter, chanting, "Quit! Quit! Quit!" *Die, was the better word—but no matter, the savages had to go!*

Almost there. Only a few hundred left. Don't let 'em win, Eric.

Nearing the finish, he felt like a Clydesdale horse clomping down the last fifteen yards—strong and powerful but slow. He lifted and drove his legs while striving to keep his posture upright and not pitch backward from exhaustion. A few hundredths of a second counts in some races, and poor posture would make the difference between winning and losing more times than not. He always had to remind himself of that, no matter how many intervals or races he ran.

Eric broke his imaginary finish line, edging out his phantom competitor, then mentally tossed his invisible baton to the infield.

"Fifty-seven point two seconds," Miklos said.

No Eric Roberts sacrifice today, he thought.

"Well done," Miklos said. His scowl was gone and replaced by an approving smile. Yet, his buoyed expression could not hide his reddened eyes, which seemed to have sunk deeper in their sockets. "Walk a lap, then run a mile for a warm-down."

After a quarter-mile walk, Eric began his warm-down at a trudging pace. He clasped both hands on top of his head and continued plodding, stumbling now and then from exhaustion.

Eric took great pride in having finished the two quarters under the 58 second goal Miklos had set for him. In the last nine months, Miklos had pushed Eric to near exhaustion only two times. The first was a long-distance interval session on the roads around the valley in December. It totaled fifteen miles that day. And the next was a track interval session the week after the indoor season had completed. Miklos had explained that he pushed an athlete when needed or to test his limits. The goal was to measure where his runner stood regarding the training plan. Maybe today's workout was a mental test, not solely physical. Eric curled a smile, thinking about his accomplishment.

He could picture himself sleeping heavy and contented in his warm soft bed. He was looking forward to that.

A lap into his mile warm-down, heavy droplets replaced the soft drizzle, showering Eric in a cold downpour. He continued to plod, his feet slipping and sliding in waterlogged shoes.

Approaching the finish of his warm-down, Eric looked over toward Miklos sitting on the bleachers. His coach was slumped over, with his umbrella flipped over on the ground. Eric bolted across the infield.

He grabbed Miklos's shoulders. "Coach, what's wrong?"

Miklos mumbled but didn't move.

"Coach!" Eric yelled. He lifted Miklos's face. His coach's languid eyes rolled to the back of his head.

What do I do? Eric thought. He could call for an ambulance. There was a pay phone in the gym nearby, but Eric's money was in his car. That would take too long. He had to get Miklos to the hospital fast.

Eric sat down beside Miklos and grabbed his coach's jacket in his fists and pulled him to a sitting position. Miklos groaned. The unsettling thought that Miklos might be dying darkened Eric's mind. *Could he get him up,* he wondered? Eric's heart rate was skittering higher from panic. Exhaustion from his workout was gripping him, wobbly legs and his body weak, completely out of energy. *Should he go and get someone to help? No,* he thought. *There was no time.*

Eric stood, turned, bent over and wrapped his arms around his coach's chest. He then straddled his legs either side of Miklos and painfully drove his aching quads upward hefting him to his feet. He moved to one side and slipped one of Miklos's arms around his shoulder. Miklos still couldn't lift his head to level. Eric gently tilted Miklos's head up to look into his eyes. "Come on, Miklos. I need you to walk." To his surprise Miklos responded, and as if Eric were the coach now—pushing Miklos to do more than he thought possible— Eric saw strength come to his coach's legs and a bit of lucidity to his eyes. "OK, we got this, Coach," Eric said and guided him toward the parking lot. Miklos's larger car would be better suited to the situation than his little VW, so he searched his coach's pockets until he found the keys. Miklos kept muttering, his breathing labored. Eric eased him into the passenger side of the car. He ignored the sheeting rain strafing his eyes. Rushing Miklos to the hospital was his only concern.

The car's enormous V-8 engine rumbled to life, and Eric yanked the steering column lever into reverse. The drivetrain clunked, and the vehicle launched backward out of the parking space. He dropped it into drive, the tires whining on the wet pavement. The rubber eventually caught and sent the old behemoth roaring out of the parking lot. Miklos had now slumped halfway down the bench seat, his head back, his shallow breath scratching like sandpaper on wood. "It's going to be OK, Miklos. It's going to be OK."

Eric breathed in halts and gasps, unconsciously mimicking his coach's dire condition. His muscles were taut from his super jacked adrenaline; he felt like he could lift a car off the ground.

The car's defogger was broken, and vaporizing rainwater was collecting on the inside of the windshield, obscuring Eric's view into the the rain-darkened twilight. He wiped his hand at the glass, trying to clear the fog. He peered out through the opening he'd made as the car screamed down the rain-slicked roads. The hulking vehicle devoured the asphalt as the centerline became one white blur. Fortunate for him and Miklos, the hospital was less than a mile from the track.

Eric guided the car to a screeching halt near the emergency room door, missing the overhang's supports by a few feet. A doctor came running out. Eric recognized Charles Doughton—the doctor who had attended to his ankle the night Buzzy died.

Doughton called to the nurse inside the lobby for some attendants. He pulled open the door. "Miklos!"

Miklos mumbled something inaudible. "We'll fix you up, Miklos," Doughton said.

Two attendants swept around the doctor and eased Miklos out of the car, laying him on a gurney. Eric watched from behind.

"Is he going to be all right?" Eric said, through chattering teeth.

"We'll do our best," the doctor replied. "But we have to get him inside quickly. I'll let you know soon. Meanwhile, go inside and ask the nurse for a blanket. You're shivering." He raced off into the emergency room.

Eric steered the car into the nearest parking spot, turned off the engine, and sat there for a moment. The rain beating against the car's roof was loud, nearly drowning out his thoughts. He said a prayer for Miklos, then jumped out and sprinted through the torrent into the hospital.

The nurse at the front desk gave him a blanket and a towel to dry off. Afterward, Eric called his mother from a pay phone to explain the situation and ask if she could bring some dry clothes.

She arrived quickly, laden with bags. "I brought you some of your brother's clothes," she said, handing him a plastic bag.

Eric's eyes fell on the brown paper bag in her other hand. "What's in there?" he asked. She didn't have to answer. As soon as he heard the clinking glass of a casserole dish, he knew what it was.

"Mom, you gotta stop doing this. I can make food for myself. I still have the food you brought me last week."

"I can't help it. You're my boy—I care about you getting a good meal."

"All right. I surrender," Eric said. "I'm going down the hallway to change."

Doctors and nurses came and went at a furious pace. Finally, Dr. Doughton came out. He glanced over at Eric before dropping papers off at the nurse's desk.

Dr. Doughton walked toward them. Eric and his mother rose, she holding tight onto Eric's arm. Haggard from the stress and the workout only added to Eric's dread. As the doctor approached, panic at what the doctor would say, drove Eric's heart rate higher again. The doctor's initial expression was grave, but started to smile as he took his last few steps.

"So how is he, Doc?" Eric asked.

"He's going to be all right."

Eric sighed relief.

"But he's still in critical condition," the physician said.

"I have a specialist coming to look at him in the morning. We may have to move him to Asheville if his case is critical. The pneumonia, I mean."

"Pneumonia?" Eric asked. "What does that mean?"

"We're not sure if the type is bacterial or viral, so we'll have to send test cultures to a lab to find out the specifics before we know what's going on."

"Can we see him?" Eric asked.

"I'm sorry, but no. Miklos is still semi-conscious and could be that way for a while. I can't allow any visitors right now."

Eric let out a heavy sigh. "I understand. When then?"

"I don't know yet—but leave your phone number with the nurse at the desk. I'll have someone call you when we have a status update." He paused. "I'm sorry I have to rush off. I still have to finish his paperwork so we can process his tests as soon as possible."

"Thanks, Doc," Eric said.

"You're welcome," Dr. Doughton said. "It's good to see you back home Eric. Heard you were running again. Your ankle doing OK?"

"It's good, Doc. Glad to be home too."

"Great. OK," the doctor said. "I better be going."

Eric stared through the window into the room where the attendants had taken Miklos. He caught glimpses of his gaunt face until a nurse walked into the room, hung an IV bag on its pole, turned, and drew the curtain across the window.

Eric's mother slipped an arm around him. "Don't worry, Honey. It'll be all right, you'll see."

"I hope so, Mom."

Eric's grandfather had passed in a matter of days from pneumonia, but he did his best to push that thought out of his mind. He had lost two essential men in his life already. He couldn't bear losing another.

Chapter 37

On Saturday morning before Eric began his drive down the mountain for the Greenville track meet, he stopped at the nearest gas station and picked up a copy of the *Greenville News*. He searched the sports section and found a four-column article about the meet. The feature reported that the race would include ten runners, besides Oberlin, listing their names and personal bests, ranging from 4:02 to 4:15. Eric fit in the middle of that group, at 4:08. The college's head track coach, Riley Johnson, was quoted as saying they were "fortunate to secure a group of talented milers for the race, which will, of course, improve the chances of a sub–four-minute time." The coach went on to explain that a sub-four had never been run in the state of South Carolina, and having Steve Oberlin at this track meet definitely improved that chance. Apparently, Oberlin was preparing for his summer racing season and was looking forward to this low-key race as the perfect preparation for a big meet the following month. He said his performance here would help him and his coach develop further training plans.

The article thrilled Eric. Having the opportunity to race side by side with a present-day American legend was a once-in-a-lifetime moment. As he steered his car down the winding mountain road toward Greenville, he focused on his race plans, but found it hard to concentrate, his thoughts drifting to Miklos. Eric wished his mile race was to be broadcast on the radio. Then Miklos could at least hear the play-by-play. Eric could picture the ABC sportscaster Jim McKay as the perfect person to call the race, using his steady, storytelling cadence to bring the race to life. Even as Eric daydreamed, he was keenly aware of the empty spot Miklos had left in his heart, as well as the empty passenger seat, where Miklos should be sitting right now. If he were there next to Eric, he'd be talking strategy for the upcoming race. Miklos would indulge in *what-ifs* and tactics for hours on end if Eric would let him. These thoughts put a smile on Eric's face and helped restore his enthusiasm.

It had been a tough week for Eric following Miklos's collapse. Monday night, when he had returned home late from the hospital, he was exhausted from his intense workout and emotionally spent from seeing Miklos so helpless. He wanted nothing more than to crawl into bed, but he couldn't. He had to study for an algebra test he had the next morning. He fought to keep his eyes open until he was confident he would pass his exam.

The next morning, his sore muscles begged for more rest, but he dragged himself out of bed and got to school just in time for his test. Throughout the exam, thoughts of Miklos jockeyed for Eric's attention, but he reined in his focus again and again. As soon as the test was over, he went to the student union to call the hospital and found out Miklos had already been transferred to Asheville, precisely as Dr. Doughton had anticipated. With this physical distance added to the mix, Eric felt Miklos slipping from his grasp.

With a low-level sense of dread in his gut, Eric headed home after lunch and crawled back into bed for a much-needed nap. When he rose, he dressed and headed out for an easy seven miler to flush the ache out of his muscles. During the run, Eric felt like his tank was half-empty. When he came to the long uphill that led to downtown Brevard, he slogged his aching legs up the incline, his shoes barley lifting off the pavement. Once he finally reached the crossroads, he stopped to hang his heels off the sidewalk's curb to stretch his calves. After a few moments, he sat down on a bench near the gas station, the infamous spot where he and Mary had fought moments before he'd left for South Carolina. Despite the bench's minimalist construction, Eric's exhausted body sank into it as though it were a comfy sofa.

For a moment the downtown traffic was nonexistent. Practically glued to the bench, Eric bent forward, allowing his back muscles to elongate. Then he grabbed his ankles to further stretch his lower back. Had Miklos worked him out too hard before such an important race this week? Would his body recover in time for the meet? What was Eric going to do for workouts the rest of the week in Miklos's absence? A wave of uncertainty swept through him, and for a moment Eric doubted this entire endeavor—not just the Greenville Race but running at all. Why had he even thought to take this sport up again? What if Miklos didn't make it? How would he ever manage on his own? An image flashed into his head of tossing all his running gear into the box of old sporting equipment in his closet.

Feeling more defeated than he had in months, Eric rose slowly and eased back into his run. He had to get back home to study for another school exam.

On the way back to the camp Eric stopped for some water at the fountain in the Brevard College gym. As he walked through the entrance hall, he passed row upon row of championship plaques, records, and trophies mounted on the walls. When he came to the track and cross-country team awards and photographs, he paused for a closer look. There was a picture of Coach Winters standing between his two Junior College All-American runners just after the cross-country national championships in 1979. Again, Eric's mind went to Miklos. In truth, Miklos had been in his thoughts nonstop since his coach had collapsed. As he gazed at the photo, he had a new understanding of his sense of defeat. He wasn't questioning his own fitness and readiness for the upcoming race. He was concerned about someone other than himself. It was the first time he had ever allowed himself to care genuinely about, and even depend on, another person. And the fear of losing that was excruciating. He truly needed Miklos.

Standing before the picture of those two Brevard runners and their proud coach, Eric knew he couldn't quit. He knew his coach would say, "Hey, don't worry about me. Go race. Have fun. Focus on your goal." Eric had to find a way to flip on his mental switch and find positive thoughts for his upcoming race. If he couldn't do it for himself, he had to do it for Miklos.

The rest of the week, Eric developed his workouts as best he could. The sessions he designed were light and restful, as Miklos would have prescribed, yet without coach there they were still mental torture. His focus did wane through the week, but he got the job done. His legs were feeling loose, his body relaxed; he had done an adequate job for his Saturday meet.

The private college hosting the track meet was situated eighteen miles northeast of downtown Greenville. Eric drove his car through the college's open iron gates. He drove slowly through the campus's tree-lined streets, getting lost on the sprawling property until he flagged down a campus security officer on a bicycle for directions to the track. Once at the parking area for the track, he found the lot spilling over with cars. Luckily, he nabbed a spot just as another car backed out of it.

Usually college track meets had few spectators other than parents or students, but the American track superstar, Oberlin, was there with his star power, attracting a larger number of college track alumni and fans. The newspaper article Eric had read mentioned that the school's athletic administration had been happy to pay Oberlin's travel expenses and fees. They would more than recover the costs from the expected jump in alumni donations.

The parking lot was situated two hundred feet from one end of the track's oval and was elevated some fifty feet above. Eric walked a gravel pathway from the parking lot that led down through two practice fields that perched above the track. Along the full length of the embankment down from the practice fields, the crowd had staked out the grassy slope that bordered the track. Blankets and coolers covered nearly every square foot. And numerous pop-up canopies were stationed in one row along the top edge of the hill.

Eric descended the slope toward the track. The spring weather was cooperating that day, relatively warm considering the blanket of gray sky. The wind was lightly brushing the leaves of the nearby trees. He was psyched by the excellent racing conditions; he couldn't have asked for a better day to break 4:05.

He had arrived a couple of hours before the start of his one o'clock race. The field events were nearly completed. As he crossed the track toward the infield, he noticed that the track's white lane lines were faded, and in a few spots, only traces of paint were visible. He dropped his gear in the grassy infield and took a lap jog in lane one to see how the surface felt under his feet. The textured rubber surface in the center of the lane, about two feet in width, had been worn down and was less springy than the rest of the track. He knew if he were running in this lane he couldn't entirely avoid the worn area, especially on the turns, but overall, he didn't think the dilapidated lane one would pose a problem for his race.

An hour later Eric started his warm-up routine: a mile-long jog, stretching, another two miles, and more stretching and resting—ending with ten hundred-yard sprints down the middle of the infield to raise his heart rate and loosen his legs.

After he finished his warm-up routine, he sat down on the infield grass to put on his spikes while the 440 relay races were finishing up. His event was after the relays.

In the time after Eric had arrived at the track, the size of the crowd had increased. He looked at the road that led up to the parking area and saw it was now lined with cars as far as he could see. The school's colors peppered the crowd's apparel like a field full of purple and white daisies.

When the runners of the final relay race crossed the finish line, the meet announcer started into his spiel, laying it on thick for the marquee event: the mile. He briefly introduced the dean of the college and the alumni director, then went straight into his mile-race buildup. Despite Eric's prerace nerves, he couldn't help but enjoy the entertainment. "The mile is our main event today," the announcer said, stretching his words and giving long pauses for dramatic affect. "We have the U.S. mile record holder here, *and* he is ready to go sub-four. It will be four grueling laps, but we have assembled *ten* talented milers to help him do it . . ." The announcer's over-the-top reference made Eric chuckle; he knew Oberlin really didn't need any help to go under four minutes, but the announcer's pitch was effective. A swath of purple-clad spectators had crowded the outer curb of the eight-lane track and gave a roar at the announcer's every prompt.

Once the announcer had worked the crowd up, he summoned the runners, one by one, to the starting line, introducing each by name and their personal best time in the mile race. The order was from the slowest to the fastest. The announcer called Eric to the track. He was ranked fifth fastest in the field of ten. Eric threw off his sweats and jogged to the starting line, taking his place in the growing row of runners pacing nervously next to the curved line. The crowd gave obligatory cheers with each runner's name called. When Steve Oberlin jogged onto the track, they roared loud. Oberlin waved and smiled while the announcer recounted his running stats and accomplishments.

Steve Oberlin took his spot in lane one. His short brown hair framed his broad, angular face, and his smile was bright and engaging. Oberlin did not have the archetypal build of a lithe distance runner. This American record holder's shoulders were expansive and muscular, his arms and legs powerful. Eric was an inch shorter than the six-foot-one Oberlin, and while Eric shared a similar muscularity, he was smaller. Seeing Oberlin up close for the first time intimidated him a bit. The well-tanned Oberlin looked like a thoroughbred stallion, a temporary captive in his lane-one starting gate. The bell would sound, the gates would fly open, and he'd gallop away—this Secretariat—as the trailing herd of triple-crown posers struggled to keep up.

And yet, here the guy was completely relaxed. Eric knew this was a low-key race for him, but couldn't he at least fake some nervousness? Eric's temples started throbbing. He placed three fingers on the carotid artery of his neck. Pulse seemed ok, but his chest felt tight. Was he too anxious? *The anaconda?* Nah! *C'mon, Eric. Focus on you, not on Oberlin or the crowd.* He wanted to take a strider up the track to loosen up, but it was too late. The starter was walking toward them, about to give the runners their starting instructions before sending them on their way.

Eric glanced over the line of runners on either side of him. They looked calmer than he would expect. Of course, like Eric, they were enlisted to help Oberlin; this race being about raising money for a new track—and setting a new SC state record in the mile, if possible; they didn't have a deadline to meet; they didn't have to run a 4:05 . . .

"Gentlemen," the lanky starter said in a thick but light-hearted Southern drawl. "Take one step back from the parabola and stand tall." The curved starting line—coined a *waterfall* start in the track community—was designed to give the runners an equal angular distance to the beginning of the first turn. A few runners laughed, but Eric did not, trying to remain focused and calm. Maybe this race was a low-key affair for the other guys, but it was all business for Eric.

The runners retreated a step.

"Go, Eric! Go," a woman's voice cried, barely audible among the crowd's cacophony of shouted names. *Does someone know me here?* Eric thought, then forced his focus back to the starter, who was now saying, "Runners to the line." The starter was pointing his left arm directly at them, then raised his right orange-sheathed arm vertical, a firm grip on a black pistol.

The runners quickly shuffled forward and settled, Eric being the last to the line.

The gun fired.

"Ughh!" Eric groaned.

A bony elbow had crushed into Eric's right rib cage, knocking him leftward into the adjacent runner who shouted multiple expletives. The elbowing runner on the right continued his physical pressure, crossing Eric's path, halting Eric's momentum as the mob drove for lane one. Eric hoped the guy to his left would give way, but no chance. It was always dog-eat-dog at the start of a race; fair was fair, so long as you didn't hold on to somebody's jersey or intentionally trip someone. The runner on the left threw a forearm back across Eric's chest. The door to the front had closed. Eric himself cussed. How had he let that happen?

OK. He was at the back. Now what? Getting to the front wasn't impossible, Eric knew, but a long sprint on the outside of this fast-moving pack wasn't smart right now. He'd expend precious energy reserves needed for his fourth lap drive to the finish.

When the field was halfway into the first lap, someone called out time splits, ". . . twenty-seven . . . twenty-eight . . ." *Too fast!* Eric thought.

As the pack swept into the next turn, Eric tried to turn off his anger and frustration—anger at his bad start and frustration at the pace and the fact that Miklos wasn't there. He was here by himself, not one friend or family member in the crowd to root him on. He tried to put all that out of his mind. *Big deal, you're racing alone. C'mon, Eric, forget about it.*

He considered slowing his pace, conserving some energy, but if he did, he'd lose crucial contact with the pack, thus losing the energy savings he got by drafting behind them. So, he'd have to endure, see how this race played out. There were still three and a half laps to run.

The timer called out the first lap splits as the pack entered lap two, ". . . sixty-one, sixty-two, sixty-three . . ." Thankfully the pace had slowed some. Oberlin was leading the race with one runner on his right, matching him stride for stride. The remaining milers filed in behind, stacked up in lanes one and two, except for one brave soul, who was out in the third lane running near the front. The guy was either very strong, or he had simply gotten caught outside and didn't want to drift back and lose his spot. There were so many choices a miler had to make in such a fast-paced race. Every race was different; you had to play the cards you were dealt.

Despite the speed-induced lactic acid rising in Eric's body, his stride felt powerful and his steps light. The bad start was behind him. He knew if Miklos were here, he'd be standing over at the second turn—his favorite spot to watch Eric at outdoor track meets—giving his runner a cautioning wave, letting him know to relax. When the pack started to exit the second turn, Eric saw a man standing near the edge of the outside lane. Imagining the guy could be Miklos, Eric pictured his mentor looking down at his silver stopwatch, then giving him a palms-down wave, cautioning him to relax. Eric lowered his shoulders a tad to ease their tightness, then focused on minimal upper-body motion, just letting the legs do their work.

Entering the back straight of lap two, Eric decided now was a good time to get to the front before the pack got stretched out and he fell farther from the lead. He swung wide, out to the third lane. The surge came easy, his quarter inch pin-spikes getting good traction off the old rubber surface; the familiar scratch, scratch, scratch was music to Eric's ears. Heads turned to see who was streaking past. Ten yards before the back straight curved into the third turn, Eric flicked five or six quick strides, then, with barley a one-step lead over the race leaders, including Oberlin, Eric dove left in front of them all, securing lane one's open track. Using his surge's momentum, he put two yards on them before settling down. He was really psyched now. He was in front and loved setting the pace. He could run free, unencumbered, not suffer the sudden pace changes among the trailing runners jockeying for positions.

A new running partner showed up on Eric's right shoulder. It was Oberlin, who'd wasted no time marking the new guy at the front. Out of the corner of Eric's eye he saw Oberlin giving him a close inspection. Eric shot him an *I'm ready to race* look.

Across the track, Eric heard the announcer going wild: "Folks, after a daring sprint down the back straight, we have a new runner at the front . . ." He paused, then came back. "I've been told, it's Eric Roberts of Brevard, North Carolina. He has a previous best of 4:08. C'mon folks. Give him a cheer." The crowd roared on cue. Eric started inching in front of Oberlin. *Easy, big fella, easy!* he told himself. *You're not running for the crowd.*

Just as Eric pulled the pack onto the second lap's homestretch, he glanced back, eyeing the runners in the curve. The pack was stretching out, twenty yards, he guessed. He was glad not to be riding the caboose anymore. At this stage of his race, the only thing that worried him was if his second-lap surge would cost him. Had he just taken a wheel off the wagon?

". . . two o-three . . . two o-four . . ." the timer called, when Eric and Oberlin approached the end of lap two.

A sixty-second 440 for Eric. Not bad, but here came the third lap. If his muscle reserves were depleting too fast, this next lap would be ugly. Doing the easy calculation, he knew he couldn't afford to lose more than four seconds off his pace, or he'd have to run the last 440 in 57 or 58 seconds to get his 4:05. He wasn't sure if he could do that. The fastest he'd ever turned a final lap was a 59 when he'd run a 4:10 mile a month earlier.

Boom. There it was. Eric knew this was coming. A few steps into the next lap, Oberlin blasted away from the field as though Eric and the other runners were standing still. Eric hesitated, holding his pace. Should he stay or should he go? By the time he took off after Oberlin, the guy had already pushed twenty yards ahead. Two milers sprinted around Eric and quickly bridged the gap, settling in behind the American record holder. Eric soon realized it was a foolhardy mistake to go after Oberlin. He made another quick calculation. Oberlin needed to run at least a 1:57 for the next two laps to equal four minutes for the mile, which Eric knew the guy could easily do. But Oberlin wasn't just going to flirt with four minutes, he would go under in a big way. Maybe not an American record 3:49 way, but likely 3:55 or so: and that meant he would be running a 57-second per-lap pace. Eric was not that fast a runner.

"Folks there it is," the announcer said. "That wonderful grace and speed. Oberlin's going need to run a sub-two-minute last half mile to get under four minutes. Cheer him on folks!"

As Eric rounded turn two of the third lap, he searched for the Miklos stand-in he'd noted earlier; he was gone. *Keep this lap steady, Eric. Hold your pace.*

For the next half lap, Eric ran alone in no-man's land between Oberlin's chasers now thirty yards ahead and three others hounding

Eric ten yards back—and closing. Was he slowing or were they running faster? He wasn't sure, his whole body duller now.

Ding-Ding-Ding!

The bell sounded the start of the final lap for the race leader, Oberlin of course. Eric wished he were up there too. He was like all competitors; they all dreamed of winning the great race. It was wishful thinking. Oberlin had at least forty yards on Eric now.

"Wow, folks," the announcer boomed, "Oberlin just clocked a 57 on that last lap. He just came through at three minutes! What do you think, folks, is he going to do it? Will he set our new state record?" The whipped-up crowd was maniacal, sounding larger than it was. Eric could barely hear the runners behind him . . . until: "Huff, huff, huff—scratch, scratch, scratch . . ." *They're on me now!* One runner took a spot on Eric's right. Eric heard the steps and heavy breaths of other runners right behind him.

"Three o-six . . ." the timer called, when Eric completed lap three.

That was 63 for the third lap split. *Not too bad, Eric. You need to turn a 59 to get the 4:05. You can do this . . .* He flashed on how tired he had been at the Tennessee meet, how he willed himself to run faster than his body wanted. *You're feeling way better than that right now.* He glanced left and saw Oberlin almost halfway round the turn. The two runners chasing Oberlin were still twenty yards ahead of Eric but looked to be tiring, each casting frequent backward glances. To catch them in the next half lap would be Eric's first goal.

When Eric was ten yards into the final lap, a young boy's voice pierced the din of the crowd. "Go Ewic! Go."

Eric snapped his head right. In the split second as he flew past the crowd, he caught a glimpse of a blond-headed boy at the edge of the track, his tiny fist raised high.

It's not Buzzy, Eric assured himself, and yet his chest was tightening. Then two palms jolted Eric's shoulder blades. "Keep your pace!" the runner behind him yelled. Their strides tangled. Eric stumbled forward but kept upright, immediately adjusting his leg turnover back to race pace. But Eric was washed in fatigue, and his chest was as tight as ever. It was the dreaded anaconda, and it had a death grip on him.

His lungs were pulling hard, as though sucking wind through a straw. Oddly, his legs felt fresh, his stride even, circling swiftly, powerful, like the pistons of a well-balanced engine, his feet tapping lightly on the track's surface, but he couldn't go faster. The runners in front of him were pulling away easily. And, to make matters worse, Eric heard the footfalls of more runners behind him. Out of the 11 runners who started the race, five were in front of Eric and four behind.

The previous night, unable to sleep, Eric had lain awake picturing today's brilliant final lap and his subsequent conquering of the 4:05 mile. He knew if he could picture it, he could do it. This was no Tennessee mile. There was a force pressing him harder. He was helpless, as though there were an RPM limiter on his heart, slowing him down.

Running the last 440 of this race was like watching a slow-motion picture. As each trailing runner passed him, his chest tightened further. By the time Eric reached the home straight, a hundred yards remaining, the last runner in the race finally passed him. Eric was now dead last.

He looked up the track and saw Oberlin crossing the finish line, undoubtedly well under four minutes, the crowd screaming wildly, others setting off ear-piercing air horns.

As Eric gutted out his last hundred yards, he could see the finish line area exploding with Oberlin fans. A different voice, not the buoyant race announcer, implored the fans for restraint and to keep the track clear, but his words fell on deaf ears. Finish line officials had to spread out on the track, making a human chain to cordon off the finish area so Eric could complete his race. But the coaches were overmatched. The swell of fans increased so fast that Eric practically had to squeeze through lane one to cross the finish line.

Eric crossed the line in a time of 4:18. He then fought his way through the crowd, making his way over to his gear on the other side of the track. He paced in one spot, eyes closed, head back, trying to calm himself, to break the anaconda's grip and get his breathing back to normal.

Once Eric had gathered himself, he sat down on the field and tried to make sense of what had just happened. He'd thought he had overcome the whole Buzzy affair. Was it going to haunt him forever? Would it always crop up at some unexpected moment? And why now? Why of all days did it have to be today?

Before Eric started for home, he decided there was something he had to do first. He wanted to find the little boy and his mother. He wasn't sure what he'd say, or even if he would speak to them at all, but he had to find them.

He walked over toward the corner of turn one, where he had first seen them. He searched the crowd on the way. There were plenty of people moving about, likely returning to their spots after the Oberlin mania had dialed down. The meet officials had finally cleared the track and the next scheduled race had started. Eric walked back and forth the length of the infield, searching the crowd. Finally, a group of people moved and Eric saw them, the boy and his mother, along with a guy he recognized from the race. He had forgotten until now that this other guy was named Eric too. He had heard about the talented Spartanburg, South Carolina, runner back in high school. He was the runner lined up two spots away from Eric on the starting line. He remembered his wavy blond hair from the race; he was the guy who had run into Eric's back.

Eric watched for a moment. The little kid was chattering away, his hands pointing, gesturing like he was recounting the race, telling the other Eric his favorite parts.

Eric walked toward them. The closer he got, the more he felt the presence of the anaconda again, and his hands shook a little. He stopped, took a big breath, briefly closed his eyes, and exhaled slowly. Then he approached the small group and introduced himself. He exchanged pleasantries with the other Eric. He congratulated him on his race and apologized for their encounter, promising that it would never happen again.

Eric then asked his namesake about his little friend. The little guy turned out to be the other Eric's nephew.

Eric looked down at the young man. "Hello, my name is Eric too."

Unhesitant, the little boy stuck his hand out and said, "I'm Jewwy."

Eric reached down and gently clasped the tiny hand. "Nice to meet you, Jerry. You must be very proud of Eric here."

"I am," said the boy, giggling, suddenly shy, letting go of his mother's hand and wrapping himself around his uncle like the boy at the gas station and his mother. Eric nodded toward the little boy's uncle. "He's a great runner." Eric made more small talk about running before saying goodbye.

That wasn't so bad, he thought. The anaconda uncoiled from his chest and slithered away.

As Eric walked across the field in the direction of his car, someone tugged his shoulder. He turned and found himself face to face with his hero, along with two autograph seekers waiting close by.

"Hi, Steve Oberlin," the winner said, extending his hand.

Eric returned the handshake. "I'm Eric Roberts."

"I liked that move you made today—gutsy! You had me worried for a second, but what happened?"

Eric explained he was trying to make a comeback from a broken ankle and earn a scholarship. *And trying to keep the snakes at bay,* he thought to himself. "Guess it just wasn't my day," he said.

Oberlin put his hand on Eric's shoulder. "Hey, you looked good out there. Put today behind you. I know you'll make that goal of yours."

"Thanks," Eric said. "That means a lot."

Then he watched as Oberlin made his way to his sponsor's tent to sign autographs.

Eric had considered asking Oberlin for an autograph, but right now there was something more pressing on his mind.

CHAPTER 38

Instead of driving the winding mountain road home after his Greenville race, Eric took the flatter, longer way around, but instead of cutting back through Hendersonville as usual, he continued north on the interstate toward Asheville.

"Hello, how may I help you?" said the woman at the hospital's front desk greeting Eric in her slow, friendly drawl. Eric recognized her voice; she was the woman he had spoken with each time he had called this past week.

"Hi. My name is Eric Roberts. I came by to visit Miklos Ionnos."

"Oh, yes, Mr. Roberts, I'm glad you're here. Did you get my message this morning?"

"Sorry, I didn't. I was at a track meet," Eric said. "I came straight here afterward. Is everything OK?"

"Yes, yes," she said. "I called to tell you that Mr. Ionnos can have visitors now. I'll let the doctor know you're here." She picked up the phone and dialed.

"Dr. Jansen be out shortly, she shouldn't be long, Mr. Roberts," the receptionist told him after hanging up. "Have a seat if you like." She gestured to a row of uncomfortable-looking plastic chairs along one side of the lobby.

The doctor came out within a few minutes. "I'm glad you came, Eric," she said. "Mr. Ionnos expressly asked for you. I've been informed he has no relatives here. He said you rent an apartment from him, correct?"

"Yes."

"He has improved much these last few days. He should be able to go home in a week. He's making great progress. We'll move him to a regular hospital bed on Monday. I'm sorry I had to restrict visitation for this long, but his critical condition warranted the quarantine; he was going in and out of consciousness until today. But he has stabilized now. I'm happy you're here. He kept asking for you. He kept mentioning some mile race . . ."

"Yes, I was at a track meet today."

"How did you do?"

"Thank you for asking," Eric said, "but can I tell you later, Doc.".

"Sure. I know you're eager to see him," she said. "I can only allow a visit of half an hour. He's still drowsy from his medication and might not be able to hold much of a conversation. Also, his breathing is still labored."

"I will, Doc. I won't stay too long."

She escorted Eric to Miklos's room. As they walked in, the doctor gently said, "Miklos, you have a visitor." She turned to Eric. "He's been sleeping most of the day. He didn't sleep well last night."

Miklos opened his eyes.

"It looks like he's awake. I'll leave you two alone," the doctor said.

"Hi Coach," Eric said, dragging a chair over to the bed when the doctor left the room. "How are you?"

"What was the time?" Miklos said.

"The time? Oh, you mean the race. You are a hard-core coach, aren't you?" Eric said, grinning. "I ask how you are, and all you want to know is my mile time."

Miklos gave a weak smile. "I've been better."

"Well . . ." Eric started, "I have a story to tell you."

Miklos's face tightened with confusion as his smile slipped away. "A story?"

Eric squirmed in his seat. "Well . . . This is how it went down. Last week's training was great. I tried to design workouts like yours, and I think I succeeded. I wrote them down so you could look at them later. I know you like to keep meticulous records."

Miklos smiled.

Too nervous to sit, Eric stood up, stepped to the end of Miklos's bed then turned around. "OK, here's what happened at the race . . ."

After Eric finished his story, his face flushed from his lively accounting of the race, he came over and slumped into the chair next to the bed, exhausted—as though he had just rerun the whole race.

"I'm sorry, Eric," Miklos said.

"The weird thing is I've always been able to tune out problems or distractions when I race. But I couldn't do it today. I thought I was over that whole night . . ."

Miklos patted Eric's arm. "It's OK, Eric. We're all human. We want to think we can shrug off our worries, but some take longer than others."

Eric nodded. "Thanks, Coach."

Miklos's voice was soft and caring, like an understanding father. "I know our relationship has been landlord and tenant, coach and runner, but soon might be a good time for us to sit down and talk more about the things you're dealing with, if that's something you'd want."

"Thanks, Miklos. I would like that."

"When the hospital releases me," Miklos said. "We'll go have us a nice lunch at Marcel's and chat." He hesitated, his face earnest. "Please know Eric, I'm not trying to be your father. I'm not prying into your life."

"Thanks, Coach. I know."

Miklos motioned for Eric to come closer. When Eric did so, he placed his fingers against the side of Eric's neck. "Your heart rate is better now, yes."

Eric giggled.

"So . . . changing the subject," Miklos said. "How's the camp doing?"

"It's fine. I called your partner Professor Fried. He forwarded the phone from the camp to his house. I'm glad he was available. I'm not sure I could have handled the camp calls along with my work, training, and school."

"You did good," Miklos said, his voice scratchy. "It's always prudent to have a partner like Fried as a backup. Having a lifelong friend—a wife—is essential too. Maybe you and Mary will tie the knot one day," Miklos said, his eyes brightened.

"We'll see. We'll see," Eric said, humoring him.

"Can you help me with these pillows?" Miklos said, attempting to sit up against the headboard. Eric adjusted things for him, and Miklos turned to business: "What did you do for workouts this week?"

Eric explained the general specifics of his workouts as best as he could remember, hoping he was giving enough details for Miklos to get a general idea of each interval session.

"Sounds good. Are you doing the same this week?" Miklos asked.

"I don't know. I wanted to ask you, but I don't think you're in any condition to plan anything."

Miklos chuckled, then coughed. "Ordinarily, I'd do it anyway, but with all these medications in me right now, I can't put many thoughts together. But I know what you *can* do." The old man picked up a water glass from a side table, took a sip, then cleared his throat. "I want you to go to my personal office and take out the notebooks I have in the bottom drawer of the file cabinet. You know where I'm talking about?"

"Yes."

"Good. The notebooks are labeled." Despite his coach's condition, Miklos's face seemed to come alive as he spoke, the red puffiness around his eyes fading, his voice growing steadier. Miklos was determined to impart his coaching advice, pneumonia be damned.

"Your notebook is in there," Miklos continued, "but there is one I want you to look at in particular—the one on Tim Donaldson. Go over it, concentrating on the track seasons for now. But, remember, you are not him, so don't run your workouts exactly as he did. Use them for comparison. Most of all, feel what your body wants. It will tell you what it needs."

"I can do that."

Miklos's words soothed Eric's nerves, the tension slipping out of his body. He knew Miklos needed recovery time, but Eric couldn't stop himself from asking: "Hey, will you be able to go to Raleigh? Of course, you know, it's a few weeks away. Has the doctor said how long it takes to recover from this kind of pneumonia?"

"I don't know, Eric. The doctor is hopeful, but we haven't discussed any exact dates yet. Let's see how I do. I've never been this sick before." Miklos pulled his bed covers closer to his chest.

There was a knock on the door. The nurse tipped her head in. "Sorry, fellas. Time's up."

"OK, Coach," Eric said, rising. "I'll come back soon." He gave his mentor a gentle hug. At the door, he turned. "Do you think I can do it? Can I run as fast as Coach Winters from State wants me to?"

"Come back here a minute, Eric," Miklos said.

Eric closed the door and sat back down on the bedside chair.

Miklos held Eric's gaze for a moment, then said, "It's OK to doubt yourself. No matter what the outcome is, know that it's all right to fail. You've worked as hard as you could, and I'm proud of you."

"Thanks, Miklos."

As Eric reached for the door handle, Miklos said, "I believe in you, Eric."

Eric flashed to that first day in his coach's office when Miklos asked him "Do you believe in me?" When Eric turned back to Miklos, he first saw a man late in his years, frail and weak from sickness, but Miklos's inner strength still lay in his words.

Eric rubbed at his eyes and momentarily covered his mouth trying to quell his quivering lips. "I believe in you, too, Coach."

Chapter 39

It was near the end of April. Springtime was at its zenith in the Carolina Mountains. Emerald green leaves, not yet fully darkened for summer, shimmered in the sun. The season's bright and cheerful radiance inspired Eric, his excitement building as the Raleigh meet approached.

The weekend following his visit to the hospital, Eric had returned to Asheville to pick up Miklos and bring him home. The doctor had asked Eric to stay in the house to keep an eye on him—at least until his next checkup. So, for now, Eric was sleeping in an upstairs bedroom. The doctor had also advised Eric that Miklos was not to overexert himself, and as a precaution, Eric should travel with him if he wanted to leave the house.

Once Miklos had settled into his new post-hospital routine, he took a look at the workouts Eric had designed for himself and commended Eric on their thoroughness and creativity. Examining the handwritten workouts, Miklos said, "You understand how to train yourself now. You're getting a better feel for what your body needs and when." Then Miklos chuckled and said, "You don't need me anymore!"

"I could barely get through two of those interval sessions," Eric objected, but privately he felt flattered and encouraged by Miklos's compliments. "But I need you more than ever for Raleigh," he told his coach.

Eric finally had come to enjoy crafting his own practice sessions, but having Miklos back home and creating his workouts for him gave him a huge sense of relief. However, for now he would need to complete his intervals without Miklos's supervision. Miklos needed rest.

Miklos scheduled a late afternoon workout for Eric to do alone at the college track on the Monday before the Raleigh meet. Eric had knocked out two exams that day and was eager to complete his interval session and return to his studying. He hustled through his warm-up and was ready to begin. As he crouched over and placed his finger on his wristwatch button, a shadow appeared on the track in front of him.

Eric straightened. "Miklos! Where'd you come from?"

A broad grin was plastered Miklos's face. "I snuck around through the gym so you wouldn't see me." Miklos let out a triumphant laugh.

It was nice to see Miklos so lively, so much so that Eric forgot for a moment about the doctor's orders. "Hey! You're not supposed to be out and about."

"Oh, I'm all right," Miklos, said, claiming a spot on the bleacher. "Besides, I have an appointment next Monday, and she'll say I'm well enough when she sees me."

"But—"

"No buts. I'm the coach here, and it's time to start the workout. Hand me your watch. Change in plans," Miklos barked.

A bit flustered, Eric handed over his watch and waited next to the starting line.

"So, what's the workout?"

"My teams back in Chula Vista liked to call this workout the "Hades Mile." It's four one-lap intervals with a one-minute rest, no recovery jog. The goal is to accumulate the lowest total time by running each repetition as fast as possible. It's fun but very challenging. The trick is trying to decide how fast to run each lap." Miklos chuckled.

"You know, I'm not sure I liked that little laugh at the end there, Coach. I think you're going to enjoy watching me suffer."

"Maybe yes, maybe no," Miklos said, raising his eyebrows. "You're ready to start, no?"

"Yes." Eric liked seeing the gleam in Miklos's eyes and hearing the giddy tenor of his voice. His coach's workouts usually maintained a disciplined thread; he rarely kidded around. He must have missed their coaching sessions.

"OK, we start . . . GO!" Miklos punched the watch's button.

"Oh, crap!" Eric said as he sprinted away. But how fast should he go? Sub sixty? He tried for the middle fifties for a start. It was weird to do this without a goal time, but he'd give it his best shot.

Four hundred and forty yards later, Miklos called 57 seconds. He pulled another stopwatch from his jacket pocket and started it for the one-minute rest.

Eric waited patiently. *Not bad. I can recover in one minute,* he told himself. "How much time left?"

"Don't worry," his coach said. Moments later: "To the line. Go!"

"Argh!" Eric groaned.

He finished the second lap in fifty-nine seconds.

Selecting a lap time and meeting the goal was challenging and enjoyable at first, but after two laps, the simple workout had lost its fun. Now the name "Hades Mile" made sense.

The minute rest before the start of this third interval ticked away and Miklos motioned for Eric to approach the start line. *That was only ten seconds, I'm sure. Coach must be cheating.* Miklos sent Eric off for his third circuit. The maxed pace and lack of rest deadened his legs, and his thumping heart rate bombarded his temples. Sixty-one seconds later, he lugged his body across the line. He panted, hands on his head, hoping this rest felt longer than the last one. His body was screaming for oxygen, and his mind, like an overworked computer, was shutting down all unnecessary processes. He walked a few yards down the track.

"Don't go too far," Miklos said.

Before he knew it, Miklos sent him off. And, as if his head were in a space-time continuum, his mind was hurtling down the track on a different path than his body. The white lane lines on the black asphalt had merged in a jumble of white strings. *Was he still in lane one? Where was he?*

The lap blurred by as Eric's pulse rate shot far into the red. Sixty-three seconds later, Eric's tormented, languorous body welcomed the end of the workout.

"Good workout, no?" Miklos said. "Your total time was four minutes."

It was nice to hear the total because he sure couldn't calculate it at this instant. After Eric had collected himself, he said, "I survived." He threw his coach a quizzical look. "What was that about?"

"I wanted to see how you would react to an off-the-wall workout. See if you would respond to something outside your normal routine. But my real goal was to shorten your workout and keep you fresh for the race on Saturday," Miklos said.

"Did I pass?"

"A-plus."

"And now a mile warm-down, right?" Eric said.

"Yes, that's right."

"OK, but don't go anywhere, Miklos. I'm following you home."

Miklos gave a nod and a smile. It was nice to see him returning to his old self.

Chapter 40

When Eric had returned to Brevard, he had expected the worst. The reception he'd received surprised him. Except for the occasional indignant glare, most people appeared to have forgotten, or at least forgiven him, for his past transgressions, but there was, one thing that still nagged at him. He hadn't yet made amends to Buzzy's parents.

The Connor family lived two houses down from Mary. Buzzy's mother had been a stay-at-home mom, his father a foreman at a successful machine shop in Brevard.

Eric hadn't attended their son's funeral. His feelings of guilt about Buzzy's death had sapped Eric's courage. How could the alleged killer of his classmate pay his respects to the grieving parents? How could he change anything by showing up to witness their one and only child being lowered six feet into the earth change anything?

Throughout these last three years, Eric had had time to reflect on his past decisions. He had apologized to those he had hurt and made amends to most everyone close to him. The Connors had been last on the list, and for a good reason; he feared they would never forgive him. Before Eric's post-graduation escape from town, a rumor had been circulating that the Connors wanted nothing to do with Eric.

Buzzy's parents, had been extra protective of their handicapped son, Mrs. Connor, especially. She'd kept Buzzy on a short leash, limiting where he could go and who with. When he did go out, there was usually someone there to chaperone him, like Mary on that fateful night.

The Connors were members of the Episcopal Church that Eric had attended regularly; he had stopped going in order to steer clear of the Connors. And while the Christian ethos was to forgive, it appeared that Mrs. Connor couldn't bring herself to do so, and Eric couldn't bring himself to ask her forgiveness.

It was finally time to break that stalemate.

Eric pulled up to the Connors' house at three o'clock in the afternoon. He knew Mr. Connor got off work at two thirty and would be home by now. Eric wanted to speak to Mr. and Mrs. Connor at the same time.

When he reached their door, Eric noticed that he wasn't as anxious as he'd expected, only a slight elevation of his breathing and pulse.

Mrs. Connor opened the door halfway. She was an imposing woman, standing at six feet without heels, wearing a pair of blue jeans and a red bandana wrapped around her head. She was wiping her hands on a dirty kitchen towel, the smell of furniture cleaner wafting in Eric's direction.

"What do you want?" she said, eyes glaring, a look of disgust on her face.

Eric blew out a long breath. "Hi, Mrs. Connor. I—I came by to speak to you and Mr. Connor."

Buzzy's mother didn't smile, no neighborly friendliness. With her eyes fixated, robot-like, boring right through him like two focused laser beams, he next expected to hear: "Get the hell outta here." *Hang in there,* he told himself. *Tough this out no matter what she says.*

"What about?" she said.

"Well, I . . ."

The door swung open further, and Mr. Connor appeared.

"Hello, Eric," he said in his gentle baritone voice. Mr. Connor stood half a head taller than his wife. His hair sported a flat-topped crew cut that had grayed early. He was stout with thick arms and chest that bulged underneath his white T-shirt. He rested one of his large hands on his wife's shoulder. Despite the man's imposing features, he had a firm but gentle touch when you shook his hand. Eric had never known the man to raise his voice around Buzzy or anyone else.

"What can we do for you, Eric?" Mr. Connor said.

Eric looked up at Mr. Connor. "I came to apologize," he said.

"We appreciate—"

Mrs. Connor cut her husband off, "There's no forgiveness for what you did."

"But," Eric said, "I wanted to say I'm sorry . . . to make amends."

Mrs. Connor pointed a finger at Eric, but before she could utter what surely would be heated words, Mr. Connor reached over and pulled her hand down. "Excuse us for a moment," he said and steered her inside, leaving the door partially open.

Words flew between the Connors, their quarrel loud enough for Eric to hear without leaning in. At first, there were angry barbs and pointed opinions both ways, before the dispute quelled. Sniffling and sobs ensued.

The door drew open, and the two parents appeared. Mrs. Connor, tears streaming down both cheeks, took a tentative step forward, but then hesitated. Words were catching in her mouth. Her husband gently rubbed her shoulder and spoke softly, "Go ahead honey."

Mrs. Connor's face had lost its earlier rage, but her tight eyes and pursed lips told Eric there was more. She dabbed a tissue at her wet eyes. "Eric," she said, a slight treble catching her throat. "I talked with my husband and we appreciate you coming over. But I do want to know one thing. Why didn't you come to the funeral? I think that was what made me mad the most."

Eric had try to prepare himself for this particular question earlier today when he thought about what he might say if asked. He figured it would be on top of her list, and rightfully so. "I—I," he stuttered, his speech warbling, his mind racing ahead of his mouth. "I was scared. I felt you and Mr. Connor hated me, and felt I killed Buzzy. I just couldn't bring myself to be there. I couldn't bear your disappointment. Staying away was easier for me, and I thought easier for you. But I was wrong. I was a coward. I should've apologized sooner."

She opened her long arms. "I'm so sorry, Eric. We forgive you. I'm sorry for being so bitter these last three years," she said. She motioned for Eric to come closer. As he did she wrapped them around Eric's shoulders. Mrs., Connor hugged him tighter than he expected. It was like she was hugging her son through Eric.

After the tears and reconciliations had ended, a conversation emerged. The three caught up on the painful past, sharing their deepest feelings about the night at the house. When Eric described the night's events in relative detail, both Connors' eyes widened with increasing understanding of how Buzzy had died. Mrs. Connor burst into tears again when Eric described him reaching down the stairs for Buzzy and the subsequent failure of the railing. Out of respect and decency, Eric limited the details of his description where necessary. There was no need to burden Mrs. Connor with the image of her son lying contorted on the floor with blood seeping from under his skull—a memory that still haunted Eric.

Both of Buzzy's parents offered appreciation to Eric for coming by in person. Before he said goodbye, Eric asked permission to visit Buzzy's grave. "Of course," Mrs. Connor said. "You go make your peace with our Buzzy."

Ideally, Eric would have wanted Mary and Rodney to accompany him to the grave site, but both were still away at school. He would have loved their support, but he knew he needed to make his peace now.

The moment Eric drove away from the Connors' house, relief swept through his body like water spinning down a wide drain. The Connors had forgiven him and bestowed their blessing. After stopping at a signal light where three roads converged, the little hatchback picked up speed, the four-cylinder droning out lazy revolutions. Fertile farmlands stretched out to Eric's right, the corn plantings now a dark lime green, the sky a pure blue.

Two miles later the car rolled to a stop in front of the cemetery's half-open gate, the rectangular iron door angled down, dragging the dirt, a crescent shape gouged in the soil. Eric stepped out of the car. He turned and looked back at the expansive farmland, noticing the tufts of shrubbery and hedges poking up above the plowed fields, the greenery clinging to the French Broad River's banks. It was barely a half mile from here that his father was buried—or more accurately, where his father had been *poured out.*

When his dad had been alive and coherent, he had always reminded Mrs. Roberts that, if he died before her, he wanted his body cremated and his ashes poured into the river that had played a large part in creating the town's valley. He'd said he wanted to ride the currents to the ocean.

On a side road, just off the Greenville Highway, at a small bridge, Eric's mother and her two sons had sent their father off on his voyage, Mrs. Roberts slowly pouring the ashes from Mr. Roberts's urn into the French Broad.

Now today, for the first time in his life, Eric felt a sense of respect for the man who was his father, a man who wanted to go with honor and knew how he wanted it to happen.

Buzzy's burial site was in an old family plot located outside of town on the Greenville Highway. The graves were situated on the crest of a little hill.

Eric grabbed a brown grocery sack from the passenger seat and got out. He then slipped through the half-open cemetery gate.

The graveled pathway that looped the cemetery was gutted in places and was more like a trail than a road fit for an automobile. The unkempt grounds had become a thick forest, foliage crowding the plots and narrowing the road. Eric walked, deliberate, funeral-procession pace, the weight of Buzzy's death pressing his more heavily on his shoulders with every step.

While the ground around Buzzy's plot was kept well and clear of sprouting trees and bushes, the heavily forested cemetery kept most of the sunlight from reaching the gravesite. A green patina of mold and patches of lichen capped Buzzy's white marble headstone.

Buzzy's marker was unique. The headstone designers had fashioned the top in a Fleur-de-lis shape, a sharp contrast to the generic rectangular markers that dominated the other gravesites.

He kneeled close to the headstone. "Buzzy," he said, "I talked to your mom and dad. They said I could come by and visit you."

The last few years, whenever Eric had a brief thought about Buzzy, the gruesome night always dominated those memories. But, at this moment, Eric only pictured Buzzy playing pinball and how his face lit up when the boys asked him about the winged-foot charm his mother had gifted to him. These images calmed Eric, but metaphorically facing Buzzy at his gravesite still choked him up.

"I'm so sorry about that night, Buzzy. It should have been me and not you. I'd trade places with you right now if I could. And I'm sorry I wasn't the friend I should've been. You deserved better than that."

Eric unrolled the brown paper bag, took out the contents, and set the bag on the ground. Placing his first gift in front of the headstone, he said, "Buzzy, these are for you. I bought you a brand-new pair of running shoes. I hope you can run up there in heaven." Next he pulled out a framed photograph enclosed in a clear plastic bag. "Also, I have—"Buzzy seemed to appear right before him, his face wearing his customary gregarious smile, waiting to plaster a bear hug around Eric's shoulders. Eric sniffled, then cleared his throat. He tried to smooth out the plastic bag's wrinkles so he could see it more clearly. In the photo the trio were standing in front of a yellow school bus before they were to leave for an away track meet. Buzzy had leaned in just before the shot was taken. The final result included Eric's angry face and blurry arm as he tried to push Buzzy out of the way. Eric leaned the photo against the base of the stone. "I brought it here for you. I wanted your best friend Mary to be with you." Eric gave a muted laugh. "And I hope you're OK with that other goofball being in the picture too."

Chapter 41

Eric penned the final sentence of his spring semester's fifth and final exam. He handed his bluebook to his history professor, took a deep breath, and let out a long, satisfied sigh. Now that his first year of college was complete, there was only one goal left—his last race, and his last chance to make his 4:05.

It was 11:00 a.m. on a Friday, and he was to leave for tomorrow's Saturday race in Raleigh after lunch. Today's destination, at Mary's request, was her grandparents' house in Apex, North Carolina. She wanted him to spend some time getting to know them.

When he arrived at the camp, he rushed into the house. Miklos was lounging in his easy chair watching television.

"Miklos, I did it," Eric said, triumphant. "I'm done. I made it through a year of college!"

His coach rose slowly and shook his hand. "That's great, Eric. I'm proud of you." He reached for the TV's remote control sitting on a small table next to the lounge chair and clicked off the set. He picked up a bulky letter-sized envelope from the table and handed it to Eric. "I have something for you."

"What's this?"

"Look inside."

Eric unfolded the tab and found a bundle of $20 bills inside. "Miklos, there must be three hundred dollars here. I can't take this. I mean—"

"Don't worry. I have plenty. It's a present. And besides, you need some spending money for your trip," Miklos told him.

"Man, this is too much, Coach!"

"I can take some back if you like," Miklos said wryly.

"You know what I mean."

"I know," Miklos said, chuckling.

"Thank you, Miklos." Eric closed the envelope, slipped it in his back pocket and said, "Well, I better go get ready for my trip. I'll be back to make us lunch."

Eric hurried to his apartment and packed. Before closing his suitcase, he stopped to double-check, not wanting to forget anything critical. And sure enough, his racing singlet was missing. He stepped to his dresser, knowing the exact one to wear for his finale. The singlet's white nylon material had, the word FLORIDA silk-screened in blue letters across the chest, and below them was an image of an orange. The garment was the product of a Florida surfing trip with his uncle. He hadn't worn it yet for a race.

In the September before Mary's January ultimatum letter, he and his uncle had chased hurricane swells down the peninsula on Florida's eastern shoreline. Their final surf session culminated at Sebastian Inlet. After surfing waist high swells for three straight hours, they dragged their exhausted bodies from the dying surf. On their return home, they explored the requisite surf shops along A1A as they traveled north. But when they stopped for lunch in Melbourne Beach, his uncle had broached the subject of him running again. Once back on the road, Eric became consumed with nostalgia for his former sport. While traveling through Melbourne, Eric asked his uncle to stop at a running store he had spotted along the roadside.

Eric bought a shiny blue pair of New Zealand Splits running shorts to match the Florida singlet. For daily training, he didn't care if anything matched, but he liked to look sharp when he raced.

Eric folded the singlet and tucked it into the suitcase and zipped it closed. He rushed downstairs, skipping steps as he went before tossing the bag into the open window of his car. Then he went to fix Miklos's favorite lunch—grilled cheese sandwiches with a slice of ham.

When they finished eating, Miklos piled the dishes into the kitchen sink. He reached up and retrieved something from the top of the refrigerator. "Here," he said, "I have one more thing for you." He opened his closed fist. "I thought I'd give you this, too."

Eric's eyes flew open. "That's—"

"Yes. It's the red ribbon you stuffed in my hand the night you lost to Wardlaw."

"How did you get that? I mean . . . I gave that back to Jen. I told her I didn't want it."

"Yes, I remember you telling me that story of how she pranked you with it. So, I thought I'd touch base with her and see if she still had it. Mary gave me her phone number."

Eric appreciated the efforts his coach put in, but the reason left him confused. "So why did you get this from Jen?"

"I wanted you to have a reminder of your past and how far you have come. Read the back."

Miklos had written the time of Eric's two-mile race that day, and a note below it: "Pride before the fall. Always be humble."

Eric hugged Miklos. "Thank you, Miklos. I'll remember." Eric moved to leave, but Miklos stopped him at the kitchen door.

"I want to tell you something," Miklos said. "It won't take long."

"Sure, Coach, I have time."

Miklos cleared his throat. "Well, I wanted to tell you about Bob Schul's 5000 meter race in Tokyo. More to the point, I want to describe the last lap."

Over the past nine months, Miklos had told numerous stories about athletes he'd known personally, helped to train, or watched in races. His coach had mentioned Schul, but only relating to his training with Mihaly Igloi, imparting nothing about his races. Eric's skin tingled in anticipation of a story about a great Olympic runner.

Miklos glanced out the window for a moment, remembering. "When Bob approached the last lap, he was in the front pack with a bunch of runners, and it was coming down to a kickers race. Coming out of the second turn of the bell lap, Michael Jazy from France—a world-class miler in his own right—took off.

"When Jazy made the jump, he created an enormous gap. Bob and the rest of the group followed a few yards behind. As the lap progressed, Bob worked his way to the head of the trailing pack. He cleared Jazy's remaining chaser with 150 meters to go."

Eric was trembling. The vivid picture forming in his mind made him want to lace up his spikes right this moment.

Miklos stopped his story momentarily, went and grabbed a pencil from his side table next to his lounge chair and then the salt and pepper shakers from the kitchen table. He placed the pencil on one end of the kitchen table to signify a finish line, then he took the two shakers in both hands sliding them on the table's surface as if they were Schul(salt) and Jazy(pepper) racing the final meters in Tokyo.

"When Bob caught Jazy with a 100 meters to go he made his final burst," he said, sliding the salt shaker faster, "and pulled ahead for the victory."

"Oh, man. That is so cool," Eric said.

"Do you know why I wanted to tell you that story?"

"Because Bob was really fast?"

"Well, he did have excellent foot speed. But no, it's because he came into the race with a plan and he ran his race, without panicking when Jazy took off."

"I see," Eric said.

"So, what I'm saying," Miklos said, looking Eric in the eye, "is to remember everything that you and I have discussed. Know your strengths and weaknesses. Don't panic because it's your last race. Consider this: Olympic athletes have one chance, sort of like you do tomorrow. It's the best prepared and mentally ready athletes who usually win."

"Thanks, Coach. I'll remember."

"OK. Now take off. I've jabbered enough for one day," Miklos said, pulling open the kitchen door.

Before Eric stepped out, he said, "I wish you were coming."

Miklos clapped a hand on Eric's shoulder and held on for a moment. "I do too. I'm sorry. I wish I could be there to witness your greatness. I know it'll be perfect."

Eric spoke in an even tone, doing his best to hide his disappointment. "No problem, Coach. I know you had a hard week and you're still recovering."

As Eric pulled away from the house, he called to Miklos through the car window, "I won't let you down."

Miklos, still standing on the porch, smiled and waved. "You better not," he called back.

After three hours of driving, Eric was approaching Greensboro and was ready for a break. At the next exit ramp, he eased his car off the interstate and found a decent-looking gas station. The station was old, but it looked well kept. He pulled the car to a pump and stepped inside to pay.

While Eric pumped the gas, he noticed a folded newspaper among the debris of an overflowing trash container next to the pump, its front page flapping in the breeze. He stooped over for a closer look. "Greensboro Runner Sets Mile Record" the headline read. Eric stopped pumping when the dial read five dollars. He placed the gas nozzle back in its slot and picked up the newspaper. Below the headline, there was a picture of the runner and his coach. The article described the details of the athlete's performance at the state finals.

The picture reminded him of a photo Miklos had taken of him at the meet in Tennessee, after he'd run such a good race. His coach had had a larger print made, framed it, and hung it next to the great athletes and coaches on the office wall. "I haven't done anything special enough to be up there with all of them," Eric had said. Miklos had replied, ever so tactfully, that many on his picture wall were friends too and that Eric deserved to be up there as much as anyone. Then he added, "Don't worry, your greatness is coming soon."

With an ache in his heart over Miklos's absence, his mind wandered to the next day's race. He pictured himself rounding his final lap, the last few yards, seeing his time on the race clock until a car horn jolted him back to the moment. With only four pumps at the station, it was a busy Friday afternoon. "OK, OK, keep your shirt on," Eric said. The driver scowled.

Eric tossed the newspaper onto the passenger seat and pulled his car away from the pump and into a parking space. He wanted some gum before he got back on the road. He reached to the ashtray in the center console, where he kept extra change. *Why is my ashtray closed?* When he pulled it open, he was surprised to see it full—sitting atop the change was what appeared to be a rolled-up ribbon. The blue half-inch-wide ribbon unspooled and then stopped with a clink. A gold, disc-shaped object sat in the metal tray. He grabbed the disc, flipping it between his fingers and rubbing his thumb over the embossed surface, its sheen dulled from oxidation. Eric couldn't read the language, but the "#1" on it told him all he needed to know.

"Miklos," he said, "you devil, you." It was the third thing Miklos had given him that day. For Miklos to entrust him with one of the treasured medals from his past was overwhelming. A rush of anger welled up, and Eric pounded on his steering wheel. "You should be here, Miklos, you should be here!" He knew Miklos needed to rest to fully recover, but it just wasn't right that, after all his coach had done for him, he would miss his big day.

Chapter 42

On the Saturday morning of Eric's final race in Raleigh, his car was dead-stopped on the highway to the track meet. The blaring scream of a siren rose in Eric's ears as a North Carolina Highway Patrol car flashed by on his right in the narrow emergency lane, the vehicle's tires kicking up dust from the edge of the embankment. Eric eyed his rearview mirror and saw an ambulance coming along the emergency lane. He set his parking brake, flipped off the ignition switch, and said to Mary, "This traffic is crazy." He thumped his hand on the steering wheel. "I can't believe this. We've moved *one* mile in forty-five minutes. It's a parking lot. If we don't start moving soon, I'll miss my race!" He let out a disgusted sigh. "And the off-ramp is backed up, too."

"We'll make it," Mary said calmly.

Eric glared at her, wherein Mary flipped him an indigent face.

He reached over and rubbed her hand. "Sorry, I'm on edge . . . and I'm running out of time."

"I know. It's all right." She squeezed his hand. "I'd be freaking out too."

"Thanks," Eric said. "Do you think your parents are caught up in this traffic?"

"I don't think so. They're driving the scenic route. I don't think this mess will affect them. My dad wanted to take the scenic route and stop at his favorite drive-in; it's like the Cardinal. You remember that he grew up here, right? My mom says the food is disgusting, but she indulges him."

Eric chuckled. "I guess a lot of folks have their favorite drive-in where they grew up."

"Yeah," Mary said. "I joke with him that he's so old the car hops skated on stone wheels."

"Ha. That's funny. You must have gotten your sense of humor from your father."

"Probably," she said. "Hey, I'm glad you got to stay at my grandparents' house last night. My grandfather likes you. He told you all his favorite jokes. He told me it was fun having you there."

"Speaking of fun . . ." Eric flipped his wrist to check his watch. "I have an hour and fifteen minutes till post time."

"What, are you a horse now?" Mary joked.

He stared straight ahead into the sea of cars.

"What are you thinking?" Mary asked softly.

Still staring, Eric said, "How far is it from here to the track?"

"You're not thinking . . ."

"How far?" he asked again, his voice calm and even.

"Three, four miles, I think. Are you thinking of running to the track? You'll be too tired. You'll—"

Eric placed a gentle finger on her lips, leaned close and looked her in the eyes. "I don't have any choice."

Mary pulled his hand away and held it for a moment. "OK, I'll tell you how to get there."

"Thank you," he said.

She explained the directions as best she could, advising him to stick to the main roads, and gave him a few landmarks to look for, too. He stepped out and surveyed the highway's parking lot of cars for signs of traffic movement. Not a budge. He went to the back of the car and retrieved his racing spikes from the trunk. He threw them on the driver's seat before stripping off his warm-ups, leaving him in his running shorts and racing singlet. The surrounding drivers jeered and whistled.

Eric picked up his spikes, one in each hand, before he set off.

Mary came around the car and met him by the driver's door. "I feel like you're heading off to war and I'll never see you again."

"Aw, that's sweet."

"Eric," she said, "I . . . I want to wish you luck. If I don't make it on time, know that I'm with you in spirit." She slid her arms around him and buried her head into his shoulder with a firm and lingering hug. The warmth from her embrace was even better than "I love you." He kissed her head. "I know," he whispered. He brushed a tear off her cheek and said softly, "I hope you make it." He reached to her necklace and picked up the winged-foot charm in his fingertips. He rubbed it gently and said, "I wish Buzzy were here."

She reached behind her neck and unclasped the necklace. "Take this," she said. She held it out to him, "He would want you to have it."

"But—"

She reached around his neck and clasped the neclace together.

He understood. He gave her a quick kiss, grabbed his spikes and singlet, and strode off.

Eric trudged at first, stiff from sitting in the car so long. The next exit was a half mile away, but the sea of automobiles made it appear farther. He hoped he could remember Mary's directions.

Hoots and hollers rang in his ears as he passed car after car. He smiled at the attention. The jokes and taunts were an amusing distraction. Responding to some catcalls from a group of pretty college girls in an open convertible, he strode over one lane and high fived them as he ran by. When he jogged up onto the highway's overpass, Eric stopped and shielded his eyes from the sun. He tried to spot Mary and his car far down the road, but the rising heat from the pavement blurred his distant vision—colors blotched together into indiscernible shapes. He gave a hopeful wave, anyway.

He sprinted across the road on the overpass when the traffic was clear and gave the wreck a closer inspection. From the higher advantage, he could now see what had caused the backup.

Below him, a tractor trailer had overturned, mangled like an accordion spanning the breadth of the three lanes. A family station wagon lay wheels skyward in the median. He winced at the sight and didn't want to imagine what the outcome had been. He felt bad for the accident victims. The Fire Rescue Squad were still using hydraulic power tools to pry people out of the battered vehicles. The wreck would take longer to clear. When he set off for the track, he noticed a few cars edging around the wreckage on the highway's outer safety apron. "*Now* they start moving," he muttered.

Breaking a good sweat, Eric stopped and peeled off his singlet to carry it and keep it dry. He wouldn't have much time when he arrived at the stadium, and he didn't want to stand around in sweaty racing gear. It was hard enough to relax without the bother of sticky clothing. He checked his watch. It was almost noon. An hour to go. If he ran a relaxed seven minute pace he'd make it to the track in about a half hour if Mary's mileage estimate was correct. He worried that a half hour or less rest before his race would be enough. *It's going to be close,* he muttered as he jogged along the bridge's sidewalk.

The images of the wreckage had stayed with him. To push them back, Eric tried to concentrate on the race strategy he and Miklos had discussed before he'd left for Raleigh. *Eric, you have to get this right,* he thought. *Most but not all the guys in this race are trying to qualify for the NCAA regional meet today.* He knew this because Miklos had called Coach Winters for race details. Besides telling him how many runners would be gunning for the regionals, the coach had also said that Trey had been struggling to lower his mile time. His personal best, the same as Eric's, had only improved to 4:08 so, he too would be trying to qualify here. That bit of info about Trey wasn't news to Eric. Mary had told him Trey had been laboring all spring.

They'll likely want to go out fast and not wait for it to become a kickers race in the last lap, he thought. *That will be good for me. I can let the leaders work the pace.* He hoped they all would have the same idea. But Eric had no competitive knowledge of the other runners except for Trey and two others he had raced against during indoor season; the latter two wouldn't pose a critical challenge to Eric. Also, there'd be some guys there vying to squeeze in one last race for a late-season personal best. He figured, of the sixteen runners entered, many would fall away early if the pace were high. Miklos also said there might not be many runners with blazing speed, but that Eric should take nobody for granted.

Eric considered the scholarship goal time Coach Winters had picked. The 4:05 time was the NCAA Championship qualifying standard for the mile. *Maybe Coach Winters figured if I couldn't make that time, I'd be of no use to him,* Eric thought. He couldn't blame the coach for picking such a tough challenge. Eric understood now that the goal wasn't so much physical as it was mental. He figured Winters wanted to know if Eric could handle the stress, if he could compete and do the hard work it took to be a great runner again. At practice this week, Miklos had encouraged Eric to focus not only on his time goal. Miklos said he was ready and told him to be confident, concentrate on winning the race, and if he paced within his limits, he would have a good chance.

One landmark Mary had mentioned to help Eric gauge the distance to the stadium was the Quick-Stop gas station. She said when he passed the station, he'd have approximately three miles left from there. Two intersections later he found the station. Deciding to stop for a drink from the inside water fountain, he stepped into the building's office. Cold air from an ancient, wall-mounted air conditioner strafed his hair, infusing his heated skin as he sipped at the fountain. On his way out, he turned to the employee at the cash register and asked how far it was to the track and field complex. The man confirmed Mary's mileage estimate.

A few minutes after Eric resumed his run, he searched for a turn Mary had described. She'd said the road would tee into a four-lane road. And there it was—a green sign with white letters marked, NORTH CAROLINA STATE. An accompanying arrow pointed left. "Well, that's obvious enough," he muttered.

Catching the traffic light perfectly, Eric safely dashed across the intersection, then hopped the sidewalk's cement curb, turned left, and settled into his steady warmup pace.

As he cruised the final miles to the stadium, he worried for his friends and family traveling to the meet. Were they stuck in traffic as well? Their outpouring of support had overwhelmed him. Jen and Jonathan would be there; Jen was attending NC State, and Jonathan was nearby at UNC Chapel Hill. Eric's mother, Uncle Joe, and Mark were coming, too. His mother and Mark had left early that morning and should make it in time for the early afternoon race. Uncle Joe was coming from Charleston. He wished Rodney could make it, but he knew he was still training at Tennessee for the Regional NCAA track championships.

A quarter mile later, the road narrowed to two lanes, entering a heavily wooded neighborhood of small, cookie-cutter homes, perfectly spaced on their tiny lots. Massive oak trees planted along the sidewalks towered over the houses and road, their overabundant acorns crunching under Eric's shoes. He had run through similar neighborhoods back in Brevard, and he found the idyllic setting comforting.

The comfort, however, was cut short when he remembered Mary's words, which jagged him back to his coming race. Where were those light towers? She had said he'd see the light towers of the track complex when he started getting close, but she couldn't give him any accurate mileage for this stretch. For now, that horizon marker was occluded by the giant trees. *It must be a ways to go,* he thought, a panicked tension creeping into his shoulders.

With no distance landmarks to go by, Eric had to rely on his watch. His time guide was a conservative seven-minute mile pace. Some minutes later Eric figured he'd gone another mile. Now running through another housing development, a newer one, no large trees to block his view, he still saw no light towers in the distance.

It was twenty-six minutes past twelve. Time was running short for his one o'clock race. Guessing he was about four miles into his run, he looked for one more distance marker Mary had mentioned. She said once he came to a large train trestle, he'd have about a half mile left to go. Not having seen the trestle yet, Eric twisted his watch to the outer edge of his wrist to stop himself from looking at it so much. The track spikes and singlet he was carrying, which weighed next to nothing, were beginning to feel heavy. He was also thirsty again, and he still had no idea where he was. He resisted looking at his watch.

"Mister! Hey, Mister," a kid's voice shouted.

The grinding of plastic on concrete drew Eric's eyes downward. Traveling low and fast, like a submarine's torpedo, a child pedaling a yellow and red Big Wheel was on a direct course toward his ankles. Eric dodged right, and the end of the plastic tricycle's handlebar grazed his calf. Stopping and looking back, Eric watched the tyke continue his headlong course, the child never turning to look back.

Momentarily amused, Eric cleared his fuzzy mind and got back to his run. A minute later he came to the iron train trestle. Relieved, he passed under it, entering a business-like district. Up ahead, above the roofs of the businesses, the track's silver light towers gleamed in the distance.

Chapter 43

Eric jogged through the gate of the Track and Field Complex. *"Attention!"* a voice blared from the stadium's overhead speakers. *"First call for the mile run—Attention, first call."*

That instant, a twinge of adrenaline tugged at his heart, its sudden palpitations responding to the familiar verbal cue, his body anticipating the coming task now only minutes ahead. *Not yet. Stay calm, Eric.* He glanced at his watch. Twenty-five minutes left until his one o'clock race. From past experience, Eric knew that the time between first and second calls were generally ten to fifteen minutes. These calls reminded the athletes to check in with the race clerk for their next event. Eric set out to find his friends and family. Eric stopped at the track's outer fence along the backstretch and scanned the home-side bleachers across the infield. He spotted a group of people sitting in the first few rows closest to the start/finish line. Breaking into a brisk jog, he circled the track's perimeter, knowing his family and friends would be fretting as to his and Mary's whereabouts. Her parents, without question, would be distraught by her absence.

When he approached the group, their worried faces brightened, but only for a moment. "Where's Mary?" Mrs. Kline said, urgency in her voice.

"She's fine," Eric assured her. "But she may not make the race." Eric's mother was sitting next to the Kline's; he gave her a kiss on the cheek. Then he explained to them all, as quickly and clearly as possible, what had happened.

"We were so worried" Mrs. Kline said.

"We heard news about the accident," his mom added. "We were terrified you two were in it."

"We weren't directly affected," Eric assured them. "Just the traffic. Mary's OK, and the car has plenty of gas."

"We nearly called the highway patrol," Mr. Kline said. "Thanks for letting us know. We know you wouldn't leave her stranded."

"No, sir," Eric affirmed. "I apologize, but I've got a race to run. I better get moving." He bent down to his mother and whispered, "Love you, mom," then bounded down the bleachers, as everyone called out their *good luck* wishes.

After a cheerful woman at the check-in table checked off Eric's name, he searched for the nearest water fountain and restroom. On the way, he noted the sparse attendance in the stands. He wasn't expecting an overflowing crowd for a meet like this, but he remembered what racing at the state finals had been like back in high school. Raucous parents and fans filled the bleachers, with cheering so loud you couldn't hear your panting breath or pounding feet on the track. Even now, with the full support of his family and friends, Eric couldn't help but feel vacant. After nine months of training, the two most significant people in his life were missing his race. Hard as it was to ignore that reality, he stuffed down those feelings to focus on his race, only minutes away.

After his restroom and water stop, Eric's stomach panged. As he walked past a snack stand, a small open box on the counter stuffed with packages of candy, drew him like a Hummingbird to nectar.

You have a race to run. Why are you standing here?

Just forget the candy.

"You want some M&M's?" Called an eager teenage girl from behind the counter.

"Oh, ah . . ." he stammered, embarrassed that the girl had caught him starring. "I'm sorry. I don't have any money, and I don't have time to go back to my friends—"

"—That's OK. I could lend you the money, and you could pay me back after your race, if you like."

"Attention, second call for the mile run."

"Really? That's so nice. You'll be here after my race? Can I give you the money then?"

"That would be OK."

"Tell you what," Eric said, "I only need a few. You keep the rest, but I'll still pay for the whole bag, is that cool?"

"Sure, that's cool." The girl handed him a bag. He tore it open, poured a few M&Ms into his hand, and gave the bag back to her.

"Thank you," Eric said. "I have to go. Wish me luck." He grabbed his things and hustled off.

As Eric stepped across the red, rubberized track, he felt the sugar enter his bloodstream, giving him the lift he needed. But an even bigger lift came as the familiar fragrance of fresh-cut grass hit his nostrils. That was the smell of competition. That same aroma had hit his senses before every outdoor race all over North Carolina and beyond. And it made his blood pump faster.

He took a deep breath and imagined Miklos telling him to relax. He found a spot on the infield where he could start his stretching routine. Sitting on the grass, he strapped on his favorite pair of racing spikes. They were still in fair condition, even after two years of neglect at the bottom of a cardboard box. The spikes colored stripes had flaked off, and the soles were thin, but he wouldn't trade them for any fancy new pair right now.

Eric hadn't even thought about Trey until he heard the familiar, booming voice of Trey's father. No surprise. In fact, he realized, laughing inside, that he would be disappointed if Trey's dad weren't here. He turned and saw the man standing thirty feet away, arms folded, overseeing the conversation between his son and Coach Winters. Winters seemed agitated, shaking his finger at Trey, then pounding his fist into his other hand. When Trey turned and gestured back to his father, the coach threw his arms up at Trey and stormed off.

Eric tried to forget Trey and the father and studied the other milers as they warmed up. They milled around with grim, game faces, shaking legs and arms, trying to loosen up. Eric checked his pulse, placing his fingertips against an artery next to his throat. The vessel was pulsing in long intervals. A good sign but his stomach's usual prerace turbulence was there too.

"Last call for the mile. Please report to the starting line," the loudspeakers crackled.

Eric jogged over to check in with the race starter. After the clerk marked his name off the list, Eric caught sight of two men coming around the corner of the bleachers It took a moment for him to register the familiar faces—very familiar—because they weren't supposed to be here. It was Miklos, wearing his cowboy hat, with Dr. Doughton at his side.

Eric's heart thumped with joy. He didn't mind the extra jolt of adrenaline at this time. Having his coach here just might be the extra kick he needed.

Eric looked toward the starting line and noticed the race starter wasn't assembling the runners yet. He decided to stride the infield's length a few times to stay loose. He eyed his wristwatch. It was approaching 1:00. *Almost post time,* he thought. He glanced over to the timing tent and noticed a coach inside arguing with the officials. *That might mean a delay,* he thought. He could use a few extra minutes of rest.

Since he had arrived at the track, Eric had had little time to concentrate on his race. As the starter lined up the runners, he gave himself a pep talk: "Don't overthink, Eric," he said under his breath. "You know what to do."

The sixteen runners stood abreast along the curved start line that spanned the eight-lane track. The clerk placed Eric in the seventh position from the tracks inside curb. From here he had a balanced view of his competitors on either side. Trey stood two runners left of Eric. When their eyes locked, Trey glared, but Eric kept his eyes calm and focused.

"Well, Roberts," Trey said, with his usual snark, "one last try, huh?"

Eric turned away without a word, lifted the winged foot charm on Buzzy's necklace, kissed it, and looked at the sky. "It's you and me now, Buzzy . . . give me wings."

The starter instructed the runners to take one step back from the starting line. Eric's muscles tensed waiting for the starter's call. On his command, they rushed forward, toed the line, and settled. Eric focused on the starter perched atop his tiny ladder twenty yards ahead, his right arm vertical, holding his gun high like Lady Liberty's torch. To prepare for the chaotic crush for the inside lane, he angled both his elbows outward, pushing back against the arms of his feisty rivals on either side.

The gun fired.

The runners drove forward and swarmed for the inside lane as they bent into the first turn. A runner's arm jolted Eric, pitching him right, and several runners spilled hard to the track. Several seconds later the official's gun fired twice, calling the race back for a new start. The runners grumbled as they trotted back to the starting line. Nobody liked being called back, but the basic rule was: If a runner fell in the first one hundred yards, the race had to start over.

Eric was a little annoyed that it had taken the officials so long to fire the gun. The runners had been near the seventy-yard mark when the double blasts had signaled for a restart. To allow his spiked heart rate more time to calm, he sauntered back to the line. As he neared his starting position, his eyes focused on Miklos standing at the fence next to the starting line, his favorite timepiece cradled in his hand. His coach nodded a few times as if signaling that everything would be all right. Eric flashed him a quick smile.

The officials gave the runners a little extra time to settle elevated heart rates before the restart. The gun fired for the second start, and in the crush for places, arms flailed, and bodies bounced off each other like steel balls against the bumpers of a pinball machine, but nobody's skin found the track this time. To stay out of trouble, Eric eased his pace and slid to the back of the pack to draft. It wasn't the ideal position to be in, but for now he would be fine. He would assess the first lap pace before he moved to the front.

For a few moments, he couldn't hear his friends or the paltry crowd, only rapid breaths, and scratching spikes on the firm rubber surface. *Geez, the pace is fast—these guys really want to qualify.*

Trey had beelined to the front, dragging the clustered pack through the first lap in a furious fifty-nine seconds, Eric trailing one second behind. Considering Trey had only run a 4:08 coming into this race, Eric didn't expect him to hold that pace for four laps. A sub–four-minute mile pace was out of his range. Eric strode fluidly, but he knew that first laps could be deceptively easy, and never a place for overconfidence. The second circuit was the time to settle down and relax.

Without warning, runners groaned, voicing complaint, their hands jabbing into the backs of the runners in front. Trey had slowed the pace abruptly, catching the group off guard. The sudden pace change stacked up the runners, with a few squeezed out into lanes two and three. None of the runners seemed to want to run the extra distance in the outer lanes, But Eric didn't mind a little energy sacrifice right now. He knew the slowing lap increased the probability of someone making a jump. So, he edged around the group and maneuvered closer to the front, wanting to be ready if anyone tried. Other runners followed Eric's lead. Once Eric had staked out a spot three rows behind the leaders, he had to throw a few elbows to defend his precious claim.

Eric watched the seven runners ahead of him trying to guess who would be the next one to make a move. Maybe the tall guy near the front or the thin guy with the bouncy stride next to him. The tall guy looked impatient, and the bouncy runner exuded speed. *Forget them, Eric. Worry about you,* he scolded himself.

"Sixty-three," the timer called out as they finished the second lap. Slower but not too bad—a 2:03 half-mile split was perfect.

Eric waited. No moves yet. *Two laps left to go.*

A hundred yards into the third lap, the pack was nearing the end of the second turn. Seven hundred yards remained to the finish. It was clear now that neither the tall guy nor the bouncy guy had any intention of making a jump. But Trey did. With a decisive move, he broke the race apart, casting out a line of baffled runners in his wake. *He's going for it this early?* Eric thought, hardly believing it. *That's either gutsy or crazy.* As he puzzled over the implications of Trey's move, more runners slungshot around Eric, as though Trey had them on a rubber band; where he went, they would follow. Eric now found himself in tenth place. His first instinct was to move up, fight for a better spot, but he waited, while continuing to match their pace.

Not yet, Eric. Not yet. One more runner blasted past him, and Eric tagged along with him. Deep down, he wanted to match Trey mano a mano, but remembering the blunder he'd made the previous fall at the cross-country race in Raleigh, he stuffed that dog-eat-dog impulse. Now wasn't the time for heroics. He couldn't throw out everything Miklos had taught him about racing smart. He'd be wasting nine months of training on one egotistical move. So again, Eric held back. *Chasing Trey with six hundred yards to go was too far—too far out!*

As the runners zipped around the next turn, Eric studied Trey's form. Every stroke of his powerful, rangy stride was consuming the track, laying the field to waste. The guy was going for broke. But why this early?

When Eric approached the bell lap, the timers shouted 3:02 for Trey's time, a 59-second third lap. Eric's 62 put him at 3:05.

When the bell rang, signaling the start of the last lap, a Pavlovian response swept through Eric, his body switching modes, robotic and conditioned. The sprint was coming, and the reward waited at the finish line.

The runners who had covered Trey's move were not gaining much. Like Eric, they seemed to find Trey's move was too difficult, too early, and gave up the chase. But no matter, Trey was still rolling along at a good clip. Having the race of his life? Possibly. Or he was downright insane for trying to break a mile race open this early. Eric had never seen a guy go for victory that far out in a mile race and succeed.

Eric repeated Miklos's words to himself: *Be patient, and you'll have a chance for the win—and a good time.* But Trey had fired the first salvo, and the battle was on. Eric wouldn't betray his coach's advice, but he wanted the victory, always wanting to win, no matter who led the race. He had to be smart and run his race. That's where the success lay—in a good plan and proper execution.

Eric pressed himself to erase the five yards between him and a procession of runners in front of him. Inspired that the gap was diminishing, he reeled in his competitors. Eric now held seventh place coming out of the second turn with three hundred yards remaining. And though the rigors of his race besieged him—tightening shoulders, lactic acid levels rising—he wasn't blown up yet. He still had gas in the tank.

His confidence boosted when he saw the line of runners in front of him tiring, bunching and squeezing over into lane two again. Now he had to move around them.

But could he catch Trey? Would he be too late?

He hadn't heard Miklos yelling from the fence near the finish line for the last two laps. As Eric approached the backstretch, he caught sight of his mentor standing at the fence—the end of turn two—his coach's favorite spot to watch him. Miklos caught Eric's eye, gave him a steady, purposeful stare. He had a tiny smile on his face, and his eyes gleamed with approval. They had examined last-lap strategy dozens of times—where and when to make your move—and without words, his coach was telling him it was time to go.

Come on, Eric, let's give your coach something to remember.

As he bombed down the backstretch, he swept around the remaining stragglers; he was in second place now. The two runners he had noticed earlier in the race covered his move. They challenged his pace for a few yards, but Eric kept pushing and broke them thirty yards later, nonetheless keeping them in the back of his mind.

With a half lap to go, Eric resisted the urge to look over at the finish line. He didn't dare look just yet. *Don't get ahead of yourself, Eric. Focus on the hunt in front of you.* It was more fun to be the hunter than the hunted—and his prey was slowing.

Step by step, the finish line drew him closer. The emotional and physical suffering the human body endured during the last quarter of a mile race was a cross combination of joy and ache. But, for him, the ache always won out; the joy was afterward. Right now, his level of suffering stood at three-quarters on the dial, and his body's tank of lactic acid was topping off quick; he hoped the overflow wouldn't come too early.

When Trey started into the last half oval, about 200 yards to go, he shot a few backward glances. *Does he know it's me?* Eric—now twenty yards behind—close enough now to get a good view of Trey, saw him grappling with fatigue; he was running taller, losing his forward lean, his bouncy lope gone, and his head was bobbing in long arcs.

With a hundred and fifty yards to go, Eric pulled aside with Trey.

Eric stared straight ahead but caught Trey's repeated glances from the corner of his eye. Eric returned no inspection, not wanting to give him the pleasure of eye contact. *I've got you now,* he thought to himself, surging forward.

Trey matched the pace for another fifteen yards, but Eric snapped his foe's rubber band.

Eric edged around Trey. With successive strides, the gulf between them swelled. Confident that Trey was cooked and no longer a threat, Eric maintained a guarded eye for the previous two he'd passed on the backstretch. One runner's coach was whooping his support from the infield. The coach's voice was hitting the back of his ears, so Eric suspected he had maybe a ten yard separation. *Come on, Eric, don't take any chances. Lift your legs!*

With his legs leaden from his prodigious effort, he glanced back with fifteen yards remaining. He was clear of Trey now, thirty yards at least, but the tall and bouncy runners who trailed him had closed some yards.

Eric fought his freezing muscles with every stride. *Almost over. Five more yards!*

He watched the race clock panels flip, his thoughts syncing with the falling digits. *Maybe . . . yes . . . maybe . . . yes!*

He dove through the line, arms back, head down, in beautiful form.

There it was—4:02 and some change. But the exact time didn't matter—the scholarship was his. His last lap split was fifty-seven seconds like he'd done in practice.

Eric gasped. He stumbled a few yards, then turned to watch the tall and bouncy runners swooping for the line. Trey, several yards back, was struggling to fend off some other competitors, still accomplishing a reasonable mile time despite his early gamble.

Eric's body calmed quickly. He dashed over to the fence and jogged by his cheering section, giving them high fives. Mary was there too. He was relieved that she made it to the track safely and got to see his race. He continued his cooldown lap in the outside lane before the next event commenced. He punched his fist in the air. "It's yours, Eric, the scholarship is yours!"

Coach Winters yelled from the infield, "Hey, Roberts! After you finish your victory lap, find me, and we'll talk scholarship." The coach gave him a thumbs-up sign, and Eric returned it.

As Eric started around the curve for his victory lap he saw Miklos walking toward him along the outside perimeter fence. When Eric reached Miklos he decided to can the victory circuit. He jumped the three-foot fence in front of Miklos.

"You are not tired, Eric?" Miklos said, a smile spread ear to ear.

"Maybe a little," Eric said.

"You ran fast today, no?"

Eric nodded. His voice stuck, almost shy. He watched some runners flash by, warming up on the track. He looked back to Miklos. "I want to say thanks, coach—thanks for taking a chance on me."

Made in the USA
Columbia, SC
20 July 2021